Praise for Shani Mootoo and *Valmiki's Daughter*

"*Valmiki's Daughter* is an intensely moving story of buried hurts and private desires in conflict with the inherited legacies of class and culture. It's a novel for both brain and heart: at once wise and smouldering..."
— Scotiabank Giller Prize Finalist Camilla Gibb

"A fascinating meditation on the complexity of race relations... Mootoo's prose is vivid, poetic, and passionate... This is a writer who knows how to satisfy the reader." — *NOW Magazine*, NNNN

"... wise and skillful... A stand-out novel." — *Montreal Gazette*

"[*Valmiki's Daughter*] is possessed of a droll, knowing humour... [Shani Mootoo] gives us a view of Trinidad we have not had before."
— *Globe and Mail*

"[A] beautifully rendered story... This book shimmers with passion... Heavy with smells, rich with flavours, and throbbing with music, it is a feast for the senses. The landscape serves as a metaphor for sexuality: the dangerous jungle of unleashed desires vie with the manicured lawns of nature suppressed... Readers can look to this book as a tropical respite from a bitter winter's chill." — *Winnipeg Free Press*

"Vividly set, full of elaborate physical details... highly charged and downright explosive... Mootoo's description of Viveka's sexual awakening is one of the most poignant I've run across." — *Xtra*

"[A] beautifully detailed look at a culture that on the surface appears to be as easygoing as any island paradise, but in reality is bound by social conventions." — *Edmonton Journal*

"Shani Mootoo elevates her material through deft characterization, an ever-building sense of urgency, and her obvious love for an island landscape..." — *Georgia Straight*

valmiki’s

shani mootoo

daughter

Hardcover edition first published in 2008 by House of Anansi Press Inc.

This edition published in 2009 by
House of Anansi Press Inc.
110 Spadina Avenue, Suite 801
Toronto, ON, M5V 2K4
Tel. 416-363-4343
Fax 416-363-1017
www.anansi.ca

Distributed in Canada by
HarperCollins Canada Ltd.
1995 Markham Road
Scarborough, ON M1B 5M8
Toll free tel. 1-800-387-0117

House of Anansi Press is committed to protecting our natural environment. As part of our efforts, this book is printed on paper that contains 100% post-consumer recycled fibres, is acid-free, and is processed chlorine-free.

13 12 11 10 09 1 2 3 4 5

LIBRARY AND ARCHIVES CANADA CATALOGUING IN PUBLICATION

Mootoo, Shani, 1957–
Valmiki's daughter / Shani Mootoo.

ISBN 978-0-88784-837-7

I. Title.

PS8572.O622V35 2009 C813'.54 C2009-903909-5

Cover Design: Ingrid Paulson
Text design and typesetting: Ingrid Paulson

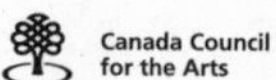

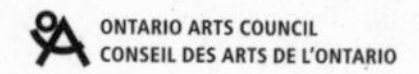

We acknowledge for their financial support of our publishing program the Canada Council for the Arts, the Ontario Arts Council, and the Government of Canada through the Book Publishing Industry Development Program (BPIDP).

Printed and bound in Canada

For SJD

Contents

Prologue

24 Seconds

SHE IS SEATED ON THE BED IN A SEA OF BRILLIANTLY WRAPPED PRESENTS.

He watches her, grinning, and he makes silly comments as if he fully agrees with all that is happening. The grinning hurts, but if he doesn't grin he will cry. He'd rather switch off the light in the room, throw a net over her, wrap her tightly in his grip, and flee with her. Take her deep into one of the forests hunting with him. Just the two of them. Never to return. Instead he stands still, jokes about the presents. What he wishes he would or could do and what he actually does are related only by being perfect opposites.

Once, she doted on him. Then, suddenly it seems, she sees right through him. He is sure of it.

Suddenly. Everything has happened so suddenly.

His wife certainly saw through him long ago. But he credits Devika with a vision larger than that of his daughter. Devika's vision encompassed her own long-term welfare as well as that of his two girls, their girls — young women, rather. Devika's vision, too, held dear nothing but respect, the utmost, for how things are expected to be. He and Devika have these values, if nothing else, in common.

Of course, it isn't really so "suddenly" that his daughter reared up and threatened to undo them all. What is sudden is him seeing her for who she is, as if for the first time. Even so, he has done not a damn thing to help her, he taunts himself, and now she is on the verge of leaving. He knows this is good for them all, or at least for those who will remain behind. He has no idea if it will be good for his daughter. If only he could take her away. Tell her his own story so that she might create a different one.

He can only hope. Such a frail thing, hope.

He needs, for his own sanity, to point to the moment, to the specific sliver of time when his eyes began, finally, to open, when he might have done something — or everything — differently. The point on which he might hang regret.

Regret is so much more palpable than hope.

Was it just that day, that rainy September day — a year ago now — that had begun with his daughter barging, even before he had fully awakened, into his and Devika's bedroom, insisting on having her own way? He should have stood up, not to her, but to his wife. He should have let his daughter do all that she wanted, be all that she was. But in a place like San Fernando, that was impossible.

I San Fernando

24 Hours

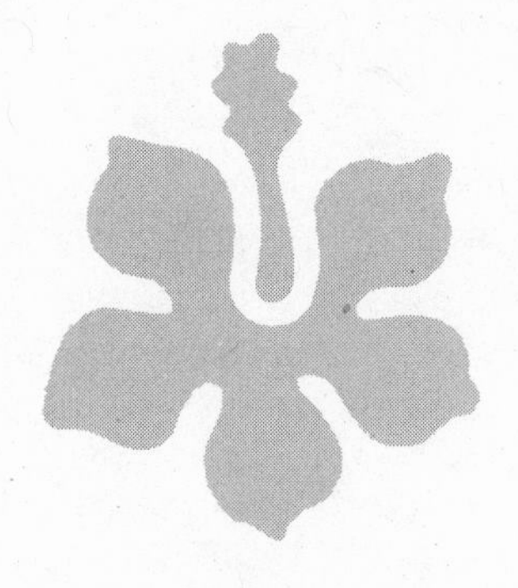

Your Journey, Part One

IF YOU STAND ON ONE OF THE TRIANGULAR TRAFFIC ISLANDS AT THE top of Chancery Lane just in front of the San Fernando General Hospital (where the southern arm of the lane becomes Broadway Avenue, and Harris Promenade, with its official and public buildings, and commemorative statues, shoots eastward), you would get the best, most all-encompassing views of the town. You would see that narrower secondary streets emanate from the central hub. Not one is ever straight for long. They angle, curve this way then that, dip or rise, and off them shoot a maze of smaller side streets.

There is, at that Chancery Lane intersection, a flow of traffic around the white-painted triangular concrete islands that involves some nudging, constant car-horn blaring, frantic bicycle-bell ringing, face-reddening expletives, and curses of one's forefathers and progeny. Streams of cars jerk forward, halt too suddenly, and then as if by magic, flow forward effortlessly, traffic lights and wardens momentarily rendered unnecessary.

Imagine you are a tourist let down from the sky, blindfolded, in the middle of a weekday, onto one of those traffic islands. Your senses would be bombarded at once. You would descend into a cacophony of sound, and a cacophony, yes, of smell. Car horns would hoot and toot in varying lengths and tones, sounding, with a little imagination, like a modernist noise symphony that would include outbursts of the nut seller's arcing melody, "Nuuuuhts, nuts, nuts, nuts, nuuuuhts, fiiiif-ty cents a baaahg." You'd hear theatrical steupses, and people hawking unabashedly, dredging the recesses of their craniums before spitting — should you open your eyes prematurely — amphibian-like yellowish or greenish globs hard onto the sidewalk. You might be lucky enough, if you arrive at the right time of the day, to hear rounds of clarion bells on a descending partial scale. The church's organ would no sooner soar upward than the choir would be heard in practice: short bursts of a phrase repeated, repeated, repeated until it is mastered, then longer sections practised until the entire hymn is finally belted upward ever more. Outside the church, people would be hurling greetings at one another. Some would be hailing taxis, and at least once a day there is bound to be the theatre of a spurned lovers' quarrel, all the better when not two but three are involved. The taxi drivers at the several stands in the area, and the nut sellers perched like ground-bound gargoyles at every intersection, could probably intervene as witnesses or judges, for from their positions they might well have seen the affair unfold from beginning to end. But in the interest of business as well as their own longevity they stay out of the fracas, which sometimes involves knives or cutlasses that make the proximity of the emergency ward useful. From many sources you will hear radio commentary on a cricket match. Sailing in on a breeze from one of the side streets, the faint music of a steel-pan orchestra might also be discerned. Human-like cries overhead might startle you at first, but you would soon easily distinguish the sounds of greedy competitive seagulls from those of agony and despair emanating night and day from the various wards at the hospital.

Despite the aural melee, what might well overwhelm you are this intersection's odours. Before you remove the blindfold and see the blue haze caused by the exhaust fumes of cars, scooters, and trucks, your nostrils will have stung from it, and your skin will have tingled and turned greasy. The aroma of roasting peanuts, of corn boiling in garlic-infused water, of over-used vegetable oils in which split-pea fritters with cumin seeds have been fried, of the cheery, spicy foreignness of the apples and grapes being sold in the open-air counter on the corner, would activate your tastebuds, and in spite of the surrounding unpleasantness, even if you had eaten not long ago your stomach would argue that it was ready and able again. A person might pass near enough for you to be assailed by his or her too-long unwashed body. And you might well be assaulted by the equally offensive fragrance of another passerby's underarm deodorant, which, having been called upon to do its duty, swelled uncontrollably in the heat. The stink of urine would, of course, be there, and surprisingly, that of human excrement, rising high on crests of wind and then thankfully subsiding. And sailing in, all the way up to this high point, on a breeze from the Gulf not too far away, would be the odours of oil-coated seaweed, dried-out barnacles that cover fishing vessels beached at the wharf below, and scents from foreign ports. If this olfactory mélange were audible, it would indeed be cacophonous, made more so by the terrible nostril-piercing stench of incinerated medical wastes and bed linens, intermittent effluxes from two tall chimney stacks set at the rear of the hospital. Your stomach, opened up moments before in greedy receptivity, might feel as if it had been tricked and dealt a dirty blow. Then again, it might be the season when the long, dangling pods of the samaan tree (the unofficial tree of the city, planted and self-sprouted everywhere), which resemble a caricature-witch's misshapen fingers, split—and the entire town is drenched in an odour akin to that of a thousand pairs of off-shore oil workers' unwashed socks, an odour as bad as, but more widely distributed than, the effluvia from the medical waste incinerator.

The air temperature would be high, as befits an equatorial midday. If you remained standing on that exposed traffic island too long, your skin would redden and become prickly in no time, as if it had been rubbed with bird-pepper paste.

SO, TAKE THE BLINDFOLD OFF. OPEN AN UMBRELLA AGAINST THE SUN and have a look around. But where to begin your visual introduction? The long view in any direction seems better than the one before, especially if you ignore the closest—that of a row of beggars sitting on their haunches on the sidewalk, with arms outstretched, reaching for, but not touching, the clothing of the passersby. Those beggars attempt to hook pedestrians' eyes with their own, muttering their plaintive invocations: "God bless, God bless."

You might or might not have noticed, depending on where you have dropped from, that the people on the streets are mostly of Indian and of African origin. Indian or black. You'd likely notice that most of the beggars are Indian. But you might not.

You will realize that some of the teeth-sucking you've been hearing came from pedestrians on the hospital side of the intersection forced to cross over the sleeping body of a homeless man, or having come upon the pee-sodden body of a young and out-cold drunk woman.

Well, perhaps it's not all that difficult to know where to begin your introduction. If you can lift your head up, away from the beggars, the homeless, and the drunk on the sidewalks and take in the six-storey buildings of the General Hospital, you will see that they form an imposing and eerily beautiful backdrop to one side. Painted stark colonial white, the hospital rises higher than any other building in view, yet each section is capped with the traditional V-shaped roof of a simple family house, a shape meant to quell its simultaneous grandeur and foreboding.

Outlining the edges of the hospital property is a low white concrete fence topped with tall silver-painted iron spurs, V-ed like the blades of an overly long sword. There is a formal entrance, with a sentry's concrete hut dividing entry and exit lanes. The sentry box is often empty, and cars and pedestrians usually come and go at will. But the sentry is there today. He is outside of the box, dressed in his uniform of starched and pressed khakis, with a khaki cap pulled low on his forehead. He leans — only his shoulders touch — against the side of the box, his sole focus the young woman in front of him, with whom he chats through pursed lips. Only she can hear what he utters. One of his legs is raised back, its foot bracing against the wall. His arms are folded high on his chest. If his eyes were fingers the young woman before him would be at his knees. Cars still come and go at will.

At this entrance, also, is a group of men huddled over a radio. It is from here you heard the cricket commentary, and the men who listen seem, from their clothing and demeanour, to have nothing in common but their interest in cricket.

Because you can still hear it, you look around trying to spot where the sound of the steel-pan band comes from. The music seems to come from one side of the town one minute and then, whipped away on a breeze, from another direction. You try to hold on to the mellifluous sounds, but they float in and out quickly. Behind the entry and fencing, well-tended lawns spread out and surround the hospital, and lush islands of Calla lily — reds, yellows, purples — direct the flow of pedestrian traffic. The driveway that cuts through the hospital grounds is bordered by a single row of palm trees whose trunks, from the ground to a height of about six feet, are washed in the same white paint as the fence and the buildings, a holdover from colonial days when paint was thought to deter destructive bugs. Some concrete benches in a semicircle, painted that white again, are set on the lawns under the spreading shade of flamboyant trees whose trunks were not spared the whitening either. The benches were originally meant for use by patients and their visitors, but serve more often, day and night, as beds for the homeless and the uncared-for insane. Across each and every one lies a spectre of a figure, a body bound in rags that reek, knees pulled up to chest, one arm pillowing the head against unyielding concrete.

The regulars at the hospital, in addition to some long-term-care patients who won't be going anywhere in a hurry, or ever, include nurses, and Drs. Peters, Rajkumar, Krishnu (who also has a private practice in the town centre), Tsang, Chu, and Mahabir. Turn around now and face the north. Your perch, after a spread of some ten yards or so, drops down a steep road, Chancery Lane. The slope is like the long handle of a ladle. To one side at the bottom, the ladle's bowl, is the hospital's and shopping district's principal parking lot. On the other side is a descending row of colonial-style buildings, the offices of lawyers and notary publics. The commercial main street begins at the base. There, just before the main street turns and disappears, you can see a gas station, its red-and-white Texaco sign spinning, The Chase Manhattan Bank, Khan's Clothing and Household, Bisessar's Furniture and Rug Emporium, and part of Samuel's Sporting Goods Store. Then the street curves away and disappears around a bend. If you were to continue around that bend you would find a supermarket, a building of doctors' private offices — Dr. Krishnu has his there, and a hairdressing salon is on another floor — Maraj and Son's Jewellers, and the city's only bookstore.

Raise your eyes; keep looking out into the distance to where the yellow and silver waters of the Gulf of Paria are studded with red-and-black oil tankers awaiting their turn at the refinery's docks. Between that high horizon and the town at the bottom, you see a sea of green — the fronds of palm and coconut trees mixed with sampan, flamboyant, Pride of Barbados, mango trees — dotted with a confetti of colourful roofs — reds, greens, silvers, blues. These mark the residential neighbourhood of Luminada Heights. It is here you find the residences of the city's more prosperous citizens, including Dr. Krishnu — who, with his wife and their two children, lives in an architect-designed house — and the Prakashs. When the Prakashs bought land here several years ago — their son, Nayan, had just become a teenager — they built a mansion Ram Prakash had sketched out on a foolscap sheet one sleepless night: four bedrooms for his family of three, and three baths. The Morettis (not rich, but white) still own a house in Luminada Heights even though they long ago returned to wherever it was they sprang from in search of paradise and independence. Their house, just up the way from the Krishnus, is leased now to an off-shore drilling company, and in it lives a single American man who makes good money working in the Gulf on one of the rigs he can see from the patio of the house.

Look behind you, to the south, down Broadway Avenue. The avenue is wide, divided by a high island of tended grass, down which runs an uninterrupted row of Pride of Barbados trees. On the left and the right sides you will see two-storey concrete houses, all set behind concrete walls whose paint has long washed, or been peeled, away. The shoemaker, some of the hospital's nurses and workers, clerks in the law courts nearby, some taxi drivers, teachers, servants, an ironer, the piano teacher who has her "school" in the living room of the top floor of the house she rents, an ageless man who lives by himself and wears dresses (he had ambitions to be a fashion designer and dressmaker but was unable to find clients and sews only for himself now), and a midwife are among those who live on Broadway. As that avenue curves off and disappears, taking with it an old, once-prosperous neighbourhood, your eyes are naturally carried eastward toward a narrow band of more private houses and more trees. The lushness and the randomness of vegetation suggest that much has sprung up of its own accord, without discouragement. Behind and between are snippets of yet more houses, but you are unable to see clearly the shape and nature of all that lies there, so you gravitate right back to the busyness of your intersection. All around you, cars, mostly simple compacts, some held together, it seems, by duct tape, slide around the islands, near accidents only just avoided by the long, hard, loud engagement of horns.

Unexplored as yet is Harris Promenade. You have to step off the island and make your way very, very quickly, across the street, making sure to catch the eyes of the drivers as you do so. The sun, however, almost directly overhead, reflects and glints wickedly off the cars' windshields. If the tinted windshields and windows — purple is the fashion here — ward off glare and heat for those inside the cars, they make it doubly difficult for a pedestrian to see if she or he has caught the eyes of the drivers. So take extra care in crossing.

Even as you cross, you will notice off to your right, which is also to the right of the promenade, several policemen, and you will wonder why none directs traffic. The police mill about the mouth of the police station, which yawns wider as you approach the promenade proper. Groups of them seem to be waiting for something, anything, to happen, and so to be called for an assignment, but they do not act unless ordered by their superiors.

The promenade is a remarkably wide thoroughfare that shoots off the intersection in a relatively straight line toward the east, and is flanked on either side by churches — first, on one side, the Anglican Church with its modern bell tower; then the fire station; followed by the Town Hall, a long, three-storey building that houses the offices of aldermen and the local offices of the Ministry of Health (the main offices are in the capital of the country). There are some other government buildings in the colonial style, but these are not open to the public, and no one knows what really goes on inside them. Past these are St. Patrick's Catholic Church and a colonial-style house that is the administrative home of the diocese, a home for the local officiating priest, and the Catholic Church library, and past this, a building that houses several government licence-granting offices: hunting, fisheries, vehicles, vending, births, deaths, marriages. Here, just after the Woolworth Store, the promenade ends. Traffic follows this course in one direction. An island as wide as a three-lane city street divides the flow.

Beginning on the hospital end again, on the other side now, are more buildings that harken back to the town's colonial past. On the corner, there is a row of lawyers' offices. Clerks and clients mill about the narrow doorways of the two-room offices built in the late 1800s, structures that are falling apart — their filigree woodwork broken and dangling in places — and are not being modernized. Yes, there is still no running water, and the lawyers and their modest staff are obliged to walk to the updated law courts to use the public facilities there. Farther along is the police station. The scene before you, of three prisoners handcuffed together, being led barefoot along the scorching asphalt by eight police officers carrying guns, is not uncommon. These men have likely just been arrested and are being taken to the short-term cells next door. Pedestrians, hecklers, and concerned citizens alike, among them relatives of the prisoners or of their victims, line the street and watch the spectacle with a mix of awe and fear. Past the short-term gaol is the police barracks, followed by the law courts building (with public toilet facilities), more lawyers' offices, and then, stretching for a good distance, the lands of the Sisters of The Immaculate Conception, which includes one of the town's major secondary girls' schools, and finally the Convent of the Sisters of the Immaculate Conception. The convent itself shares a wall, but only that, with an Indian movie theatre. The movie theatre is at the end of the promenade, directly opposite the town's public library.

The promenade itself is a pedestrian-only island. Its asphalt paving is brilliant orange, carpeted with newly fallen flowers from the trees planted along its length. Walking in the shade of the trees, on this hushing carpet of bright colour, one encounters first a raised, roofed bandstand, with ample room around it for an audience. A railing runs around the platform, which is accessed by a wide staircase that faces the Town Hall opposite. A police officer stands on the platform of the bandstand. He wields a baton in one hand. The baton is aimed at a body prostrate, and in deep sleep, on the ground. The young officer, a thin man of African origin, seems unsure of what to do. The person on the ground is clearly homeless, but there is a "no trespassing" sign on the railing of the stairway. The policeman walks around the body, and his gait, if you were to force a reading on it, seems to say, "Let the man sleep, na. But, then again, this is the only work I might get. Also, if anyone is looking on, getting the man to move might look as if I were doing my job well. On the other hand, if I wake the man up, who knows what might happen. If he is mad, it might cause a bigger problem than there is now. If he is just sleeping and I awaken him, where is he to go?" The policeman turns his back to the man and walks, baton still gripped, to the railing. He leans on it and looks out toward the busy intersection.

Beyond the bandstand is a paved area. A bronze box, like an overturned orange crate, is anchored in the centre of this area, known as speaker's corner. A tall thin man, of Indian origin but with pale yellowish skin, circles the box. He walks with his head bent, as if looking at the reddish clay tiles of the area, his hands clasped behind his back. He is balding. And he appears to be talking to himself. He is not like the other people who make Harris Promenade their home, but he is often found here. He travels by taxi from his house in a nearby town to spend the day walking around the speaker's box. He arrives at the square at 8:30 a.m. sharp, and leaves by taxi again at three in the afternoon — the hours of the school at which he once taught. He had been a bright young English literature teacher who wrote what some people called poetry — two of his acquaintances who also wrote what looked like poetry called his writing this — and, indeed, a foreign magazine had published some lines of his writing, and paid him, too. The editor of the magazine had contacted him later and requested more of these poems, and had suggested he think about submitting a manuscript for publication. He put his mind to the task of producing such a thing and the other teachers at his school ridiculed him, his family teased him, and his students lost respect for him. They joked behind his back that he was a mamsy-pamsy writer of flowery lines. He wrote and wrote and wrote, never satisfied with what he had written, and the editor of the foreign magazine eventually changed, and no one from that magazine was ever in touch with him again. He remained unpublished thereafter, and the staff and students of his school, and his own family, who had worried about their welfare had he decided to turn writing poems into a career, were pleased about this. The man, however, left his job to polish lines such as "*River, oh river rise, and quell the fields of bellies emptied.*" His family gasped, snickered, and then left him. But that was more than twenty years ago. No one in the square remembers his name, but he looks up and then quickly turns away if he is called "Sir," which is how his students once addressed him.

Just before moving onward, you will be hit with a strong, sweet whiff of garlic, scallions, and ginger as they are sautéed, a street away, in peanut and sesame oil. You will smell, but you won't see, The Victory Hotel, which houses The Golden Dragon Chinese Restaurant, the best hotel and the best restaurant this side of the oil refinery. The hotel is mostly used by visitors to the island, but it is known to be available on occasion to certain businessmen and professionals who are willing to pay the daily double-room rate for the privacy of their illicit pleasures. The Golden Dragon is where the aldermen, the mayor, and lawyers take their lunch, and where some of the doctors take theirs too. On occasion you will find Dr. Krishnu there. He usually requests one of several private dining suites at the back of the restaurant. He will, of course, not be alone, but the staff is discreet.

Despite the distraction of the aroma from The Golden Dragon, know that there is street food higher up, exceptional and unusual food, near the gates of the girls' school. You will want to sample that, to buy it from the vendor there, so have courage and steer the promenade tour onward.

Behind speaker's corner is a large, shallow, round pool, with a fountain at its centre, a bronze mess of scaly fish entwined and with open mouths that once spouted water. But the fountain has not worked in years and its pool is empty of water. The ceramic blue-tile floor is covered in a carpet of freshly fallen orange petals. There are benches around the fountain, and these are occupied by court-hearing attendees, office clerks, and idlers. Nut vendors walk up and down the promenade, cream-coloured canvas bags slung from their shoulders. Their outstretched hands show off small brown-paper packages of unshelled peanuts. It is nearly the town's official lunchtime, and the air is fragrant with the scent of foods from vendors' outdoor cooking and from the jeeps parked near the promenade's far end, out of which hot dogs and hamburgers are already being barbecued and sold. The scent of food rising up from all corners of the city is a blessing.

Huddled at the base of tall stately trees are people who have staked claim on these meagre spots and will ward off anyone who trespasses with shrieks, curses, and lunges, armed with frail fists and fearsome body odours. Even the police leave them alone. If you look closely, you will see sleeping figures in the densest sections of shrubbery planted by the town's gardeners. Past the fountain is a towering bronze pedestal, on top of which is a disproportionately smaller, pigeon-blessed statue of Mahatma Gandhi, dhoti-clad and stepping briskly forward. He seems about to step off his base and into the air. Behind the Gandhi statue, in the centre of the tree-shaded promenade, is the biggest statue of all, a full and highly detailed bronze of Queen Victoria in ample skirt, every fold rendered, sporting crown and sceptre, also streaked in dried-white pigeon droppings. Fading into the distance are more water features, none of which function, and more statues of past governors, past mayors, and business benefactors.

The high school attached to the convent has just recessed for lunch. The electronic wrought-iron gate grates and rumbles as it slides open, and the girls, rowdy and excited, spill out. They head for the doubles vendor, whose daily intake revolves around this very moment. When they cross the boundary line of the gate that separates the world of commodities and desires from that, supposedly, of learning and restraint, the girls seem, one by one, to take a vertiginous step, to misstep, falter, and land a little off to the side, or illogically, too far forward. If you were to videotape their exit/entrance, and play back the moment in slow motion, you would discover the cause of that odd blip in the girls' appearance and gait: you would see their hands grabbing the waistbands of their skirts, and smart flicks of the wrist to turn the waistband under, once, twice, sometimes even three times, in order to shorten the skirts to well above the knees, a movement studied and practised until it is executed so swiftly that a casually watching eye sees a jump-cut in life. The collars of the girls' white shirts are normally pinned tight at the neck with a brooch, but by the time the girls reach the food vendor, house badges have been whipped off and necks exposed.

All morning the vendor has been preparing for this lunchtime crush by frying on the spot batches of split-pea flour patties, and heating up a large vat of curried channa she carted from her home. Buzzing around the vendor already are sixth-form students from the boys' college three streets away. They have come for the girls first, and the doubles as a kind of side order. And now the girls have arrived. Vashti Krishnu is here. Her parents, Dr. and Mrs. Krishnu, who consider themselves to be of high-calibre Indian ancestry, prefer not to know that their two daughters buy and eat street food. They know it is fashionable. The food section of the daily paper often praises the inventiveness and culturally hybrid taste of Trinidadian street food—the doubles, aloo pies, tamarind balls, pone, sugar cake—hailing it to be among the tastiest in the world. But still Dr. and Mrs. Krishnu can't bring themselves to eat food prepared by people whose sanitary habits are unknown, food served in the germ-filled and fly-infested outdoors. Pria Castano, whose father's law office is at the top of the promenade, is here, too. And so is Felicia Clark, whose mother works as a clerk in the police station. Lloyd Gobin is also here. His mother teaches at the convent and his father is the manager of the furniture and rug store in the town centre. Being a more open-minded kind of Indian, Lloyd's father would see nothing wrong with his son being here but would not contradict his wife's judgment.

Prefects from the girls' school have been stationed to make sure the girls do not stray. The rendezvous between students from the two schools, orchestrated to look like little more than coincidental line-ups of boys and girls who happen to find themselves elbow to elbow, lasts no more than ten minutes, that being too long even so for buying this quickly prepared street food, which the girls must take back behind the gates to consume. Boys and girls take care not to be caught chatting or directly facing each other or acting as if these meetings have been planned. But those ten minutes will be the stuff that keeps them from hearing anything that goes on in class that afternoon, and the stuff, too, of that evening's, that night's, confused and excited longings.

The vendor's helper — a girl, perhaps the vendor's daughter — takes care not to look into the eyes of the students, many of whom are older than she is.

Vashti Krishnu knows better than to stand out here too long or to get caught chatting with the boys, so she orders her doubles — the vendor pulls a yellow chickpea-flour flap from a pile in a tea towel, readies a little square of greaseproof brown paper in the palm of the other hand, places the bara flat on top of that, then slaps its centre with a tamarind paste, and in the cup she has made with the back of the paste's spoon she slaps on top a heaping tablespoon of curried channa and then pulls another flap over that, and folds the lot in two, and with a twist and flick of the paper's ends she has created one order in less than fifteen seconds — and Vashti pays the daughter and heads back to the gate. She is about to cross the street that separates the promenade from the school when a bedraggled woman who had been hidden in some shrubs nearby hobbles with surprising speed toward her. Vashti hears her name. She spins around, and when she sees the woman her heart thunders. The woman appears to be old and haggard, but Vashti knows she is only a handful of years older than she is. The woman is, in fact, the exact age of Viveka, Vashti's sister. The woman is thin, with the depleted meagreness of the alcoholic. Her long black hair is oily and clumped. She wears what was once a white shirt, a school shirt from not too long ago, but it is yellowed and soiled, and the trousers she wears, men's trousers, are covered in dirt, dust, urine. They are several sizes too big for her, held high above her waist with a belt and, as if that were not enough, a length of heavy rope. She is barefoot.

Vashti wants to pretend she can't see who has called her. She wants to pick up her pace and hurry across the street and back through the gates. And as much as she wants to do these things, she also wants to go to this woman, stand with her and ask if she can do anything for her. But she does not want her friends, anyone on the promenade, even people who are strangers, to see that she knows this woman about whom rumours have spread far and wide. People have driven their cars here on a Sunday to see if they could spot this woman. She is said to give her body to men, right here on the promenade, behind statues at night and in the bushes in the day, in exchange for a cigarette or money to buy a flask of rum. It is much discussed. Vashti hears the talk, and in this moment, as she lets her eyes meet the woman's, it is as if she, too, is saying these things: "But if she is doing this sort of thing, what they say about her can't be true then. It can't be so that she is a buller. If is woman she like, how come she doing it with man? Well, maybe is not a bad thing, then. That might cure her. And from such a family, too. It is killing her parents. No wonder they put she out the house."

But Vashti knows this woman. Merle Bedi. She used to come home to visit Vashti's sister, Viveka, and Vashti and Viveka would sit in the living room and listen to this woman play Beethoven on the piano. And Debussy. "Au Clair de la Lune." Their favourite. And when she played, she forgot the world around her. It was as if some unearthly understanding of the meaning of every note she played arched through her body, filled her lungs, and weakened her. Watching her made you breathless. Her fingertips touched each key, and the keys gave themselves up to her, as if they too had been waiting for her. Vashti and Viveka knew that Merle would be a great pianist one day. That is what Merle had wanted. But her parents insisted that the piano came too easily to her, and for that reason it should be her passion, not her job. They insisted that, since she did well also in the sciences, she was to study medicine. If only, Vashti finds her self wishing now, if only the other students, and the people staring as she walks slowly toward Merle, could know how brilliant and talented she is, and that playing the piano is her calling. Or was.

"Vashti, can you spare some money?" Merle asks.

Vashti is taken aback. She thinks Merle might have asked how she is. She instinctively holds out her brown-paper package of doubles. "No, but you can have this."

Now that she has stopped and faced Merle, she wants to ask her something, to say something more, but her mind goes suddenly blank. Merle does not reach for the doubles but says, "You don't have any money? I need some money."

Vashti says, "I don't have more on me," in such a soft, scared voice that Merle does not hear and comes closer.

"Vashti, listen, can you carry a message for me? Take a message from me to Miss Seukeran, please."

Vashti steps back in horror.

"Wait, Vashti, wait. Do this for me, please. I need you to tell Miss Seukeran something for me."

Vashti shakes her head emphatically and hurries across the street, tears welling in her eyes. At the gate, before going through, she turns, but Merle has already disappeared.

The convent, oddly, shares a wall with the cinema next door and if you listen just now, you will hear the lunchtime programming begin. The cinema's walls are not soundproof, and in every direction the soundtrack of movie trailers can be heard above traffic sounds, and the laughter and chatter of students, vendors, and passersby.

Across the road, a half-minute walk down the promenade, is the last of the official and once-grand buildings along this strip. This point is known as Library Corner. It is here that the promenade's glory peters out. It ends at a ragged intersection whose many converging streets and lack of traffic lights, and whose apparent system of blind trust, mirrors its more glorious front end. On either side of you now are private commercial structures that were built not to impress or to contribute culturally to the community in which they exist, but with materials and design meant purely to maximize the money-making potential of every square inch. A narrow roadway lined with dilapidated buildings leads to a public park that includes a football field, a running and cycling track, and several netball, volleyball, and basketball courts. Bleachers encircle the park. Behind them is the foot of the San Fernando Hill, a once-magnificent natural promontory and wildlife paradise in the heart of the town, a forest of bamboo, silk cotton, poui, and flamboyant, a bird watchers' haven, a reptile sanctuary, a nature lover's refuge, disfigured now with treeless trails that ensnare it, tractors and trucks crawling up and down its raw bruised sides, moving whole cubic acres of its yellow and white bedrock daily, its most perfect beauty pulverized for a most singular profit.

IF ALL YOU DO, HAVING JUST PLOPPED DOWN FROM THE SKY, IS STROLL down one of its streets, gawk at the buildings and monuments, and take cursory note of the local folk you pass and those who pass you by, a new place will reveal only so much of itself to you. A much better way — one might even say a more responsible way — to acquaint yourself so that you can truthfully proclaim: yes, I visited that place, I know it, is to move right into the homes, into the private and public dealings — into the minds, even — of some of its citizens.

You've met Dr. Krishnu and one of his daughters, Vashti. We might as well stay with them, meet the rest of the family and some of their friends. In due course — no hurry; after all, you're operating on Trinidad time now — we ought also to pay a visit to at least one other part of the island, for to know one corner alone is not at all to know a place that is so miraculously varied geographically, environmentally, socially, linguistically. It sounds like a hodge-podge of a place, but it's more like a well-seasoned, long-simmering stew.

For now, let's just slip into the world of Dr. Valmiki Krishnu.

Valmiki

IT WAS THAT SEPTEMBER DAY, ONE YEAR EARLIER, WASN'T IT? THAT rainy September day— exactly. The door behind his last patient had barely closed, and Valmiki Krishnu, still seated in his swivel chair, exerted a tremendous effort simply to lean forward and prop his elbows on his desk. Rain hit the galvanized overhang that protected the louvred window of his office like a torrent from a fire marshal's hose. He had not wanted to get out of bed that morning. He wished he had not.

The address book on his desk was open to the page with Tony Almirez's phone number in Goa. There was a nine-and-a-half-hour time difference between there and Trinidad. In Goa, it was midnight. Valmiki would awaken Tony if he were to telephone him—and Tony's wife, too. But it was Tony alone in all the world with whom he wanted to speak. Two decades before, he and Tony had been medical students together in Scotland. That was a long time ago, and much had happened for both of them since, and still every minute of their time together was indelibly etched in Valmiki's body and mind—even though they hadn't seen each other in twenty-something years, and had spoken on the telephone not more than a dozen times or so, all the calls initiated by Valmiki, the last one a year ago. Still, whenever Valmiki felt as disoriented as he did just now, it was Tony, not his own wife or any of their friends on the island, he reached for.

Valmiki's palms made a tower, and he tapped together the tips of his first three fingers as his mind bloated with the previous night's and that morning's aggravations. If it wasn't one thing with his wife, it was bound to be another with his daughter. His second daughter, Vashti, was as placid as the Gulf of Paria. But Viveka, the elder, had never been placid. At least, before going to university, she had been manageable. He opened his palms and let his head fall into his waiting hands.

He would not call Tony, he decided. Even if it had been Tony's midday instead of his midnight, he would not call him. That was how it had been for some time. The desperate lurching for Tony, the equally swift realization of the futility in that, and then Valmiki making do, turning to Saul. Saul, with his unreproachful, smiling eyes. Those long eyelashes. But Saul's comfort was limited. He could not offer Valmiki more than the physical—a respite from home, certainly, but always a shortlived respite and always on the sly. No one could help him.

THE TELEPHONE'S INTERCOM BUZZED. ON THE OTHER END, VALMIKI'S receptionist, Zoraida, expressed surprise at not spotting him at the door of his office. Valmiki normally saw a patient to the door, one hand light on the patient's back, ushering him or her out with nothing more than a suggestive nudge onward and a brief parting sentence of encouragement that made that nudge feel more like a gentle launch into the world rather than an expulsion from his office. But an expulsion it was, as he usually had an overflowing roomful of hacking, restless, not-so-patient patients to see, several of whom would have to be turned back at the end of the day with promises they would be seen first thing the following morning.

But today he had not even stood up as the man he had been treating exited. It was old-fashioned, he and his peers would agree, but most patients thought of their doctors as demi-gods able to make them well and whole just by poking and prodding the surface and orifices of their bodies. None of the doctors discouraged their patients from such thinking, but the load of being a healing god — the patients seldom did a single thing to heal themselves, the doctors would grumble — sometimes wore Valmiki down.

It was that, but not only that, which provoked within him such resistance to being where he was and contributed to his feeling of being trapped. Nor was it merely the altercation with Viveka that morning, nor the one immediately afterwards with his wife. And nor was it the troublesome one the previous night with both Devika and Viveka. After all, not a day seemed to go by without some unpleasantness from one, if not both, of them.

No, it was the weight of pretense. The weight of responsibility in general.

Had Valmiki been at the door to let his patient out, he would have been privy to one of Zoraida's coded gestures. Given the lack of reliable electricity and telephone service on the island, Dr. Krishnu and Zoraida had between them what Zoraida, who had been with him for twelve years now, liked to think of as a secret language. Her desk was angled for this very purpose, and the seating in the waiting room arranged so that Valmiki, his door, and a patient entering and exiting were out of sight of those awaiting their turn. A particular gesture from her would let him know that his wife had arrived and was in the waiting room. Another would indicate that certain individuals whom he might not want to keep waiting — family, old and dear friends, his bank manager, his solicitor, a number of people who not so coincidentally were white-skinned, and certain women acquaintances among that latter group — had arrived for their appointments or had shown up without appointments. Yet another gesture would inform him that both his wife and a queue-jumper were in the room. These gestures, flicks of the wrist, hair-arranging, specific numbers of fingers resting on her cheek, had been all initiated by Zoraida herself. She had even provided him with a de-coding chart. This initially amused him at her expense, but he came rather quickly to appreciate and rely on their system. More than once, her antics had saved him his marriage. Indeed, his attendance upon particularly privileged queue-jumpers had so often coincided with the unexpected arrival of Mrs. Krishnu that one might wonder if fate was complying with a subconscious wish of Valmiki's that he be caught out. Zoraida, in those instances, had enjoyed her part in staving off the possibility of public fiascos. With the barest hint of something that resembled a knock, she would officiously barge into his office, part of which, behind a curtain, was also the examination room, to inform her boss of the situation. The woman in his room would immediately be turned out, led by a massively important Zoraida down a private corridor and into another room where she would render herself presentable. Valmiki would be given just enough time to make himself the same before Mrs. Krishnu, none the wiser, or so one thought (for no wife is that dumb), would be ushered in, also by Zoraida. It was an orchestration Zoraida relished.

But Valmiki was not at his door this time, and therefore Zoraida did not get to perform her antics to inform him of the unscheduled arrival of one of his newer lady acquaintances, Tilda Holden. In any case, that day he did not care. He just wanted to run out of his office and leave everything behind. Every single thing. For good.

One thing had simply led to another, and now he was at that point, random on the one hand and precise on the other, where he had had enough. He had been doctor, boss, lover, husband, father for twenty weighty years now, and even so, in regards to the latter two especially, he still felt as incompetent as the first day, and not too much more willing.

While Valmiki had been attending to that last patient, a Mr. Deoraj Deosaran, he had been up and about, taking the man's pulse, rapping his knuckles on the man's sallow back and bony front as he listened through his stethoscope above the thundering of the rain on the roof, depressing the man's tongue with the palette stick and peering as far as he could down his windpipe, even hazarding a breath inhalation to see if his nose might pick up what his eyes, hands, and ears had not. He had, in other words, been attentive, absorbed even, until the end of the visit, an end that he had determined, there being nothing more to do, but an end that was still premature for the patient. Mr. Deosaran wanted to tell Dr. Krishnu the story of his life, as if Dr. Krishnu's knowing this story would alter his prognosis and prescription. Accordingly, he had talked about when he was a licle-licle boy, so small'n'tin nobody ad a think he'd a make man, he so licle and walking two mile one way to reach he school barefoot in the heavy heavy rain, rain worse than that week's rain, splashing up and duttying he clothes, and he holding his even licler brother by he hand — and the doctor's mind floated out of the room. Mr. Deosaran must have sat there telling his story for another several minutes, but Dr. Krishnu had heard nothing of it.

Mr. Deosaran had watched Dr. Krishnu's eyes grow dim and saw that he had withdrawn, but he noticed too that Dr. Krishnu had not risen, as he had in the past, to indicate that the visit was over. He spoke on some more, a little less certainly, but now it was to watch Dr. Krishnu. When he saw that he no longer held his audience, he dug his feet into the parquet tiling and shoved back the wooden chair in which he sat. The action made a sound like a car breaking a corner, but Dr. Krishnu seemed not to have heard that either. Mr. Deosaran lifted his khaki felt hat from his lap and rested it hesitantly on the desk in front of him. He leaned forward and his voice rose above the rain.

"Everything okay, Doc? You look like you seeing a dead."

When he received no answer he became perplexed and rapped the table with his knuckles. "Doc!" he said, sharp enough to snap Dr. Krishnu out of his blankness but not so sharp as to disturb the balance of power between them.

Only then did Dr. Krishnu catch himself. "Sorry, Mr. Deosaran. You took me back to another time."

A SIMPLER TIME, REALLY. VALMIKI MUST HAVE BEEN ABOUT TWELVE. For no reason other than to trouble him, his uncles, his father's brothers, used to unleash their curled thumbs and middle fingers at his ears, flick the tips and make him run squealing. His own father was a soft but strict man, and had never hit Valmiki. So he couldn't help but remember the first, albeit the last time, he got skinned by his father. Valmiki had been a fair and plump boy, with fat red cheeks and an insatiable taste for the desserts his mother, his aunts, and the servants made daily with milk from their own cows. He looked like the pampered child he was. His father was the area's most affluent citizen, a man whose family had built up and passed down to Valmiki's father and uncles a dairy business situated on the same property on which they lived, just south of the town of San Fernando. They were Brahmins, and so didn't touch the cows themselves. They managed the business from an office in the main house and hired men from the village who did the manual work of feeding and milking the cows and cleaning the pens that were some distance from the house.

Valmiki was his parents' only child, and seen as the one who would one day inherit a good portion of this thriving business. From the workers' point of view, Valmiki, even though he was a child, was their boss too. So when he took the three boys (he shouldn't really have thought of them as his friends, but he did — they were classmates who jeered at him for his plumpness yet relied on him to help them with their homework, as he was the brightest boy in his class and they the dimmest) into the barn, the workmen who knew that he should not be going in there were not confident enough of their position to stop him. He had already changed out of his school clothes and wore short pants and a yellow, red, and brown striped T-shirt that his father had brought for him on a trip to England. His friends, as he would call them, wore the white long-sleeved shirts and the grey long pants of the school uniform. None wore the grey-and-white striped ties that were also part of the uniform, having removed them once they were off the school grounds and bound their stack of school books with them. The boys had come around to the back entrance of the house, knowing better, as children of poor villagers, than to approach the house from the front, and had asked the servant for Valmiki. Valmiki heard her loud steupses. The servant, even though she too was from the same village as the boys, took offence to them coming to play with her employer's child. Her disdain was clear. "He drinking his tea now. What you want him for? It is a school day, the middle of the week. Why you not home doing your homework? He have to study. He can't come out to play; he have homework to do."

Valmiki was annoyed that the servant had acted as if she were his parent. He heard the boys laugh, and mock back, "He drinking tea. And what he eating? He eating bread and jam, cookies and cream?" One of them asked the maid if he could have a biscuit, please, he was hungry. She asked him if he had no shame, begging so, and what his mother would say if she knew? Valmiki pushed his plate away and ran to the door. He pushed the maid aside. He and the boys both knew that he could not invite them inside his house or offer to bring them mugs of hot, sweet, milky tea or the semolina pudding, which he knew they were bound to love in spite of such teasing. But he was overcome with the desire to give these boys who ridiculed him so much, and yet came to his house looking for him, something of his that they themselves did not have. He pulled the hands of two of the boys along with him. He led them under the wood fence of the pasture where cows stood motionless except for their tails, whipping flies off their backsides. As they side-stepped heaps of cow dung the boys continued to tease Valmiki, asking what kind of tea he was drinking and why didn't he bring a biscuit with nice cream in it for them. One of them asked him what he was studying so for. They didn't have a test that week, and if there had been one, he would still pass it. The boy added, "You not dunce, but you dull, dull, dull. Dull, for so. What is better? To be a dunce, yet the kind of fellow everyone wants to spend time with, or to be bright and coming first all the time, and can't talk to ordinary people because all your head is full up with is information?"

Another boy piped up, "Five times nought equals nought five times one is five five times two is ten five times three is...five times three is what? I forget."

They cackled at this, and then the first boy continued, "Krishnu, tell we, na. You ever try talking to one of them school books? You ever sit down and ol' talk, and have a good laugh with a science book, boy?"

Valmiki nodded thoughtfully and he even managed a small laugh, as if to say the boy had made a good point. He did not show his hurt.

Old samaan trees with verdant umbrella tops spread a cooling shade across the acres and acres of undulating land that had been in his father's family for seventy years. The sky, and the trees' foliage, and their trunks, took on a yellow tinge with the evening light and the treetops trembled with parakeets. The birds made a racket with their incessant twittering and the fluttering of their restless wings as they landed, each one hopping about urgently, searching out the right spot in which to pass the approaching night. In vain the boys combed the soft rich earth beneath for rocks with which to pelt the parakeets. They tried using fallen sticks and bits of branches that had dried, but these were too light and the boys did not have the power to launch them high enough. They pelted doodose mangoes and then used fallen bird-pecked ones to try to bring down others. They climbed into the generous cradle of the governor plum tree because it was low and easy to climb.

For a while Valmiki was pleased that his father's property could provide these boys with entertainment. But they became bored quickly enough, and picked up again and carried on mercilessly the theme of Valmiki's biscuits and tea. He said nothing, shamed that he had been gorging on his second helping of pudding. Being the son of the wealthiest man in the area was more of a strain than something to revel in. These boys, whose fathers were labourers on the sugar-cane estates or in the nearby sugar factory, and whose mothers were government-paid water carriers for the road works programs, had the ability to easily make him feel inferior, powerless; they could tease him about his privileges, about his family's fancy ways, but he dared not say a word about their poverty or narrower future prospects. Suddenly, he realized that he had the power to be more benevolent than they, and he decided that he would exercise this power. He would offer them something more tangible and special than the chance to throw sticks uselessly at birds. So he led them through the pasture to one of the sheds where more than thirty cows were housed. He had heard it said that no one in the area kept cows anymore. His father, Mr. Krishnu, owner of the cattle estate, wouldn't allow it, others said. Whether this was true or not, reasoned Valmiki, the cows would be a novelty.

No one but employees and Valmiki's father and brothers were allowed inside the fetid barn with its miasma of cooped-up, hot cow bodies, the milky sweetness of newborn calves, bales of dry grass—some rotted and fermenting in the heat—spilled milk that had soured, and the stench from two brimming open-mouthed pits along the centre aisle into which dung, sometimes a loose slick, sometimes stubborn, matted straw and syrupy urine, were hosed twice a day. But Valmiki marched in confidently, doing his best to ignore the odours and completely ignoring, as if they weren't there, the same men who greeted him, and whom he greeted, mornings and afternoons as he left and returned with the chauffeur for school. The three boys with him, meanwhile, gagged at the stench. They shoved the toes of their school sneakers under the edge of the piles of grass stored in the aisle, dragging out strands onto the uneven concrete path. They made lewd gestures at the cows, which stared back with eyes bulging but unfazed while chewing their cuds and used their tails to lash at sultana-sized flies that crawled on and bit their bodies. The boys mooed, and when a cow mooed—either back at them or simply because it did — they made a racket of mooing sounds.

Rakes and shovels leaned against a post, and one of the boys headed for these but Valmiki sharply told him not to touch them. To his surprise, the boy acquiesced immediately. Valmiki himself then lifted a large galvanized iron pail off a hook on another post, dragged it with a ruckus along the ground, and then slid with it under the slatted gate of one of the pens. He had to brace himself with one hand on the ground. The ground was wet. In the low light he could not see what he had put his hand in. He wanted to smell it, but he knew that if he did, and if it were cow-excrement, not only the smell but the idea of it would weaken his resolve in front of his friends. He wiped his hand on the side of his pants. One of the workers made his way over. The cows, hearing the metallic sounds made by the bucket, shifted their weight from side to side. Restless, their tails whipped about. When the other boys tried to follow Valmiki under the gate, Valmiki stopped them. He patted the cow on its side. It tamped the grass beneath its feet, moving its body closer to Valmiki as if to nestle against him. One of the boys managed to slip under the gate.

"Bayta," the worker mumbled, not enjoying contradicting the actions of his boss's son, and more so in front of the boy's playmates, "your pappy ent go like for you be in here. You go dutty up your clothes."

Now, as an adult, Valmiki recalled the man wearing a white button-down shirt, the sleeves rolled to his elbows, and a white cloth tied around his head like a rough turban. In his memory the man wore grey trousers and he was barefoot. The man's clothing, as far as he could recall, was spotless, but then he doubted his memory, for reason would suggest that anyone working in a cattle barn and dressed in white was bound to get the stain of grass-feed on his clothing, if nothing else. For an instant Valmiki wondered how much of his memory was reliable, how much of it he had invented or doctored. Hadn't he felt his face go red with anger that the man would talk to him like that in front of those boys? Hadn't he told the man sharply that his father didn't know he was in there, and what he didn't know wouldn't bother him? He was able to hear, as clearly as if it were yesterday, one of the boys outside of the pen tease, "Let's get out of here, man. This place stinking fuh so. Ey, Valmiki, you living by a stinking place, boy. Even the open drain in front my house don't smell so bad."

Valmiki remembered ignoring the boy and all that followed. "You want to taste some nice fresh milk?" he had persisted.

He slipped the pail beneath the cow. In response, the worker who had spoken with him before swung open the gate. The man was suddenly stern. And Valmiki remembers him now, his clothes in Valmiki's memory now gleaming, and the man standing straight and tall. "Bayta, that cow give milk for the day. It need a rest now."

Valmiki clenched his teeth and ignored the man. He knelt down beside the cow. The man sighed hard. Even if the boy was only twelve years old, this was the boss's son. Valmiki grabbed hold of the teats and worked them one at a time, as he had seen done, and as if he had done it a thousand times before. He was determined. Fortunately, a forceful stream of white milk shot into the pail noisily, opaque bubbles rapidly forming. The other boys were finally impressed. They bent down to watch and whistled in awe. Valmiki, sweating, released the teats and stood up only when the pail was half full. The others wanted to try. Valmiki knew better than to let them. That would have been going much too far. He tried to lift the pail himself, but the milk sloshed from side to side. Some of it spilled, and the man rushed to take the pail from Valmiki. "What you want to do with this?" he asked, showing his anger and frustration by not addressing the boy with the usual affectionate Hindi word for son. Valmiki told him to empty the milk into three bottles. He sent each boy home with a bottle.

Valmiki was whipped that night on his raw backside with a guava switch for not staying in to do his homework, for going into the barn, for taking boys from the village there, for showing off, for getting cow dung on his hands and on his pants, for milking a cow, for milking a cow that had already been milked for the day, and for giving away milk to neighbours when those very ones, like all others, were accustomed to buying it.

Valmiki pleaded weakly, "It was just milk, Pappa. Just three bottles. I will pay you back from my allowance."

Valmiki's father retorted with the violent calm of the one wielding the switch, which came down on his son seven more times: "You BETTER LEARN the VALUE of business FAST, you hear? And take THIS! For not being MAN enough to STAND UP to those boys, for LETTING OTHER children lead you into doing wrong." His father, finished, pushed Valmiki away. Valmiki tried to pull up his underpants, but the bite and burn of his buttocks was too great. He put his hands on his backside to calm the pain, but the heat of them only made the fire burn more. Valmiki's mother finally took him by his shoulders and ushered him toward his own room. His father's voice grew loud again. "Let him go and live in the village for a day or two with those same people. He wouldn't last a minute. You think I hit him good? They will beat his ass to a pulp."

Valmiki's mother rubbed aloe on his buttocks until his sobbing eventually subsided and he lay limp. The sheet about his face was wet from his crying, and about his body it was drenched in the sweat of humiliation and anger at his father. All the while his mother cooed, "Bayta, don't mind your pappa. He have a temper. He love you, child, but he find you too soft. Mamma love you, too." She held his face and turned him to face her. "Just so, just how you stay. Don't mind Pappa beat you. He is not a bad man, he just want you to toughen up a little." Valmiki was perplexed at the softness his parents saw in him, and from then on he pondered how he might fix that.

He hadn't seen those boys, men they would be now, in more than thirty years. Trinidad wasn't a big country, but still their paths wouldn't readily have crossed. He only thought of them and this incident because of his patient's story. He wondered where those three boys — men — were now. If he knew and called them up right that minute, could he have said to them, Let's go find a cow to milk, or a bar to drink dry and catch up? And would they go? They might have continued the old teasing in a good-natured manner, and in a good-natured manner he would have accepted it because they would all see that he had changed and was no longer the boss's too-soft, mamsy-pamsy son.

BACK THEN, HE HADN'T WANTED TO BE WHERE HE WAS RIGHT NOW, that was for sure. If his own son were still alive, he couldn't help but think — and he imagined a boy of five or so, not a youth of eighteen, which would make chronological sense — he would have that second got into his car and taken the boy out of school, driven with him to the foot of the San Fernando Hill or into the forested lands of the central hills, and taken him hunting, or at least to catch birds there. This, in spite of the fact that he had never actually taken his son anywhere, his son being a sickly boy from the day he was born until he died at age five. Instead, he had several times taken Viveka, older than her little brother by two years, to the forested lands, and walked her along a cutlassed path so that he could show her where he hunted. He used to be big in her eyes then, bigger than he was in anyone else's, ever. How could a child, your own daughter, unsettle you so, without you knowing exactly why?

"Those were different days then, weren't they?" Valmiki mumbled, returning to his patient, raising his eyebrows as if in surprise at himself.

Mr. Deosaran offered, in a quiet tone, "Sometimes the doctor might need to see a doctor too, not so, Doc?"

Valmiki rubbed his mouth with a circular hand motion. Finally he said, "You know, the truth is that the doctor can't fix everything."

Thinking that his advice was being solicited, the man grew bolder. "Well, I could take it if the doctor can't fix heself. That make a kind of sense. But I hope the doc still good with his patients."

At this, Dr. Krishnu snapped back fully. He looked Mr. Deosaran directly in the eyes, assured him that while everyone else was easy to care for, the doctor himself was typically the worst patient. He muttered, "Physician heal thyself," to which the Mr. Deosaran said, "That is a good one, Doc. They should make that a saying. Is a good one." The man picked up the umbrella he had left by the door, lifted his hat to his head, and tapped it into place. Then he backed out of the door.

And that was when Valmiki leaned toward the table, tipped the swivel chair forward, and dug his elbows into his desk. He brought his palms together as if to pray, although he was far from doing any such thing. He tapped together the tips of his first three fingers, opened his palms, and lowered his face into them just as Zoraida rang.

“Yes?” His voice was muffled because of the hand pressed against a portion of his lips. Still, his terseness with Zoraida in that one word was palpable. He resented having put himself in the position of needing her. She knew — not everything, but certainly a great deal about him, and he hardly anything of her. And he certainly didn’t want her thinking that because he had intimate dealings with more than one of the women who paid him visits in his office, she had any chance of falling in among them. It must have naturally crossed her mind — for what perks might come with that! — but she surely saw the similarity among the women he favoured. They were — the exception being his wife — foreign white women, all beautiful in the way that men commonly — or common men — liked their women. No doubt she knew better than to try to cross any more lines than she already had.

She *did* take liberties. For example, sometimes he sent her to buy his lunch at the doubles vendor on the promenade. One or two dollars in change should have been returned to him, but more often than not, they were not. Two dollars was nothing to him, but the boldness of her actions, and the fact that he felt he had no choice but to allow her this audacity, made him fume. If she put off doing a task, like letting office supplies run out entirely before reordering, he fumed then, too, but to himself. Occasionally he dared chastise her, but she would interrupt him almost kindly. “What you said, Dr. Krishnu? How you talking as if you not feeling good today?”

She also had her by-the-way reminders of his illicit acts and her indispensability. “Did you call back Mrs. Alexander? That was close yesterday, eh! She and Mrs. Krishnu almost met. But I got Mrs. Alexander out as soon as Mrs. Krishnu pull up in her car.”

Valmiki sometimes complained about her to his wife, Devika. Only certain things he told her, of course, but usually it was enough to make her take Zoraida's insolences personally: "Who does she think she is? She is too familiar with you. She is behaving like your wife. Why do you let her get away with this behaviour? Let me have a chat with her, I will straighten her out so fast!"

Of course, he would allow no such thing. How he sometimes wished, though, that stories of his philandering would leak — no, rather explode — throughout the town, and cause such a scandal that his family would toss him out like a piece of used tissue or flush him from their lives, and he would be forced to leave the country. He would be freed. He revised his thought: perhaps he, forever concerned about appearances and doing the praiseworthy thing, would never really be free.

If philandering had been for him a sword, it was the double-edged kind. On the one hand, it was a suggestion of his more-than-okay status with the ladies (not one, but many) and so worked against suspicions of who and what he was at heart. A man was certainly admired by men and by women for a show of his virility, even by the ones he hurt. On the other hand, since philandering had never been a shame in Trinidad — a badge it was, rather — for a man who wanted to be caught, broken, and expelled, it was a problem.

These days, Saul was the object of Valmiki's most powerful and basest desires, yet Saul could have come to Valmiki's office every day and not even Zoraida would have had the tiniest somersault in her brain regarding that. But still, he wouldn't let Saul visit him here. Saul and his friends — they had became Valmiki's friends eventually — would get together on the occasional weekend. Saul and Valmiki usually started their visit on the Friday night. They would drive all the way up to Saul's cousin's house, a two-room wooden structure in the Maraval Hills. The cousin would leave, and Valmiki and Saul would spend the night there. In the early hours of Saturday morning Saul's accepting male friends would come up and meet them, and they would all head deep into the northern range to hunt. Hardly anyone minded or wondered about that. In fact, the hunting itself, as unusual as it was for a man of Valmiki's background, was seen as his little quirk and a recommendation of his widely admired viritilty. Even though the group hunted less frequently these days, there remained the perception in his social world that Valmiki was still quite a regular hunter. Valmiki and Saul now met at The Golden Dragon, and even at The Victory, once in a while.

"DOCTOR? HELLO, DOCTOR? BUT, EHEH, WHAT HAPPEN TO THE PHONE? Doctor, you there?"

Valmiki had been quiet for what must have seemed on the other end an unusual while. Then he spoke. "I heard you, Zoraida. I heard you. Give me a minute. I will call you when I am ready."

But Zoraida was insistent. "No, Doctor, I didn't see you let Mr. Deosaran out and now Mrs. . . ."

But Valmiki instinctively did not want to hear. He cut her short. "No. Look. Not now, I said. I don't know what I am doing." He spoke more sharply than usual.

"What do you mean you don't..."

He snapped at her, "I said wait. Just wait." He slammed down the receiver.

Had he listened, he would have found out that a woman he had met some days before, Tilda Holden, and had paid a great deal of attention to — an inordinate amount, he later admonished himself, at a doctors' dinner, on an evening when Devika was not feeling well and so had not accompanied him — was in the waiting room. She had arrived without an appointment, complaining to Zoraida first of headaches, and then, kept waiting too long, of a pain in her chest. Had it been any other day, Valmiki would likely have seen the woman right away, and the rest of his scheduled patients in the waiting room might have been left a good half hour, fanning themselves, or steupsing with frustration over the long, long, long wait in that hot, airless, germ-filled room.

But today was different.

The night before, when Valmiki and his family had sat down to eat supper together, his eldest daughter, Viveka, had announced she planned to stay at home the following day to study in the library at the back of the house. The library had been built especially for the children when Viveka was eight and Vashti four, and although the intention was for Valmiki and Devika to remain in that house for the rest of their lives, and also to have the two girls attend university, this room they called the library — to instill in the children a sense of serious study — was built for a small child's needs, with low shelves, not too many, and desks too light for spreading out university-weight texts. It was less than three years ago, when Viveka had entered the University of the West Indies, that they had replaced the two pint-sized desks with ones more sensible for the needs of young women, but this had reduced the already small space by half. Still, this more than any other place was where Viveka preferred to hole up. It was where she had learned to think beyond the words of a book, and where she sometimes leaned back in her chair, staring up at the ceiling in almost the exact manner that was her father's unconscious habit.

Last evening, just before supper and not long after Valmiki and Devika had had another of their regular tiffs — tension still between them, and Valmiki worn out by now — Viveka had barged into the house in a flurry of excited huffs and puffs as if she had had a most noble and terribly long day at the university. As they sat down to eat, she had announced, as if it were a present she was giving the family, that she would not make the trip up to the university the following day. The family library, she glowed, was perfect, still perfect, even though one would have thought she and Vashti had by now outgrown it. Valmiki and Devika, in spite of the chill between them, had discreetly exchanged nervous glances at this touch of congeniality, but when nothing untoward immediately followed, they relaxed. The main part of the meal was eaten in an atmosphere of hesitant amicability.

Then, just as Devika finished serving out the cherry cheesecake and placed on the table a saucer of Rimpty's chocolates that their chocolate-making neighbours, the Prakashs, had sent over, the dreaded subject of extracurricular activities came up. And not just any extracurricular activity, but volleyball. That damned volleyball subject yet again! thought Valmiki, even as he tried to appear unfazed. But the subject hadn't simply come up, of course. Viveka had introduced it in a contrived way. Throughout the meal Vashti had been talking to Viveka, and Valmiki, perhaps because he had been anticipating some unpleasantness, had noticed that Viveka seemed unduly irritated by Vashti's chatter and appeared to be listening to the conversation going on between him and Devika. Valmiki had been telling Devika that the Medical Association was having their annual dinner and dance soon, and was wondering if he should secure tickets. Devika had responded that there was a clique of wives who were social climbers, using their husbands' professions — professions that the husbands only had because education and scholarships were available to any and everybody in the country — to give them all kinds of licence they wouldn't otherwise have, and that those women liked to gossip too much. Those women were smiling and paying you compliments one minute, and the moment you had your back to them they were prying into your life and crying you down, all to build themselves up. She really hated those dinners.

Just then, Viveka piped up. "There seems to be a general human need to form cliques and join clubs, doesn't there?" Valmiki knew instantly where she wanted to go with that statement. Both he and Devika bristled. There was a local women-only sports club, not connected to the university but a local community club that met on Tuesdays and Thursdays for practice at the public park at the far end of the Harris Promenade, and a few weeks ago Viveka had expressed an interest in joining it. Devika had asked her if she was crazy, wanting to go and play a game in a club that was open to anybody and, of all places, in that part of the city. Whereupon Viveka had reminded them that Helen, daughter of their financial adviser, was on a team that played there. Devika had responded, "I don't care if the Queen's children play on that court, my children are not playing there. You should know better than asking."

And now Viveka had burst into their dinnertime conversation, bringing up the subject again. "You know, the interesting thing about a community sports club is that it does allow for the intermingling of the different social classes and the many cultures our county is blessed with, don't you agree, Dad?" Although Valmiki knew the question was rhetorical, he was about to grab the rein with some clever and diverting response, but Viveka didn't wait for an answer. "I mean, after all, we are a small island, and rather than form cliques we should indeed be learning from and about one another, helping one another upward, you know what I am saying?" She looked from her father to Vashti and carried right on again. "As you yourself have said, Dad, strong individuals make for a strong nation, a strong country within and without." If Viveka's little sermon prevented her from hearing her mother's sudden heavy breathing, Valmiki was aware of it, and this panicked him even more than whatever Viveka had up her sleeve. Devika bit her lower lip. She pushed her plate up the table. Valmiki couldn't help himself. He had to smile. His daughter was bold. Bolder than he was. Vashti put down her fork, scrunched up her mouth and forehead, and looked at her sister in confusion.

But Devika was not about to play this game with her daughter. "Look, get to the point, Viveka. You are talking about joining that club again, aren't you?"

"Well, Mom, Helen..."

Viveka's tone immediately went from the pulpit one she had managed so calmly to a high-pitched one, but she got no further than the mention of her friend Helen's name. Her mother lashed out, "Look, I don't want to hear about Helen. Helen is not even Indian. At least, not *properly* Indian. Her father is white—which, let me remind you, not just you, but you *and* your father, does not mean that he is one bit better than us. Most of those foreign whites who leave their countries and come here are not from our class. They come here because they can't do better for themselves in their own countries. They come behaving as if they are superior, lording it over us. They have no social graces whatsoever, and people like you and your father fall for all of their nonsense."

Valmiki was irked. He gasped at the manner in which he was so suddenly insulted, but knowing better than to get trapped by either his wife or Viveka, he simply threw his hands up in mock defeat and shook his head.

"On top of that, Helen's mother is a brassy Port of Spain Indian. Those Indians from the north like to think they are too different. They do whatever they please without thinking of what others might say. Mix that sort of attitude with a little whiteness and they have their children joining swim clubs and tennis clubs, prancing about like horses, and you hear about their children attending all kinds of parties they have no right being at, you hear things about them, things that I would be ashamed to repeat to your father. Those town Indians have no respect for their origins, they forget their place, they ooh and they aaah over curry as if they never had curry before, and they give their children names like Helen. You are not joining that club."

Viveka opened her mouth but was cut off again.

"You tell me, are there any other Indian girls on that team? Go on. Tell me." Devika asked this with a confidence in the answer that both annoyed her husband and inspired awe in him.

"Women," Viveka corrected, albeit in a less confident tone now.

"As long as you're living in my house I will call you what I like."

Valmiki slid one of the Rimpty's chocolates off the plate and his hand hovered in front of his mouth. He could smell the sugar in the candy. In a softer manner he tried to employ a different tactic: he and her mother didn't think Viveka joining the team was a good idea because it might affect her studies, he said. Devika inhaled loud and long to let them both know that she thought this was pandering, and she did not approve of it.

Viveka sulked back that playing a sport did not mean her grades would suffer or that she would not qualify with a degree. Valmiki asked how long each evening's session would last. Before Viveka could answer, her mother snapped: Time didn't matter, what mattered was that club days were during the week. When neither Valmiki nor Viveka said anything, Devika added in her inimitable tone that weekdays were impossible.

The topic had first come up several weeks previously. At the time, Devika had expressed her worry to Valmiki that since Viveka already lacked a certain finesse one wanted in a girl, engaging in team sports and competition might only make her that much more ungainly, and whatever polish she, Devika, had tried so hard to impart would certainly be erased. But other things were on Valmiki's mind, then and now. He could not imagine either of his daughters being at that park late into the evenings. Young men idled there, men of African origin in particular. But he knew better than to say this out loud, as Viveka would then have asked about his friendship with Saul, who was of African origin, and that would have derailed everything. She would certainly have jumped, too, on the racism and sexism implied. If she had used the word *hypocritical* he would have understood, but Devika would likely, in a single action, have stood up and flung her hand across Viveka's face. In short, provoking Viveka further would only leave room for a litany of examples of how old-fashioned and everything-phobic he and Devika were (none of which Valmiki minded being), with the result that Viveka would end up looking like the noble, victimized member of the family.

Valmiki did worry that, in all innocence — for how could Viveka be anything but, as she had no experience of the world as he knew it — his daughter could be encouraged into an easy manner with unsavoury young men precisely because of all that so-called progressive university-nonsense she came home with, nonsense that always had terminology suffixed with the dreaded "ism": sexism, feminism, paternalism, Marxism, racism, antiracism, activism. Of course he had said none of this to Viveka, nor to Devika.

But something more had nagged at Valmiki last evening at dinner, and now continued on into his office hours — the knowledge that while team sports involved various kinds of camaraderie and, yes-yes, all that important exercise, it had the potential to involve something else: complicated kinds of physical contact. He knew something of this; he had played soccer with boys from his high school and, later, soccer and cricket at university. And even as he sensed the foolishiness and futility of trying to protect her, he couldn't bear to give his daughter, this one in particular, permission to enter an arena that could stir within her, like it had in him, a confusion she would absolutley have to keep to herself. He wasn't entirely sure that this would happen, but it nagged at him that it could.

Valmiki had not been overly enthusiastic about sports when he was in high school, but on the soccer field during mandatory physical education period he proved himself to have a special talent for sliding by the other players, seemingly out of nowhere, and scoring goals. Several older students — brash, loud fellows who played soccer every chance they got, during the lunch break and after classes — noticed his talent. Among themselves they carried on a kind of roughousing that included a good bit of deliberate touching-up, which at first he thought was strange for boys who teased one another so much. He noticed that they would fall into spontaneous, out-of-control wrestling bouts, and that the physical education teacher would come out and shamelessly land himself in their midst. They shoved and pushed one another, grabbing onto one another's privates, shrieking, cackling, getting hoarse, almost choking on their fun as they made one another hard by the sheer act of this kind of play. They all, every one of them, seemed to enjoy it, and fell into it over and again — even though, once off the field, none of that sort of touching continued, or was even made mention of. In the change rooms where they showered, two boys to a concrete stall with a half door on it, the boys only half-naked — their underpants remained on — there was the strictest hands-off protocol.

But Valmiki was taken under the wing of a self-appointed guardian, an older student who, when they were in their shower stall together, would insist on giving Valmiki's growing limbs a good rub down "to help keep that kick nice and strong," as the older boy would say. The torrential flow of water out of the shower head hit their bodies hard and felt good to them both. Valmiki liked what the older boy did to his body, soaping his hair, massaging his scalp, riding his thumbs under Valmiki's meagre scapular and up and down either side of his spine. Across his chest, his buttocks, hard down his thighs — his "quads," the boy would say. His calves. And even his feet, one foot held in the boy's hands as Valmiki leaned his shoulders back against the mossy concrete wall of the stall so as not to slip in the soapy pool collecting about them. One toe at a time the boy soaped and pulled, and Valmiki would laugh and kick and pull back his foot, doing a sort of dance to balance himself that made them laugh to the point of tears. "How a lil fellow like you could kick so big and hard and direct, boy?" the older boy would ask, and Valmiki would feel as if he had been lifted high into the air.

But then one day the boy, while soaping Valmiki's back, slipped his hand inside of the waistband of Valmiki's underpants, a soapy finger sliding into the crease of his bottom. Valmiki spun around fast and backed away from the boy, who, grinning widely, put his forefinger to his lips. The boy reached into the front of his own pants and pulled out his hardened penis. Valmiki stood still and stared. The older boy stepped toward Valmiki and put his free hand on Valmiki's shoulder as he pulled at himself until his penis spluttered its semolina-like fluid. Valmiki's face burned with a sudden terror, but his body trembled with excitement. His own penis had hardened, but the older boy only patted him on the face and laughed. He turned his back to Valmiki and washed his face rapidly with soap, breathing out noisily against his hands and the onslaught of water from the shower head. Valmiki's curiosity had been piqued. Even as he knew better than to make his interest obvious, he began to keep the older boy in sight, to shift his body this way or that in an attempt to catch the boy's attention. But the boy had changed. He kept a distance now, even during the physical education period. Come shower time, he would make a show of entering a shower stall alone. Valmiki watched the older boy as he stood with groups of other students chatting and laughing among themselves. He felt scorned, and shame blossomed soon enough into anger when he imagined the boys were watching him, as if they knew.

One day, when there was no physical education class, not minutes after the bell rang to announce the start of the long lunchtime period, Valmiki buckled his courage and with a studied calm walked across the field, far away from the school building, to the edge where the unfenced property was marked by the neighbouring one, an unkempt stretch of overgrown razor grass and guava trees. Valmiki knew the boy would see him go to the bushes. He looked back, caught the boy's eye, and then carried on. He could only hope, and sure enough, the boy waited until Valmiki had entered onto a narrow path and disappeared into the grasses that closed in behind him. He crossed the field, entered the same path, and caught up with Valmiki, who had stopped among the guavas to wait for him. They held hands as naturally and as easily as if they had done it before and

Valmiki led the older boy as he ducked in and about the trees. Suddenly, the older boy pulled Valmiki to a stop and suggested they take their long-sleeved white school shirts off so they would not easily be seen. Shirt and tie off, they drew each other farther along to a spot where they could, through the foliage, still see bits of the school building, but where they were sure they themselves could not be seen. Even now, decades later, Valmiki could conjure up the cloying perfume of that guava orchard, and remembered how the cuts from the razor grass there stung his legs, his bare back, and his chest. The memory of this concoction made him feel at once ill and nostalgic.

Their tongues had hesitantly touched.

The memory now caused a lurch in Valmiki, from his waist down to his toes. The older boy had undone the zipper of Valmiki's short khaki trousers and taken Valmiki in his hand. He and the boy continued to stick their tongues out of their mouths so that only the tips touched as the boy fondled Valmiki until Valmiki's penis grew long, thick, and harder than he himself had ever managed to make it on his own. He trembled and the boy bent his head and put his mouth on it. Valmiki came in the boy's mouth instantly, and a horror overtook him. Revolted, he kneed the boy under his chin so hard that the boy accidentally clamped his jaws shut on his own tongue and blood spewed out of his mouth. The boy stood there holding both hands to his mouth, tears blurring his vision, and Valmiki ran, pulling on his shirt, buttoning it and tucking it back into his pants. He ran, tears of anger and horror in his eyes, until he was right out of the school gates. He made his way home, ducking into the tall grasses that lined the roads whenever a car passed by. He slipped into his house unnoticed, and went immediately to the shower. He was in a rage, crying as he bathed himself, scrubbing his entire body — although he was barely able to bring himself to touch his penis — until his brown skin was raw, pinprick-size beads of blood reddening the surface of his skin. He spat and spat, and rubbed the soap against the tip of his tongue as he attempted to erase the taste and feel of the other boy's tongue from his mouth. He couldn't have hated that boy any more, and he hated himself in equal measure.

For weeks he was terrified that word of what he and the boy had done in the bushes would spread and he would be beaten up, kicked off the soccer team, perhaps pulled into the bushes by other boys and the same done to him by one or a group of them, older, stronger than he. But what he was most afraid of was that word would reach his parents. Then he would surely kill himself. He had planned how he would do it, and waited day and night for the indication that his dreadful, unnatural activity had been made public. But until this day, no word of it had ever been spoken. The boy left school at the end of that term. No teacher had offered a reason, and no one seemed interested in finding out why. Valmiki had always assumed that it might have had something to do with — not so much what the two of them had done that day in the bush, but with whatever it was that had made him do that kind of thing in the first place. Even as he fondled himself in his nighttime bedroom, his heart racing full tilt as he imagined the same boy bent into his lap, and he experienced the same uncontrollable shudder at the memory of the boy's mouth on him, how it felt as if his mind were about to be blown apart and his body to shoot right into outer space, he didn't mind never seeing the boy again. These fantasy moments usually ended with Valmiki suddenly shoving the boy off him, giving him a solid undercut with his fist, a knee under the already bloody chin, and a shove into a wire fence where he imagined the boy holding on, crying and begging forgiveness. How Valmiki hated that boy and what they had done together.

He practised bouncing a soccer ball on his head and on his knee. He made a point of engaging in disparaging jokes about women and "faggots." He developed the affectation of spitting, velocity and distance becoming markers of his manhood. He launched, too, into a display, at school and in front of his parents, of noticing girls, commenting almost to the point of excess, sometimes with a lewdness that did not suit him.

Intimacies, albeit of a lesser degree, he came to see were something sporting fellows never outgrew; at medical college abroad he played soccer and cricket, and there the men gave one another stout congratulatory hugs, pats on the shoulders, playful but harder slaps on their backsides, pats on the face that sometimes felt as nuanced an exchange as one might expect in an engagement between a man and a woman. He watched closely for signs that might have exposed secrets between the men, but he saw nothing that resembled his much-regretted exchange with the boy in his high school. He was careful, regardless of how he felt, not to touch or respond to any teammate in a manner that might provoke that teammate to lash out at him the way he himself had done to the boy in high school.

Then along came Tony, the student from Goa who was to tutor him in a course he had failed twice. Tony: not athletic, but muscular. He was short, one might even say stocky, and brown like Valmiki himself. Tony had grey eyes, unusual for an Indian, and he had short curly hair. He reminded Valmiki of sculptures of Grecian young men he had seen in the museums.

Valmiki didn't know if "feeling each other up" during games was strictly a guy-thing, but he suspected and worried that girls and women might get on with their own version of that sort of thing, too. He wanted Viveka spared the horror, the confusion of the kind of experience he had had but never revealed to anyone.

In adulthood Valmiki might have played golf, as did several of his colleagues and other men from his social world, but he took up, instead, hunting. It started with an invitation from Saul, one of his patients, an electrician who lived on a fringe of the city and who could not have entered Valmiki's social circles. The pupils of Saul's eyes were a yellowish brown and light always seemed to emit from them. They reminded him of Tony's grey eyes. Saul would look directly at Valmiki with those eyes as if he could see through Valmiki. He was not like other men, not afraid of long, insistent eye contact. Saul Joseph was lean, ruggedly muscular. It was precisely the fact that he was partly of African origin that heightened the unlikeliness of there being a bond between the two men, and that drew Valmiki to accept Saul's invitation. No one would pay any attention. Valmiki went with Saul one Saturday into the forested central hills, awkwardly toting a rifle the man had spared him for the day.

By the time darkness had fallen on the hills that first day, Valmiki was sold on the particular camaraderie that went with that sport. That week, accompanied by Saul, who had in a sweet instant risen from status of patient to peer-of-sorts, Valmiki bought a shotgun and a box of ammunition from a villager, a cacao farmer who moonlighted smuggling these and other contraband onto the island.

The hunting circle was elastic. One week it might include just the two of them, and another there might be four men altogether, but rarely was there ever more than that, and never was there anyone among them who would have known Valmiki in his other life of city doctor, San Fernando professional, and socialite.

None of these men Devika liked or wished to entertain in her house. She bristled when Valmiki brought them onto her patio. If he offered them drinks, Devika made sure they were served—and certainly not by herself—in tumblers that only the maid and various other workers were supposed to use. These men looked to her more like security guards, or house builders, people who would work for them rather than visit with them. When Valmiki talked to her of going hunting with "Saul," Devika said, "So, what now? He calls you Valmiki?"

Valmiki could truthfully answer, "As a matter of fact, he and the others call me Doc." Why he went with these men Devika could not fathom, and although Valmiki had a practice of cajoling her in almost every way, giving up this particular pastime or his communion with these men he would not do. With them he knew an affinity he simply did not share with her. It was a world of few words, more silence, and hard, immediate, and sure handling of one another that was as loaded, as sprung, as the guns they carried. The act of looking out for one another in the most primal way gripped him. It was not just him looking out for them, but them looking out for him too. An equal caring. With gun in hand, and knowing there was a wild cat or a startled diamond-back mapipire in the canopied darkness of an evening forest, every man had to look out for himself as well as his friends. When you reached a hand out against your friend's chest to hold him back, that touch was like a lightning rod of information, intent, opinion transferred. Such camaraderie made Valmiki bristle with life in a way that not even the practice of surgery had ever done for him. In the forest with the men he might have been duty bound, but he was not weighed down by it. He was no one's father, husband, employer, or healer. He was one with them. They were one with each other.

Valmiki was not a gifted hunter, though. That is why Saul taught him how to set the bird cages with pieces of banana or a coating of laglee on the parallel rods, so that at the end of the day there was still the possibility they would return to where the cages hung in the bushes and he would find a peekoplat, a semp, or a banana quit in the cage. He would have something to take home, to show for his day away. Still, at the end of a hunt, over drinks by the open trunk of his car, the other men clapped his back and said, "Next time, Doc, next time," desiring nothing more from him than he go with them soon again. How they admired him, if only because the town doctor left the comfort of his tamer world, of his social network, and went deep into the dark dank forest with them. They would spot the agouti, or the deer, or the lap, and point it out to him. They invariably let him take the first shot. He would watch it through his binoculars, then nestle the rifle's butt into his shoulder and lift its long barrel, catching the animal in the target sight. Aim. Shoot. Nothing. Yet the clean, clear animal rawness he felt with these men friends, his sporting friends, enlivened him. It wasn't for his correct or effective aim, for those were sorely lacking, that they called him "a real man," but rather for his trust in them, for his courage to go with them time and again and then to sit with them, either right there in a clearing or on the roadside by the car, or in the dusty clay yard of one of the men over a hand-built fire as they cooked an animal someone had shot.

If they were at Saul's house in Fellowship Lands in Marabella, there would suddenly be a platter heaped with lengths of limp sugary plantain that glistened in a slick of the oil in which they had been deep fried until they looked, but were not, burnt. The others knew Valmiki liked the candy-like fruit, and someone would excitedly race like a person with a holy mission, not the day before, but the instant they arrived, and hack off a hand of fresh ripened-on-the-tree plantains, which Saul's wife would then fry especially for Valmiki. She would leave after cooking and go to a relative's house for the night. The other men ate with their hands, but they always gave Valmiki a thin, light spoon that bent with the slightest pressure, or a fork, each of its tines making off in a different direction, and a knife. But he would use his hands, and then he would lick his fingers, one at a time, each one deep in his mouth, down to the knuckle almost, pulled out slow, his teeth gripping and scraping off the very last tastes, with an indiscreet pop. Saul would bring out a bottle of Johnny Walker Black Label that he had bought and kept under lock and key especially for Valmiki. Or if they were at the home of one of the others, Valmiki might be served home-brewed puncheon rum or pineapple babash. His eyes had filled with water, tears of shock, when he had first tasted the babash. But then he got used to it and looked forward to the bite of the fermented fruit singeing the length of his esophagus.

He sometimes drank babash or scotch enough that by the time he got home, after driving very slowly to remain steady on the dangerous pot-holed road back into the city, Devika would be either asleep or disgusted by his drunkenness, the searing odour of wood fire in his hair, the smell of wild meat, and the testosterone-enriched sweat on his sticky body, a combination that might have appealed to a different woman but certainly not to her, and she would not want him near her — just as he had hoped, as he did not want to contaminate the thrill of an excursion where his friends all reeked similarly, as if this were the mark of an unusual affinity.

SO IT WAS THAT AT THE TABLE THE NIGHT BEFORE, THE TENSION caused by Viveka's relentless desire to play volleyball was at an all-time high. Still, there might have been more discussion, but Viveka had given that laugh of incredulity, one she had been honing for months now and that she knew would irk Devika and himself. Devika shoved her chair backwards, and the screech might as well have come from within her. With that, Valmiki knew she intended to bring an end to the subject. Viveka began to say something, but barely had sound come out of her mouth when Devika shouted, "NO! I don't want to hear another word. I said no. Don't you understand? NO!"

Valmiki and his younger daughter, Vashti, shared a weakness for cherry cheesecake, particularly Miss Myrtle and Miss Mary's. The sticky yet tart topping of carmine-coloured Bing cherries. The deep middle section of sweetened Philadelphia cream cheese that had a consistency right on the nameless line of texture between velvety and a cheese that had been baked. And then there was the shell with its contrasting texture — the scratchiness of buttery, sugary, graham crackers crumbled fine. No part was complete without the other. Valmiki and Vashti would usually make a show of their enjoyment of this particular dessert that would delight Devika and irritate Viveka.

As Vashti watched her family spar, she was, Valmiki could see, aware of the growing possibility of a dessert-curtailing blow-up ahead. And so she quickly ushered into her mouth one spoonful after another, cut from the top through to the bottom of the pie, mushing all three layers at once, intending to finish up the wide wedge she had cut for herself before the meal was destroyed, as it was bound to be, by Viveka. Valmiki, on the other hand, didn't even bother to cut himself a piece. He leaned back in his chair and held his breath because a snickering laugh from his elder daughter told him that Viveka had no intention of leaving the matter alone, regardless of Devika's outburst.

Viveka, they all knew, had her strategies. The next round would surely come. Valmiki wasn't sure when, and it exhausted him, the thought of waiting, of not knowing what would happen next. When Viveka and Devika quarrelled the air went out of the house. Vashti would would watch as if taking lessons, and her father only hoped it was in how *not* to behave. He would usually make his way to the bedroom if the fight had not already travelled there, and turn on the air-conditioning, which blocked out the shouting and the pleading and the crying and the harsh words flung so carelessly between two people he loved — one because she was his own flesh and blood; the other because he had first grown used to her, then to appreciate all she had done to run the house and keep the family, and then, finally, to love, at least like one might love one's sister — but neither of whom he understood. If the altercation had travelled to the bedroom, he would find a chore somewhere in another part of the large and sprawling house, and retreat there.

In spite of the evening's unpleasantness, that morning when Valmiki stirred in half wakefulness he had not at first remembered the quarrel. He had been awakened by the distant rumble of thunder, thinking of Tony. No, not thinking of him, but with a feeling of him in his belly, in the muscles of his thighs, and an ache in his early-morning sleep-hardened penis. It had been twenty plus years since he had last seen Tony, and still this. So often, still this. He opened and shut his eyes. The light through the windows of the room was a fast fading pink. The birds in the mango trees at the back of the house were well into their usual morning bickering session, louder in anticipation of rain. With a sudden conviction that he could go into the study, use the phone there, and call Tony in Goa, just to say hello, he came completely awake. And awakening so fully, he felt the heat under the blankets of another human being. Devika. He closed his eyes, turned on his side, and scuttled closer to her. The ache in his body dulled, his penis limped. There was, instead, a more tolerable numbness. He brought a hand up to rest on Devika's shoulder. Her shoulder, however, was not heavy with the weight of sleep. He opened his eyes again. Devika was already well awake, and he was immediately aware that she bore the brunt of last evening's quarrel still. He could hear sounds outside of their door.

"You okay?" he whispered hoarsely. Devika did not answer, but her breathing sharpened.

He said, "What is it? Is it still Viveka? Are you still on about her?"

"Listen to her. She is storming about outside. She is the one who is not finished. I don't want to start my morning like this. Why did you leave me to deal with her alone last night? She is as own-way as you are. You are the one she takes after."

He pulled his hand away and returned to his favourite sleeping position, flat on his back, his face to the ceiling, fingertips resting on pelvic bones, and he shut his eyes again. In an instant the door to their bedroom was opened, the attempt to do so quietly clearly halfhearted. Seeing both her parents awake, Viveka charged in to say that she was leaving for the day, that she had changed her mind from last night and although she had no classes she would spend the day studying at the university library.

Valmiki's heart lurched. He could see that if his son Anand had lived, these two children, particularly because of Viveka's angular facial features, her lankiness, and her short hair, would have been unmistakable as siblings. He wished Viveka would grow her hair longer like all the other attractive young ladies he and Devika knew, at least to her shoulders.

Viveka's aggression first thing in the morning wore him down instantly, and he had not even got out of bed as yet. Valmiki asked her only how she was going to get to the university. She grumbled that she would take a taxi. There was a long silence while each waited for the other to respond. Finally, Valmiki asked Devika if she needed her car. Devika pursed her lips tight. He tried again. "Didn't you say you don't have anything to do outside of the house today?"

"So I have to report to you everything I am doing now?"

Viveka groaned audibly. She said, "Forget it. I am not driving on the highway in any case."

"Listen, it looks like it's going to rain again. Why don't you take my car and your mother can drop me to work in hers?" Valmiki offered.

Devika immediately protested. "But Viveka just told you she doesn't want to drive on the highway. She isn't confident to drive on the highway and you are going to give her your car. You don't see how ridiculous you can be? Why can't you stand up to her just once?"

At this Viveka looked as if she was trying to shout, but a whisper came out. "I said I will take a taxi. I don't want to drive."

Valmiki shook his head in feigned disbelief, but making sure to employ a smile he told Viveka that if she waited half an hour he would get the chauffeur to take her. Viveka replied that practically everyone got to the university by taxi, even the professors. Valmiki winked in an attempt to cajole his daughter and said, "But do they all have access to a chauffeur? It's no trouble, sweetheart, I don't need him today." He turned to Devika. "Do you?" His wife was sitting up now, propped against the pillows, and she looked at her hands clasped on her lap. A terse "No" came from her, like a cleaver falling onto a dry board.

But Valmiki ignored this and went back to Viveka, who had not ignored it. Before he could say more, she snapped, louder, "I will take a taxi."

Her father pleaded, "In the rain?"

"It's not a big deal. I won't melt. You should try taking a taxi sometime. I'll get a ride home with Helen. I'll probably be late." She marched out of the room.

Devika snapped again at Valmiki, "Why are you always trying to please her?"

Valmiki hadn't ever expected this kind of relationship to develop between Viveka and himself. She used to be a real tomboy, full of curiosity and adventurousness, but not argumentative like this. Lately, she elicited the kind of emotion from him that he was more familiar with in his dealings with Devika.

And just as Devika had expected, Viveka was not finished with them for the morning. Devika had braced herself, waiting, and sure enough, Viveka returned, with less haste in her manner. She set herself down at the foot of their bed, pinning the blanket so that the toes of one of Valmiki's feet were forced forward and those of the other backwards, strapped immovably there. Viveka asked in a softer tone if they had reconsidered allowing her to play volleyball. She baffled her father with such boldness, such obstinance. In lighter moments he would have seen potential in the boldness, but at the moment it infuriated him. He let Devika field this request.

Devika said, calmly, "We told you it is not the kind of thing girls from families like ours do — wearing those kinds of skirts in public, prancing about like that. That kind of thing might be all right for other people's daughters, but not for ours. Besides, look at you. Playing sports is just going to make you even more unladylike than you already are. The time for you to have grown up, Viveka, has long past."

Viveka breathed in so deeply that Valmiki thought she was going to implode. It was a relief, almost, when she burst out, "You know, I don't understand you all. You're both supposed to be so enlightened. And Dad, you above all people should know that playing sports is good for your health. I can't help how I look, okay?"

She clearly had more to say, but was unable, stuttering instead with hurt and fury. Devika snapped back, much too loudly for first thing in the morning, that when Viveka got her degree and was her own woman she could do whatever she wished, and until then, her parents said no, and that required no explanation.

Viveka stormed out of the room, lashing out behind her, "You are so old-fashioned. This is ridiculous. I can't believe you're criticizing me. I mean, I am twenty years old. I shouldn't have to ask…"

She was interrupted by her mother shouting, "As long as you live in this house you are a child, and you will do as we tell you." Then, when she was certain that Viveka had left the house, Devika turned to Valmiki. "This is ridiculous, in truth. You are behaving like a country boukie with her."

"Look, neither of us agrees with her playing volleyball. We have different reasons, but in the end, neither of us wants it. All kinds of things go on at that park," Valmiki said quietly. "What if, next thing, she wants later to go to one of the islands to play in some competition or the other? One thing will just lead to another and this whole thing could get out of control. I don't care if I am old-fashioned or a country boukie. I am not letting her play."

"*You're* not letting her? You don't even say a word to her. You leave it up to me, and that is causing a lot of coldness between her and me. You can't even stand up to your own daughter?"

Valmiki said to his wife, feebly, that it was not his job to discipline the children, that he had a job already and couldn't take on another battle. It was in these moments that he just wished he could pull the covers up over his ears, shut out the light of the day, and go back to sleep. Or get up and go with his rifle and his buddies into the forest.

AND SO, LATER IN HIS OFFICE, HE WAS STILL HARASSED BY IT ALL. Viveka had become like a stranger to him. She offhandedly interrupted and contradicted him, sometimes laughed in overly dramatic disbelief at something he said, and he felt silly, for he seldom understood what it was that she was getting at. She diminished him. That was how he felt in front of her. What had happened? If he were a young man just meeting her he would find her, he hated to admit, uninteresting, a little too smart for her own good. She wasn't charming. She wasn't willing to flatter, to let someone else's faults or ill-conceived notions go unmentioned. Who on this earth would marry her if she continued like that? On the other hand, he couldn't imagine a man who would indeed be good enough for her, for either of his daughters. He was as infuriated as he was proud that he had fathered a girl more strong-willed than he ever had been.

Valmiki had never indulged in the hope for a child of a particular sex. When he was at medical college, he had known that his particular bond with Tony would have to end. He had known that upon qualifying he would return home — to Trinidad, that is — and marry. He had known that was what he had to do, but he had not been able to formulate an image of himself as husband or father. He tried to picture himself with a woman, he and she walking side by side, she pushing a pram with a baby in it. There was no face to this woman and the baby was always substituted — his mind insisted on the joke — with a dachshund pup in a baby bonnet. It was not the kind of joke that made him laugh, but cringe.

No matter how much he and Tony suited and cared for each other, Valmiki had been determined to return home and to fall into whatever role was expected of him, or at least to adopt some form of numbing complacency. People talked, and he had heard of others, men he knew, who lived a double life. He didn't want to be talked of in such a manner.

In his office now, feeling a flash of fear, he thought of calling Zoraida back and asking which of his women friends was out there, telling her to send the woman in. But he had no heart, or mind, and certainly no body, for that kind of thing right now.

The times over the past twenty years when he had spoken from Trinidad with Tony on the telephone, Tony had been aloof. He spoke as if with just any old acquaintance, filling in a few well-chosen blanks, no real details. He spoke little of his practice or anything related to medicine that might create camaraderie between him and Valmiki. What he dwelt on was his children, how well they were doing at school, how they were like members of his family or like his wife and her family. Valmiki and Tony's past together had been erased by Tony. There was no overture, not even nuanced acknowledgement of how close they had been, and Valmiki sensed better than to insert himself. No one would have guessed that Tony was once willing to risk a rather hefty inheritance, his family's highly respected name in Goa, and his life to be with Valmiki. Valmiki had had much less to lose, his family being well enough off, but with not nearly so much nor such a public presence as Tony's. But in a place as small as Trinidad, Valmiki was much less ready to risk any of it, and most of all he was not willing to raise the ire of his father or (as he thought he might do with such revelations about himself) kill his mother.

Once, when student examinations had ended and a two-week break was to start, Valmiki's father had asked him to return home. Tony asked him, rather, not to go to Trinidad, but to go with him to Tony's family's house in Goa. Tony was going to tell his older sister there about their relationship, and get her support. He was going to tell his sister that he had met the person he wanted to spend his life with, break it to her that it was a man, this man from Trinidad, whom he had fallen in love with. It was the true kind of love, Tony wanted to tell her, the kind they had seen in the movies and were brought up to believe was possible. He and she used to come home from a movie and act out the dancing, and they would wish for each other love that was full of passion, integrity, and the will to endure regardless of all obstacles. Tony would tell her, as he always told Valmiki, that he had found it.

With Tony's request, Valmiki was faced with the reality of breaking such news to his parents, the seriousness of this thing he was doing with another man, and he began to withdraw from Tony. He told Tony he would think about the request to go to India, but as the holiday drew nearer he began to treat Tony's persistence like pestering. A fracture, inexplicable and devastating to Tony, began to form between them. Valmiki not only went directly back to Trinidad for those two weeks, he got in touch with Devika Sankarsingh, the pretty daughter of a good family known to his parents. Mr. Sankarsingh was a businessman who gave liberally to charities and wasn't afraid to spend his money on himself and his family. Valmiki, the doctor-in-the-making, made overtures to Devika and her family, got pleasantly teased by his own extended family, and was treated with the admiration and respect of a boy who was about to embark on the natural journey of a man.

Left alone one evening with Devika, he did what he had done with no one else but Tony. He had sex with her, cementing, in case of a dip in his courage, his determination to marry her. He meant only to have sex with her. That would have been enough to bind them. He hadn't expected that one round of it, the first time he had had sex with a woman, would be sufficient for a pregnancy to ensue. It was not until he learned of Devika's pregnancy that he understood what he had done to himself. All of a sudden, he was to be a married man, a regular man with the usual ordinary expectations imposed on him. He was to be a father. To have a clockwork life. There would be no hard body to butt against. No shared knowledge of a particular touch or wanting. He thought of middle-aged men back home, and saw himself destined to develop a paunch, even shrinking in height as if from a burden on his shoulders, and certainly from one in his heart. He would turn into a man who was dead in spirit but whose physical body was trapped in everyday Trinidadian limbo.

But in the end, Valmiki felt quite pleased with himself for what he hoped the fact of pregnancy publicly confirmed about him. He ended his relationship with Tony, left the apartment one day when Tony was not there, and even when he heard that Tony had tried to kill himself, he felt there was nothing he could have done differently. In the deepest recesses of his heart and mind he congratulated himself again and again on his astuteness in making sure that he had had sex with that girl back home.

Six and a half months into married life, the child was born. He had delivered mothers of their babies, and held the minutes-old wriggling things in his arms, but suddenly, in the delivery room as a father rather than a doctor, he was paralyzed. He stood back, transfixed and terrified, staring dumbly at the wrinkled baby covered in a film of grey waxy vernix, eyes scrunched tight as if to refuse final entry into such a situation. Devika's mother tersely ordered him to touch his child. He awkwardly worked his pinkie into one of her minute fists and she immediately clenched that fist so tight, as if to lock his finger to her — by will or natural reflex it didn't matter — that she hooked him. He stood there contemplating the strangeness of touching something that was independent of him, yet carried in it, in her, his history, his essence.

Stubborn and wilful she was from the very first day, his wife complained. But this in itself was enough to further endear this girl to Valmiki. Devika's mother, in a show of wilfulness of her own, and without consulting the family's pundit, had named the child Viveka, the union of his and Devika's names.

Valmiki never fell in love with Devika, but from the start he was entranced by this daughter.

Time was the ointment he, Devika, and even Tony far away in Goa, needed. Over time, Valmiki grew to feel something akin to possessiveness — a form of responsibility — for his wife. He thought of this as an aspect of love, the kind that develops in arranged marriages and that enduring marital unions and family life could be made of. Would he say that he loved Devika? He loved his children. Therefore, how could he not love their mother and want the best for her?

Devika seemed content with the respectability and comfort of being Dr. Valmiki Krishnu's wife. She and he slept in the same bed, shared children, a bedroom, a house, a life. She was not an unfeeling woman, and she was not unaware. But Valmiki felt her resentment slowly set in. For years, words had remained necessarily unspoken. Finally, with the arrogance of Valmiki's friendship with this man Saul from "the back of nowhere," words came to her. At least — she said to him once in the midst of one of their frequent fights — he had the decency to make a public ass of himself fooling around with women. He did not ask her to explain what she meant. And thank God, she continued, he had the good sense to run around with women who were not from their world, their backgrounds, their culture. The potential damage was, to an extent, contained.

Valmiki felt only the smallest amount of remorse or pity for Devika, as he had realized long ago that he and she used each other to advantage. Wasn't it the way of the world? People stayed in seemingly unsavoury situations, not because they were trapped there but because they in fact were getting something they needed. It was an exchange.

And whenever Devika felt the threat that Valmiki's oddities would become fodder for public ridicule, she threw a party at their house. Let the world come in and see for themselves that she was not suffering, that she had more than most people had. Valmiki didn't blame her for taking whatever she needed.

There wasn't a woman Valmiki had been with who could have satisfied him. He had well-drawn parameters. A married woman was, of course, safest of all, as there were built-in hindrances to continuation for them both. And the married foreigner, the white foreigner who had no ties to Trinidad, to whom their Trinidadian and Indian communities had no loyalties, was best of all. Such women served Devika well, they served him well; and he, no ordinary local — a doctor to boot — served them just as well.

Still, Valmiki did dream. He imagined a time when the two girls would be married off — hopefully not to a man like him. He would not leave Devika. But he imagined coming and going as he wished. Falling in love even. Maintaining his obligation to Devika — there was no question about that, he would do that for her — but loving someone, a man, a man from his own world with whom he would share another life. In Valmiki's mind, this man had something of a face and a shape — much like Tony's — but he was always in shadow. There was enough of him, though — the thickness of a man's body, the muscular hardness, the resistance to Valmiki's push, something to shove against, a force that could bear a weight. Valmiki just wanted the chance one day to feel something more than obligation. He dreamt of that day, a day he knew would never come.

As it was, in the present he settled for meaningless flings, his Friday nights here and there with Saul, the occasional Saturday hunting, wrestling a shot animal to the dusty or damp forest ground, he and his Saturday friends blood-stained and sweaty, their hearts thundering in the forests, showing off their manliness to one another — and a night here and there with Saul who was, in the end, not from his world.

What he wished he could do right now was leave his office and go out with Saul and those fellows and hunt down an animal. Something as big and as small as himself.

VALMIKI SLUMPED BACK IN HIS WOODEN CHAIR. THE CHAIR cambered back and swung a little. He steadied it. He laced his hands behind his head and tilted to face the ceiling. He closed his eyes.

Suddenly, Valmiki jumped up from his chair. He rushed to the louvred windows and opened them. It was still raining. That didn't matter. A soaking wasn't going to hurt him. It might even help. A cleansing of sorts. He'd never gone into the forest by himself before. He'd make a detour into Fellowship Lands where Saul lived and look for him, but if Saul were at work — a colossal courage washed over him — he knew the paths well enough. With the haste of a doctor in an emergency, he snatched up his car keys, yanked open the door to his office, and, before Zoraida had time to turn her head in his direction, made his way hastily down his private corridor, out the back door of the building, and down the flight of stairs to the underground parking.

Breathless, Valmiki opened the trunk of the car. The .22 rifle, a pair of binoculars, and the safety-locked metal box that contained, among other paraphernalia, a knife, a coiled length of rope, flashlight, gloves, batteries, and a box of ammunition were there. Neatly folded in a canvas bag was a change of clothing so he could return home not covered in dirt and wildness after a day in the forest. There, too, was a jacket — a plaid long-sleeved flannel one — that was entirely unwearable in Trinidadian weather, but that Vashti had seen in a magazine, and because it looked to her like real hunting gear, mail-ordered from a clearing house in Houston, Texas, for a birthday present. His black rubber boots were also there, and a bird cage, and, just in case, there was a tarp to keep the trunk clean. He got in the driver's seat and headed directly to Marabella, to Fellowship Lands. He intended this time to shoot and kill something.

When he reached Saul's house, Valmiki remained in the car with the window rolled down only a few inches so that he could call out through it. He saw a window closed against the rain at the front of the concrete two-storey house. The curtain parted slightly, but he could not see who was behind it. It fell closed again. He expected Saul, but it was Saul's wife who came through the front door. Valmiki knew that she was aware of the nature of his relationship with her husband. He wanted to drive off but she had by this time looked over from the veranda at him and tilted up her chin in acknowledgement. She held a thick wad of newspaper over her head and made for the stairway at the side of the house. It was too late to escape.

He put the window down an inch farther. The rain came in so he leaned away, but in vain.

"Saul not here. He leave for work six o'clock," Saul's wife said. A pause followed. Valmiki shrank from it. She continued, "He working by Mr. Kowlessar new house. They putting in the electrical now. You know where Mr. Kowlessar new house situated?"

Valmiki wondered if indeed she knew of his and Saul's relationship. She showed no animosity toward him. And he knew that he couldn't go to Malcolm Kowlessar's house. He dared not be seen going there to meet a tradesman, pulling this worker out to go and fritter away a day with him. People would talk. They would wonder if he had lost his mind.

Valmiki remained silent, and the woman's manner softened as she continued. "Well, he leave real early to beat the traffic, so he might come home any time now."

Having unintentionally involved Saul's wife in his impudence, Valmiki now lost the feeling of needing to see Saul. Saul might have offered the reassurance and sort of stillness that usually calmed Valmiki. But ultimately, Saul could not really help Valmiki, and Valmiki knew this too well.

If going into the forest is what he wanted to do, Valmiki could accomplish this by himself. He would drive off immediately.

But Saul's wife was saying, "I know about him and you, you know, Doc. I know he real take to you."

Valmiki's face flushed. He stared forward, put his fingers on the key in the ignition. Mrs. Joseph spoke quickly now, undeterred by the rain. "Even though he and me married since we young, and living that long together, we used to be like neighbours to each other. But that was before he and you."

A sweat broke over Valmiki's entire body. Before he and I *what*? He wanted and didn't want, at the same time, to know what she was saying. He bit the side of his gum like a child who had no explanation.

"It used to be that he minding he own business, me minding mine. But he come like a brother to me since."

Since. Since what? But Valmiki was glad that she had not said more on this.

"We don't have relations, but I have to say what we have is better than that."

The rain wetting her dress seemed immaterial to Saul's wife. Valmiki reached for the ignition, and she put her hands on the glass of the window, hooked the fingers of both hands on its edge. "No, Doc. I did want a chance to tell you I don't have no bad feelings. Nobody can expect me to feel good as a woman, but I don't have bad feelings either." She pointed to the house and quickly returned her hand to grip the window. "You see this? He work hard and with his hard-earned money he buy the house."

Valmiki turned and looked at her directly, but when she spoke on he looked away again. "Saul does sleep in one room. I in the next. Why I wouldn't be a little sorry for myself? But he treat me all right. Doc, we are not rich people. I can't get up and leave just so. Leave and go where? I have to stay and make do. Saul happy, and I happy for him. It might be a strange thing, but I will say it, I happy for him because he happy and he is my husband. Is only strange if you not in the situation yourself and you watching-judging from outside."

There might be some queer openness between Saul and his wife, Valmiki noted, yet not so great a one that Saul would reveal that it was Valmiki who had bought that house. Rather awkwardly he mumbled that it was a slow day in the office, and he had just taken a chance that he might see Saul to talk about some electrical work he had for him. But, he apologized between gritted teeth, he had better get back; he was expecting a full office later in the afternoon.

He wondered if he should put a stop to this thing with Saul immediately.

VALMIKI HAD LEFT THE HIGHWAY AND PASSED SEVERAL SMALL SETTLEments along the way to the western edges of the Central Range. He arrived in an area of forest he had visited in the past with Saul. Here, the road conditions changed. He pondered all that Mrs. Joseph had just said to him, and wondered too, in his embarrassment, who was the wiser in the degree of their discretion, his wife or this woman? He went along a narrow two-way road that was thinly paved with a mix heavy in gravel and light in asphalt. If a car were to come from the opposite direction, he or the other driver would have to pull off the pavement, exercising caution not to slip too far down the gully that ran along either side. Arriving alongside a cutlassed path into the forest, Valmiki brought the car to rest on a well-padded section of knotgrass that was usually kept low by hunters for this very purpose. He shut the engine off. A path of dirty grey skylight mirrored the roadway. In an instant, the windows fogged up. He switched back on the ignition and lowered the windows a fraction all around. The glass cleared, but he saw nothing save for a blur of shivering greens and the darkness of the forest magnified.

The rain tapped relentlessly off the car's metal and glass, on the asphalt and gravel, off the leaves. The ground was coursed by muddied vein-like rivulets. Even while it rained, birds could be heard chirping in the trees. Caws and squawks in call-and-answer patterns came from all directions. Through the incessant and loud ringing of innumerable cicadas he heard the occasional grunts of howler monkeys. No human sounds could be heard. He mumbled nonsensical sounds just to hear himself.

This forest was dense and dark enough that at any time of day it offered good hunting opportunities. In the rain the animals would have hunkered down beside the wide trunks of trees, on the inside of one of the wall-like roots of a balata tree, or under the umbrellas of wide-leafed trees. They would be easy prey like that.

Valmiki hesitated at the rain and mud. Then, with a jolt of determination, he opened the car door, got out, and stood in the rain until he was thoroughly soaked. He went to the trunk and opened it. He unfurled the rifle from its pouch. He licked the trickles on his lips. His own salt had already begun to break through, in spite of the rain washing over him. A grin set on his face.

It did not last long, though. Once the car and roadway were no longer visible he tensed and moved one deliberate step at a time. By himself, without someone to watch his back, he had the sense that anything could fall out of the trees onto him, or that he could be pounced on from behind. He tiptoed, even though the falling rain drowned the sound of his presence.

He hadn't gone out or used the rifle in the rain before, and wasn't sure how he and it would fare. And, he remembered, snakes got washed out in this kind of weather. In spite of the tall heavy rubber boots he wore, he felt that he could be bitten and die right there. In the forest. Alone. Like a man. Devika and the girls would live the rest of their lives wondering what on earth had made him leave his office and go into the forest by himself. His heart raced.

He walked a hundred or so yards into the forest. Suddenly, he stood still. He could hear something. Fear caused a thundering pulsing in his head. He did his best to listen beyond the sound of his own fear. He watched with the painful acuity of one whose life depended on it. Soon he could hear a steady, fast-paced panting. A whimper. He bent down and looked through the binoculars that hung around his neck. Rain covered the lenses and the forest was an undecipherable mess of fractured shades of green. Again, there was that sound, a wince or a whimper. He looked with his eyes, the water globbing on his eyelashes almost blinding him. About ten yards or so away, he could just see something that seemed out of place. A honey-coloured shape, huddled in the stalks of a stand of baliser. He couldn't see its face, but judging from the shape, the heaving body, and the paler hanging folds of skin knobbed with rows of teats, he knew it must be a dog that had been recently nursing. Rabies came to mind. He watched for a while, until the dog ducked its head under and out from the heavy dripping fronds of the baliser. He aimed the rifle. In its hooded target lines, he could see the dog's face. Its eyes were soft, its face soft — almost timid. The dog shivered. He lowered the rifle and looked around. The dog seemed to be alone. No pups, no sign of a person nearby or a squatter's lean-to or shed. He lifted the barrel again, and let the scope's target lines roam the face of the dog. He let it run down the dog's body. Its neck. Its visible hind leg. He lifted it toward the chest. There. Between its ribcage. He steadied himself and cocked the rifle.

Suddenly, above the patter of rain falling he heard what could be nothing other than the clearing of a man's throat. He was so startled that he made a fast turn, slipped on the slimy floor of rotting leaves, and fell over. He quickly righted himself and looked about. About the same distance away as the dog, but off to its side now, the glow of a cigarette revealed a man whose face was obscured by a straw hat with a brim wide enough to permit him to smoke in the rain. The man was stooped in the root system of a balata tree.

It horrified Valmiki to think he had not seen that glow. The man remained on his haunches, as still as if he were a bird asleep on one leg. But the lit cigarette gave away the fact that he was watching, and his well-timed throat-clearing said that he disapproved, and intended to interrupt whatever it was that Valmiki had been contemplating. Valmiki wondered if the man was alone. If he hadn't seen this man, he wondered, what else was he missing? The man did not look like someone Valmiki had met in the village while travelling there with Saul, and made no sign of rising, or wanting to talk, or even to quarrel. Valmiki, still hunkered on the ground, was terrified that the man might also carry a gun. His temples throbbed. He suffered an acute shame, like a schoolboy caught in the act of doing something wrong. He had the real, albeit fleeting thought, of turning the gun on himself, if only to handle his self-inflicted humiliation. The barrel of the rifle would have been much too long to accomplish even this, and he imagined himself further mortified by yet another incompetence.

Hastily, he stumbled backwards, keeping an eye on where the man stood, wary that a bullet from the gun the man might carry might be racing in a crippling hurry toward his spine. Finally, he turned and ran forward, arriving back at his car his only desire now. He sweated, and was drenched in a way that no rainfall could have matched.

WHEN VALMIKI FINALLY REACHED HIS CAR, HE SPUN IT AROUND AND got out of there — not caring about the bumpy road — out of the village, out onto the main road, and made his way back into San Fernando faster than was legal or safe. All the way he shook his head, as if trying to dispel the act and the knowledge that he might have, that he could have, that he almost pulled the trigger on a sitting, nursing, shivering dog. He didn't know which was worse, to have been so close to doing this or to have been caught in the act. He had also to find a plausible, acceptable reason for running out of his office in the middle of the day without telling his staff, and with a room full of waiting patients.

Back in town, he went to The Victory Hotel first, where the staff knew him well. They were not surprised to see him on a workday — but to find him drenched, his clothing mud-splattered, his shoes caked, him looking like a fugitive and without a woman? They gave him a room, no questions asked, expecting that a woman was bound to arrive looking for him. However, in record time, the staff noted, he had changed — not into his usual work attire but into the clothing that was kept in the trunk of his car: khaki slacks and a white golf jersey — and was out of there. He was a handsome man, the staff, both the men and the women, agreed, and so gentle, they said, adding: no wonder all those women he comes with here like him so much.

Valmiki arrived at an excuse that involved him making a stop at Maraj and Son Jewellers. Under the guidance of the owner, Sunil Maraj, he would buy Devika, Viveka, and Vashti a piece of jewellery each. The explanation would be partially true: having just seen a patient who had the effect on him of making him think of his family, he was overcome with appreciation for each one of them, and wished to express this, so he had left the office early in search of the perfect gifts. He would buy them the best there was, and perhaps they would ask no more questions. The bonus, he thought, would be that Devika might be placated, at least for a short while, and Viveka, through some heaven-sent generosity, might settle down and behave herself.

Viveka wasn't home when he returned. He handed Devika and Vashti the presents. They were surprised, speechless, and made a gaggle of sounds that were lost on him. His mind was on something else: his relief that he hadn't had time to pull the trigger.

Viveka

EARLIER THAT SAME DAY, VIVEKA WALKED DOWN THE HILL FROM Luminada Heights and from there took a local taxi to the stand just outside of the San Fernando General Hospital. The umbrella she sheltered under did nothing to keep her feet dry. The legs of her jeans were damp and clung to her thighs, and her feet were wet and splotched with debris from the street. She stood in a huddle with several other people under the ample awning of the taxi stand. A doctor who knew her as Valmiki's daughter drove through the gates of the hospital, spotted her, and pulled up his car. He drew down the window and greeted her. She knew he was bound to be wondering what she was doing waiting in the rain, outside of the gates of the hospital, for a taxi, but wouldn't come right out and ask. She saved him the trouble with a harmless lie: "I am doing a project that involves public transportation." The look on the doctor's face brightened. After that she positioned herself a little behind another waiting passenger and made sure to duck down whenever a face she knew from her family's world of friends passed by.

The wall behind her stank of urine, the odour like a vapour leached by the rain. The woman at Viveka's side held a handkerchief to her nose. There didn't seem to be any judgment in this; she just held the kerchief there as if it were the most natural thing to do. Viveka thought of doing the same, but felt that if she did she would certainly appear to be aloof and disdainful. The woman turned to her and said, "I don't know why they don't do something about the beggars sleeping under here, na. Is like every wall in this place is a public toilet." Viveka smiled but remained quiet. From the way other passengers and passersby looked at her, some of them taking in her entire frame in a slow examination, she knew she seemed out of place at the taxi stand. She wondered which was easier — enduring all of this or just mustering up enough courage to sit behind the wheel herself and drive. Since getting her licence more than a year before, she had driven only a handful of times, and never unaccompanied by her mother or her father. Given the way people drove their cars — "as if they owned the streets," people would say, and regardless of rules — and given the number of accidents and deaths caused by careless driving, she had no desire and even less courage to drive.

The waiting people chatted easily among themselves, even the ones who were clearly strangers at the stand, about the environment, the rain, the heat, the price of tomatoes, the morning's newspaper headlines. Viveka felt unable to engage with them, and while the others watched her, no one but that woman had addressed her directly. Viveka looked across at the promenade to see if she might catch a glimpse of Merle Bedi. Cars passed between where she stood and the promenade, and she willed her vision to leap over the traffic, to zip through the rainfall all the way across the road, into and under bushes. She saw no one resembling her old high school friend and happily entertained the thought that Merle Bedi might have been taken back into her parents' home.

The combination of rain and heat intensified the pollution caused by exhaust from the jam of cars. The hospital's incinerators spewed their noxious gases into the sodden air. The nearer smells of urine, unwashed bodies, and too highly perfumed ones produced a dizzying cocktail that finally got the better of her. She was about to act as if she had just remembered something and quickly head inside the gates to one of the wards to which her father sometimes sent his patients and where she knew several of the nurses. She would call her father and tell him that the taxies were running late, and ask if he could, after all, send the chauffeur for her. Just then, the taxi that went from San Fernando to the stand in Curepe, near enough to the university, arrived.

Thank heaven for air-conditioning in the maxi-taxi in which she travelled. The low-lying land on either side of the road just outside of the city bobbed in a stew-like concoction of rain and the debris its flood waters had dredged.

As the taxi arrived in the central part of the island, the rain ceased, and the sun came out in a sudden burst for the first time in about ten days. The distant tree tops instantly glistened. The vehicle inched forward through a jam of traffic that stretched the length of the Sir Solomon Hochoy Highway, the island's north-south corridor.

Viveka stroked the case that held her CD player and a new CD she had won in a late-night radio contest. The contest had been held almost six weeks before, but she had only days ago received the prize in the mail. The night of the contest the Krishnu house had been in darkness, Vashti asleep in her room, and Viveka's parents in theirs some hours ago. Viveka was unable to sleep, as usual, and had her CD player tuned to Radio Antilles. She was plugged into it with earphones. The host had offered a CD of rock's greatest hits to anyone who could identify the last five songs that had been played, in order. Contestants had to mail in their answers by a certain date. She had never entered contests before, but in one of her usual impetuous moves she decided to enter and was shocked to hear her name, and her region in Trinidad, called on the air in the middle of another night ten days later. She had listened to the CD only once before today, and was more thrilled at having won it — won anything — than with the music itself. Now she wanted to listen to it again, to give it a second chance, but she did not want to offend her fellow passengers by shutting out their congenial chatter.

The four rows of passengers — twelve in all, resigned to their cramped seats in what was essentially a mini-van — and the driver were used to travel delays. When they first saw the queue of traffic up ahead, before the car had slowed to a crawl, one of the passengers had sucked her teeth and whispered, "Man, if it ent one thing, is another." The driver, by way of apologizing, but not accepting any fault for this delay, offered, "Years I driving, and every time it rain is the same thing. The swamp lands does flood and it does overflow onto the road. And nobody would do anything. They could make a levy or fix the drainage. And when the same road dry, if you see how it mash up because of all this flood. You could believe this island have a lake that bubbling pitch day and night?"

The woman just behind the driver sighed audibly. She was an Indian woman with skin the blue-brown colour of sapodilla seeds. She wore her oiled black hair tightly pinned into a bun at the back. She wore, too, a scent reminiscent of oleander that was so strong it was as if a vial of it had spilled in the vehicle and spoiled in the heat. She said, "Is only skylark in this place. The people who could fix this road don't have to use it. They only fixing-fixing the airport. And who you see using the airport?

Not me. Only in Trinidad, yes!" At the back a man raised his voice. "Fire the whole lot of them. Tout bagaille. Bring in fresh blood. This country good only for government officials and white people. Is they who does get everything, and people like we? Nothing, nothing, nothing." Then, "But you know, don't make a mistake about this: it don't matter the colour of the skin of government — white, black, Indian — all of them, once they get in, would be the same damn thing." An older black man with grey hair and a hoarse British-accented voice commiserated, "It's all about power. Power corrupts. No one embarks with bad intentions, but it is the nature of power. Power corrupts, I tell you. What are you going to change anything for, then? You must, of course, know the saying: better to stay with an evil that you know rather than a devil that will surprise you." There was a moment of silence after this man's interjection. Viveka wondered if the people in the car had been caught out by his accent or his inflected sagaciousness. Then the rumblings in the car piped up again, with the Indian woman offering, "Well, at least the rain holding up. I glad for the sun, too bad. The roads go dry out by this evening, God willing. But all you, look how this island small, na. Look over to the Central Range. The sun shining here, and over there you could see the rain falling hard-hard still."

Viveka looked toward the Central Range. It was where her father and his friends hunted. What a weird man he was, she thought, killing things for sport. He was sort of brave, she supposed, going into the forest as he did. She had met his friend Saul, and of all her parents' friends she was most drawn to him. Well, he wasn't her *mother's* friend. Why her father didn't bring him around to the house she couldn't understand. She could only put it down to the facts of Saul's race and class. Saul seemed so unassuming, so unlike most of the men in their more regular social circles. Her father really was weird. Brave on one hand, a coward on the other.

THE SOUND OF THE OTHER PASSENGERS' CHATTER LULLED VIVEKA. She felt no draw to contribute, but still a thrill to be in this closed-in space, privy to ideas and ways of speaking and being that were not part of her family's everyday. She slipped the CD player between her thighs, rectitude washing over her, intent on being part of the travel experience. This feeling drew the morning's quarrel with her parents to her mind, and without realizing it, she soon left the passengers behind with their chatter. That morning, after storming out of her parents' room, she had gone into Vashti's and plunked herself down on the bed as Vashti dressed for school. Vashti tried to placate her. "Last night Mom and Dad said that playing volleyball would just make you rougher than you already are." At this, Viveka was on the verge of bursting with anger again, but she knew that if she controlled herself Vashti would tell her more. She feigned calmness and said, "Rougher?"

"Well, face it, Vik, you're not like other girls. You walk so fast, and you don't stay still, and you don't dress up or wear makeup. You don't even talk about boys. Are you still friends with that boy, Elliot?"

"Yes, and Elliot is *just* a friend. Why is it that every time a girl has a boy friend, I mean a friend who just happens to be a boy, everyone gets so excited or concerned? You haven't said anything about him to Mom and Dad, have you?"

"No. You told me not to."

"So you think I am rough, too?"

"Well, not really. A little, I suppose. It's just that you wear the same 'uniform' day in and day out."

Vashti was sounding like their mother, but Viveka still needed to hear more, so she held the volatile responses accumulating in her head.

"When we have to go to a party or to dinner, " continued Vashti, "it's always a major harassment because you only have one dress that you will wear and it's not even dressy. Everyone else enjoys deciding what to wear, what will match with what, but you end up sulking and..."

Viveka listened. It was good, in one way, to know what they all thought. For the length of a sigh she wished she were more like Vashti. Then she answered, "They will see. I will be successful regardless of what I wear or look like. I will be strong, not flabby like Mom..."

"Mom is not flabby," an indignant Vashti flashed back.

"Well, she is not strong — I mean *independent* — either."

"Mom said playing sports will make you muscular."

"What did Dad say?"

"He agreed with her."

"What did you say?"

"Nothing. I was just listening. Nobody ever asks my opinion."

"Well, I am asking for it."

This made Vashti smile. "Okay, Vik, just stand in front of the mirror."

"So?"

"So, look at the way you stand."

"I'm looking. What am I supposed to be seeing?"

"Well, look at how you push out your chest, and how your arms stick out from your side."

"What! Well, so what? This is how I am." That boxiness, as she thought of it, had served her well in her physical training classes in high school.

"But you look like one of those body builders in those weird competitions on TV. We females don't stick our arms out so much. And walk with our chests so high in the air. Drop your chest a little."

Viveka did so, and Vashti followed with, "Now, tuck your arms closer to your sides."

Viveka didn't dare say it, but it flattered her that Vashti thought she looked like a body builder. She sucked her teeth and relaxed her body; her chest rose and her arms sprung out again. "Vashti, what does this have to do with anything? It doesn't feel natural for me."

"Okay, you do look kind of tough for a female."

"Christ! Say girl or woman, but not female. That makes it sound as if you're talking about a cat or some other animal."

"Whatever. I am trying to say that you have a tendency to be muscular. I mean, really: do you want big calves and harder arms — which you will get if you play sports? That's so ugly on a . . . whatever. It makes us look mannish. Mom says *you're* sort of mannish."

That was enough. The word *mannish* was unacceptable. Not wanting her parents to hear them, Viveka kept her outburst as low as she could. "Well, I just don't want to have someone carry two bags of groceries from the cashier to my car, like every other woman we know does. It's not just about strength. It's about exploiting others. And about not realizing one's full potential. It's not like we're incapable, you know. Do you see those women walking on the side of the highway with bundles on their heads and heavy bags in either hand? They can't pay others to do it for them, but they are women, and have no choice but to be strong. Tell me they are mannish! All this dependence we are taught is not natural, it is class related. I don't know why it is admirable in our little claustrophobic world to be pretty, weak and so dependent."

Vashti looked perplexed. She said, "Vik, sometimes you sound like you're not really talking to anyone in particular, just lecturing."

Viveka said nothing, but she was still chewing over the word *mannish*.

"Look, it's getting late, I have to hurry. Please let me dress now," Vashti pleaded. "Should I wear these earrings or these?"

Viveka pointed to one pair and said, "In my day"—at which they both smiled—"we couldn't wear any jewellery to school. Now look at you, with eyeliner. I hope you study as well as you look."

But just as Viveka got to the door, Vashti said, "I saw Merle Bedi yesterday." Viveka stopped. This information, immediately following a conversation about mannishness, made her feel ill.

"So?"

"She asked me for money."

Viveka yearned to know more, for the state of her old friend distressed her. But she couldn't bear the thought of being judged unfairly through association. "Where did you see her?" she asked casually, as if barely interested.

"On the promenade. At lunchtime."

"What were you doing on the promenade?" asked Viveka harshly. She tried to suppress the memory of Merle confiding her love for their science teacher, Miss Seukeran. When they were in fourth form, Viveka had had a long conversation with Merle, trying to make her understand that what she felt was admiration, the desire to be whatever Miss Seukeran was. But Merle had eventually told Viveka that sometimes she felt like she wanted to hold Miss Seukeran in her arms, and kiss her lips, and that these thoughts made her whole body tingle and shake. Viveka's heart had pounded. She didn't know if this was from anger and embarrassment at being party to the knowledge of such a thing or from the fear that she knew something of what Merle felt.

For Viveka, it was Miss Russell. Miss Sally Russell. But the feeling hadn't lasted. Miss Russell had been her and Merle's physical education teacher two years earlier. She had just arrived from England. She was tall, very thin, and angular for a woman. She had longish hair that was parted on one side. It was mostly kept back in a bun, but strands would hang down over her face and cover one eye, and she was always having to push them back behind her ear. Sometimes when she was lost in thought she would take some hair between her fingers and, as if she had made a paint brush, she would swipe, softly, back and forth along her lips. Viveka had studiously tried to make a habit of that very action, but for one thing, her hair wasn't long enough. The other students used to try to describe the colour of Miss Russell's hair to each other. It was auburn; no, it was blonde; no, it was honey-coloured. It was more like hay. As if they knew the colour of hay. Actually, it was golden. Rays of sunshine itself. And Miss Russell, her face was the sun. Everyone was taken aback by her eyes, which were a kind of blue, a shimmer to them like the iridescent blue side of the wings of a morpho butterfly. Her leanness was envied, yet no one would really have wanted to be so thin for fear of being called meagre or sick. It looked good on Miss Russell, though. And the way she moved about — swiftly, *mannishly*, they said, quickly adding that, regardless, she was more feminine than most of the other teachers on the staff. The other teachers in comparison were motherly and grandmotherly. Girls came to school with their hair piled on their heads just like Miss Russell's, and wearing long dangling earrings like hers, and even Miss Russell was obliged to tell them to remove those earrings as jewellery was not part of the school uniform. Girls brought a salad to school for their lunch and ate that instead of doubles and rotis, hoping that they might lose a little of their roundness. But emulation peaked there. Miss Russell confused everyone. They all agreed that she was unusually glamorous for a teacher, but in the next breath she was criticized for being too strong, too serious, for walking the grounds too fast, even during lunchtime and recess when everyone slowed right down. And there were days when her leanness was questioned. "What it have on her for a man to hold?" they asked.

Miss Russell gave tennis lessons and coached netball and throwing the javelin and discus. She had a boyfriend, a local white man who the students, through their mysterious and sometimes questionable methods, found out was an oilfield worker. He would come and pick her up after school on his big growling motor bike, and the instant she saw him, it was abundantly noted, Miss Russell lost all of her physical-education teacher ways and became like any of the other women on the staff—save for the nuns. Suddenly her gait changed and she was all smiles. She would loosen the bun on her head, pull on the helmet, and hop on the bike with more grace than when she was walking the school grounds. She would slide in tight behind her boyfriend, throwing her long sharp arms around him to hug him first and then sliding her hands to his sides, where they came to rest as he took off with such a jolt forward that the sixth-form girls knew he was aware of their eyes on him. With that helmet on, leaning tight against her boyfriend, Miss Russell was everything most other girls wanted to be. Not Viveka, though. She found herself angry with Miss Russell for being so intimate with her boyfriend in public, in front of her students, and knew even as she felt this that she was being silly. Still, she felt what she felt. She and her friend Merle Bedi thought the other students shallow for gawking at Miss Russell's boyfriend the way they did. Viveka also watched him intently, but she knew that her watching was different. She wondered what it was that Miss Russell found alluring about him. She compulsively imagined the motorcycle rider, the oilfield worker, and Miss Russell in a hot bedroom, a red and blue afghan rug on the floor, these two lying on top of the rug, he on top of her—*perched* was the word that always came to her—his mouth on hers, his body pecking away at hers mercilessly.

There were two Miss Russells. The teacher who paid Viveka every attention, who laughed with her and showed her how to do things right; and then that other one—an entirely different person as far as Viveka was concerned—who, once she exited the gates of the school, became as common as everyone else. Viveka wished she could save that Miss Russell from the fate of ordinariness. Miss Russell coached one of the older students who, outside of school life, took part in track competitions and won them. Viveka wanted to be coached in track, too, but Miss Russell, after putting Viveka through certain trials, had dissuaded her, saying that her body type suggested she would not be a good candidate for track but would do better in field—at throwing the discus and the javelin. This was certainly one way of saying that she was chunky, boxy, Viveka had thought, but no one else had been picked for the discus and javelin, and so she also felt special. She imagined the discus in her clutch, spinning it-spinning it-spinning it until she was giddy with untold power and strength, then releasing and launching it far out across the field with an enormous force, all of this with Miss Russell's eyes on her. Viveka's eyes were almost always on Miss Russell.

For a time, Viveka's life revolved around a measly eighty minutes per week of physical training. During school hours she found herself looking out of the classroom window to see if Miss Russell was anywhere in sight. If she did see Miss Russell, she would suddenly be overcome by a tickling feeling throughout her body and dizziness, and she would want to burst into a run, longer and much faster than she was capable of in reality. She knew then, in spite of what Miss Russell had told her, that such power was pent up inside of her. When Miss Russell put together a school team to compete in intra-school sports, Viveka tried out for the discus and javelin to see if she was ready for competition. She did strength, endurance, power, and jump tests. Viveka was weak in the endurance tests, yet she could jump higher than most of the students, and this surprised Viveka herself because of her boxiness. And she tested better than anyone else in power and strength. She went home and boasted to her parents and sister. Her mother showed no interest, but Vashti said, "You would jump to the moon for Miss Russell. If Miss Hollis or Sister Veronica were our PE teacher you would be sick for every class."

In the end, Viveka was chosen to be on the school's sports team, but her parents absolutely refused to allow her to take the time after school and on weekends to train. And Miss Russell lost interest in Viveka after meeting with Devika and Valmiki to try to persuade them to let Viveka train and compete. Viveka's parents had informed Miss Russell that there was no future in that sort of thing, and that Viveka, being weak in math and in French, would be taking after-class lessons in those subjects, starting immediately. Soon after that, Viveka heard that Miss Russell and her boyfriend were getting married, and a terrible acne broke out on Viveka's face.

It was two years later when Merle Bedi told Viveka about wanting to kiss Miss Seukeran. Saying these words out loud was craziness. But Viveka understood something of it. That kind of talk, she felt, could get them both in trouble. A clash of thoughts, incomplete ones, incomplete-able ones, resounded in her head. She would be implicated in Merle's craziness: there was Viveka's very public and close association with Merle, Viveka's well-known affinity for sports and things *mannish.* And there was Miss Russell — Miss Russell leaving, Miss Russell engaged, Viveka's coinciding acne problem, and in the instant of Merle Bedi saying she wanted to kiss Miss Seukeran, Viveka knew that she, too, had wanted to throw the discus and javelin because it was her way of kissing Miss Russell.

She stood up, looked down at Merle, and snapped, "I wouldn't go around announcing that if I were you."

Merle's eyes were bright, as if she was seeing some kind of saving truth. "I want to tell her. I need to tell her. It's so real and so good. I feel like a kite, Vik. It's unbelievable. I can't study or think of anything else. *She makes me feel that way. She does it.* She *must* feel it. Come on, Viveka, can't you see how she pays attention to me, more than to anyone else?"

"Merle, I really think you should keep those feelings and all of that kind of thinking to yourself. I don't want to carry on this conversation. Don't say those kinds of things. Not even to me."

But Merle was beside herself, composing music for Miss Seukeran, writing Miss Seukeran cards in flowery language expressing her admiration. Even if she had not actually expressed her dirty thinking, Viveka thought, it would have been obvious to a moron. Saying those words out loud was a kind of suicide. And indeed, there had been some camaraderie between the teacher and Merle, but it was shortlived. Suddenly Miss Seukeran stopped noticing Merle, no longer stopped on her walks down the hallways to say hello to her, and seemed almost to shun her. Viveka wondered if Merle had told Miss Seukeran how she wished to kiss her.

THAT MORNING, VIVEKA RECALLED, VASHTI HAD SULKED AT VIVEKA'S unwelcome authoritarian manner, a manner oddly prompted by the mention of Merle Bedi.

"I got a doubles for lunch. What does it matter to you?"

"But why are you eating doubles for lunch?" Viveka persisted. "You should know better than that. They are so greasy. You'll get pimples. Why don't you take a proper lunch to school? You don't even have to make it. Get Pinky to make you a sandwich and a salad."

"I am trying to tell you about Merle Bedi, and you're going on about my lunch. In any case, you used to buy doubles too. How come you can eat it but I can't? Why do you have to disagree with everything and make others feel like they're wrong or stupid? You are so contrary."

"Contrary!" That was not a word that Vashti would use on her own, Viveka reflected. Her suspicion was confirmed when Vashti sheepishly responded: "Mom says you're contrary and I just happen to agree."

Merle had clearly suffered from Miss Seukeran's rejection more than from the hush-hush gossip that eventually ensued. By the last year of high school, she withdrew even from Viveka. From the time she had begun high school, Merle had been the top student in her particular stream. Suddenly she was failing every subject, and grinning about it as if that was an achievement. By the time Viveka had entered university, Merle had started living on the street. It was said by some people that her parents put her out, and by others that she left home, on her own, this act being part of the same craziness that had her loving within her own sex.

"Christ, Vashti. You're like a clone of Mom. Why can't you just think for yourself? Well, perhaps you *do* think I am contrary, you just have to have the vocabulary fed to you."

With that, Viveka slammed shut Vashti's door. The loudness of it brought her father from his bedroom. He glared at her, but said nothing. She glared back at him, thinking, "You're such a coward, Dad." Instead of trying to bribe and cajole her with the offer of the chauffeur, why couldn't he have spoken his true mind to her mother, or to her, or to both of them. How could the two of them be her parents, she their child? She felt betrayed in myriad ways.

If the altercation with her parents had made Viveka wish she were not part of her own family, this one with Vashti had left her feeling a little frightened, but she wasn't sure of what, exactly. As she was dressing for her trip to the campus she had tried on a skirt her mother had long ago bought for her, but which she had not yet worn, and a pair of black low-heeled, open-toed shoes. In the mirror she saw a stranger. The waist of the skirt, and the way her shirt fell over it, brought notice, she felt, to her already shapeless torso. She considered the thick, naturally muscled legs before her. Her legs were dry and needed shaving. All she had to do was to pull on a pair of flesh-tone stockings and, despite her age, she would have passed for a dowdy high school teacher. She flinched.

She left the house feeling more comfortable, but a little graceless, in her uniform of button-down collared shirt, blue jeans, and Indian-style leather slippers.

SCABBY LOOKING STUMPS OF BRUSH STUCK OUT OF THE WATER IN THE swamp fields closest to the road. Red-breasted blackbirds, their black feathers bright and shiny as if polished by the rain, did their mating dance, hopping directly into the air as if bounding up from a trampoline and floating down again to land on the same few inches of visible, bare scrub top. They looked to Viveka as if they had alighted on something that either burned them or pricked them and so they flew up in utter surprise and a-flutter, only to alight on the same spot again and to have the same effect occur. Over and over. Such pretty birds and so silly, she would normally think, but today her mind was elsewhere, and the dance of the birds was nothing more than that, an animal dance.

With such slow progress along the highway Viveka was thankful that she didn't have a class to attend this morning. She hadn't really wanted to go to the university campus, but it was better than staying at home in the presence of her mother. This way, she didn't have to make the choice of prolonging their disagreement or giving it up, either out of wariness or real defeat. By travelling to the university in this public manner, without the aid of the family's chauffeur, she hoped her mother would in her absence have the time and chance to come to the understanding that she was wrong and Viveka right. Besides, travelling like this she felt apart from her family, able to take part in the ordinary life of her country, something her mother knew nothing of, and something her father liked to think he understood because he had patients from all walks of life. Yes, it was true that he hunted with a few black men who were skilled labourers. If any of the other passengers had been watching Viveka they would have seen her shake her head, and curl her lips as she thought scornfully, "But if we were to have a party at our house there is no way he would invite them, his so-called buddies. What did I do to be born into this hypocritical mess? I can't, I just *can't* allow myself to become them."

Sometimes Viveka had the sensation that her arms were tightly bound to her body with yards and yards of clear Scotch tape. When she felt this, as she did now, she imagined trying to locate with her eyes one of the ends, her eyes darting, blurring, concentrating on the silvery-clear mess that bound her, and on locating a faint line that indicated an edge of the tape, tilting her head and attempting to reach it with her mouth, stretching her lower jaw until the sides of her mouth ached, down to her shoulder, and raising her shoulder up to it as much as she could, and using her teeth to pry up a tiny piece. Then, she imagined, she would hook it and yank it up without tearing it off. There in the taxi, her neck taut and her temples aching with the mere thought of this exercise, she could taste and feel uneven bits of tape. She almost gagged, imagining spitting out those stubborn flecks of tape on her tongue.

The comfort of life as lived in her parents' home bred in Viveka certain aspirations, aspirations she was beginning to suspect were naïve and unrealistic, among them to be an internationally heralded literary critic whose emphasis was on Caribbean writing. As a student majoring in English literature, she was making her way through aspects of the usual canon, but she was barely able to satisfy an elephantine thirst for Caribbean literature. The writings of Jamaica Kincaid, Dionne Brand, Jean Rhys, Derek Walcott, and Earl Lovelace provoked her to want to experience a Caribbean-ness, and a Trinidadian-ness more specifically, that was antithetical to her mother's tie to all things Indian and Hindu. At times Viveka felt like an alien presence in her parents' house. Her mother was not impressed that she was attending university. Devika, in typical old-fashioned Indian manner, found Viveka ambitious — not *too* ambitious, but ambitious — a quality that was not to be cultivated, and was not generally admired by people of Devika's generation. Viveka's aspiration to be a literary critic, tantamount to pompousness and arrogance, fell under her suspicion. She asked Viveka again and again what made her think that she had the ability to be such a critic. Her refrain — levelled at Valmiki as well — was "Ambition will be your downfall."

Valmiki, on the other hand, encouraged Viveka's interests — even though his encouragement often felt misguided. Viveka knew he didn't understand how or why one would study subjects based on what he saw as opinion rather than proven fact. But Viveka also knew she had a special place in his heart, and that he would support her. He had said to her more than once "Get a degree — law, medicine, whatever you want." (He never mentioned what she was actually doing.) "Because if anything happens at least you have something to fall back on." Devika had once interrupted his benevolent speechifying and answered back, "Something? What you mean *something*? And in any case, she doesn't even have the subjects for medicine. You really do talk foolishness sometimes, Valmiki. And what on earth could she do with a law degree? I don't want my daughters practising law. Standing up like that in front of a bunch of men, making spectacles of themselves."

Valmiki knew to ignore Devika. "A pretty girl like you, you're bound to get married, but suppose something happened to your husband and you were left to fend for yourself. In any case, even if you don't get married — because you're too smart for most men — having a good degree is a good thing for a girl. We won't be around to look after you forever. Get your degree, and no one will be able to take advantage of you."

Devika's family's financial comfort, and that provided since marriage by Valmiki, afforded Devika the choice to work or not to work, but she had no use for the choice: she had no imagination for work outside of the house, nor for study, and thought little of educated women. Educated women, she said, were aggressive, unladylike. The only professions she could imagine for either of her daughters in an age, she conceded, when women were demanding to spend time outside of the home, were catering, flower arranging (both of which, incidentally, could be done in the home), and teaching. The latter for Devika meant at a primary school or high school moulding young minds, not at a university. To her mind, even outside of the lecture hall female professors carried themselves like lawyers. They were grim and lacked social graces and didn't pay attention to fashions, and were a threat to the comfort of men with all their serious thinking and interruptions to correct and beggings to differ. What she understood was preparing one's self for marriage. But marriage had never interested Viveka.

Looking around the taxi, Viveka mused how her friend Elliot, who was at university with her and studying English too, was a bit like these people she travelled with. Well, not exactly like them. A bit, though. She watched the passengers, listened a little more to their conversation, and tried to think how Elliot was different from them. He might come from a similar class, she decided, but he was a university student. His concerns and aspirations were different than these peoples'. He was already living a marginally different kind of life from them, and in time that margin would widen. But at least, she thought, he would have a hands-on experience of this more real world.

What if she were to marry Elliot? Their children would be part Indian, that part from her, and from him they would inherit his black, white, and Carib ancestry. That would teach her parents a thing or two. She snorted, imagining her mother bouncing a little mixed-race boy on her knee, having naturally fallen in love with him despite herself. But this was merely one of her many subversive fantasies. She wasn't that interested in Elliot.

Of course, if her parents were to meet Elliot, they would not approve. Her mother would come straight out and voice her disapproval in the most unequivocal way. Her father, on the other hand, would not want to offend or upset Viveka. He would not commit to an opinion one way or the other, but he would joke, cajole, placate, tell her how terrific she was, mention that her friend, that Elliot-young-man, seemed like a nice-enough fellow, and as if the conversation were unrelated, state that no one, absolutely no one she had yet met was her match. He would say that he had his eye out for a nice Indian boy who could give a dowry of at least one cow, et cetera. Vashti would jump in then and correct her father and say, "It's the girl's family who gives the dowry, Dad." And her father would be only too pleased to be handed the opportunity to retort, "Not in this family. Anybody who wants one of my girls has to pay me handsomely..."

Viveka would have loved to have this battle with her parents, for their true colours would show then, and could only shame them. But she really felt so little for Elliot that she was not prepared to take on this battle and risk winning it. Her parents, therefore, were unaware of his existence.

Elliot had seemed recently to have only one goal in mind. Given the slightest opportunity, his hands found their way underneath Viveka's shirt. He would inch them this way, then that, his fingertips circling the small of her back in non-threatening playfulness. In time, and that time could be as long as it took for him to feel that Viveka had relaxed and would not resist him, his fingertips would dance along the waistband of her pants.

Viveka wasn't as unaware as Elliot imagined. She knew that if she allowed him too many inches in the vicinity surely he would expect (and what if he were to demand?) the whole mile. The instant those fingers entered her waistband, she would start talking of something she felt might arrest his attention. She would take hold of his arms and in a casual, non-confrontational manner, move them. On one occasion recently, he had waited for her to do this, and then locked his arms around her, pinning hers to her sides. He walked her — a graceless, almost frightening backward stumble — to the wall. There, he pressed his body to hers, trapping her against the cool wall, and he brought his lips to her ear. She giggled nervously and tried to push him back, but he was intent, and did not laugh with her. She tried to raise her arms, but he had them well caught. She said, "Oh Elliot, come on." And he said back seriously, "No, you come on. What's this? I mean, what are we to each other? I spend all my time with you. You spend all your free time here in my apartment with me. What do you expect? Isn't this what you want, too? Tell me it isn't. Go on, tell me."

Elliot's unusual seriousness and sudden focus on this matter had surprised her. She did not want to offend or disappoint him, and did not quite know how to answer without doing either. He carried on, "This is what *I* want." More quietly, more gently, he added, "Come on, I need this from you." That he *needed* this disheartened her, but that he needed this *from her* tamed her resistance. He lowered his crotch to hers. Hard as a stump of guava wood there, he pressed into her pubic area. She felt a tingle in her lower back, and her pelvis, as if it suddenly had a mind and agenda quite apart from her, lurched forward to meet him. It felt horribly good. An uncontrollable desire and the dregs of her reserve co-mingled. She shifted her weight from one leg to the other, intending to brace herself and engage her brain in decision-making, but he took advantage of that split second to spread her legs with his knee. He was saying something in her ear, but she was unable to make out the guttural sounds. The weight of his whole body against her, and the insistence of him between her legs, was stifling. She placed her hands on his waist intending to push him away, to quell the rising quake of his body against hers, to put an end to an unintentional desire swelling in her and betraying her, but the moment she touched his waist he began to breathe more heavily, gasping hot wet air into her ear. Her ear was unpleasantly drenched in heat and spittle, and the desire between her legs instantly numbed. Suddenly, his body convulsed, he was rigid for a few seconds, and then he slumped slowly down onto her, heat rising from his body as if from asphalt at midday. He stayed there for some moments like a wholesale-size sack of flour on her chest. Her body tensed against the weight. She breathed shallowly. She wanted to push him off, but was pinned not just by his weight, but also by a confusion of emotions. She had experienced in her breasts and pubic area an awakening that in moments made her want to lose her mind in pleasure, yet now it was as if a bulldozer had run over and crushed a part of her.

When Elliot released her, Viveka fixed herself and left without any words. But in class the next day Elliot sat next to her, and they resumed their friendship as if nothing had come between them. His advances had left her cool, and now she had drawn an imaginary line that she would not let him cross: She decided that as long as he didn't try to remove her clothing, she would not try to stop him.

THE NEXT TIME THEY WERE ALONE TOGETHER, ELLIOT LEANED AGAINST the counter of his student apartment, again strapping her arms against her body. She was nervous and rambled on about one of the Trinidadian authors she'd been reading. He slipped one hand under her shirt. That hand was splayed, and she leaned back on it as if it were a wall. "He makes Indians out to be ugly, stupid, concerned only with their narrow knife-edged slice of life. He's criticizing his ancestors, but these are *my* ancestors too, and by implication he is criticizing me. And yet, I keep wanting to read on. He gets it right, but so what? Does he have to write it at all? I don't think he really hates us so much as he is gravely disappointed in what we have not become."

"And what is that?" Elliot's voice was distant.

"I don't know. White? Brighter, whiter than the conqueror himself?"

"Conqueror?" asked Elliot distractedly.

"Well, the British, who else? Oh, come on, Elliot. Stop it. Pay attention to me."

"But I am. See?" Elliot unfastened her bra with one hand. She pushed him hard. He laughed, but the laughter was chalky, choppy. His eyes had narrowed and his pale skin had turned a drunk-man's red. He walked some paces away from her, and in the midst of her rambling on about this author he cut her short and said he was tired and still had a paper to work on. The simultaneous feelings of relief and of being rejected left her dazed. All the feminist rhetoric she was able to spew easily and brightly in discussions or could write for A-grade papers burrowed into the farthest recesses of her mind. It was her father who came to her mind — the sense that while Valmiki might have disapproved of Elliot, her lack of desire would have disappointed him. It was as if she had just betrayed her father, and it was that feeling, rather than whatever it was that had gone on between her and Elliot, that distressed her. She must try to do better next time, be more like her affair-crazy father, she scolded herself.

Next time, she let Elliot pull the top of her bra down far enough to reach the nipple of her breast. Something like a small animal taking refuge in her underwear suddenly bolted up.

Elliot felt this excitement in her too, and he took the opportunity to lift off her shirt before she had time to stop him. He pushed her still-clasped bra upwards to release her breasts. He held one breast with one hand, and put his mouth to it. He put his other hand between her legs. She gasped with the suddenness of the whole thing, at his strength, and with unexpected pleasure. He began to undress her, not everything, he said to her hesitation, just her shirt and bra. He said in a light tone, *No penetration, I promise*, and she knew instantly that she didn't want him this close to her. He pointed out that Helen and Wayne were doing it, and nothing had happened to them. No one even knew they were doing it, he said. But that was not what she was worried about. Hard as she tried, she really didn't feel connected to Elliot. She wished it were different, but it simply wasn't.

Later that that same week, Viveka and Helen had studied late at the library. As they drove home afterwards, an accident on the highway had created a traffic jam that moved a car length every ten to fifteen minutes. When they reached the entrance to the mall at Valsayn, they decided to stop there to eat dinner and wait until the traffic had cleared somewhat. At the Indian restaurant she and Helen talked about books, authors, volleyball, and family affairs, but neither of them brought up Wayne, Elliot, or boyfriends or marriage or their futures. On the drive home, they were quiet. Every so often Helen hummed a tune that was unrecognizable, perhaps made up. She was driving and in a world of her own.

Viveka had leaned her head on her seat's headrest and kept her eyes on the darkness ahead. She thought of Elliot wanting her and him to be naked, and of how she had felt when he had touched her nipple and put his hands between her legs. She shifted her eyes, but not her head, and glanced at Helen's legs. Helen had pulled the flounce of her long Indian-style skirt up above her knees, and her legs were pale in the darkness of the car. She imagined Helen was her, and she was Elliot watching Helen's bare legs — or her own legs as she saw them in her imagination — and she felt that same heat, that same jostle inside her underwear and the rush of wetness there. When they arrived at Viveka's house, Viveka turned away from Helen as she opened the door to get out, but Helen put her hand on Viveka's back and stopped her. As Viveka turned to face Helen, Helen moved forward to give her the usual goodbye peck on a cheek but in a confused moment, their lips met. It was quick, the barest brush, but they were both startled. They laughed, and in their laughter was a show of indignation. Viveka blew air out of her pursed lips and hurriedly mumbled, "Oh my god. That was weird. Too weird." And they laughed again, soft rattled laughs.

The next time, they were more careful. And for a time Viveka was more tolerant of Elliot's desires. He was able to touch her breasts again, and knead her nipples with twirling fingers and with a tongue that flicked with the speed of a hummingbird's wings. No matter how painful her nipples became under his kneading, she would say nothing, and Elliot's quiet, his fatigue and spaciness after, was almost worth it. In turn, Elliot grew more patient with her. No doubt he thought that since he had come this far, if he continued to be a little more patient, in time she would consent to touching him.

When Viveka was on her own at nights with the lights off, Vashti's breathing telling her that she had the privacy she needed, she would try to re-create that feeling she had experienced the first time she had had an orgasm with Elliot. She had had others with him since, but none were as surprising, as delightfully confusing as that first one. She tried imagining him touching her, but that left her more sore than excited. So she would imagine herself driving a car, but she would also imagine that she was Elliot sitting in the passenger seat, and that she, Elliot, was riding his hands up her bare legs, inching up to her crotch, finally slipping her/his fingers inside the elastic of her panties, and that feeling, like the first time, would come to her again. It was a tingle that crept up her arms, down her legs, circled her hips, gripped her feet, her toes, and shook her with numerous explosive convulsions. She got to this place every time on her own, but never again with Elliot. Rather than let this worry her, she decided that since she was perfectly capable of arriving at this delight on her own, her reluctance with Elliot was because he was not the right man, and she was waiting for that man to come along. In magazines she browsed through at the hair salon, she had read that when the right man came along you knew it, you simply knew it. She was nagged, however, by an irrational conviction that the right man would never come along. Her father had a saying that all men were bastards, that he should know. She hated when he said that, but didn't doubt that he should know. Deep in her the memory was some long-ago family unpleasantness involving her father and a former neighbour, Pia Moretti. Viveka had an actual memory of the situation with Pia Moretti, but that memory was so bizarre she had often wondered if she had built pictures around bits of overheard fighting between her parents, and these imagined scenes had worked themselves into what she experienced as a memory.

Viveka suddenly realized that in the public space of the taxi she had been thinking about sex, and that if she were to call up that bizarre memory there would be even more sex sifting into the psychic space of the taxi. She wondered if any of the passengers was a mind-reader. Her face, she feared, might have given her away, for she had felt a burn in her cheeks thinking of Elliot and of Helen. She would stop all of this crazy-making thinking; Elliot often said that she thought too much. By way of relaxing her brain, she tried to focus on the landscape through which the taxi travelled.

They were well past the swamp now, red-breasted blackbirds replaced by opportunistic corbeaux flying low overhead, their heavy heads angled downward as they ploughed the land with their red-ringed eyes for the swollen carcasses of animals that had drowned in the flood. The road here was raised, and the land on either side sat below. Although the roads were now dry, the water had still not drained from the low-lying fields. On the left were plots of coconut. There would normally be a delightful spread of crocuses at the foot of the tall trees, lime green fronds studded with brilliant orange tulip-like flowers, but the ground was completely submerged. In clearings were people's homes, one-room structures no bigger than Viveka's bedroom, made of mismatched planks of wood with roofs thatched from palm branches. Although these houses were on stilts, the water had risen up to the doorway of several of them. A man stood in the open doorway of one. The brown water was up to his ankles and Viveka imagined that the floor of his house was underwater. The driver of the car could be heard, "You woulda think they'da build up they house off the ground by now. Flooding in this area is not a new thing. Some people don't learn, I tell you."

Viveka let her head fall lightly against the turned-up window, aware that a thousand other heads had likely greased that same spot before her. She guessed — hoped — that head lice didn't live on glass.

She liked thinking that the flood and the havoc it wreaked would not have made one iota of difference to the pace of travel along this route, whether she was in a private chauffeur-driven car or in this public taxi. But for the man standing in the doorway of his partially submerged house, having choices might have made a difference, she mused. He probably couldn't afford, or didn't have the technical knowledge, to build any higher. She ought to have said this to the driver, should have been less shy, Viveka thought. The classroom at the university seemed to be the only place where she was not shy or demure, or where she thought her plain looks were not a disadvantage. Here in the car, her plainness contributed to her reluctance to speak up. She wanted to bet that if she had spoken up, no one would have heard her or someone would have begun to speak over her voice, blocking out whatever she was saying. Or the correctness of her grammar and the pronunciation of her words — in short, her accent, though a Trinidadian one — would have pegged her as a local but not one of the usual taxi-travelling clientele and therefore her contribution would either have been ignored, rebuffed, or experienced as a silencing of the others. Suddenly she was wishing she had worn lipstick — even just a faint colour, nothing like the dark purple worn by the Indian woman up front — or even a push-up bra, something her sartorially savvy and more well-endowed sister had suggested more than once.

In her mind somersaulted partial phrases. "When the right man comes along." "All men are bastards." "Some people don't learn, I tell you." She glanced discreetly at the faces of the other passengers to see if there were any mind-readers in her midst. If she could change one thing about herself it would be how demure she became outside of her parents' house.

SHE HADN'T ALWAYS FELT DEMURE. SHE USED TO THINK OF HERSELF as a blond-haired boy who was strong, powerful, peaceful, and could do anything and everything. He had a horse he could ride. He didn't speak much. He was kind. His name was Vince, short for "invincible." He was not in the least the bastard her father said all men were. Vince loved being outdoors. There was that time when she, or rather Vince, had been out in the yard. There was a butterfly net. He had been waving it at a butterfly.

But whenever this particular memory came to her, this last confused her: the boy she had imagined herself to be wasn't the type who would capture any living thing for sport. Memory and imagination collided. Was she seven years old then, or was it five, or was she eleven? Was Anand alive then? If he was, she would have a clue with which to work out her age when this incident took place. She tried to remember something in school or something about how and why she had got the net — if there was, in fact, ever a net in their house. If there had been one, it had long ago been discarded. How she wished she could anchor the events in this particular memory, more than in any other, and separate out what had actually happened from her propensity to bridge the gaps in logic with invention. Asked about a net, her mother had one day vaguely remembered there being one once, but then on a different day long after had said, no, she didn't remember any such net. In any case, the memory went like this.

Vince was barefoot. He skipped about the yard following a rather large morpho, the biggest he had ever seen, the size of a small child's head, of Anand's head. It was sapphire one minute like the tropical sky at night, as silver and turquoise as the waters of coral reefs the next, and the beauty of the thing lured her boy-self through the front gate of his parents' house and up the road past several houses until he found himself standing at the gate of a neighbour's yard. The low gate was unlatched, and slightly ajar. The butterfly alighted on a sign on the gate: Manetto Moretti, Painter and Contractor, Residential and Commercial. *When it took off again, up the high wide red-painted concrete stairs of the Moretti's shrub-and flower-surrounded bungalow, the boy followed it. There, on the terrazzo-tiled veranda, the blond and heroic boy was suddenly breathless. He perched on the railing of a wrought-iron balcony.*

In her mind's eye, sitting in the taxi, Viveka saw the house up the road from her own, and there was currently no stairway with a railing on it. Ah! That was the tear in her memory. The incident couldn't have happened because there was no balcony and no railing on that house now. But the memory, like a piece of music, marched onward relentlessly.

Perched on that wrought-iron railing that surrounded the open balcony, Vince stretched out his arm, the net agape, and he reached even farther for the flying thing, such a perfect thing, bigger than a newborn baby's head—impossible, Viveka thought, but the memory was compelling, persistent. *The butterfly flew lithely over the railing and was caught in a swirling current of air. It flapped its wings, and gaining control, rose above the yard, above the clotheslines on which billowed colourful dresses belonging to Pia Moretti, and several pairs of Mani's white-but-paint-flecked overalls. The morpho winged higher and higher until it was above the rooftops of the neighbourhood, and then it ceased to flap and merely glided.*

No matter how often Viveka had replayed this mind-tape, when she came to this part her heart beat faster and she felt the excitement of the almost-ness of a moment, and she was pleased, even as she questioned the reliability of her mind, that she had the good sense not to try to follow the butterfly-bird over the railing.

About to head back down the stairs, Vince, her invincible boy-self, noticed that the wall-length sliding doors that led into the Moretti's house were drawn invitingly wide apart, yet no one seemed to be about. "Mr. Moretti?" the boy whispered with neighbourly concern from the balcony. There was no answer, so the boy raised his voice and called again. "Hello, Mrs. Moretti? Mr. Moretti? Anyone here?" He, or anyone else so inclined, could have been a lucky thief that day. On tiptoe still—and now, in the taxi to the university, Viveka's heart raced again, this time because she really wanted the scenes to miraculously change and to remember something entirely different—*Vince entered the house. He could feel the coarse sponginess of the high-pile blue-red-taupe Afghan carpet*—this is the detail that had always made her think there must be truth to the wretched memory, for it was not likely that her child-self would otherwise have seen an Afghan carpet, there being on the tropical island no need for such an item—*and he stepped over a leather belt that had been dropped on the carpet along with a hammer, a pair of pliers, a wire clipper, a screwdriver, and a wrench, and then walked down a corridor that ended at a closed door through which low sounds wafted*—Viveka pressed her ear to the glass of the taxi, but in the memory she pressed her ear to the door—*and he heard a groan. Not an urgent or ugly groan, but still, a groan. The blond boy called again, "Hello?" The groaning persisted and he, if he could have been heard, was ignored. He turned the door's handle, waited, and called again. Then, unnoticed, he stepped into the room and immediately bolted out again. He held his breath and pressed his face to the crack between the door and the wall to which it was hinged. Through the crack he studied his father, his cacao-coloured skin. The arc of his back. Vince watched Pia Moretti beneath his father. Her eyes were shut tight, a frown on her face. Pia stretched and arched her pelvis upward, and Viveka's father's pelvis flicked at her. Suddenly his father's body collapsed in exhaustion on top of Pia.* Viveka's heart pounded, resounding in her ears.

She had no actual memory of what might have followed, but Viveka always imagined actions that would have made sense, would have knitted the memory, if that is what it was, into a logical, sensible whole. Doing so calmed her: she, or rather blond

Vince, did not go straight home, but ran around and around the neighbourhood until, dripping with sweat, he limped, feet swollen, blistered, and bleeding, through the front gates of his parents' house.

How could she have made any of it up, she wondered, when there were bits and pieces, like the heaving and the humping, that she would not otherwise, at that age, have been enlightened about, and so could not have imagined them? And how else to explain the coldness that had followed between her parents?

IN THE LIMBO OF TAXI TRAVEL THE DREADED WORD CAME TO HER again. *Mannish.* An onomatopoeic word that sounded as disgusting as what it suggested. It occurred to Viveka that her father was mannish, and she meant that in the derogatory sense—hunting helpless creatures on weekends and almost flaunting those affairs he had with women. When he and her mother quarrelled about his affairs, it was as if they did so in private, yet it seemed as if her parents were in fact making sure that Vashti and Viveka overheard them. It confused and irritated Viveka that her parents were both simultaneously secret and public about the subject.

Viveka sat up suddenly with a little jolt that startled the passenger next to her. She, her boy-self Vince lingering inside of her, had a sudden, compelling desire to know where Pia Moretti was. She had a vague notion that Pia and her husband were no longer on the island, but she wasn't sure if this was actually so. She looked at the cars crawling down the other side of the highway to see if anyone resembling an aged Pia Moretti might be in one of them. She was oddly compelled to know that Pia Moretti was safe. Safe from her own beauty, and certainly safe from men. Men like her father. She wanted to keep her mother safe, too. Safe from Pia Moretti. But if loyalties regarding her mother tugged at her one minute, in the next they repelled her. "Serves her right," Viveka thought, "for putting up with all those affairs. How could any woman be so accepting? I can't stand what Dad did and probably, for all I know, still does to her. Still, I'd rather be like him any day, than helpless and accepting as Mom is."

Her taxi-musing now circled back to the altercation about volleyball. She would find a way to play volleyball, she decided, even if it caused an ungulfable rift between her parents and herself. Volleyball, after all, meant more than volleyball.

Travelling on dry roads much farther inland now, the taxi was to arrive at Viveka's stop in front of the university library in less than five minutes. The sky had already set up. It wouldn't be long before the rain began again. She would meet Helen there, and she and Helen would study for part of the day. She would meet Elliot, too. He would, no doubt, want to go to his apartment with her, and once there he would, again no doubt, want to lie on his bed with her. Today she was determined not to go near his apartment. She would, rather, suggest seeing an exhibition of paintings at the Cipriani-Butler Gallery on campus, and in the evening, if the rain had stopped early enough and the courts were dry, she and Helen would play volleyball in the park at the foot of Harris Promenade, exactly as she had done the previous week. And she would hope again that her parents did not find out about either Elliot or the volleyball.

Devika and Valmiki

THAT EVENING, DEVIKA AND VALMIKI SAT ON OPPOSITE ENDS OF THE patio, facing each other. The newspaper Valmiki was reading shielded him. As she fingered the ruby and diamond pendant Valmiki had arrived home with, Devika reflected: Whatever he had done to warrant buying these presents was Valmiki's business; half of her good-sized collection of jewellery, selected from the best available on the island, had been given to her by him for no reason she knew of. What she did know was that he gave his gifts sheepishly, the red glow on his face suggesting some sort of guilt; if she were to try to sort *him* out as well as Viveka, she would go crazy.

It was time for her to do what she excelled at. She hadn't thrown a party in almost a year. She was willing to bet that people had noticed and were wondering if something untoward had happened in her family — if finances were down, or an embarrassing and hush-hush illness was keeping them low key, or if Valmiki and herself were fighting, if he was running around again, or if something unseemly had happened to her daughters. For some time now she had wanted to send a flare up into the sky that all was well. And now that she and her daughters had been presented with this unexpected jewellery, she had better do something fast. She would host a party, tell the world that the Krishnu family was just fine.

In the past she had been able to handle throwing big parties — not just handle them: she excelled at them. But in the last year or so, she had felt an exhaustion that made no sense to her. After all, she did nothing that required great physical energy. What she wanted was not so much to throw a *big* party as to host a small one that would bring her the same kind of glory and admiration as the big ones did. She reasoned that basically the same work was required for any number of guests from twelve to forty. It was marginally more work to adjust from forty to sixty-five or so. It was only when you started hitting seventy and above that you required the kind of stamina that at her age — no, not at her age, just these last few months — she no longer had. She had been told enough times that she looked a good decade younger than she was. She simply wasn't feeling happy-happy. A party would brighten her up, unite them all in a common purpose. Well, maybe not Viveka; Viveka always found a way to sabotage their happiness. A party was a good medium. But she wouldn't let Viveka run their lives or ruin hers. So, how many people should she have?

She looked around. The rain served the garden well. It was lush. The ferns and philodendrons had firmed up. They looked ripe. Bougainvillea didn't flower in the rain, but its foliage, which formed a backdrop to the swimming pool, was at least rampant. She'd get Sheriff the gardener to snip off the old dry leaves, the gold filigreed skeletons interrupting running clumps of bright light green. She had the good taste, he the green thumb — although their friends always complimented her on having the green thumb. Sheriff would freshen up everything. If anyone could, it was Sheriff. The Antigua Heat spread like a red rash along one section of the fence. The flowers of the halyconia in a corner hung like the characters of a foreign language, and the baliser punctuated it like eternal flambeaux. Most of the work of the garden was done by nature itself. The lawn, as green as if it had been fertilized, was all that would really need looking after. It grew overnight in weather like this. Devika could imagine people standing on the thick carpet of grass. It was not necessary for them to actually notice every detail of the garden, but her tending to these details, or rather having Sheriff tend to them, would aid in relaxing her guests, give them the sensation of being in a paradise without knowing why. She liked that. Indeed, she preferred that her guests not know what it was, exactly, that made *her* parties what they were. She imagined the guests. Heard the sounds of their glasses tinkling with ice, felt their fingertips wet and cold from the glasses they held, the beading from the cold wine inside meeting the warmth of the Gulf air. Oh yes, cocktail napkins. Well, that would fall under the list of things she'd have to get. She wouldn't have them monogrammed. Everyone was doing it, and it had become quite tasteless. The gullies that divided lawn from beds would have to be lined with fresh manure. She'd order that right away. And the food. It would be out of this world. Appetizers, a full meal, courses served one at a time. Or perhaps a buffet, with several choices of meat. Followed by desserts.

Then there was the choosing and renting of cutlery, and chairs, tables, ashtrays, vases for every table, napkins and tablecloths. The ordering of flowers and candleholders. Hiring a deejay, or a solo musician for the entire evening, or perhaps a lone pan player or a classical guitarist for the cocktails, and a small band for the rest of the evening. After-dinner drinks. Well, she'd leave the drinks to Val. All of this made her feel tender toward him.

Valmiki turned into a different creature when there were parties at their house. She felt unusually close to him then, more so than at any other time. She enjoyed his surprise and delight when, not having paid attention to the goings-on around him, on the afternoon of the party he would arrive home earlier than usual and see that she had pulled so much together seamlessly. This never failed to have the same effect. When he had seen how much she had done, how marvellous the house looked, the lighting and decorations just right, the tables set and only the candles left to be lit and the food served, he would invariably put an arm around her shoulders and say, "When did you arrange for all of this?" And she would suck her teeth, smile with triumph, and say, "All of this has been happening right here in front of you for the last several days, but you, you never notice anything." He would ignore her comments because he would be thinking of how awed their guests would be, of how good she makes him look. He would take her hand in his and lead her to the bedroom. She would ask, laughing, "What are you doing? I've got things to do." But she would follow him.

He would shut the bedroom door and she will face him, grinning yet protesting in a whisper, "But what are you doing? I am needed out there." He will close his eyes, lick her lips, the inside of his mouth tasting sourly of instant coffee, and her words will rise hesitant, and hoarse, and muffled in her throat, "Valmiki, Valmiki, don't. I'll have to shower all over again. We can't be long, Valmiki." He will hold her tight to him, and with his body pressed against hers he will guide her backwards into the bathroom and he will shut that door behind them, too. She will lean her back against the door as she mumbles, "People will be here in a couple of hours, Valmiki," and holding the collar of his shirt she will draw his face to her, but he will push her back, pull his face away from her, and staring intensely into her eyes, he will grab the cloth of her dress about her thighs and slide it up against her legs until his hands are at her panties.

She will feel triumphant, for in that moment he would be — he is — a man, taking her like that. That other thing that happened on weekends, that odd friendship with Saul, whatever it was, that nameless thing, was an aberration that she could not understand, especially in someone who took her like that. Aberrations were not to be encouraged, but very smart, busy people with heavy responsibilities should be allowed an aberration once in a while, and all that should be asked of them is that they do not flaunt it. In any case, perhaps she had incorrectly imagined what Valmiki and Saul got up to.

Valmiki would lean into her and position his hardened penis at her crotch. He would close his eyes, and with hers open she would see the red thickness of his stiffened tongue come toward her mouth. She would open her mouth for it, while in her mind a pleasing image flashed of the tables in the garden covered in white cloths, aglow with silverware, water glasses, silverplate bud vases that each held one red carnation and a sprig of baby's breath, and candles that were waiting to be lit.

With one hand pulling the band of her panties down, and the other unzipping his pants, Valmiki would reach into his underpants and retrieve his penis. His tongue would seem even fuller and harder in her mouth now, and he would already be panting into her mouth. She would push his tongue back out, pull her face away, and bend sideways to pull her panties down the rest of the way. She would unhook one foot, but leave the panties caught around the other. That act in itself, being free of the garment yet having a part of it touching one ankle, would be enough to cause her to forget about her party, to wish that it was not scheduled for that evening. Valmiki would brace himself with one hand, palm firm against the door, the other cupping the glistening head of his dark penis, while his knuckles, rubbing against her thick hard hair would open a slippery path into which he would guide it. She would move her pelvis in the circular motion he likes, and grip the band of his trousers, shove them down enough to allow her hands in so that she could caress his ass, and hold him against her. She would arch herself, try to brace her self against the door, and he would attempt to pull her legs up by her thighs. She would make small hopping-up motions as she tried to help him, but they would both realize they can no longer do this as easily as in their younger days.

She would think again of time, hoping the bartenders would show the precision she hired this lot for, and not have drinks ready so soon that they were served watery from long-melted ice cubes or so late that people would mill about with empty hands. She would push Valmiki back and, grabbing hold of his once hard and thick legs — how flabby he has grown, she would think with heightened affection — would slide herself down to her knees. Valmiki would arch his back and hold his penis, pulling and pushing at the skin of it until she had fixed herself on her knees and was ready for him. She would look at its weeping eye, wrap both hands around its length. She would look up at him to find him looking down at her, biting his lower lip, and she would open her mouth. He would throw his head back and mutter something, but she would hear only the word *head* and just then he would come in one small but forceful shudder. She would think of the white napkins again, folded in triangles, pinned to the table by an upturned shiny fork.

It will all go well, Devika felt — more confident now than even in her most confident moments before. It would be a party like none before. The best she ever gave.

Valmiki would slump back and lean against the adjacent wall and Devika would slowly get up, her mouth filling with the constant release of her saliva. Her face would be tense. She would turn on the tap at full strength and spit, again and again, rapidly into the sink, saying between her spits, "Oh my God! Look at the time. We have to hurry now." She would rush over to the shower and turn it on full, then rush back to the sink and put toothpaste on her toothbrush and take it into the shower as she said, "I've got to shower right now. I can't let my hair get wet. I am going to shower right away, what are you going to do?"

All of this Devika thought while watching the newspaper that hid Valmiki's face. They had been married twenty — or was it one? — twenty-something years now and had held, say, six parties per year. That would be about one hundred and twenty-six parties. Perhaps more. The incident she had just now remembered so well had happened when Anand was a baby. Just that once. But she remembered it, and she still held the feeling in her body. What were the chances that he would ever do that with her, to her, again? In the past fourteen years she and Valmiki had had sex once, and that once was seven years ago. Perhaps every seven they would have sex and a round, or a bout, of it was pending. Perhaps it would happen just before the new party she wanted to host.

What did Saul and his wife do? she wondered. His wife, what did *she* do? Women from those classes had more resources. They could fight in public, they could let it all out, they could leave or throw their husbands out on the street for several days or for good, but women like Devika had to behave themselves, take it all and smile in public and defend their husbands even if they were tyrants or bastards or useless in the privacy of their homes. Well, it wasn't exactly so anymore. Times had changed. Younger women from her class weren't putting up with what their mothers did. But she was too old now, and even if it was imaginable that she could leave the man hiding behind his newspaper she wouldn't know how to begin life afresh. She didn't have those kinds of skills. Leaving one's husband was done when the children were small; that is when she should or might have done it. But time was not on her side then. Or now. She wouldn't have left the children, and she wouldn't have been able to take them with her. Do what with them? She had done the right thing. And look at her now: sitting on a reclining chair on a patio surrounded by a garden that looked like it came right out of a home and garden magazine. And soon she will go into her house and sit down to a dinner prepared by her cook (whom she *did* have to teach everything, but the cook learned well and fast) and eat off china that was bought on holiday in Italy, and she wouldn't have to wash a dish herself afterwards. The pendant around her neck was the least of her gifts.

Perhaps Saul was different, and was able to do it with his wife as well as with her husband. She didn't even know for certain what her husband and Saul did, and she didn't want to be sure of any of it. The harassment of not knowing was better than certainty. There had always been talk of some wife or the other fooling around with her husband, but she felt disdain for that sort of rumour. She was the plug in the hole of their marriage and family life. If she were to pull out, everything would come tumbling down. And her reputation (she couldn't bear the thought that anyone would know that she had married a man who, although he was known for his affairs with women, actually preferred the company of other men) would fall with it. No one knew how strong she was, and that aloneness was her burden to bear. Valmiki, sitting just some feet away from her, had no idea that such thoughts filled her head.

Devika had once met Saul's wife in the Mucurapo Street Market when, in an unusual move to tour the local farmer's market, she had accompanied the cook there. The cook had gone off to make a purchase of ground provisions and seasonings and had left Devika in a clean wide thoroughfare, watching the commotion of the market, which was very different from the quiet supermarket shopping she knew. The chauffeur stood like a sentry, a decent distance from her. Saul's wife came up behind her and said, "Mrs. Krishnu?"

Devika hadn't known who this person was.

"I am Saul Joseph's wife," the woman explained. "Saul is Doctor's good friend."

Devika's instinct was to be gruff, to ask this woman what she wanted and tell her to keep her husband away. But the softness of Saul's wife's voice, her manner and warm smile, stopped her. She said only, "Yes. I know of him." Surely this woman didn't encourage or approve of the kind of man her husband was, and so, naturally, Devika would try to be civil. After all, the two of them were in a quandary together.

But Saul's wife blurted, as if they were in the middle of a longer conversation, "Well, what to do? Just look at our crosses, na. You and me, we in this thing together. You know what I am talking about, eh?"

Devika did not mean to answer, but, in an attempt to discourage any lengthy explanation she nodded, albeit tersely.

Mrs. Joseph leapt at the opening. "The consolation is that the good Lord gives us no more than what we are capable of handling, not so? Take a look at me, Mrs. Krishnu. I am managing, you know. I know women living right on my street — my short street have two of them — who don't come out they house for days because they don't want nobody to see how they eye black or they lip bust. Me? I don't have a mark on my body. I am not starving and I have a roof over my head. I have plenty to be ashamed of and to hide but I also have much to be grateful for. Life is a blessing itself. How you managing?"

Devika's skin burned with embarrassment but there were no words to hurl. This woman had a point. She was, however, incensed by the woman preaching and commiserating in such a familiar way, as if the two of them — she had used the words *you and me* and *us* — had to stand arm in arm, as comrades, and bear the whole nonsense. Perhaps — but it wasn't for this woman to make a side out of them. Condone it, is what Saul's wife seemed to suggest. How dare she ask how I am managing? Devika had thought. She was livid. Imagine talking like that about women being beaten. Of course, she herself knew of one woman in Luminada Heights whose husband, one of the more well-known businessman in San Fernando, beat her so much and so regularly that she, too, hardly left her house. That woman wasn't the only one from their social world rumoured to suffer such abuses. But this sort of thing was not something people chatted about so unabashedly, and especially in a public place such as the Mucurapo Street Market. What people did behind their closed doors was their own business. Not hers. Devika was nervous about how much the chauffeur had heard, and what he would have made of it. She said, "Look, Mrs. Joseph, I have no trouble bearing my own burdens, thank you. In fact, I welcome them. I can't stop to talk now, I have to see what my cook is buying." And she marched off in the direction of the cook.

But the words came back to her now: *I don't have a mark on my body. I am not starving and I have a roof over my head... I have much to be grateful for.* And to those words she added, *Even Valmiki. And my troublesome daughter.* Yes, she would show her gratitude with a party, by doing what she did best.

Organizing the details was the easiest part of all. She would have to hire extra help — servers, bartenders, one person dedicated entirely to washing up. But managing people, getting them to do exactly what you wanted them to do, required stamina. No matter how many times she might tell and show them how a particular task was to be done, she knew that unless she stood there watching their every move, they would do it how they liked.

And there was, of course, Viveka's attitude to be dealt with. While Vashti liked to dress and to preen, to come out and mix with guests — sometimes a little too long into the evening for Devika's liking — it was difficult to get Viveka to wear a dress, to put a little makeup on her face, even just some lipstick, much less make a polite token appearance. Viveka would bury herself in some novel or other book in the study and remain there for most of the evening, going to bed early without saying goodnight to anyone. She didn't seem to be shy, and in general she wasn't unsociable. She was simply, to Devika's mind, difficult. There were moments, Devika admitted — to herself only — when she was relieved that Viveka didn't show herself. She made hardly any effort to make herself attractive, and after what had happened with that Bedi girl, living like a street person on the promenade, Devika worried about her own daughter. She would not form a sentence even in the recesses of her mind to say what it was, exactly, that worried her or why. The only words that come to her mind were, *Wives know what their husbands won't tell them, and there isn't a thing that a mother does not already know about her child.*

THE SUN WAS JUST GOING DOWN AND THE PATIO WAS AGLOW IN AN orange light. The electric patio light was switched on in anticipation of the usual speedy nightfall. Valmiki reclined in the wicker chaise-longe, his feet aimed directly at Devika. If he hadn't turned the pages of the paper once in a while she would have thought he had fallen asleep. He raised his lower body, the left side, a couple of inches or so off the chaise, and there it hovered for a good few seconds. He would have looked up at her with a lame and apologetic smile if there had been an accompanying sound or a foul scent. But since neither emanated, he lowered his body and continued his reading. Animals had better scent perception than humans, Devika reckoned, for the birds in the four cages that hung from the patio roof, one sporting a Mohawk-like arrangement of feathers on its head and bearing a name she couldn't pronounce suddenly became ruffled and hopped about in agitation. The newest addition scuttled defiantly on the cage's metal tray, nervous and distressed. Valmiki shifted his body again, this time into a more comfortable position, raising one leg at the knee, and tucking the foot of that leg under the thigh of the other, as if to warm it there.

Devika watched him, wanting to remind him of her achievements as a hostess, as his wife. Wanting him to put down the paper and come to her, take her hand, and lead her to their bedroom, or better yet, to their bathroom. She loved it when he or the children remembered one of her parties and went on and on about what a terrific hostess she was. But that rarely happened. It's different for him, she thought. If he needs a little boosting he will talk about an occasion when he rewired a lamp or did something else that was particularly remarkable, such as repairing a spindle that had come undone from the back of a dining-room chair. These were not skills he had honed by making a practice of doing repairs around the house, but one-off things he would impetuously jump to when the mood caught him. They were able to afford the cost of handymen and tradespersons to do repairs and make additions or alterations, but saving money was not in Valmiki's mind at these moments. If Devika were asked, she would say that God alone knew what his motivation was. But she had her suspicion: he wanted to be the man about the house for his daughters. She wished that he would stick to prescribing medicine for them when they had the flu or a gastrointestinal problem. Then he was not man alone, but a god to his daughters. On the other hand, more than once his repairs had to be redone by a professional tradesperson called by Devika — without Valmiki's knowledge. Still, when he wanted a boost, he would make a casual reference to one of these tasks, and Devika and Vashti — seldom Viveka — never failed to rise to his bait, and in no time at all he would be the centre of their conversation, both of them affectionately extolling his cleverness and teasing him about his "unusually innovative" techniques.

This had happened just the day before, here on the patio as they sat exactly as they did right now. Valmiki had begun with, "Phil Bishop has been on my mind lately. I don't know why. I wonder how he is doing. The last time I saw him was at the Medical Association convention three months ago. He was there with his wife." And he had no cause to say anything more, for Devika recognized the pattern and was hooked by habit. "Yes, he was there," she piped up. His shoulders relaxed in gratitude. Devika continued, "I didn't speak with them, but his wife waved at me. I haven't seen them since. That was the night you gave that speech about the necessity for a health insurance plan for the elderly. People are still talking about how well you spoke. I met Millie Morgan in the grocery yesterday and she said her husband Phillip says all the time that you're one of the few doctors in the country who is a true visionary, and that it was too bad that you were such a good doctor, otherwise he would tell you to form your own party and enter politics."

Devika said all this with a certain quiet pride in how well she knew Valmliki, how well she knew how to handle him. But in an instant, as if a coin had been flipped and its other face revealed, her delight soured when he retorted, "So, do you think I might make a good politician? Can you imagine being the wife of the Minister of Health? Or Her Excellency Lady Devika Krishnu, wife of the President?"

The words that pooled in her head were: "Wife of the homosexual Minister of Health, you mean." The words she let fly were: "What? You're not serious? Don't let Phillip put any nonsense into your head, please! I am not interested in any sort of public life where people would know my business even before I knew it. I don't want myself and my children subjected to any sort of scrutiny, thank you. People here are too damn fast, and gossip much too much. Not a family doesn't have a skeleton in a closet, but in this place people like to clean out other people's closets before their own. Your affairs are one thing, you might not mind people talking about those, but there are other things I will not be able to tolerate in public. I don't give a damn what people say but I do not want my children embarrassed, thank you. I have no aspirations to be the wife of a politician. Not one bit, but thank you for asking."

Valmiki had sighed. His eyes had hardened, and he clenched his jaws. Seeing this, and with her tirade ringing in her own ears, she had added a more positive spin, "Politicians don't even make the kind of money you do, Valmiki, unless they're doing something they shouldn't be doing. You make enough money and do enough good from where you are. You don't need anything else, and I and the girls don't want more than we already have."

He had swallowed, and she took that as reconciliation. But she could not leave well enough alone. In a voice low and weary, she had asked, "I don't know why you have to be so ambitious. What is wrong with where you are now? What more do you want? We have it good here, Val. You have provided us with more than most men can give their families. Everything is not ideal, but no one is complaining. No one has a perfect life. Some people have it damn hard. I know you would have liked a different life, but you would have had to stay abroad, given up this place. Given up your past, your history." She knew she was talking to herself as much as to him, but she couldn't stop. She needed to hear the words even if they came from her own mouth. "Look, just leave well enough alone and let us try to be as happy as possible in spite of everything. It's from you that Viveka gets all her ideas about being more than she needs to be. Let's just be happy as we are. Can't we do that?"

He had grunted, "I wasn't even serious. There is just no joking with you these days."

"Well, I thought you were serious."

"And what does Viveka have to do with all of this? What good is it to drag her into this?"

Devika didn't answer. Seconds, and then a minute passed, and still she answered his last two questions only in her imagination. He closed his eyes. When he did this her blood boiled. She hated being shut out. She simply couldn't let him have the last word, but she made sure that hers were as caring as she could manage: "You know, Valmiki, you don't complain about things as they are but you always seem so remote, as if you're living in another world."

Now, Devika wondered how much of last evening's acrimony had stayed with him. She would steal into his quiet and make an offer of some pleasantness. She would tell him she wanted to have a party. Perhaps the pendant Valmiki had given her this evening was not an indicator that he had done something wrong today but an acceptance of her words from last night. An apology, an admission. She would accept these without mention of any of it. Even he must agree that a party would do them all good.

"I want to have a party of my own. We haven't thrown one in a good while now. What do you think?"

"What do you have in mind?" Valmiki muttered behind the paper. He had not really been reading it, contemplating still how close he had come that afternoon to shooting a dog.

"Not a sit-down. Something bigger. With a live band. Like we used to have."

Valmiki closed the paper, rested it on his lap, and looked at her quizzically. "Am I forgetting something? Is there an occasion?"

"Have we ever needed one? But no, there isn't one in particular. I just have an itch to organize something. Dinner, dancing. A good old-fashioned fete."

He folded the paper, the rustling of it at odds with his pensiveness. He dropped it on the terrazzo floor. She expected him to recall a very particular one of her parties — not the one she had minutes ago remembered, but the one a while later that had exploded into a scandal without parallel. How could he not recall it? It was at that party that the nature of his relationship with Pia Moretti was made perfectly public. It had been a great party otherwise, later talked about for many reasons.

The complication had first arisen on a Sunday thirteen years ago, in the days before Valmiki spent the better part of his weekends hunting with Saul. Valmiki was down in the living room that day, trying to mount brackets to one of the concrete walls. He intended to erect three shelves to hold his growing collection of beer stein. Shelves, he told Devika, that might one day be encased, glass doors attached. He described to her how he could see the completed thing in his mind: the cedar stained to mimic mahogany, gold hinges, clasps, keyhole, and knobs on the doors. He could imagine it there off to the side, a thing of beauty. But Devika knew that he had no idea how to build it, other than to nail brackets to the wall and set pre-cut slabs of wood on the bracket. She reminded him that they could afford to buy a shelving unit or a cabinet, or even hire a carpenter to do it quickly. But Valmiki wanted to build it himself. He wore the tool belt Devika and the children had given him that Christmas past. He wore the belt low, like a gun belt, and from the leather holster he would pull the hammer out by its head and aim the handle at Devika or the children. It made them all laugh, and even though Devika had no confidence in Valmiki's meagre abilities, it pleased her that he enjoyed wearing the belt and fooling with it. During the initial spurt of fixing things, he had taken off the light switch plate in the living room and replaced it with a decorative one. When he finished, the plate was askew. Devika asked him to straighten it, so, a little peeved, he removed it, and put it back, swearing that to his eyes it was fine. She shrugged, twisted her mouth in small despair, and left it at that. And soon she became accustomed to these halfway measures and left him alone to enjoy this play that kept him in the home, close to them all.

That fateful Sunday, Devika could see that Valmiki enjoyed being watched as he imagined the shelf. He stretched his hands and peered through the set square he had made with his fingers. He tried to draw it on paper for Devika, but his lack of skill left her clueless as to his intentions. He said to her, "Honestly, I know what I am doing. Here on paper it is exactly as I want it. I don't know why you can't see it; it's so clear."

Devika was not convinced, but accompanied by Anand, who clung to her, his nose runny as usual, she sat in the same room, not contradicting in the least, but picking up the nails that dropped from between Valmiki's teeth or from between his fingers as he tried to hold them against the resistant concrete, or the hammer when it fell, and it fell often, or the tape measure that more than once sprang hard out of his hand while he awkwardly perched on an upper rung of the ladder.

That is where he was that Sunday when the telephone rang. Devika heard Viveka answer it from the hallway. She had taken to rushing to answer the phone before anyone else could, delightedly blurting out, "HelloDr.Krishnu'sresidencewho'scallingplea se," her seven-year-old voice and greeting attempting to emulate that of their housekeeper. Devika and Valmiki looked at each other, rolled their eyes and smiled. Viveka hopped into the living room to announce that it was a lady wanting to speak to Dad. Devika said, "Did you ask who was speaking?" Viveka became shy. Yes, she said, but I can't say her name. It is the new lady. She speaks funny.

Valmiki began to descend the ladder. Devika asked him who that would be. He seemed perplexed. "I don't know. A lady who speaks funny? I wonder if it's not the people who moved in up the road a couple months ago. The ones in the house with the front porch."

Devika asked, "Are they your patients now?"

"They came once. She had something wrong with her back. I sent her to see Peter. I think he's seen her already, but I haven't spoken with him since."

"But I think I have seen her. What's wrong with her back?"

Valmiki didn't answer. Devika carried on, "He is a painter, or some such thing? There is a sign on their gate. They have a Spanish name, a name with an accent, I think."

Valmiki half-smiled and muttered, "Italian."

Devika continued, "The sign says he is a house painter, I think. I wonder if he is any good. What's the name, again?"

As Valmiki made his way out of the room to take the call in his home office, he said, "Mani and Pia Moretti."

"Pia Moretti. Hm! That really is a lot of syllables," Devika said, opening her eyes wide as she looked at Viveka. Viveka drummed her small hands on the coffee table in time to her repetition of the name: Pia Moretti, Pia Moretti.

Valmiki returned some minutes later to say that he had to make a house call, and oddly, it was not as a doctor but as a plumber. Mani, he explained was not at home, he was working on a house where there was no phone, and the Moretti kitchen faucet, which had already had a small leak, was suddenly beginning to gush water. The faucet, Pia worried, was likely going to pop right off the housing any minute.

Devika was puzzled. "I don't understand this at all: you're on a first-name basis with every Tom, Dick, and Harry! And I don't understand if she is having a plumbing problem why she called *you*."

Valmiki's testiness when he responded—"Oh, God, Devika, she is new in the country, hardly speaks the language, and doesn't know any other neighbours"—put her suddenly on edge.

"She obviously doesn't have any trouble communicating with you. And you, all of a sudden, you know about *plumbing*? Well, that is a good one." She wasn't laughing.

"Well, it can't be that big a mystery," said Valmiki. "I mean, you just have to shut off some vales — they shouldn't be hard to locate — close off the main, tighten a few things, and turn it all back on. With this handy little belt you all gave Dad, Dad can accomplish anything." He winked at Anand, and walked past Devika saying, "I think you need something like *washers*. We must have washers somewhere in the toolbox, and that stickyish white tape — plumber's tape. I'll go look for them."

Devika snapped, "So, what about lunch? It *is* Sunday. What about Sunday lunch at home with the family?"

"Her house will be under water if I wait. I'm already taking too long in leaving. Why are you being so difficult suddenly?"

"Well, why don't you call our plumber? I mean, what on earth can you do for her? Here, I will get the number." She made a step toward the hall where, on a small table, her address book rested.

But Valmiki leapt at her, grabbed her wrist, and pulled her to him. "Hey! Let me at least try. Besides, I will get there faster than he will. Look, don't make a big thing out of this. I will be back as soon as I am finished." He put his palm on her cheek and looked into her eyes. "In any case, I have seen plumbers do these things before, right here in our house. I can at least try. I will learn something at the very least. I'll eat when I get back. Don't wait for me. And don't worry."

All he had to do was touch her face and look at her like that, and Devika gave in to him, even when she didn't totally believe him. In a softer, more conciliatory tone, she said, "Well, just don't go and break anything, for God's sake, and then find that you end up paying their plumbing bills."

Devika had decided that she and the children would wait until Valmiki returned from his plumbing mission so they could all eat together. But after an hour the children became cranky with hunger, Anand crying in a low monotone wail that made her want to run out of the house, and so they ate without Valmiki. Devika took her sickly boy to nap with her in her bed. After he had fallen asleep, she went out to the back gate and looked up the road. She could see the fence of the Moretti house, but the house itself was obscured by the one before it. She went back inside, to the bathroom attached to her bedroom, and closed the lid on the toilet seat. She sat on the lid, and lit and smoked a cigarette out of view of the children. It made her eyes burn and her throat ache, but it had a calming effect. She thought of her two girls. Vashti was in the study combing the shiny yellow synthetic hair of one of her dolls. Viveka was in the backyard, trying to catch butterflies and grasshoppers with an aquarium fish net.

What Devika didn't know was that sometime later Viveka had taken it upon herself to go up the road to look for her father.

Later that night, as Devika and Valmiki and the three children sat at the dinner table, just about to tackle their dessert (Valmiki had finally returned in time for supper), Viveka asked Valmiki why, when Pia Moretti was groaning, he had continued to lie so long on top of her.

Devika stopped breathing, She stared at the tip of the fork in her hand.

Viveka waited for an answer from her father. Valmiki glared at his daughter, but in his peripheral vision he was observing Devika.

She put down the fork slowly and reached for her glass of water. She gripped the glass. Valmiki gripped the edge of the table, bracing himself against his chair. But Devika simply lifted the glass, as if, oddly, to offer a toast.

Viveka whined, "Tell me, na, Dad. What were you doing?"

Valmiki sat up briskly and lifted his glass to comply with Devika's raised one, but Deivka merely brought the glass to her pursed lips and sipped the ice-cold water, thoughtfully. Valmiki was spared having to answer to Viveka's question when Devika, in a chillingly soft voice, said, "I need to have a party. I need to have a big party. Right away. With a band. Food. Every single person we know."

Valmiki lifted his glass higher and said, "Yes! What a good idea. I'll drink to that!" and Viveka immediately forgot her question.

"WHO DO YOU WANT TO INVITE?" VALMIKI SAID, INTERRUPTING Devika's reverie.

"The usual, and others whom we haven't entertained as yet but owe an invitation."

Their chatter was interrupted by the sound of the back gate being unlatched. They looked at each other puzzled, as no one was expected. Devika sat up, pulling the skirt of her dress over her knees. Valmiki instinctively checked the zipper of his trousers and stood up. There came a friendly rustling of leaves from the bird of paradise shrubs that crowded the path leading from the gate to the patio. Devika hoped, even as the thought unnerved her, that it was Viveka returning from her day at the campus library.

A man's voice filtered through the shrubbery. "Uncle? Auntie?"

It was Nayan Prakash, their good friend's son. His family and theirs were not related by blood, but like any decent young man he still called them uncle and auntie. Only this past month

Nayan had returned from five years of university schooling in Canada, and he returned a married man.

Nayan rounded the garden path, followed by a slight white woman — the woman people were already talking about. Until three weeks before his return, Nayan's annoyed parents had informed Devika and Valmiki, no one, not even they, had known of the presence of this woman in his life. Worse, he had married this foreigner, this stranger, a Frenchwoman, without their knowledge. No, it wasn't a shotgun thing. The only sense they could make of it was that it was the passion of youth, impetuousness, the influence of North American ways, of that kind of culture, with its lack of consideration for family and for what people might think and say. They weren't pleased, they felt obliged to express explicitly. They had had no hand in choosing this woman. She certainly would not have been on any list of possibilities for their son. (Devika had later told Valmiki that she almost felt that Nayan's parents were apologizing to *them* for him having married this woman. She had itched to assure them that neither Viveka nor Vashti were upset when they heard he had married.)

This woman, the Prakashs had carried on, eyes wide with wonder, was white and not a Hindu, and English was not her first language. She didn't even speak it well. They didn't know a thing about her family — what class she came from, which, they were quick to add, was not the most important thing, but it was something, wasn't it? What about her and her family's medical history? They knew nothing of this, of any madness or hereditary diseases. And what was the matter with Nayan, in truth, for he had never spoken a word of French before meeting her? And still he only knew a handful of words — and she a handful of English — and the whole thing just drove them crazy, especially as they lived all together in the same house and had to listen to this tortured back-and-forth quarter-English, quarter-French, and-the-rest-I-don't-know-what between the two of them. And how many parents had spoken with them in the hopes that their daughter might marry him? Some of those young women had steadfastly refused other shows of interests. Well, even if they were after the money, at least they were known families, Hindus — and regardless of class, this above all else was important.

There had been talk, not idle Valmiki and Devika could see now, that Nayan's wife was a remarkably beautiful woman, in a glossy, foreign-fashion-magazine kind of way. This had not impressed Nayan's parents but had rather irked them. Valmiki and Devika, on the other hand, were immediately impressed. Before Nayan could introduce them, Devika had already taken good note of the glistening double-gold chain that hung heavily from his wife's neck.

"Auntie Devika, Uncle Valmiki, this is Anick." The young woman uttered something Devika imagined was a greeting. The words were not only inaudible, but accented — perhaps not even English. Devika repeated *Anick* a few times, trying to get its pronunciation. Awkwardly she said, "It's French, eh?"

Anick said, *Mais, oui*, with the tone of someone saying, *But obviously, why wouldn't it be*, and Nayan rubbed his wife's back and laughed as if to say, *Isn't she lovely and funny*? Devika flattered back, "Well, I will just have to call you Mrs. Prakash, won't I? I won't get that wrong."

Valmiki informed the pair that Viveka — their eldest daughter, he enlightened Anick — was still at the university, and Vashti — the younger one — was expected back any minute from an after-school extra-lessons class in preparation for the advanced level exams the following year. Devika watched the model-like features of the young woman, her long neck, minute waist — stomach flat, flat, flat — and the provocatively protruding pelvic bones. Anick's nose was slim and ran straight down, no bumps or humps — a perfect angle. The skin on her face was flawless. There was not even a blemish from, say, a scratched pimple. Had she never had chicken pox? Her complexion was not fatty or puffy. It was thin, lean skin. Her eyes were brown, and although Devika had seen brown eyes on white women countless times, she noticed that Anick's were unusually alert — a well-mannered and unintimidating alertness. Her eyelashes were long, but they weren't false. They were definitely hers. She didn't seem to be wearing mascara. If she were, it was obviously of a good quality. Her eyebrows arched perfectly, the arch itself in exactly the right place. Hard to do. There had to be help from nature to be able to do that. And they were not too thin or too thick. Her lips were pink, but she didn't seem to be wearing lipstick. A little lipstick might have been a good idea, thought Devika, but she conceded that Anick might not have expected to have been brought to meet anyone on her stroll. They were shaped by the hand of God himself, Devika mused. She watched hard, trying to see if Anick really wore little makeup or if it was of such a quality and so well-applied that it looked natural. She thanked God that Viveka was not home, for next to this beauty Viveka would be rendered even plainer than she already was.

Nayan intoned apologetically that he had been taking Anick for a walk around the nieghbourhood and, spotting Valmiki and Devika through the shrubbery against the fence, had wanted to say a quick hello and introduce his wife. Devika invited them to come right in, come and sit down, have a cup of tea — or, Valmiki interjected, a glass of sparkling wine; there was a chilled bottle with no other but their names on it. He added that he had heard from Nayan's father that Nayan had become a discerning wine drinker. Nayan raised his eyebrows and, chuckling said, "Discerning? That couldn't be the word Dad used!"

"What would he have said?" Devika provoked.

"He would more likely have said I became a snob, and he might have used a qualifying expletive, too."

Valmiki sought to quickly throw water on this by saying that Ram, Nayan's father, had told them himself how proud he was of his son going abroad, graduating, and returning to his roots, qualified now to run Rimpty's and Son. No one pointed out that Nayan's marriage was not on that shortlist of accomplishments.

Valmiki insisted again on them coming right in for that drink and a slice of fruit cake. It was a display of hospitality that obviously pleased the young husband. He declined, saying that his mother was expecting them back shortly for dinner. Devika noted that he had grown into a lovely young man — not rough-around-the-edges like his cacao-farmer-father-come-to-town at all — and so gentle.

"Well, you will all have to come over soon and introduce… Anick…" Devika said to Nayan, a question mark in her voice, "to Viveka and Vashti."

Then she said to Anick, "My eldest daughter likes your husband, you know. You will have to watch out, he is quite a catch."

"Yes, I know, everybody tell me this," Anick managed with a shy smile.

Valmiki slid in, "Well, clearly Nayan is the lucky one. You make a fine couple, Nayan. You did well. You did well."

It was Nayan's turn to laugh, to be shy and proud at once.

Valmiki inquired after Nayan's parents.

"Mummy is good. Cooking a lot these days. And Dad, well, he is as usual. Everyday he goes to the office or up to Chayu, so we don't see him too much, which is not a bad thing."

Valmiki asked if Anick had seen the estate as yet. She had been asking to go, Nayan replied, wanting to see the countryside and the rich lands that he had told her so much about, but it was crop season — his father wouldn't let her go when the workers were in the fields. He added, "You know how it is," implying what didn't need to be said — a pretty white foreign woman among the workers might have incited slackness and bravado. Anick said, in her small voice, "He think I do not know to take care of myself."

Nayan smiled, but he was unable to properly hide his slight peevishness at her comeback. He asked "Uncle" if he still hunted, and told Valmiki that the other day he had seen an agouti on the estate. He invited Valmiki to hunt there on a weekend when less work was carried on.

When Nayan and Anick left, Devika said, "Hm! Well, he will have good trouble with her. She is one beautiful woman. You don't think so?" Val raised his eyebrows, noncommittally. "He is one lucky man," Devika persisted, "but he will catch his tail! You know how men are here. And you didn't see the thickness of that gold around her neck, Val? I wonder if he gave it to her, or if it was his parents who gave her that." When Valmiki still didn't respond, she pushed. "Don't tell me you didn't see it. Everybody is saying how pretty she is, but I never imagined her to be *so* beautiful. I wonder how she will fare in that family. They shouldn't be all living in the same house, at all. That is a recipe for disaster, yes — she is a lot more cultured-looking than they are. You know what I mean?"

Trying unsuccessfully to hide the irritation in his voice, Valmiki retorted, "How can you tell that?"

"I can just tell. I mean, just look at her. Can't *you* tell? She will have him watching his back like crazy. That calypso is right: *Never marry a woman prettier than you.*"

THE SUN HAD GONE DOWN BELOW THE GULF'S HORIZON AND THE SKY that had been red minutes ago had turned to a sooty black full of diamond-bright twinkling stars. Valmiki removed the bird cages from their hooks. The newest bird was jumpy. As he brought the cage down it slipped off its perch, its wings fluttering wildly behind it. Valmiki lifted the cage to his face. He looked through the wire bars directly into the bird's eyes. It climbed back up and hopped along the perch to the far end. Finally it moved its head, first a little to the left, as if to see better with that eye, and then it spun its head almost 360 degrees to watch Valmiki with the other eye. Valmiki was as still as could be, watching the bird with softened eyes. Through all this he heard Devika. She was goading him, "But then again, you married a woman prettier than you, and I am the one who has been catching hell. So it doesn't always work out as is expected, eh?"

This brought to Valmiki's mind the line, *Marry the one who loves you, not the one you love.* He lowered the cage and asked wearily, "So, what about your party? What date are you thinking of?" He and Devika walked inside, both of them carrying a cage in either hand. Valmiki pulled the door behind them. He latched it tight. Devika went ahead to the entrance of the dining room and switched on the patio lights. They would remain on until after the girls' return. He had long ago installed the plate for the light switch and it was crooked. That was more than fifteen years ago, and Valmiki knew that every time Devika passed it, it bothered her.

Seeing Nayan settled and happy had prompted in Valmiki thoughts of Viveka and how she unnerved him, how, lately, an image of her would come to his mind, but it would be as if she alternated in a constant and rapid tremble between being uniquely herself and adopting the perfect semblance of Anand. He and Devika were losing Viveka. He could feel it. Of course, he wanted her to soar. She, more than anyone else, would know what to do with opportunities that came her way, how to make something grand of life. But he worried there would be significant costs. What if, along the way, she lost herself? What he meant by that he wasn't sure. He had the strongest desire to snatch her up in the palm of his hand as if she were a little gem, close his fist tight around her, and keep her there. On the contrary, however: he would let her be whatever she wanted, everything she wanted. Except this, and this, and this, and that.

Viveka

HAVING PLAYED VOLLEYBALL THE NIGHT BEFORE, HAVING GOT HER way, even if it was on the sly, Viveka awoke the next morning feeling generous toward her family. Even if her mother had not got past their altercation, Viveka had. She left her room ready to enter the heart of the house, sprite and congenial. She was ravenous.

As she approached the kitchen she heard her mother on the telephone, devising a menu with the caterer. On the kitchen table she saw a guest list: there were more than twenty couples on it. It took no time at all for a series of gripes to ripple through her gut. These were soon accompanied by a general feeling of weakness and nausea.

Perhaps, she thought, this was the effect of eating doubles purchased the day before from one of the vendors stationed outside the university gates. Elliot had eaten them, too. She should call and see how he was.

In spite of the queasiness in her gut, out of habit she opened the fridge. Numerous plastic containers of this and that sat atop one another. Saucers with slices of chicken, papaya, sardines, plastic wrap stretched tight over each. Paratha wrapped in foil. Cheese. Guava jam, peanut butter, marmite. She stared blankly for a long time, listening to her mother trying to decide between a North Indian-themed meal and a Chinese one: No, no, definitely no pork or beef, and the Chinese food would have to be done without a hint of pork, as there would be Hindus and Muslims at the party. Fish, chicken, duck — all three. Shrimp is fine, but you know how quickly it can turn in the heat. Nothing but the best, everything done with, with, with a European flair, if you know what I mean. Authentic Indian, authentic Chinese, whichever, but arranged and served with European — well, not just any European — more like *French* class and flair.

Viveka opened the oven door to see if anything left over from breakfast was being kept warm for her. A tea cloth draped a dish in which lay a wedge of coconut bake. There seemed to be no air in her chest. She shut the door and went back to the fridge. Her indecision caught her mother's eye. Devika glanced over at Viveka, and while remaining engaged in her conversation, she snapped her fingers. When she had caught Viveka's attention she pointed sharply to the oven, her forefinger wagging in insistence that Viveka take the bake there. Viveka hid behind the open door of the fridge and poured herself a tumbler of orange juice. Then she sat down at the kitchen table, her back to her mother and both hands wrapped around the cold and sweating glass. She felt badly about how she had left Elliot last night.

After she had refused to accommodate his desires a few weeks ago, he had withdrawn from her and they hadn't seen each other for a while. Then, yesterday, they had seen each other at the doubles stand, and after an awkward few minutes of catching up they were walking hand in hand. She didn't mind. In fact, she realized how much she missed him. They had spent the entire afternoon together at the library, and then Elliot invited himself to Viveka's and Helen's practice game. He kept his eyes on her and on Helen as they pranced about the court like colts.

The coach had left the team to play without instruction, as he sometimes did. They played harder on such days, knowing well that the coach was noting the strong and weak points of each player, making the kinds of decisions that coaches make. One of Viveka's teammates, Franka, of whom Viveka felt somewhat scornful for no reason she could identify, grabbed every opportunity to make contact with her — touching Viveka on her arm, her back, her waist. It was uncomfortable, in particular on an evening when Elliot was watching them play.

After the game Viveka and Helen went with the other players, as usual, to the pub. Helen's boyfriend, Wayne, was meeting them there, and Elliot decided he would tag along. Wayne and Helen had been sweethearts since high school. Wayne was comfortable with the other women, and they with him. Of course, he and Helen sat next to each other. At times he seemed to envelope Helen, and she would disappear into his large warmth willingly. But she would never disappear for long, and when she reappeared, her dominance in that group of fighting players dwarfed him, and he accepted this easily. He and she were like waves and weeds, each taking a turn at nipping and tickling the other.

Viveka had tried to work out in her head the consequences of reconnecting with Elliot, of so quickly getting close again. Should she sit next to him? Or should she make it so that he ended up sitting between others, perhaps across from her but not next to her? Elliot, however, decided the matter. He pushed his way in through the throng of women, ushered Viveka along the bench, and slid in beside her. She angled her body away from him, but made sure to turn back to laugh a comment to him once in a while so as not to be accused of slighting him. But when Franka, on the way to the bar to buy a drink, came around to Viveka and stooped to whisper in her ear, asking if she could get her something from the bar, Viveka instinctively leaned against Elliot. She turned to face Elliot, and then looked up and smiled her decline to Franka. She made a fist and rested it on Elliot's knee, thumping it occasionally.

Later, the four of them walked to Helen's car, Wayne and Helen with an arm around each other's waist, and Elliot clutching Viveka's limp hand. Wayne and Helen were doing their long-goodbye thing, some feet away from the car. Viveka led Elliot directly to the passenger-side door. She opened it and turned to give Elliot what she intended to be a warm and friendly hug. Their conversation in the library earlier that day rang in her ears. She had enjoyed hearing all that he had been doing during their little hiatus. He had been working with an art gallery, helping them to locate the works of James Boodoo, Hing Wan, Kenneth Critchlow, Ralph and Vera Bainey, and Samuel Walrond that were in private collections; a public exhibition of these works was planned. He clearly wanted her to know that he was busy and doing big things with himself. She was impressed. She missed his conversations about painting and art, missed talking with him about the books she was reading. She really did want a close friendship with him, she decided, but nothing more — something like what she had with Helen.

Beside the car, Elliot held Viveka's face in his hands. She became confused, then annoyed. She weighed what she should say and how she should act. She didn't want to lose him again, but she didn't want this either. He was too insistent. When he put his mouth to hers, she extricated herself by asking what his plans were for the following day. Elliot bit his lower lip, breathed in hard, and then said sharply, "I already told you. You know very well what I am doing." He put his lips to hers again. Despite the discomfort of his tongue inside of her mouth, she garbled,

"Yes, but I can't keep your schedule in my head. Tell me again."
He withdrew long enough to say, "Just kiss me, Vik," and so she did. Or rather, she let him kiss her. He had his hands on her back, and now he moved them in slow circles, each time dropping his hands a little lower. She stiffened her back. Just as she feared he would, he slipped his fingers under her shirt. Fatigued by the same old feeling of not wanting to seem rude or unfriendly to him and wondering if there was something wrong with her, she jerked her face away and put her hand to Elliot's face, the gesture on his cheek a cross between a gentle slap and a stroke. There was a heavy silence between them, which Viveka broke by asking him if he had finished reading *Mr. Biswas*. Elliot sighed. Resignation in his voice, he breathed out the words, "No, Viveka. I have not finished it."

Noting his tone, she carried on. "He is like a painter, Elliot, but with words. He uses landscape as metaphor." She intended to continue with, "For the oppression of communal family living. The Indian, the Hindu family style of living, covertly incestuous. I know you'd find it interesting." But she stopped herself, for she knew it sounded hollow.

Elliot continued to hold her, but she felt as if she were a folded-up shirt he was barely pressing against his chest. "God, Vik, nothing has changed, has it? I was hoping the time apart would have made things different between us. Art and literature are not all there is in life, you know. I like to talk with you about these things, to go to shows with you and that kind of thing, and I want to read all your favourite books, all one thousand and one of them, but I want to do other things with you, too."

"I know, I know, but it's not what I want. I want other things, different things." She was pleading, apologizing, and sympathizing with him all at the same time.

Elliot let go of her suddenly. Viveka imagined herself, the folded-up shirt, slide down his chest and fall, crumpled, to the floor. She hadn't expected to feel so dropped by him. She reached out a hand, intending to lay it against his cheek in a decidedly softer gesture, but he caught her wrist in mid-air, held it there and stared at her hard. She pulled her hand free and clutched that wrist with her other hand to suggest that he had hurt her. Perturbed, she got into the car and shut the door. The window was rolled up. Elliot stood where he was. Slowly, she rolled the window down. He walked away, looking back only to signal to Wayne that he would catch up with him later.

This morning, though, Viveka had an excuse to phone him to see how he was feeling—to see if the doubles had upset his stomach. Still, she hesitated. She slapped at mosquitoes that lived in the relative dark beneath the table, and scratched at old and new bites. Her mother got off the phone and greeted her with, "Is that all you're having? There is coconut bake in the oven." She was obviously not over her terseness with Viveka. Viveka reached to scratch a bite on her ankle. She muttered, "This is enough for now," and in an even lower voice added, "Thanks." Then she tapped the guest list with her forefinger. "What's this?"

"We're having a party."

Viveka picked up the list and rolled it into a loose tube shape. She pressed it to her lips and blew into it.

He mother snapped, "Don't do that. I need that list. Put it down."

The admonishment was at least an engagement, and Viveka felt relief.

"You'd never guess who came to visit last night." Devika had suddenly brightened.

Viveka wasn't in the mood for guessing. "Who?"

Her mother adopted a playful tune. "Well, don't you want to guess?"

"I don't know. Who?"

"Nayan. We were sitting on the patio and he just came in. He brought his wife."

Viveka pushed her chair back, ready to get up. "Yeah? Did he come with his hands swinging or did he bring chocolates?"

"Why do you have to be like that? But you're right: he didn't bring any chocolates. They had gone for a walk, and he saw us on the patio, and took the opportunity to drop in."

"Gone for a walk! Nobody walks around here. Was he showing off his wife to the neighbours or the other way around?"

Devika chuckled. If only Viveka could be more like this more often.

"Well, is she all they say she is? Does she speak English?" Viveka persisted.

"Not one word is a lie, when I tell you! She is gorgeous. White, but you can tell she is not a local white. You should have seen how she was dressed, and all they were going for was a walk. Minty and Ram said she doesn't come from money herself, but it doesn't show. Not with that kind of beauty. She has a lot of class, the way she carries herself. I don't know where she would have got that from. But you know French people. All of them have that flair."

"Flair is the same as class?" asked Viveka, in a tone that suggested her question was not to be answered but was supposed to be instructional.

Her mother was not interested in being educated.

"Well, she has landed herself a good catch. I am sure a lot of families here are disappointed."

"Does she speak English?"

"A little. And Nayan doesn't speak a word of French."

"Oh, I bet he knows a word or two by now."

"I only hope there is enough love between them. He better behave himself, and not become like men here. It will be very difficult for her here. I am willing to bet she won't put up with any nonsense whatsoever."

"Where are they living?"

"Right here. Not in their own home, but with Minty and Ram, I mean."

"Oh my God. In the same house with Uncle Ram!"

Devika pursed her lips and nodded. "Minty and Ram don't like her at all. They are not pleased one bit! Yet, if you see the gold chain she was wearing around her neck. That was no eighteen-karat chain. It was one heavy twenty-two-karat thing. I could tell by just watching it. A rope design. They must have given it to her as the wedding present. He is their only son. She is the only daughter-in-law they will ever have. It doesn't matter if they don't like her. She will still get everything."

Viveka knew better than to voice her thought that these days marriage wasn't a guarantee, that modern women didn't necessarily put up with all the things that women of her mother's generation did. "What's her name?" she said instead.

"It's a different name. Anki, or something like that."

"Are they coming to your party?"

"Yes, they're on the list. Aunty Minty and Uncle Ram, and the two of them. I hope you will make an appearance and not hide yourself away as usual."

"What are we having for lunch?" Viveka asked while contemplating an image of Nayan. Or, not an image of him so much as the feeling of his tongue in her mouth a few years ago. She must have been about fifteen and he nineteen. Several of the young people in the neighbourhood had gathered at a house to while away a long August day. They decided to play spin the bottle. On one of Nayan's spins the bottle pointed to Viveka, and his task was to arm wrestle the person if that person were male, or to go behind the wall for one minute and kiss if the person were female. Viveka and Nayan had both rolled their eyes, and Viveka had never thought for a moment that this longtime friend, family friend, would execute the task. But he had, and she was shy to push him away, felt it would have been childish to have done so, and at the same time she was confused by his initiation. Afterwards, she learned that every girl in the neighbourhood had at one time or another been kissed by Nayan in that manner. She had never been able to look at him squarely after that. And now she had little interest in seeing him or his new wife. It was beginning to irk her, in fact, that this woman's beauty seemed to be the only attribute people talked about.

Viveka told her mother about her stomach gripes.

"When did they start?" The question was like an accusation.

Viveka defensively answered, "Just minutes ago. I was fine when I woke up."

"Do you realize, Viveka"—and there was that terseness again—"that every time we even suggest having a party here, you get sick? If it's not one thing it's another. Your head. Your eyes. Your stomach. Look, don't start with this now. I am asking Helen's parents. Why don't you ask her? And I want to ask Anne and Pat Samlal to bring their son, the older one, Steve. He is such a nice young man. It is time for you to be meeting some nice men. Don't roll your eyes like that. I am not asking him here for anything in particular. It is just time you learned to chat about things other than books and ideas. What do you think?"

"Helen is going away that weekend. She is going to Matura to see the leatherbacks. They're laying their eggs now. She asked me to go with her."

"Who is she going with?"

Viveka hesitated to say that Wayne was going, but the alertness in her mother's tone, the question itself, suggested that Devika had guessed. Viveka's response was to curl her lips while looking at her mother as if to say, *You very well know, so why are you asking*?

"Well, I can tell you right now. Don't even bother to ask your father. I mean, you don't really expect your father to let you go, do you?"

"Oh, Mom, why do you have to leap so far ahead? Did I even ask? I just told you that she invited me. I don't *want* to go."

Helen had asked Viveka to come and bring Elliot. Vivkea had never seen the turtles coming ashore en masse to lay their eggs and would have liked to, but she didn't want to — couldn't — ask Elliot to go away with her for a weekend, and she had no desire to be a third wheel. Trudging through damp sand, buffeted on all sides by the east coast's cold night breezes at two in the morning, or three, or however late it was that the turtles ambled out of the sea, did seem somewhat adventurous, but in effect she would be alone. No doubt Wayne and Helen would be locked together, fording the wind in unison while she trudged along hugging only herself, conversation futile because the wind would whip their voices in various directions. Never mind that she knew her parents wouldn't consent to her going — she had no desire to be the one to make a crowd.

She picked up the thread of the original conversation. "I know Steve. He is nice enough. Sure, whatever. Go ahead, ask him if you want. It's just that I don't feel comfortable with so many people here, Mom."

"When are you going to stop this? Listen, Viveka. I know you still carry in your head what happened so many years ago. None of us have ever forgotten. That entire year was a nightmare."

Viveka could have imploded with shock at these words. Hardly a day went by without her wishing that someone in the family would bring up what had happened in the past and get it all out in the open, once and for all. And now, suddenly, she didn't know how to react.

"But why is it that you have to act as if you are the only one who it affected?" continued Devika, oblivious. "We don't talk about it, not because we don't care but because we have to move on. I am going to try to explain some things to you. I don't even know where to begin. I'll start with your brother. Anand was sick from the time he was a baby."

Viveka looked down into the cup of orange juice in front of her. Anand. Her mother had said his name aloud. In doing so she had pulled Anand from Viveka's grip. To steady herself she concentrated on a partial ring of bright white light reflected on the surface of the juice. She was grateful, and yet she wanted to run away or to begin a fight with her mother again. That would be so much more comfortable for them both.

"Your father and I knew he wouldn't survive. But you and Vashti, you were too small to understand that he was not going to make it."

Viveka wanted to ask her mother when, exactly, the party had happened — the party she could never erase from her memory. It always seemed strange — no, not strange but horrible — that her parents had held a party in the same month as Anand's death. Now, suddenly, it dawned on her that the party might have been held just before he died, or even long after. She was about to ask her mother but she hesitated, unsure of what it would mean to have everything on which she had based her understanding of her family turned inside out.

Her mother opened the oven and pulled out the covered dish. She set the dish on the table and peeled back the cloth. From a drawer she extracted the cloth placemat and spread it before Viveka. Viveka sat back and let her mother set before her a plate, a knife, and a fork taken from the draining board by the sink. As she reached in the fridge for butter and a slab of cheese, Devika said, "His death changed things between us all."

Viveka wanted to shout out, *No, it wasn't Anand's death, it was Dad's involvement with the woman up the hill.* But she had already learned her lesson regarding that one. So she gathered her courage and asked about the party, when it had been held.

"I was planning a party before Anand died, " Devika said. "Then, when that happened we, of course, shelved the idea. We didn't entertain until a good year later."

A year later. What had happened between her brother's passing away and that party? Nothing came to Viveka's mind. An entire year of her life, a blank of time.

"That is the party that caused us all so much trouble, and you," continued Devika, "I think you saw too much for your age. I don't know what got into your father at the party. But that was a long time ago, and he has changed. Besides, if I have forgiven him, why haven't you?"

Viveka slit the bake and buttered both sides. How was she now to separate the image of her father lying on Pia Moretti, and of the memories that quickly followed: playing the game of fish in the car with Anand, and of Vashti slapping Anand's hand during the game and then him crying, crying, crying, — the last memory she had of him — and of Mani Moretti in his painter overalls, and of the party? They had always collided in her memory, playing out as if they had all occurred on one long and jumbled day.

Viveka cut slices of cheese and packed them inside of the bake. She bit off the tip of her sandwich. At that her mother pursed her lips, pleased.

VIVEKA WAS GOOD AT DETAILS. HER MEMORIES WERE FULL OF THEM. But whether they were real details, or the results of an admittedly fertile imagination coupled with the need for all the dots to line up sensibly, she no longer knew.

She sat playing with the bake and cheese sandwich, staring at it as if there was knowledge to be had from it. And she watched her mother, already busy again with her list of this and that regarding the party. In this rare moment of truth-telling, of openness, should she ask another question? Dare she? She would have to admit to prying:

She had been about twelve. It was a Saturday. Her father had gone to Maraval with his friend Saul and her mother was at the hairdresser's. The house was quiet. Vashti was lying in bed reading a novel. The maid was in her room with the door closed. Viveka stole into her parents' bedroom. She looked at their bed, made up with a bedspread that had peacocks embroidered in a hundred shades of iridescent turquoise on it. She had tried to imagine her father lying on top of her mother there. But she could not. Whenever she tried, she would see instead her father and the Moretti woman. He would be relaxed and easy, even as he worked himself into a sweat. She couldn't imagine him like that with her mother. The ceiling of the house, lined in highly polished hardwood, squeaked and creaked as it expanded and contracted in the heat. Through the window of her parents' bedroom came a strong ocean breeze, the melodious sounds of blue jay tanagers and semps in the coconut and Julie mango trees, and once in a while a car lumbering up the hill or descending carefully outside.

She stole in farther, into her parents' bathroom. The doors of the cupboards were always locked when Valmiki and Devika weren't at home—locked against the prying eyes and idle hands of their hired help. Viveka went to her mother's dressing table and in a bone china dish found a hairpin. She straightened the pin and stuck it in the lock of her father's cupboard door. She had done this many times before, to no avail, but this one time there was a surprising click and the door popped open. Her heart thumped. She hadn't really meant for it to unlock. How would she lock it back, she wondered, trying to hold the door shut and manipulate the key in its lock again. When she couldn't get it to relock she tiptoed hastily out of both rooms, taking the hairpin with her. Vashti had fallen asleep with her novel on her chest. The maid was now mopping the kitchen floor. Viveka slipped past her into the garden. She looked about to make sure no one saw what she was doing, and threw the pin over the fence at the back of their yard, into a section of the neighbour's yard that was overgrown with philodendrons. Then she ran back into the house, all the while hoping, imagining, trying to transmit brainwashing messages to her mother, that her mother would simply assume she had in her haste left her father's cupboard doors unlocked.

The phone was ringing as Viveka entered the house. The maid answered and Viveka heard her say, "I don't know, Madam. They was in they room, reading. The house quiet-quiet. I mopping the floor. What time you coming back home, Madam? I have to call and tell my son when to come and meet me." Viveka stayed still. "So, I could tell him come for me by three o'clock so?" Viveka could see a clock from where she crouched. It was 1:25.

Her mother would obviously be away for some time yet. Even if she were to immediately leave the salon on the far side of downtown she would not make it back for at least half an hour. Viveka's heart beat harder with a new idea. She had time, now that the cupboard was unlocked, and now that she had convinced herself that her mother would think she herself had left it unlocked, to have a look inside.

She listened for the mop's handle hitting the metal of the pail, the swish of water in which it was washed. She eased open the top drawer in her father's cupboard. It was full of white socks and underwear. She waited and listened again. The drag of the mop along the floor could be heard by one intent on hearing it. She was afraid to touch her father's underpants but slipped her fingers under the socks. She felt the smooth cool bottom of the drawer. She shut that one and opened another: black and brown socks, and white vests. She reached into its back corners. In one corner there was an oily-feeling bottle and an almost empty tube of ointment. She tried to read the tube's label, but it was too mangled from use. Under the clothing she found a folded-up piece of paper. She pried under the clothing to see exactly where and how that paper was angled and she removed it. She opened it carefully. It was lined, and torn on one of its sides. It held four numbers written in fading blue ink. They were underlined in a swift, off-hand manner, the line slightly arched. Nothing more. The writing was not her father's. It could have been her mother's, for the letters slanted in the way her mother's writing did. But there was a boldness to them that made Viveka think otherwise. The numbers meant nothing to her. She smelled the paper. It smelled of the wood of the cupboard. She folded it back and placed it as she had found it. There was something remarkably empowering about knowing that in her father's drawer was a piece of paper on which four underlined numbers were written, and that her father did not know that she knew of it.

She opened another drawer. Leaning against one wall of it, hemmed in by neatly folded pyjama tops and bottoms, was an envelope containing about a dozen black and white photographs, all so old that they were more in shades of yellows than blacks and whites. They were photos of her father's family. Her mother had once shown them to her and Vashti. It didn't matter to Viveka why they were now in his drawer. Next to that envelope was another with a receipt from a company called Rahamut's Co. Ltd. What it was for had been filled in by an illegible hand. She could only make out the price of the item, $1,178.

Although she was looking for nothing in particular Viveka was disappointed. She closed that drawer and with some difficulty opened the last one. It was crammed tight with T-shirts, and underneath the piles were magazines. She withdrew one. It had colourful photos on the cover of women with their breasts bared. The breasts were strangely bulbous and the way the women sat made their chests protrude. They wore panties that looked like triangular patches on strings. She turned the pages carefully, her body perspiring, her heart racing. She felt odd sensations, like those one had swinging high up, or plunging fast down on a garden swing. There were men in the photos in what must have been a man's version of a panty, skimpy and black. The bulges inside of the men's underpants were large and there were little points in them. She opened the sock drawer and took out a sock. She rolled it tight and shoved it in her pants, then looked at the outcome in the mirror of the nearby dressing table. She compared it to one of the photos of the men, rearranged it a bit and compared again. She pulled out the sock, wiped it on her pant leg, and replaced it.

There was also in the final drawer a calendar, an old one, from about four years ago. It was of naked men. She looked at two of the pages, and although she did find the men's private parts curious, in general she found the calendar of little interest. The magazine had been much more interesting, the one with the women, showing how the men held the women, where their hands rested on the women's bodies and the women's hands rested on theirs. It occurred to Viveka that she would have to pay another visit to this cupboard. She would not linger too much longer, only see what else was there for the future.

Under the magazines was a large manila envelope. Perhaps, she thought, full of boring bills or photos, or — and this thought made her ticklish again — perhaps another magazine of women with men. She pulled it out. But there were only documents in it: her parents' passports, old passport photos, her and Vashti's birth certificates. She had seen these before. But there was another paper she had not seen before. It was her parents' marriage certificate. Her parents' friends held wedding anniversary celebrations, but her parents never did. The children, peeved, wanting to celebrate their parents' anniversary too, had asked more than once about the date. They were always given the same hesitant and faltering answers, each parent giving a different date, even. Now here was the certificate, with the date — the day, the month, and the year. Her heart pounded, for how would she be able to tell her parents that she knew the exact date, inform them of it, remind them of it, when this was how she had found out — by snooping? Then, suddenly, it was as if she had been hit in her stomach. The year on the certificate was the same one in which she had been born. She tapped out months on her fingers, in almost the exact way her mother had whenever Viveka and Vashti had asked about the marriage date. She counted it out again, taking their marriage and her birth date into consideration. She did it a third time. And she concluded that her mother must have been pregnant for four months before the date on the certificate. No wonder.

Trembling, Viveka could barely hold the document in her hand to replace it. She had no recollection whatsoever of the order in which she had found it, nor could she remember how the envelope had lain on the drawer bottom. There was pounding in her ears, in her brain. Her eyes brimmed fast with tears. She fumbled the drawer shut and the cupboard closed, and ran to the washroom. She had instantly tried to think of herself as special, as the vital cause from which a family flowed, but she sensed the meaning of the forgotten and fumbled date. She shut herself in the bathroom for a good hour, her tears endless, and she pinched the soft flesh of her inner forearm until cherry-like spots blossomed there. After that she never brought up the question of her parents' anniversary again.

Viveka glanced over at her mother. Devika was on the telephone to the caterer again, still making changes to the menu.

Although Viveka understood her own talent for filling in blanks in her memory, making sense of what didn't easily add up in her mind, she was sure, too, that she had made up none of that memory. Every detail was real. It was the one memory she could recall in perfect sequence: the sound of the birds through the bathroom window, the ping of the mop against the pail, the water splashing on to the floor, the maid's journey from the far part of the terrazzo floor to the part nearest the carpeted bedroom section. She remembered the moment of discovering the marriage certificate and then the moment of understanding, of wanting it to mean that she was special, and how her body had trembled after.

No, she would not ask her mother about any of that. Theirs was a house of secrets, and she would keep it like that. Her mother was finally sounding content; the decision about the menu had been made. There would be mini pastels, crab-backs, sweet-and-sour shrimp on toothpicks for starters. At least, thought Viveka, her mother knew how to pull together a menu. Devika now spoke to the caterer with a new excited authority. The colour of the napkins, the pattern of the cutlery, were the current issues.

Her mother safely occupied, Viveka continued to think about her memories, about the time just before and after Anand's death. She certainly had not forgotten asking her father why he had been lying on top of the groaning Mrs. Moretti. She thought of that moment at the dinner table with embarrassment, not for her father and what he had done (or whatever it was she imagined him doing), but at herself for asking a question she instinctively knew, even then, would cause a stir. It was the events that had followed upon that question that her fertile mind seemed entirely incapable of arranging satisfactorily.

After Viveka had posed her unfortunate question, her mother had become anxious and watchful. She seemed to cry incessantly. Perhaps, Viveka thought now, it had to do with Anand's death, and she had confused the chronology of events. But she remembered asking her mother at the time why she was crying so much. In a burst of sobbing her mother replied that she was suffering with a cold. Yet, Viveka noted, her father didn't rub her mother's head, or bring her a cup of tea or aspirin, and he slept in the guest room. The two girls were told that this was because Valmiki didn't want to catch that cold. Sometimes Viveka's mother and father spoke, but it was as if they didn't know each other. How Viveka wished to become a big strong boy who took care of his mother, made her happy. Perhaps, she used to think, if she were a boy, a brave blond-haired boy who could walk on rocks barefoot and shoot an arrow straight and far, her mother would have been kinder to her.

She remembered a day when there was some calm. They had all got into the car and her father took them for a drive to the San Fernando Wharf. On that trip he spoke to her mother tenderly. He parked against the retaining wall that acted also as a long bench on which people sat to watch the oil tankers in the Gulf, to see the sun set, and to eat corn from the vendors who set up their bike-carts there.

The entire family got out of the car and made their way to a vendor. Her father bought three steaming corns in their husks, one for him, one for her mother, and one that was broken into thirds, to be shared among the three children. They had found themselves a place on the sea wall that was free of seagull droppings, but not minutes later they were driven back into the car by the sandflies and there they ate their corn. Her parents turned around, one at a time, to make sure that they weren't getting corn kernels or juice on the seat of the car. They both smiled, wearily, at the children. Anand, seated between Viveka and Vashti, stood up at one point, and reached his little hand out to his mother in the front seat, and when she turned to face him he brushed her hair off her forehead, and even though his hand had flecks of sticky corn on it and they had gotten on her hair, everyone said to him that it was such a sweet thing to do. Viveka saw her father's arm move then; it seemed as if he were sliding it toward her mother's arm, but she couldn't tell from where she sat, low in the back seat. But then she saw her mother's hand move toward his, and Viveka grinned so hard that Vashti asked her what was so funny, and her father glanced at her in the mirror. Then her father asked if her mother still wanted to have the party. They discussed it, and who would be on the guest list, and Viveka listened.

In those days, she loved how busy the house was just before a party, and all the food smells, and the smell of floor polish, and on the day of the party itself she enjoyed the commotion of servers milling about and the very serious bartender wiping glasses, making them squeak with his big white towel, and closer to the hour of the party the musicians trying out their different microphone levels and saying, "Testing, testing, one two three." Her parents talked of the party, Viveka tried to listen, and Vashti and Anand played fish. Anand hit Vashti's prayer-hands too hard, and before she could cry he began to wail as if he had broken a bone or something, and it seemed to Viveka that he never stopped crying after that, and not long after (was it the next day, or the day after that?), he disappeared.

But before that fish-slap — or was it after, while Anand was wailing? — Viveka heard her mother say, "I can't believe you want to invite them. Why should I have that woman in my house?" Her father put his hand to his head, closed his eyes, and asked her mother to please not make such a big thing out of nothing. She heard her mother again: "Don't you have any respect for me or for your children? I refuse to invite them. I can't believe you would even ask me to do that." Anand continued to scream but her parents didn't seem to hear him. They just carried on a conversation that had turned once more to hisses.

And was it that same day, or was it a different day, that they were in the car, the five of them — she, Anand, and Vashti in the back seat, her parents in the front — and Viveka turned her window down and head-first launched herself, to waist height, through it? She scanned the ocean, looking for oil tankers waiting to dock at the refinery's pier, which in the dusky evening was beginning to shimmer with its pinpoints of lights outlining every detail of the little city that it was. She re-entered the car — Anand was not screaming, he was whimpering — just as her mother turned to face the back seat. Tears were streaming down her mother's crumpled face. Viveka remembered one minute having the urge to hold her mother's face in her hands and stare into her eyes, and the next to open the car door and extricate herself from the claustrophobia of this bubble she felt would burst at any moment. Instead she made her way across the back seat, past the whimpering Anand, past Vashti who was busy pulling at the cuticle of one of her fingers, to the other window, to search for scarlet ibis or hanging snakes in the mangrove trees on the far side of the roadway.

It was then that Viveka spotted a man in white painter's overalls, fast and purposefully approaching the car. The man brandished a scythe and his white overalls were soaked in dark burgundy, the colour of wet blood. Viveka frantically drew back inside and wound up that window, and then shoved her way swiftly across the seat to close the other. "Go! Go, Dad," she shrieked. "That man, look! Look! He has a knife. There is blood on his clothes. Drive, Dad. Hurry, please."

But her parents continued their throaty bickering, and even though Viveka was shouting and pounding on the backrest of her father's seat, neither he nor her mother heard nor seemed to see what so appalled her. The man in the painter's overalls circled the car, and Valmiki and Devika paid no attention when he hopped on the bonnet and crawled up to the windshield and splayed himself across it, smearing a thick blood-red colour. Even though he bared his teeth and banged the handle of his scythe on the windshield, Viveka's parents did not see him. In time, the man in the once-white, now-red painter's overalls slid off the windshield and seemed to fall in front of the car, and. disappeared. No one in the car, not even Viveka, had noticed that the tide was now at its highest and the highway, which ran for a picturesque half mile directly alongside the sea, had flooded. Waves were rolling in, slapping and shattering against the concrete wall. There was a stream of traffic, the cars slowed by the flooding road. The hissing inside the car ceased. Viveka's father turned the car, very carefully. Once headed back, he flashed his lights to alert approaching drivers that the creek had flooded.

Although she had done nothing that required great exertion, Viveka slept soundly through the night that followed. She awoke to find Jess the maid sitting on the edge of her bed, staring at her with what looked like pity. Her parents had already gone out, and they had taken Anand with them. She and Vashti didn't know whether to be upset that they hadn't been taken too or to be pleased that they had been left home, as if they were old enough to take care of themselves.

Her parents returned late that day — or was it night, or was it another day? — without Anand. And when hour after hour, meal after meal, day after day, Viveka and Vashti asked where he was, both parents took turns attempting an answer. One would try, while the other would suddenly begin to weep. And whenever they were about to answer the query, Viveka would suddenly become so distracted that she could never hear what they eventually said. Soon, everyone seemed to accept that Anand would no longer — not ever — be in the house with them again. Some days Viveka felt that it had something to do with the painter in the blood-covered once-white overalls who had been attacking their car with a scythe; on the other days she felt it was because of the fish-slap; and then sometimes she wondered if it was because her father had been lying on top of a woman other than her mother. The nagging sense Viveka carried with her was that it was her fault. She hadn't been able to save or to protect anyone when it had been necessary.

Once, several months later, Viveka asked her mother why the man had blood on his overalls, why he carried a scythe, and why he had thrown himself on the bonnet of the car. Her mother looked at her as if she had gone mad. The more Viveka tried to give details, the more she confused her mother, who asked her what on earth she was talking about and if she was unwell. But it had all been so real to Viveka, and so many years later, it still was.

VIVEKA HAD NEVER BEEN ABLE TO LINE UP CORRECTLY THE CHRONOLogy that included the time she saw her father on top of Pia Moretti, Anand's crying in the car, the painter crawling on the car's bonnet, Anand's sudden disappearance, and the party that followed. That goddamned party. And, now, finally, her mother had for the first time told her when Anand had died in relation to when the party had taken place. And already she had mixed up the chronology again.

She remembered clearly, though, that she and Vashti had worn to the party white, frilly, cotton dresses studded with red velvet polkadots, and underneath the skirt part they had to wear crinolines. Vashti enjoyed the full, flared look of her skirt, but the crinoline's stiff fabric scratched Viveka's skin and she tugged at and twisted it. She hated how she looked and wanted to cry, but the blond-haired boy, ever-present just on the other side of her skin, would not let her. Her scalp hurt, too, her midnight-black waist-length hair having been brushed smooth into a ponytail, bound with a red velvet-covered elastic band. She raised her eyebrows and wiggled her ears in an attempt to weaken the grip.

Seven o'clock promptly the guests had begun arriving. Viveka and Vashti had been brought out onto the patio and into the garden at a quarter after seven to meet the guests. Out of the tops of bamboo poles set along the fence danced fat tall flames of fire. Some of the neighbours were there, aunts and uncles all. Actual relatives were there, too. And her father's banker and his wife. Uncle Ram and Aunty Minty. And other doctors Viveka recognized from going with her mother to meet her father at the hospital. She and Vashti stayed out long enough for their growth to be remarked upon, their likenesses assigned to their mother or father, and the cute divulging of what they wanted to be when they grew up. Viveka had answered "a magician," but quickly changed her mind in the face of raised eyebrows — no, no, she meant she really wanted to be a doctor. Vashti said, "I don't know. A teacher?" They were quickly taken back inside.

They had been permitted that night to lie on their parents' bed to watch television until a much later hour than usual.

Vashti had fallen asleep in front of a program, but Viveka was restless. She crept into Anand's room. Although she knew better, she slid open a drawer in his dresser. His clothing was freshly, neatly arranged. She lifted out what had been his favourite pyjamas. She buried her face in them. She slipped off her blue-and-white pyjamas and forced herself into Anand's. The pants had an opening in the front. She stuck one finger out of the opening and was satisfied that she did indeed look like her little brother. She held it with her other hand and pointed it as if into a toilet. She tiptoed and arched her back for proper aim. That felt real enough and good. The shirt was short for her, and the thin cotton strained against her body. Dressed like this, she made her way in the shadows of the house's interior down to the front and into the noisy living room. The three-tiered crystal chandelier that hung from the high ceiling cast prisms of colour that danced in time to the music on the wood floor. The air was heavy with a festive confusion of food, alcohol, perfumes, colognes, after-shave lotions, deodorants, and sweat. The room had been vacated of almost all furniture except for some chairs pulled up against a wall. Helped by the dim lighting, Viveka slid behind a *monstera delisiosa* philodendron that had dwarfed its tall blue and white ceramic pot. She crouched and was well hidden.

Dinner had already been served, the food and dishes cleared, and the dancing and drinking in earnest were just beginning. Her mother was moving about the room, chatting a minute here and another there, all the while catching the eyes of servers who seemed to need only a nod from her to know what it was that she wanted. Men congregated near the bar, each trying to outdo the other with humour. Her father stood with a group of men there, and beside him was one woman. She was tall and slim and had white skin. She wore a black dress that was strapless. Her father had his arm around this woman's waist and she had her hand on his back. Her hair was dark brown and long and wavy. Her father was hugging her, it seemed. His fingertips rested on her hip bone.

Viveka imagined her father perched on this woman. She looked away immediately, toward her mother who was outside on the patio, chatting with three women. But her mother was looking from the patio, across the almost empty living room (straight past the philodendron plant) to the spot where her father and most of the men had gathered. Viveka's mother glanced a few times at Viveka's father, always with a smile on her face, then back again to laugh at something someone in her little group had said, and then over at Viveka's father again. Viveka fixed herself so that she was taller in her hiding place, and could see better. She wanted to run out and to get her mother to play catch with her, but she knew this wouldn't happen, that she would more likely be sharply pulled inside and scolded.

She watched her father again. His fingers were still on the slim woman's hip bone. He was tapping her hip with his fingers, in time to the music. He suddenly moved away from the woman and went to speak to the deejay. In response the deejay turned in his swivel chair to reach a pile of record albums. He showed them to her father and her father nodded. The music changed from "You Keep Me Hanging On" to the most popular calypso, "When ah call yuh, answer fast." In an instant, all the guests, recognizing the tune, began to move their bodies to the beat. In sudden haste, the men and women from both sides came together into the centre of the room. Viveka's mother crossed the room, passed just in front of the philodendron, and went farther inside the house, to the kitchen, Viveka presumed. The room had filled up so fast and with so many people that it darkened. Still, her father danced his way to the light switch on the wall and dimmed the chandelier so much that Viveka could have stood up yet not have been spotted. The men were beginning, one by one, to loosen their ties and to undo the top buttons of their shirts.

Viveka watched Valmiki step onto the dance floor, bringing the woman with the strapless black dress and the long wavy hair. He kept his tie fastened and did not dance like the other men in a "break-away," but with one hand he held one of the woman's, while the other hovered at her waist. He seemed to push and pull her with that hand. Her father and the woman grinned at each other. Viveka's mother suddenly appeared, walking past her father and this woman. Her father let go of the woman, of her hand and her waist, and pulled her mother to dance with them. Her mother seemed to be smiling yet she was biting her lower lip.

She pointed to something on the patio, and Viveka's father shook his head and seemed to insist that she stay and dance. Her mother turned away and Viveka couldn't see what was happening without herself being seen. A second later, her mother turned and with some haste headed back into the house. Her father grabbed the woman's waist and pulled her close to him. One of the other men shimmied up to Viveka's father and the woman, and the man thrust his arms in the air and his pelvis toward the woman's pelvis. Viveka's father grinned, stepped back to allow the man his turn, and spun around on one heel to arrive again next to the woman. The man said something to Viveka's father, and her father lifted his face to the chandelier and had a full laugh. He shook his head as if to say, "You know!" Her father and the woman put their arms around each other, and they danced side by side. The woman put her lips to Viveka's father's ear and said something. He did not look at her but nodded. He let go of her, slipped away from her, and spun around again. Viveka's mother did not return.

The next morning there was shouting from Viveka's parents' room. She opened their door, holding it not an inch ajar, and watched. Her mother was holding the white shirt her father's had worn the night before, gripping it by the collar and showing it to him. He wouldn't touch the shirt but stood very straight, speaking to her mother in a voice that, despite the smile on his face, had no laughter in it. In between his sentences he made sounds like guffaws of laughter, but there was no laughter. He was saying that there had been thirty-two women at the party, including Viveka's mother, and that the lipstick could have been from any one of them — including her, he added. He was, after all, the host and every woman there had hugged and kissed him at one time or another. Viveka's mother lurched at her father, hit him on his chest with both hands balled into fists. She pounded and pounded, and he, laughing now, but it was a strange laughter, tried to block her punches. Finally he gripped her wrists and held them tight, and her mother screamed at him, saying, You're hurting me, let me go, you're hurting me! Viveka opened the door wider and her father saw her and let go of her mother's hands. By this time he was no longer laughing oddly, but had become darkly serious. He walked quickly past Viveka, touched her head with his hand lightly, and went out toward the kitchen. Viveka and her mother listened to his car start up, and then they didn't see him again for three whole days.

Those three days her mother had spent in bed, with her door locked most of the time. When the door was locked Viveka would press the mouth of a drinking glass to the door and her ear to the bottom of the glass — a trick she had learned from a children's spy thriller — and she would listen to her mother speak on the phone.

Now, although her mother was filling in details about Anand's death, had even said something about the timing of the party and something about her father and other women, the words remained indistinct. Viveka tried in vain to hear them against the necessary and unyielding confusion in her head.

Valmiki

THAT SAME MORNING, VALMIKI HAD ALREADY SEEN ABOUT SIX patients when his receptionist buzzed to inform him that Mrs. Prakash was there, without an appointment. One of the benefits of close friendship with Valmiki was that one could jump the queue and not have to wait in the hot room, breathing in thick, germ-ridden air.

He and Devika had known Ram and Minty Prakash for almost as long as Valmiki had been practising medicine. Ram Prakash had not finished high school, but had done well enough in the chocolate-making business that was his family's since the early 1900s. Ram and Minty had lived with his parents in the original estate house, known as "Chayu," deep in the central forested hills of Rio Claro until their son, Nayan, was born. They had their own house built in Luminada Heights at about the same time that Valmiki and Devika had had theirs built there, too. The Prakashs needed their own independence, and also wanted their son to grow up in a big town with access to a good primary school and high school. Although Ram and Minty were twenty years older than Valmiki and Devika, the two families grew close.

Minty always had a beleaguered air about her, catering to her husband and to Nayan, who had been born when she was in her thirties, and who, in retaliation against his father's heavy hand, insisted on the same kind of treatment from her that he saw his father demand. Minty suffered with high blood pressure and depression, and was one of the more regular visitors to Valmiki's office.

So Valmiki was taken aback when the Mrs. Prakash who walked through his door turned out not to be Minty, but Anick. He was struck by the particular fairness and leanness of her face in the harsh light of his office. Devika's description, "cultured-looking," came to him. He thought now he understood what she had meant, and hoped that, in the moment, he too was cultured-looking. In a deafening instant he noticed the way Anick's flimsy spaghetti-strap dress clung to her slight body and then hung off her hips. He weighed the advantages against the disadvantages of being a friend of her in-laws, of being many years older than she was, of being her doctor.

"What a lovely surprise," he said. "You're well, I hope. I would rather that this were not just a patient-doctor visit."

Anick looked at him quizzically. She said nothing, and in the momentary silence he reminded himself that the woman before him was Nayan's wife, Nayan who was like a son to him. She was only a handful of years older than Viveka. He corrected himself. "If I had known last night that you were coming to visit me today I could have seen you right then in my office at home and spared you the trouble of coming downtown."

"Thank you, this is very kind, but I decide this morning that I need to come to see you."

"What brings you here?" Anick reminded Valmiki of Pia Moretti, but not in her looks. She was nothing like Pia, really—except that she was a foreigner, white-skinned, and about the age of Pia when he had messed around with her several years ago. More than a decade ago, already! His eyes rested on the wispy baby-like hairs that strayed off Anick's hairline at her temples and clung to the tiny beads of perspiration on her skin. Pia's hair was dark and long, and wavy too. He wanted to take the handkerchief from his pocket and wipe Anick's brow. The smell of Pia's hot skin returned to him. He was thinking that these foreigners had different rules and expectations than the local women, than even the local white women. So much more was permissible and possible with them.

In answer to Valmiki's question, Anick Prakash told him, in what he thought of as charming half-French, half-English, that she couldn't really say what was wrong, but that she had little energy and felt like sleeping all the time.

Valmiki said, "Hmm, maybe you're about to start a family?"

She shrugged her shoulders, smiled weakly, and said, "No, that is not the problem. I — what you say? I bleed already."

Foreign women were more ready and open with that sort of information too.

"Are you homesick?"

"I am missing my mother and my father, is true, but homesick? No, I don't think. This is a country very nice and a good people, no? I ask you pardon for my English. Everybody laugh at me, and nobody take the time to talk, to know me."

"You're not happy here."

Anick bit her lower lip. She turned her face away as tears pooled. Valmiki came around to her side of his desk. He half-sat, half-leaned on his desk. Resisting the urge to put his hand to her head, to stroke her hair, he folded his arms.

"I ashame myself. I do not think to be ungrateful."

"Anick, I want you to know that everything that goes on in this room is private and confidential. You can talk to me, and it will be between you and me. No one else."

"Merci, c'est gentil."

"Non, c'est... c'est... de rien. Je veux... Oh, I have forgotten the vocabulary. Je... Oh dear, that's as far as I can get, I'm afraid. I studied French when I was in high school and quite liked it, but then I had to drop it and study Latin as Latin was the requirement for medical college. I must brush up on my French again. We must speak French sometime. Not now, though. You tell me what's going on. What is making you so unhappy, Anick? Is everything okay between you and Nayan? I have to say you both looked very happy last night. Are you?"

"Is not Nayan. He is good. He treat me good. He give me everything. His parents they give us everything. I do not know why I feel so selfish. I miss everything in France. This sound bizarre, no? Or selfish. Mais—but I miss to go out, I miss to go for coffee in the nice coffee shop, to go for walk instead of car, car, car everywhere. Nayan talk so much about cacao and monkey and wild flower when we first come together and now he do not take me to the estate. Is talk of forest and chocolate how we come together, he and me. We like chocolate and nuts. He chocolate, I nuts."

She laughed, but her laughter was sad.

"He tell me how pretty the cacao look on the tree, and how pretty is the forest with all the cacao tree, the orange tree when it have orange on it, the flower, the bird, the people from the village. Is nature, must be pretty, no? But I never go there. He say is dangerous. His father don't agree for me to go there. He don't want the workers see me. Why everybody in this place so afraid of workers? Everybody have workers but they afraid of them. And then, is bush, bush, bush. And snake. Is like a prison living in this country. The doors and windows in your own house—in your own house!—always lock, you cannot go outside in your own yard, you cannot even go for a drive. Is crazy, this place. No?"

"Yes," said Valmiki in a soothing tone, "but my dear, there is so much crime in this place. I mean, just look at the headlines of the papers every day. There is at least one murder every couple of days. Walking on the streets is actually dangerous. But I understand what you're saying, too. You're right; it's not like abroad where you crazy foreigners walk from one place to the next. And the estate, well, it's just not safe out there in the quiet country areas anymore. Because there are no outward signs of violence — like when there is a war and people can be seen with guns, and bombs go off around you — it's hard to believe that it's not safe. But you must know of the state of things here, don't you?"

"Yes, yes. But plenty people walk in the streets and they are safe."

"Those people are not Ram Prakash's daughter-in-law. Businesspeople and people with money have a hard time here."

Valmiki could see that Anick understood him but did not have the vocabulary to carry on this particular conversation. Instead, she said, "But is not just there that Nayan do not take me. Is nowhere. He take me nowhere. NO WHERE. Well, not nowhere, but he take me by his friend who I have nothing in common with. He do not want me to make nice friend."

There was quiet as Valmiki pondered the veracity and the graveness of this.

Anick began again. "There is no opera, and he do not go to the exposition, or the museum. Nayan say the art gallery have nothing in it. I say, What you mean it have nothing? And he say, Well, it have art but not good art. So I say, But I want to know for myself, but he say is time of waste. Nayan do not read. Nobody I meet read book. The only book he read is the one he write, the business one — how much this yield and how much that cost."

Valmiki thought fleetingly of Viveka. She barely closed a book and another was already begun. A chain-reader, he called her. He was quite certain now that he could draw Anick into an affair with him. If he were to seduce her into an affair that was not entirely clandestine — a hint of it discreetly leaked to one or two of his friends — he would be afforded the credibility of manliness. She was certainly desirable — not unlike, say, a car. A Jaguar. A piece of jewellery, say a Cartier watch, or a nice pen, a Waterman or a Mont Blanc. That was what Anick was to Nayan, Valmiki reflected, the perfect accessory. But he knew, too, that that was also his own interest in her. And he suddenly felt old and tired. Even if he were to pull her into a little something with him, he wasn't sure that he would have the energy to deal with such a young woman. Being more or less alone in the country, she would cling to him too much. She was green, one could see that. She likely wouldn't understand the nature and rules of a good affair. She would be more of a liability than a thrill. Valmiki's mind wandered to Tony. He sobered immediately and turned his mind back to his professional task.

Well, she clearly wasn't meeting the right people. She needed friends who saw her for who she was. Friends who weren't wolves like himself, and so many other men he knew, when presented with such vulnerability and foreignness. Devika was perceptive when she had said that Anick was probably used to a more culturally rich lifestyle than she would find in the Prakash family. He had never known the Prakashs to go to cultural events. He himself went to plays and launches, but mostly because of Devika, who scanned the social section of the paper every Saturday to see what was showing or playing. He wondered if there was something coming up soon that they might invite Anick to. Or something that Viveka might ask Anick and Nayan to see with her. He suddenly had the fierce urge to be the one to make a connection between his daughter and Anick.

"He want I dress up," Anick was saying, "and he want take me to meet his friend. They drink, they talk nonsense. They laugh at the way I speak, so I do not speak no more, or I speak to be funny. Why not?"

"Oh, I am sure they are not laughing at you. But your accent — can I say it? — is rather lovely. I mean you have a way of phrasing things that is charming. I am sure they don't mean to laugh at you. I would bet that they, in fact, appreciate you trying out your English. Which, by the way, is entirely comprehensible. Your vocabulary is very good."

"Oh, you too. I tired of charming."

"No, no. I don't mean it in any bad sort of way. I am just very sorry that you are having such a difficult time."

"Dr. Krishnu…"

"Call me Valmiki. Nayan calls me Uncle Valmiki, but you can't call me Uncle, now can you? You are like family." He instantly regretted saying this last, as it meant he had just sealed his relationship with her. He took refuge against resignation in the odd sensation that she must see in him the old man, not the young one he still saw. He would definitely introduce her to his daughter and put a stop to this sad lasciviousness.

"I want to say one more thing," Anick continued. "Nayan do not want me to go no place without him. He jealous. I want to run. I want to be free, to run free like the lion, to be curious. Like the cat, no? But he tell me over and over, so much time I sick of it, that is not safe for woman to go out alone."

Valmiki frowned. He did not voice what ran through his mind: Frenchwoman, even a lion is not free or safe in this place! They will capture the lion and put it in a cage to gawk at it and to say how beautiful it is, and then they will skin it for its mane, which even in this hot weather they'd wear like a shawl. And you know what curiosity did to the cat, don't you? He contented himself with saying, "Your husband, I'm afraid, is right."

"I tell him come with me, and he only laugh. He say, Why you want run, we have car? He drive me everywhere."

Valmiki managed a chuckle.

"Is funny, yes, but is not funny, too. I say I want to learn to drive. He say, No, is not safe, and I say, But your mother she drive. He say is not safe for foreign Frenchwoman who do not speak properly. Everything I hear is about pretty. I wish to take a knife and cut my face."

"Just a minute. You have no intentions of doing that, do you?"

"No, no. I should not say that to a doctor because you take me too serious. Of course not I do that."

Valmiki straightened up and looked at Anick sternly for the first time. "Do you want something to help with this low feeling? I mean, should I prescribe you an antidepressant? Or if you'd like, I can refer to you someone you can talk to more regularly."

"Dr. Valmiki, I not crazy. I just not in my skin in this country. I come in your office because I need to say these things to someone in confidence, but I don't need that kind of medicine. I not crazy. Or maybe I am, to marry this man, this family, to come to this country, to leave my own parents so far away. I need music, not only steel pan and calypso. I like jump-up jump-up, and whine, whine, whine, but that alone, all the time? Is *too* much. I need symphony, too. The Verdi, and the Puccini, and to eat cotes du porc charcoutieres, but this country don't have that, and we can't have no beef and no pork, not even thin ham slice, in his house. Everything is roti-this, roti-that, Hindu-this, Hindu-that. Me, I like Hinduism very much, but they too many rules in the

Prakash house. They don't do ceremony or go to temple or pray. But still, all I hear about is Hindu, Hindu, Hindu, and all these rules. I want to lie in the sun at the back of the house in my bathing suit, and Nayan ask me if I crazy, I will offend his Hindu father. I thought Hinduism was a tolerant religion but —"

Valmiki felt compelled to defend a religion that had been important to his ancestors, although it was not one that he or his family practised nowadays. "Hinduism, my dear, *is* a tolerant religion, but the people who practise it are not themselves tolerant."

He was rather pleased with the sageness of his statement, but Anick brushed the air with her hand impatiently and carried on. "His mother, she want me to make breakfast, lunch, dinner. They have washing machine, and they have servant, and she want me to wash he and his father white shirts by hand in the tub downstairs. Nayan, he don't try speaking French no more. He used to try in Canada. In Canada he doing everything with me. But now he drinking almost everyday, I don't know what I come to this place for. I am not a good wife. I think I can be good wife, but not the way that he want, like his mother. I want to go out. I want to do things. He and me, we used to do things before we come to here."

Valmiki nodded as she spoke, thinking to himself that, indeed, she wasn't crazy at all, but with these interests and desires she would certainly find herself isolated and a bit of an oddity in Trinidad society. He felt sure that Anick wasn't about to cut her face or hurt anyone. She might not last in Trinidad — her and Nayan's marriage might not last here or anyplace else — but pills wouldn't cure that either.

As attractive as Anick was, as vulnerable as she was, Valmiki, hearing these things, also thought her too foreign. And with that thought, he realized he had changed. He had indeed grown older, had perhaps become more settled than he had imagined before. He thought of Saul, and how there had come this time now when, although he and Saul had sex less frequently than before — that was just the nature of the beast — Saul's companionship, that hard body, his bitter smell were all he wanted. But wasn't it just as likely, he asked himself, that he had arrived at this place because — and he might as well congratulate himself on this — he had so well managed his reputation as a womanizer? Clearly, the urge to fool around with women — that cultivated urge — could still be triggered, but it wasn't what he ultimately sought, and he no longer acted on that urge. That, and not his ageing self or mere fatigue, was why, he patted himself, he could decide to leave the office yesterday when Tilda Holden showed up to see him, and why today he could leave Anick Prakash alone. Wouldn't it be just great, he mused, if he could tell Devika how much he had changed?

As for Anick, he knew that what she needed was not medical intervention but close friendships. He decided that such a well-groomed, feminine woman would do his daughter a lot of good. They already shared a number of interests. It struck him that Viveka and Anick would meet each other at the party at his house in just a couple of weeks. So he told Anick about the event being planned. Was it possible to meet Viveka before then, Anick asked, as she had a great deal of free time on her hands? Valmiki, in front of Anick, made the flamboyant gesture of a call to his house.

But Viveka, on the other end of the phone, told her father she couldn't afford the time just yet; she was writing an important paper. She asked her father to tell Anick that once the paper was written she would give her a call.

It pleased Valmiki to report back to Anick the reason Viveka was unable to meet at once. The way he said it made the literary paper and Viveka sound important. Anick was visibly intrigued, grateful for the possibility of a friend who would soon share ideas and interests with her.

And so, without having laid a hand on Anick's body or taken the hard plastic head of a stethoscope to her chest, it was apparent to Valmiki that he had already been of help. Such confirmation of the possibility of restraint and of unconditioned goodness in him caused a warm shiver to course down his spine.

II Luminada Heights

24 Days

Your Journey, Part Two

LET US SAY THAT, HAVING SEEN THE PROMENADE, YOU'RE INTRIGUED. Say you want to see at least one neighbourhood that will tell you something more about town and country. There are many neighbourhoods you might venture into, but a drive through Luminada Heights is a social lesson in itself. Besides, that is where the Vishnus and Prakashs live.

To get there, take a taxi from the San Fernando General Hospital. Don't walk — the hills are steep, the roads narrow, and traffic dangerously swift. Go down Chancery Lane, to the bottom where the land is flat for all of a hundred yards or so, and then begin your climb upwards again. Even a car, especially those used as taxis, protests its journey into Luminada Heights. You rise above the red galvanized roofs of the post office, the bus terminal, the Ministry of Works, and other government offices. You round a bend, and Fisherman's Wharf disappears. The road turns and you're hemmed in by tiny one-room houses and smaller shops on either side of a road that looks as if no more than one and a half cars ought to fit on it. You're ascending and realize that you're on a precipice to which the houses on the drop side cling precariously. In some places a stout yet mangled yellow-and-black iron railing makes a mockery of the safety it had originally been intended to provide.

Not soon enough, the land is more forgiving. The precipice blunts into rolling hills. Just ignore, if you can, the barefoot wiry man in the red merino vest and torn trousers meandering dangerously in a drugged stupor down the middle of the road, his unkempt wiry hair making him look that much more fearful. And the bent, bodi-thin woman sweeping the step of her one-room shack that opens directly onto the winding uphill road. Look, instead, beyond the orderless smattering of gutted houses and shacks, away from the clotheslines, chicken coops, outdoor latrines and shower stalls. Look through the avocado and mango and plum and dongs trees that thrive in spite of having been haphazardly chopped away to make room for one thing or another, and there it is again — the roti-flat, silvery Gulf of Paria. An excellent view of it is commanded by this prime hillside location: you'll see rigs topped by gushing orange flames, red-and-black oil tankers, flat-bottomed barges, and the refinery's pier that lights up like a string of diamonds at night. You can even see the faint pier of Point Lisas sticking out like a peninsula, while the steel factory and ammonia plant emit cloud-like plumes into the air. On the western horizon of the Gulf is a sliver of the mountainous Venezuelan coastline, a northerly spur of the Andes that sinks into the Gulf then rises again in the northern hills of Trinidad. At sunset, with some little imagination, it resembles a golden tiara.

Slowly, perhaps, but surely, these lands with exceptional views, on which squatters live in huts and shacks with no running water or electricity, will give way to the kinds of homes that are built just a little farther on — the ones with gardens designed for entertaining, all angled just so, to take advantage of the view of the gulf.

A short history of Luminada Heights as it is today begins with a family of French origin, the Rochards, who in the late 1950s — with independence from Britain imminent — sold their colonially taken and inherited hillside land on the eve of their emigration. The Rochards were cattle- and horse-breeders and Luminada was a pasture. It had always been shaded magnificently by a profusion of generous samaan trees, host to birds, iguanas, bromeliads, and philodendrons, their umbrella tops intricate as lace handkerchiefs. The Palmiste palm grew there too in abundance. Several stands of them remain, interspersed among the houses that eventually emerged. A consortium of bright young San Fernando brothers, all Indian in origin, pooled the money they had, borrowed the rest, and bought the land. They added "Heights" to the name and divided up the pasture into lots. To this day they have held on to double and triple parcels for themselves, passed on to their children now. But they, of course, made fortunes selling off the rest in smaller lots. Thankfully, they and those who bought from them were in awe of the samaan's grandeur and stamina, and the trees were, for the great part, left alone and built around.

The winding road with its gentle inclines and declines opens before you and suddenly begins a climb in earnest, offering now a chronology of affluence: just past the ground-bound shacks — homes of the fisherman, the knife sharpener, and the nut seller — you find the homes of the doubles vendor and the roti man. These, only a little bigger than the shacks just passed, stand proudly on stilts. As the road winds and rises, each tier makes its own definitive statement to rival the one below it. Each level out-designs and out-builds the one before. The modest wood house gives way to larger wood houses, and these sport wrap-around verandas, and multiple doorways and windows that open onto those verandas. These are the homes of the elementary school teachers, store clerks, and book-keepers. Baskets of lush ferns hang from their eaves, and low concrete fences brace themselves against the possibility of being rammed by out-of-control vehicles, some of which have made their threats more palpable by leaving paint streaks across the fences. These houses beget, on the tier above, low concrete structures in which the high school teachers, car and insurance salesmen, and self-employed petty businessmen such as electricians and painters live. Their houses show off terrazzo-paved patios with wrap-around wrought-iron fences and wrought-iron patio furniture, paved and covered garages, and clipped hibiscus hedges instead of concrete fences.

Now come the multi-layered, multi-roofed concrete homes with partial walls of cut and polished stone, the enclosed two-car garages, portals over the front door, the rare museander shrub punctuating a military-crisp lawn, and the relief of a hybrid bougainvillea spilling over concrete and wrought-iron fences — the concrete to discourage trespassers; the wrought iron to allow the public a view of the grandeur inside. The store managers and accountants, a couple of hairdressers, the town's printer, and the denture maker are among those who live here. These beget on a yet higher tier other similar houses, but with uncovered, paved patios, sprawling lawns, and large picture windows to take in the view of mangrove hugging the coast and the Pointe-à-Pierre jetty jutting into the gulf. Here you'll find everyone from engineers and stockbrokers to small business owners, people who work in the oil fields, and a good number of moneyed white people.

When the very top of the road was finally etched out, well before electricity and water were put in, and the land was advertised for sale in parcels rather than lots — larger, that is, than anything below — there was in San Fernando a rush for this land, as if for the last pound of rice or flour on the grocery shelves. Bidding was fierce, and some people waited to make their offers only when the bidding was so high that their offers revealed much about them. It is here that the bigger business-people live, like the jewellery store owner, and those who are in the oil or transport business. Several doctors and lawyers are here too. The access road runs at the backs of the houses, rather than at the front as they do below. These houses face the sprawl of the island northward, their view enviable, magnificent, and unobstructed. The residents here have the privilege of knowing what the top of a samaan tree looks like. From their property fronts they can see the yacht club and the moored boats, they can survey the entire refinery, the oil tanks and the flaming stacks at Pointe-à-Pierre, without using their star-gazing telescopes. They can see Point Lisas. With their star-gazing telescopes they can look downwards, unseen, into the windows of their neighbours lower down. They can see the small, traditional, rectangular swimming pools down there.

The neighbours below crane upwards, or take drives to that highest road and lurk outside of the houses there. They will their vision to bend around to the fronts of the houses, but instead they receive only furiously tantalizing glimpses of landscaped gardens, light fixtures like statues that dot the lawns, and swimming pools in innovative shapes, some taking advantage of the slope downwards, one pool emptying into another.

It is in this mix that Valmiki and Devika have their house, the least ostentatious of the lot. The Prakashes are just down and around the corner, not even five minutes away.

Eyebrows would be raised and heads would nod in understanding, if you were to say you lived in Luminada Heights.

Viveka

FOR THE PARTY, VIVEKA WORE A KNEE-LENGTH, LONG-SLEEVED kurta. It was dull blue, printed with darker stripes, and in the stripes a grey-and-red paisley design. It had been a present to Valmiki from one of his patients who had visited India. The first time Valmiki had tried it on, Vashti and Viveka thought it made him look like a movie star. He quite liked it, too. But Devika had pursed her lips and showed no interest in it. He knew she thought it looked like a dress on him. Later he took it to Viveka and asked if she wanted to have it, explaining that as much as he liked it, he knew that he would never actually wear it. It had to be altered to fit her, but it became her favourite outfit immediately.

On seeing Viveka dressed like this, Vashti rolled her eyes. Devika said, "*That* is what you're wearing?"

"I don't have anything else. What is wrong with it?" Viveka couldn't hide her defensiveness. "It's what I feel most comfortable in." The kurta reached her knees, and under it she wore narrow blue slacks and Indian leather slippers.

"Don't make it sound like you are deprived, child. It is dowdy. You look like you are going to the mall, not to a party. I could lend you something. Go look in my cupboard."

Devika's offer did not soften the criticism in Viveka's estimation. "Well, you all are always saying how muscular my arms are and that sort of thing. It hides my arms."

"She'd be more comfortable in one of Dad's old shirts!"

"Oh, shut up, Vashti."

"Shut up? Mom, why does she speak like that to me. As if I am a child."

Viveka curled her lips as she levelled, "You are."

Valmiki, tucking his crisp white shirt into his black trousers, came out to look at Vashti. He put a finger to his lips and whispered in a good-natured voice, "You keep out of this, honey."

He smiled at Viveka and said, "First of all, you have lovely arms. Everyone's jealous because you're strong for a girl. Do you want one of my shirts, Vik?"

Devika exhaled hard at him. "Rather than help me, why are you cajoling them like this? Look, they are your children, too."

Back at Viveka she snapped, "I don't care what you wear, but you will come down and say hello. If you want to look like that in front of people, that is your business." And so the banter went. Soon everyone except Viveka headed down to the front of the house to meet the guests.

To the accompaniment of instrumental music from the party, Viveka, shelving and unshelving books in the study, heard the chatter and laughter grow as each new couple arrived. Before going out to mingle with her parents' guests, she had informed her mother, she wanted to check something on the computer. She turned on the computer and engrossed herself in a chat-room debate with other students regarding the university administration's implementation of heightened security measures on the campus.

Her mother didn't hide her irritation when she came into the study for the second time to call Viveka out. "I don't care how important it is," Devika declared. "If you were watching an advertisement on TV now you would say that *that* was of some great importance. You think you know how to get what you want, but I want you to get yourself out there right away. I am not coming in here to call you again. You are behaving like a real coonoomoonoo. You *will* come and meet people, and you *will* stay out and chat with your sister, and with Anick and Nayan when they arrive, and everyone else. Why can't you be more like your sister, eh?"

Viveka glanced away from the computer. "Aren't Anick and Nayan here yet?"

"No, but everyone else is."

"Steve Samlal is here, too?"

"No. His parents are here, but he didn't come."

This both pleased Viveka and made her feel peeved.

"It is really looking as if you are being very rude. Why do I have to keep making excuses for you?" continued Devika.

"All right, all right. I am coming, but I have to shut the computer down. I will come in a few minutes."

"Vashti has already come out. She is just sitting there by herself. Turn off that computer and come outside right now."

"But I just said I was turning it off, Mom. You don't have to tell me to turn it off again."

"Look, I don't want to go outside with a sour face because of you, yes. If it's not your father, it is you. I don't know what is wrong with you all. Look, you just do what you want. As usual."

"Why are you bringing up Dad? Did something happen?"

Her mother, realizing that she might have provoked Viveka's old anxieties with her dig at Valmiki, backtracked quickly. "Just stop worrying yourself. He is behaving perfectly. Stop all this worrying-worrying and come out, for God's sake."

Another ten minutes passed, and Viveka's father came into the study. He stood behind her. "You're chatting?"

"Yeah, I'm finishing up now, though."

"I know you don't like these kinds of parties, pet."

Viveka interrupted him. "It just all feels so hypocritical. I always feel as if I don't know what's actually going on. How come your hunting friends aren't invited to these kinds of parties, Dad? I mean, you see them more than you see anyone who will be here tonight."

"Well, precisely. I see them enough as it is. Besides, you know they won't feel comfortable with this crowd."

"You mean this crowd won't feel comfortable with them."

"Both."

Viveka could hear her father's irritation and defensiveness in that one word, and changed her direction with him fast. "I just don't like these kinds of parties, Dad."

"I know that, and I know that I am to blame. I know your mother doesn't think I have changed or grown up at all, but surely you can see I have. Just come out and say hello. Everyone is asking for you. Come, make your mother happy, please, for my sake. You can come back here after you say hello."

"Have the Prakashs arrived yet?"

"Not yet. Uncle Ram said they had another party to go to first. But they should be here any time now."

"I hope they bring chocolates," Viveka said in a conciliatory tone.

Valmiki quickly jumped on the moment. "Come on out now, my pet, for a few minutes, please."

Outside, Viveka remained distracted, one eye on the entrance looking out for Nayan and his wife, and one foot ever ready to rush back inside of the house to the study. Vashti, wearing green high heels and a short spaghetti-strap cotton dress with an abstract print that flashed every colour bled from the rainbow, came and stood next to her. Their father slid himself between them, and put an arm around each girl. He could be so flamboyant when he was ready, observed Viveka. And he was certainly ever ready to party. He was indeed a good host. She looked around and didn't mind admitting that so was her mother.

Viveka fielded small talk about the university from some of the guests while one man asked Valmiki if he had sons-in-law lined up yet. Viveka good-naturedly interjected, "Marriage? I don't even have my degree yet."

Vashti rolled her eyes, "What she doesn't have yet is a boyfriend."

"But who say you have to wait until you get degree?" the man answered, thickening and flaunting the popular version of the Trinidadian accent. "Pretty girls like you, and you keeping the boys waiting? Valmiki, is Devika who make these children by herself, or what? How they pretty so, boy?"

Valmiki said, "You're right about where they got their looks. I have taste, you know that. Anyhow, listen, I am not paying any dowry, you hear? I will have to be paid for these girls, and whoever wants the privilege of marrying either of my daughters will have to come damn good, for either of my girls! They will have to make sure I can retire in the style to which I have accustomed my wife."

He said this as Devika passed by, and without stopping her march toward a group of women gathered on the lawn, she said over her shoulder, "It was I who taught you, boy. When you met me I was already accustomed to that style. Everything you know *I* taught *you*."

Valmiki kissed Viveka on her cheek, whispering in her ear, "Your mother is in fine form tonight." He offered his daughters a drink, which they both declined. Then he left in the direction of the bar. Viveka felt rather awkward, standing there with Vashti, fumbling to carry on with friends of her parents the kind of conversation that bored her. In minutes a server arrived in front of the two girls with a glass of white wine and a sweating glass of Coke, the napkin around it already damp, both set in the centre of a doily-clad silver serving tray. Vashti playfully reached for the wine. Viveka slapped her sister's hand lightly, then looked over at her father, who winked at her. She shook her head at him, but took the glass of wine and remained chatting with these friends of her parents — it was a "then and now" conversation about the quality and quantity of available street food, the vendors outside the gates of Vashti's school, and the roti shops near the university gates — until she had finished half. Then Viveka excused herself with some mumblings about research and course work. Vashti reluctantly followed her into the house but went to her own room, where she turned on the air-conditioning and made a phone call to one of her friends.

BUT IT WASN'T LONG BEFORE VIVEKA HEARD VOICES, HER FATHER'S included. He and another man, gentler sounding, were talking. She recognized Nayan's voice and panicked. She straightened herself, pushed her chair back from the computer, and slowly spun the swivel chair around to face her guests as they arrived in the study. She stood.

Her father was holding the hand of a young woman, encouraging her onward.

Viveka felt something she had never experienced before. It was as if she had been swiftly pushed high up on a swing and was coming back down ultra fast. Her body was suddenly light. She felt giddy. Anick was even more beautiful than anyone had said she was. Viveka found she couldn't look her in the eyes.

Nayan embraced Viveka warmly. They hadn't seen each other in three years. "You're keeping fit? Well?" he asked.

"Yeah," she managed. "You look good too. Nice to see you." She was aware that Anick was watching her intently, smiling all the while, but Viveka still could not return the gaze.

After an awkward introduction and some chit chat, Nayan invited Viveka to have dinner with him and Anick in a few days.

"Why not?" Anick urged. "I doing nothing but to stay by myself all day. I cook good. I admit I say myself, but is true. I cook you something from France. French food, you know, very mmm food. I good for something. Not everything, but something." At this last, she winked. She had laughed nervously throughout her little speech, a self-conscious outpouring. An awkwardness fell over the group, but the moment was quickly saved when Nayan said, "She is good for at least a couple of things, and she is a very, very good cook." He tapped the front of his shirt in the area of a slight paunch, unabashedly pushing out his belly for emphasis. "See what has happened since I married her?"

Nayan made it clear that he was inviting Viveka alone. He really wanted Viveka and Anick to get to know each other, he said, with affection that pleased Viveka even as it made her uncomfortable. His parents would go abroad in the next couple of days and would be gone for a few weeks, his father on business. She should come when Ram and Minty were away so that his father wouldn't put a strain on everyone with his demands and controlling manner.

At this, Valmiki interrupted, "Oh, your dad doesn't mean anything by all of that. He looks well. So does your mom. We'd better go on out, otherwise they will think the party has moved in here."

Viveka refused her father's request that she rejoin the party, insisting she had too much work to do. Taking his cue, Nayan quickly finished his invitation, saying he would send his father's driver to pick Viveka up and bring her to their house, a distance not three minutes by car but too unsafe to walk by one's self once the sun had gone down. Alone again, Viveka felt unsettled. Neither Anick nor Nayan was any taller than she, but still she felt short and unrealized, almost childlike, in front of them. She had the near-paralyzing sense that her slippers were insubstantial, that the kurta she wore, and that not an hour before had made her feel different, exotic even, had suddenly become baggy on her. Its style, fabric, colours — in a flash, as if midnight in a fairy tale had arrived — had all turned dowdy. She felt that she did indeed look just so, as her mother had said.

It was not lost on Viveka that if she were put shoulder to shoulder with other young women, particularly those in her family's social circle, she simply could not match them in their realization of the ideal of what a beautiful girl or woman should be. But this difference itself had always been her pride. To be like any of those women was not her dream; to be unlike them had always been her distinction. She wanted to be able to present herself in that very kurta and get away with it. Standing next to Anick, however, had put the lie to this illusion. She suddenly felt her hair to be unstylishly cut, and much too short. "Different" or "distinct" was not what she felt, but unnatural. Her heart beat fast, and she was overcome by an odd sensation of grieving. She slumped into her chair and remained quite still, afraid to experience any more of these feelings of intense strangeness.

Eventually, Viveka pulled from one of the shelves the volume of the encyclopedia that included France. She didn't have anything in mind, really. What of France did she know? She knew words. The Louvre. The Mona Lisa. Notre Dame Cathedral. The Cathars. The Seine. Voltaire, Marie Antoinette, Rousseau, The French Enlightenment. They were proper nouns in a jumbled pool in her head, buzzwords acquired either through cursory reading of mandatory school assignments, or her own natural inclination to read everything, admittedly absorbing little more than a key word here or there. But although she could make no sense of a detailed map of Paris — could barely see the tiny place names on the thin paper of the encyclopedia — she felt as if a whole new world was about to open up for her. Her conversation with Nayan and Anick played in her mind. She realized she had said barely a handful of words. They must have thought her an imbecile.

Viveka made her way to her bedroom and took a long look at herself in the mirror. Her torso wasn't flabby at all. It was firm, rather. It was just shapeless. It was a barrel of a torso she had. More like her father's than her mother's. She muttered a dry, "Thanks, Dad." Playing volleyball wasn't enough. Perhaps there was some exercise she could do. Perhaps she would ask Elliot. He liked doing abdominal crunches in front of her, getting her to count out loud for him. Perhaps she might start going to the gym with him. She wouldn't do any resistance training, but lots of cardio so that she could get less barrel-like, less muscular. Perhaps when Elliot had said to her, as he had numerous times, that she might want to try an aerobics class, he had been commenting in a sly way on her hard unfeminine body. She suddenly wanted to be more shapely. She switched off the light and threw herself on her bed.

"I cook good, I say myself but is true... French food, you know, very mmm food. I good for something. Not everything, but something." Anick's voice, her words, looped in Viveka's head. She tried to say them out loud, imitating the accent and tone.

Mosquitoes buzzed around her head. She wondered again if Nayan had told Anick that he had once shoved that bloody big tongue of his down her throat. Worse, that she just let him do it. And worst of all, that she hadn't had a clue how to respond.

Viveka and Nayan and Anick

THE TABLE HAD BEEN SET QUITE SIMPLY. VIVEKA WAS HOPING TO SEE evidence of Anick's French culture in the setting, but she saw nothing remarkable: a homey, white cotton cloth with a simple red border and everyday stoneware. It might have been a dinner to which no guests were invited, quite the same as at Viveka's house — except for the setting of the cutlery: the tines of the dinner and salad forks, oddly, faced downward. Viveka repositioned hers, correctly — she thought — tines up. If a guest were to eat at the Krishnu house, a little more ceremony would be had. She was on the verge of being peeved about the lack thereof when it occurred to her that this was perhaps a kind of compliment — a signal that she was "special."

Dinner was a one pot dish served with bread, and a salad of sliced tomatoes sitting on top of lettuce dressed with nothing but salt and black pepper. The maid had baked the bread, and the smell of it competed with the heavy, dark one of Anick's beef stew, the name of which, after several times not getting it right, Viveka stopped trying to pronounce. Nayan rather quickly acknowledged what was already well known to Viveka, that his parents exercised religion in the most meagre of ways, food being the main one. Anick had decided, therefore, to take advantage of the fact that his parents were out of the country and cook a beef dish. Nayan, you see, had come to know beef, Grade AAA no less, in Canada, and not getting anything close to that in taste or quality in the restaurants here, he missed it sorely. This beef was imported. Very, very high quality. Granted, it was a stew, not a roast or a filet mignon, but it was an authentic French dish and Anick made it so well — there was a whole bottle of quality red wine in it! — that it satisfied him fully. There was even a bit of bacon in it. Nayan said all of this as Anick brought out the dish from the kitchen then went back in and returned with the bread and a slab of butter on a bread board. His words seemed not to touch her. She made no appearance of being flattered. Viveka wondered if perhaps her English was so poor that she had not understood him.

Anick had to make do, improvise a little, with the ingredients she could find locally. So she had cooked the chunks of Grade AAA chuck with the expected local seasonings, Spanish thyme, local bay leaf, and parsley — all very different varieties than were available in France. But there were, too, mushrooms, canned of course, and of all things, pearl onions. Viveka knew these tiny white onions only as a pickled mouth-puckering ingredient in a common party appetizer. They were usually arranged, along with a half-inch cube of cheddar cheese, on a toothpick, a good number of these jewelled spears impaling a whole unpeeled, uncut grapefruit. She wasn't looking forward to eating an entire meal with such tanginess in it, but she wouldn't be uncouth, either. She held one of the little pearls between her tongue and the roof of her mouth, quite ready to discreetly douse its acidity with a drink of water or the wine Nayan made a show of pouring her, or a chunk of that fresh bread. She pressed down timidly, and the juices of the dish leaked out of the onion and spilled over her tongue. The onions had been rendered, on the contrary, sweet and aromatic.

A smile threatened to break over her face, but she contained it. She stared down hard at her plate and stroked a chunk of the tender beef with the tip of her fork. She thought with some mischievous delight that the onion's transformation could not simply have been a function of its association with the other ingredients, or had anything to do with cooking techniques and methods, but was rather a result of its close association with Anick herself. She reached for another onion and made sure not to meet Anick's eyes.

Nayan dominated the table as he told Viveka—pushing out his chin at Anick in a teasing way, he said that with his wife's brand of English it would take forever for her to tell the story herself—about how Anick got to Canada, how he and she had met, and how he had gone to France to meet Anick's parents. Yes, he had indeed been to France!

Anick seemed mildly bored as Nayan spoke. Perhaps, Viveka thought, this was because she had heard the story told ad nauseam, or perhaps she really didn't understand enough English to remain fully engaged. She tried her best not to stare at Anick's prominent clavicle or her lean shoulders, her spaghetti strap dress revealing a mix of bone and steady muscle that made Viveka want to jump up and say, "See? See? She has defined muscle *and* is enormously feminine."

"Anick is an only child. Like me. Spoilt rotten," Nayan said. "But in her case, who has to pick up where her parents left off? Me, not so?"

"He think I spoilt," Anick piped up at last. "Not like I see some children in this country. Children here, the parents they have money and they give it to they children to spend like is air free to breathe, no? Not you, Nayan. Of course you spoilt, but is natural. You are an only child too, but you, you work hard. I can complain about other thing, but not that. You work hard. Like your father. He work hard too, no?"

Viveka imagined her parents at this same table with them. Had her parents been guests here, one of them, if not both, would have picked up on Anick's sly comments and might well have playfully said something like, "Wait-wait, not so fast. How is Nayan spoilt? Come on, tell us everything." But she could never bring herself to be so bold, although she could see clearly that a little boldness might make her a better guest.

Anick had wanted her parents, unusually protective for French parents — Nayan was saying this with the benevolent authority of one who owned the information — to let her travel farther afield.

Anick shrugged and muttered, "But of course, is normal. You have how many children in your family, Viveka?'

Before Viveka could answer, Nayan said, "You know. There are two of them." He seemed mildly irritated that she would ask a question she knew the answer to.

Anick, Viveka imagined, was trying to turn Nayan's monologue into a conversation. Pleased to have been addressed by Anick she said, "I have a sister. Vashti. She is younger."

"But two is one more than one. You see..." Nayan countered, and with that, he took the conversation away again, carrying right on with his story.

As he talked, Viveka wondered what Anick's version of this story might be. That was the story she really wanted to know.

Anick's parents wouldn't let her go just anywhere, Nayan said, especially outside of western Europe. She had a cousin, Jacqueline, who had married a Canadian, Robbie, who had been taking a cooking course in France. "O-tel man-age-ment," Anick corrected, pronouncing each syllable as if to someone whose first language was not English.

"That's right, Robbie did cooking and restaurant management. He is a pretty good chef."

"What you mean *pretty good*? Of course he know to cook. He learn to cook in France, after all. We French, we know about food. You can cook, Viveka?"

Viveka felt pulled in two directions. Perhaps Anick was trying to open up the conversation again, but Viveka didn't want to offend Nayan. All Anick got from Viveka, therefore, was an ambiguous response that included a half nod and a hint of a shoulder shrug that could have meant, yes, not really, or sometimes. She wondered if Anick understood that Trinidadian women — even the ones who understood and agreed with feminist principles — wouldn't try to curtail (which was tantamount to "disciplining") their men, particularly in public.

When Robbie had finished his courses in France, continued Nayan, he and Jacqueline went to Canada, to British Columbia, and bought a restaurant in Whistler. They wrote to Anick, inviting her to visit them and to work in their restaurant for a season. Her parents had to be won over, especially to allow her to cross the Atlantic, but they finally relented and off Anick went to Canada.

Most mornings Anick skied, which she was good at, her family having owned a chalet in the French Alps, and four evenings a week she worked in the restaurant's pub. She was less good at waitressing, but every male customer wanted her at his table. At this comment from Nayan, Anick curled her lips in a show of tedium.

Viveka offered a chuckle of acknowledgement on both sides. But it sounded as hollow as she felt. She was uncomfortable. It was as if silt from the bottom of what had appeared to be a brilliant pool was slowly being stirred, and a shadowy cloud of it hovered just below the water's surface. Nayan's eyes were almost always on Anick, and throughout his storytelling a grin remained on his face. Anick's mouth was pursed and her lips puckered, as if her feelings and opinions were concentrated there. Her neck was long, her skin glistened with sweat. Her dark brown hair was piled in an unruly bun on her head. Light loose strands fell, and on the nape of her damp neck, short curled ones clung. Viveka prayed that Anick had no knowledge of the spin-the-bottle kiss with Nayan.

Nayan had been in the third year of a four-year program at the University of Western Ontario in London, Ontario. He had fallen in with students, white ones, born and raised in Canada, fellows from families with means, and for whom he, the rich brown boy from the islands, was a novelty. Unbeknownst to his parents, he took the living allowance he received monthly from them and, with a show of playboy-like bravado, went for the spring break to Whistler with these friends.

He immediately noticed the beautiful French woman working in the bar — after all, who wouldn't have? — and he preened himself for her eyes. He went to one of the ski shops in the Village and bought himself a white, streamlined ski jacket and wrap-around silver-framed sunglasses that hid his eyes, and he wore these indoors so that, undetected, he could watch Anick's every move. In the wood-fire warmth of the pub he would remove the jacket to expose a well-worked chest under a white turtleneck — he used to work out regularly in the student fitness centre at the university, and was much fitter then than he was now, he informed Viveka — and he perched the sunglasses on the top of his head, as he had seen some of the well-put-together men do. He and his friends took turns buying rounds of drinks, and he paid and tipped as unflinchingly as they did. Of course, he didn't know how to ski, and had not ever really intended to do such a thing.

Viveka noticed that Nayan was now telling her two stories — in addition to the tale of how he and Anick had met, he was revealing his self-consciousness and discomfort with those very friends he had fallen in with. Viveka's inclination, on the one hand, was to sympathize with him, but she went with the other, and merely nodded as if studiously interested in the phenomenon of this cross-cultural dynamic.

The fellows had placed bets about who would get into bed with Anick first. At this revelation, Anick pushed her plate away and hit her hand on the table. "Ah, Nayan. You too crude. You have to say this?" He stretched out his hand to grab her face, and she slapped his hand away. It was not a violent slap, or one that indicated singular offence, but more the gesture of someone firmly brushing away a fly that had come too close. It certainly seemed now that this back and forth, and the digs Anick and Nayan took at each other, was a performance between them. Still, Viveka's face burned, and the smile she had been uncomfortably wearing strained even more.

"I didn't do it. You know I didn't put any money on the table. I wanted you too much to play that kind of game. I was stupid, I could have won a lot of money."

Anick had slapped the hand of one of Nayan's friends who had patted her bum — Viveka wondered if it had been the same kind of half-slap she had just given Nayan — as she set a drink on the table in front of him, and that brought her cousin Robbie out from the kitchen to have a friendly chat with them. Employing the business-savvy gesture of camaraderie, he advised them of

Anick's lack of humour. This only caused them to become even more playful and challenging with her. One tried his rough French out on her, but she refused to speak French with any of them. Still, they imitated her attempts at English, thinking all the while that they were flirting.

Nayan, on the other hand, attempted to distinguish himself by not showing up at the usual time with his friends, but rather some hours later, sporting his newly purchased ski outfit. He would show up with poles in hand, ski toque on his head, up-to-the-minute ski goggles resting on his toque. Once, in the foyer of the pub, he tried to catch the attractive Frenchwoman's attention. Anick's response was, "This do not suit you. You do not look too good. You know to ski? I think you and your friend only know to drink. You cannot bring these to the inside." She pointed to the poles. He couldn't help but smile at her astuteness and her version of English, but he knew better than to bring notice to that. He expressed worry that the poles would be mistakenly taken away by another patron. She took them, examined them, and then placed them in a spot she had determined was safe. He expressed effusive gratitude and asked her to go out with him that evening. To his surprise, she accepted.

When Nayan returned to London, he and Anick spoke on the phone two or three times a day. It was inevitable that they would begin to visit each other. They worked out a schedule: alternating months they would take turns, he going there, she coming to London or sometimes to a hotel in Niagara-on-the-Lake or one in Toronto. He had to ask his father for an increase in his allowance, as he wanted to pay all the fares.

Nayan really did try skiing after meeting Anick. He began listening to French radio, and he read a French phrase book every spare minute he had. For her part, Anick launched into a concerted effort to learn about Hinduism, the pre-history and later history of Trinidad and of the Caribs and Arawaks, the steel pan, tropical flora and fauna. It was from Anick, Nayan said to Viveka with pride, that he learned many new things about his own country.

Nayan took time telling his story and it intrigued Viveka that he had so clearly become the kind of man who spoke on endlessly without encouraging conversation from anyone else. It continued to baffle her that Anick was party to this.

He knew better than to tell his parents about Anick, Nayan said, because he would be sent for, his money monitored, and even a marriage back home hastily arranged for him with a girl from a known family. Anick, meanwhile, had told her parents about him, that he was brown-skinned, West Indian, wealthy, and owned a cacao plantation and chocolate-making factory. Apparently they were worried that he wasn't French, didn't speak any French, and that she was sounding much too serious about him. She had had other love interests before, but none they had seen her consider so seriously. If they had worried about her interests before, now they were even more so.

At this juncture, Anick got up abruptly and busied herself in the kitchen. Viveka wanted to go with her and offer to help, but she didn't want to appear insensitive to Nayan's storytelling. She wondered who else Anick might have been interested in before, and if Nayan wasn't jealous that he wasn't her first interest. How restricting life was, she thought, here in Trinidad. The only interest Viveka had ever had was Elliot, and he wasn't really all that interesting, at least not in that way, to her. If she lived abroad, perhaps she would have more freedom, the chance to discover what kind of person might truly interest her.

Anick returned with a slice of chocolate cake for each of them just as Nayan was saying that he enjoyed telling Anick about the toucans and the leaping howler monkeys that one heard and saw while sitting on the porch of Chayu, the family house on the forest-like cacao estate. In moments of intimacy, he said to Viveka, leaning in close as if imparting a secret he was both shy about and that she had the distinction of being granted, he uttered to Anick the words *agouti, lappe, anthurium, baliser, mapipire, chaconia*. And Anick, Nayan said, was mesmerized. She had recognized words related to the forest and to the cacao trade as French, and then he had remembered that cacao was one of the principal products of the French colonizers who had come from other islands to Trinidad on the invitation of a Spanish King in the late eighteenth century.

"Do you remember the history in our schoolbooks, Vik?"

It was vague now to Viveka, but Nayan was delighted to oblige.

Trinidad in those days had been a country that no one wanted to settle. The king, so the story goes, offered land and tax breaks to anyone who would inhabit it and help to make it a viable Spanish colony. So, even though Trinidad had been a Spanish colony, it was mainly Frenchmen who answered the call and first cultivated sugar and tobacco there. But cacao was what they were most known for cultivating. Nayan's eyes were big as he said this, and Viveka understood him to be insinuating that cacao had once been in the hands of the French, and now he was bringing this Frenchwoman back to it.

Nayan and Anick had been tickled by the notion of kinship in that early Indian-French history. Chocolate, he told Viveka, details and tales of the cacao estate, the remnants of its Frenchness, and all that a tropical island had to offer, were the method and madness of his courting.

Even as Anick's existence remained unknown to Nayan's family, she and he announced their engagement to Anick's parents. He told his parents he was going on a business apprenticeship program to France for a month, and Nayan and Anick went to Paris, to Chamonix, and to Anick's hometown in the south, Perpignan. In Paris they walked everywhere — yes, along the Seine, and he went to the Louvre for her sake. He had known of the Mona Lisa and that it was the name of a painting. But even now he couldn't remember who had painted it.

"Oh, come on, Nayan. La Joconde, you know who is the artist," Anick snapped.

"Da Vinci," Viveka theatrically whispered to Nayan. Anick's face lit up. "You know! You know it? But how? You never go to France before!"

"No, no. I've never seen it. I mean, in real life. But it's famous. Who wouldn't know of it?"

Anick put one hand over her mouth and with the other she pointed to Nayan. "You see, Nayan?" she said. "Why she know and you do not know?"

Viveka quickly saved Nayan with an apology. "Well, that sort of thing interests me. But I am a little odd, everyone says."

"You not odd. You normal. I do not understand how he do not take some interest in this kinds of thing. You know is not how this peinture is called? Is name is *Portrait de Lisa Gherardini, épouse de Francesco del Giocondo. That* is the name. Not this Mona Lisa everybody like to call it."

Nayan still couldn't understand how such a little painting, such a pale and ordinary face, such a gloomy background, had ever caused a stir.

Viveka sheepishly said, "I wish I could see it someday. I mean, I have seen so many reproductions of it. You're lucky!"

Anick answered, "Yes, he is lucky." But she was looking at Viveka with sudden aliveness.

Nayan beamed. He told Viveka that he was impressed with himself that he had visited the museum whose name he had certainly heard before, but what truly pleased him was the fact that he, a brown-skinned fellow from a smallish town in Trinidad, was walking through the famous institution, in Paris, with a beautiful Frenchwoman, repeating after her French words whose meanings he cared less about than that she was exaggeratedly forming them with her lips, showing him the position of her tongue, touching her throat, as she tried to explain to him how to make a sound or pronounce a phrase.

Anick's face fell. She frowned and muttered, "You so superficial. C'est suffi, Nayan, c'est suffi, maintenant."

Viveka could only imagine what she had said in French, but it seemed that Nayan understood. He said, "No, no, no. Viveka is not just any friend. We can tell her anything. I am proud of how I met you. Let me tell my story my way."

Anick began to stir the remains in the serving dish, pushing, somewhat noisily, everything that had stuck to the sides toward a mound in the centre. She cleared off the spoon by hitting it hard several times against the edge of the dish. Nayan chuckled.

Viveka willed herself to seem ignorant. Her suspicion was confirmed that Nayan simply wanted to hear out loud, in front of an audience, his version of how he and Anick had met. (An audience of one was perhaps better than none at all, reckoned Viveka, and one who would not interrupt or ridicule, at least out loud, was likely best of all.) She wished she could be valiant, a kind of knight, able to whisk Anick away to some less one-sided and exposing situation. But she ended up being, rather, an ear for Nayan's story, a shoulder for his slights and hurts. She was certainly behaving with some success like every other woman she knew. She took consolation that other women — including her mother, and including, she would bet, her feminist cohort Helen — would all have done just as she was doing under these same circumstances.

She wished, too, that she could reach over and kindly, gently, stop Nayan, explain to him what he was doing to Anick, to her, with these intimate revelations. She felt as if she didn't know Nayan at all and realized that were it not for the old family connections, were she suddenly given a new opportunity, he was not the kind of person she would befriend.

In Perpignan, Nayan related, Anick's parents, Armand and Mimi Thiebert, had asked him about his family, their origins. He did not want to introduce himself as the descendant of indentured field workers, so he said simply that his ancestors had immigrated to Trinidad less than a century ago, from northern India. To which Armand had asked: Did they immigrate? I would have thought they went as indentured labourers after the abolishment of slavery, not so, to replace the slave work force? Nayan was forced to correct himself, and was puzzled that a Frenchman living in a town he had not heard of before meeting Anick would know this detail. He talked to them of his family's cacao estate and Nayan felt like a dark prince, owner of land, of an estate, of a chocolate-making empire, until Armand asked about the origins of the estate itself. Nayan told them it had been in the family for three generations, bought from a French planter in the 1930s. Armand had seemed suddenly quite aroused. He became serious and fidgety, and then he said, So on your land, the very land you now have, there would have been slavery, and all the ravages that went with that, then Indian indentureship, and then what was typical of the time — the Indian workers bought the estates from their bosses when the market declined. Nayan now admitted to Viveka that he hadn't actually thought of any of this before, and was pleased when Armand had showed enormous interest in this aspect of his story.

Armand had actually said, "The history of your estate, your piece of land, is the history of your island, and of the international politics and commerce of the late nineteenth century, the early twentieth century. It is part of the story of the rise and decline of empire." Nayan was provoked to find out more. The French connection to his family, he had since learned, and now laid out to Viveka proudly, was as old as history. He knew his grandfather, Deudnath Prakash, had come to Trinidad from India, but he hadn't paid attention as to why exactly, and no one spoke of it until his return with Anick, when he asked very specific questions. His father told him the details. Deudnath had come to work as an indentured labourer. Many of the people who travelled on the same boat with him were sent to sugar-cane estates, but he was sent to Rio Claro, to work on that very cacao estate when it had been in the hands of its French owner. When his indentureship contract ended he stayed on at Chayu, and in time he became one of the Hindi-speaking managers of the estate. He was lucky that he hadn't gone to a sugar cane estate, not only because the work there was brutal in comparison, but because by the time the 1930s came around there was a devastating slump in the international cacao market, and owners all over the island began to sell off their estates relatively cheaply. Sugar would not be hard hit for some time yet, and the blessing in disguise was that it took longer for the Indians who had ended up in the cane fields to get out of them.

Viveka knew that her own family on both parents' sides were, a long time ago, cane workers. They were among the fortunate few who had managed to get out early, and had obviously achieved great successes ever since, but as Nayan told his story she felt the sting of that difference between them. She didn't mind, not too much, being an audience for him, but didn't want to be made to feel any less grand around him and Anick than she already felt.

The lore of the Prakash family was that Deudnath bought Chayu — the entire forty-five-acre estate — with cash, his savings from employment there, handed over to the French owner in the very cacao sacks in which he had been saving the money. And, well, look at them today, Nayan said — evidence in truth of the decline of Empire and the rise of the Indian. He laughed at his cleverness. But *now* he knew what Armand had meant. At the time he had had no idea, and had felt a bit stunned by how little he knew, and by the fact that his family's business had indeed been a nugget in the history of a larger world.

In Perpignan he was eager to tell Anick's parents of more common, touristy things, but the instant he said the word *calypso* Mimi interrupted him to sing a few lines of a Mighty Sparrow composition, her hands slightly raised in the air, waving, her accent causing him to almost roll on the floor with laughter. He liked Mimi — she was bold and opinionated for a woman, but still very indulgent of him. Armand seemed to know something about everything, and this put him and Nayan slightly at odds with one another — but still, Armand was a really likeable chap. Both Armand and Mimi knew of the steel pan and spoke of having heard a Beethoven symphony played "rather curiously, if not convincingly" on it. Nayan admitted that while he did know of its use back home in the local symphony — which made its appearance like a comet: once, briefly, every few years — and had indeed heard well-known classical works played on it, he was not himself familiar with that kind of music, had paid it scant attention, and quite frankly preferred the pan as an instrument of the carnival season. Anick's parents seemed to already know whatever Nayan might have been able to tell them about Trinidad, and he wondered to Viveka now if this was because they were inherently inquisitive, simply well-informed, or if they had only recently done a fair bit of research — upon learning of his place in their daughter's life, perhaps.

At this comment, Anick retorted, "What you mean they do research before you come? These are things they know. They just know it. I do not know why you can not understand this. They not cretins, you know. They know of the world. They smart. They read. They talk. They think. Not to impress you, but all the time."

Nayan made a face at Viveka, as if to suggest, "See? This is what I have to put up with."

Viveka didn't want Nayan to think her rude by changing the subject, even if she knew how to do it kindly, but she also so wanted to spare Anick these stories about the arrogance of her parents and the naivete of her husband. She wondered what it was that Anick had seen in Nayan to have married him. "Hmm. You know," she said pensively, "I am still thinking about the French-Indian thing. I've been curious about the differences between 'cacao Indians' and 'sugar-cane Indians.' I bet the French influence would have something to do with their differences."

Nayan chuckled and said that it was too bad that Armand wasn't at the table with them, as he might be able to expound on the differences between the two.

Anick got up and slipped away from the table. Nayan watched her leave, then continued regaling Viveka with stories of his visit to France. Knowing that he and Anick had met in a skiing village, her parents took them to Chamonix in the French Alps, to a chalet in which they had shares. They had planned a trip to take him to see France's largest glacier, La Mer de Glace, but he didn't want them to learn how incompetent and fearful he would have been on such terrain. "Can you imagine," he said to Viveka, "traipsing about on a mountain of ice with big gaping cracks in it, so big you could fall in and that would be the end of you? What for? What kind of an end would that be for a boy from the tropics?" Anick's parents didn't hide their disappointment, and he and Anick were on edge with each other because of it. But what was a holiday without a little drama? Anyway, if he had been searching for some soupçon — Anick's word, he added — of familiarity with Anick's world, he found it in the brand name of the pen that certain Trinidadians brandished. Nayan winked at Viveka as he pronounced, "Mont Blanc." Unlike those people who liked to whip the pens out of their pockets to lend to you the instant you started patting your shirt pocket for a writing instrument, he now knew, he boasted, that it was not simply the brand name of a pen, but the name of a mountain in the French Alps. And he had actually seen that mountain. Being able to make the connection between pen and place had given him a momentary thrill of worldliness. But he made the mistake, he told Viveka, of asking Mimi if there was any relationship between the two. His question provoked unexpected hostility from Mimi: of course it is named after our mountain, and that diamond logo represents the snow-cap, but the pen company was originally German. This, she tartly said, was clearly an appropriation, and as if Nayan had been accusatory she added, "But there is nothing anyone can do about that."

Although Anick's parents attempted to be good-natured about it, Nayan could tell that his timidity to go on the glacier had tainted their impression of him. They stayed in the village of Chamonix and he witnessed a bristling camaraderie between Anick and her parents. He envied it. He had never done such holidaying with his parents, nor had he ever had that kind of easy back and forth with them.

As Nayan talked, Viveka's mind trailed after Anick again, and again she wished she could get up and go to her. She wouldn't know what to say to Anick, though, if it was the two of them alone. Perhaps there wouldn't be any need to talk. Perhaps, after all that listening, Anick would welcome some silence. Viveka could have offered her silence. It was strange. She had never felt so drawn to anyone, nor so protective before. It was strange because she didn't think she was capable of protecting anything. And although she had just finished a meal, a delicious, filling one, she felt as if she hadn't eaten in a long time.

It was there in the mountains, Nayan was saying, more than in Perpignan or Paris, that he had felt like an outsider. He was aware that, because of him, Anick's family had tempered their enthusiasm for the mountains and ski resort they so loved. Back in Perpignan they showed him the coastal towns. They went on day trips to Collioure, to Banyuls, and wherever they went there was an abundance of food and drink. And always they played classical music in the house on Impasse Drancourt. Mimi plied him with local sheep's milk cheeses, with sheep's milk yogourt, and bread she sent him down the road to get fresh from the bakers. He told Viveka how he had to ask for a bag to put the baguettes in, as the bakers had expected him to just carry it in his hand with only a little piece of greaseproof paper wrapped around the centre of it. Mimi made local dishes such as the one with anchovies, eggs, olives, and a Banyuls vinegar, and it was in fact very good, and with everything they ate there was wine from the area. They took him to restaurants that served the local

Catalan food, sausages and a rice dish that resembled a pelau but was full of shellfish, mussels, crayfish, scallops, squid, everything a bright orangy-yellowy colour because they had put saffron in it. He sometimes felt that a little jeera would have made it that much better, and he wanted to try that dish back here, adding jeera and a dash of curry powder.

The restaurants Anick and her parents took him to in Perpignan lined squares where there were churches, like the one — and he struggled to remember and then to say it — like the eleventh-century one, the Paroisse Cathedrale Saint Jean in Place Leon Gambetta (on cue, Viveka raised her eyes in a much appreciated salute to his memory and pronunciation). Everything inside the church was so black and dirty and old that you were afraid to touch the pews, even. And every building they passed seemed to have a historic plaque on it, and a story that Armand was ever ready to expound.

The food in the restaurants in these squares Nayan found to be very good, and Armand, Mimi, and Anick thought the food good too, but they always had to find some small fault. Some small *but* to everything. Just so that they could dissect and argue.

The food in France was good, he would admit, rich, but — his "but" was a different kind of but — but good. Still, he missed curries, a good shrimp curry or goat meat curry, and a real pelau, and salt fish and buljol. At least when he lived in Canada he would cook these for himself.

At that Viveka said, "I didn't know you cooked? Do you still?"

"I could, but I don't have to. You know how well Mom cooks. And we have a maid. I'm too busy now, man. Too many responsibilities. A wife and a house to keep up with! And can you imagine if my father came home and found me in the kitchen? In any case, do you know how much I am worth?"

He waited for an answer. Viveka shrugged, the smile she managed becoming yet more painful.

"Three hundred dollars an hour. *Three hundred.* What do I want to spend time in the kitchen for? I can't! Time is money, Vik."

Nayan leaned toward Viveka and lowered his voice. "Dad already thinks I let Anick get away with too much. She isn't like women here, you know. She isn't into taking care of family and house and garden and all of that, all the time. She cooked today, but that is unusual. She really wanted you to taste her food, French food. But, otherwise, she doesn't cook usually. In any case, they wouldn't really like her style of food. And can you imagine, really, if Dad were to come and find me in the kitchen cooking? Man, I would be up shit creek. I can cook quite well, I enjoy it even, but still, he'd want to know who wears the pants in my family — I mean between Anick and me! He already has his doubts."

Anyway, Anick's family took him — he had already been chuckling, but now he guffawed — to the opera, and the symphony. Him! He had actually gone to an opera. He fought to stay interested, to stay awake even. He was pleased to have seen that aspect of European life, but most of what Anick and her family took very seriously left him unmoved, baffled. He didn't know if they really enjoyed all these things they took so seriously. There didn't appear to be much happiness at these events, but a lot of frowning and head-nodding. After performances, Armand, Anick, and Mimi argued endlessly. They spoke English when he was present, to engage him as they — well, maybe not *argued*, but *discussed* the merits and demerits of everything they experienced together. He merely nodded his head, he laughed, he scowled when it seemed appropriate, but he could not participate and did not understand why such a lot of heated dissection and analysis was necessary. The three of them were full of opinions, and seemed to make sure to have diverging ones only so that they could argue.

One evening, Armand and Mimi invited some of their friends over for the sweet wines of Banyuls and Collioure, and for dessert. They had, unknown to him, spent the previous days searching out in his honour a collection of chocolates. Among these were milk ones, dark ones, truffles, and some with spices in them. There were three kinds that were made from cacao beans imported from an estate in Trinidad. It was at that point, he confessed to Viveka, that he felt really uncomfortable in front of them. He knew of the estate from which the ones made with Trinidad cacao came, but he, the son of a cacao estate owner and all-things-chocolate maker, wasn't familiar with such dark chocolate. He knew none of the other chocolates they had amassed, all of which were quite unlike the sweet milky ones that Trinidadians were used to, the kind Rimpty's made. Of course, in Canada he had seen dark chocolates in the shops, with the percentages of cacao — 65%, 70%, 80% — advertised in big bold figures, but he had dismissed them as a gimmick intended to appeal to some of the kinds of Canadians he met in university, ones who liked throwing around numbers that rated the heat of the various pepper sauces in their collection. The dark kind of chocolate, in his estimation at the time, was bitter, and he could never quite understand why anyone would like it.

But now the Thieberts and their friends, to a background of classical music, were breaking off tiny bits of the dark chocolate, putting them on the tips of their tongues and masticating very animatedly, grunting their analyses, judicious with their displays of pleasure, all as if they were critics evaluating wines. Armand would eat, chat, drink, and in particularly melodious sections, conduct the music with his hands. Nayan was indeed intrigued by the chocolates with the spices, for they were reminiscent of the balls of raw cacao that some of the villagers in Rio Claro made for their own private use.

Viveka, too, knew of these cacao balls. Sometimes the workers on the estate would be given a certain amount of a crop for their own use. They would roast the dried fermented beans with peppercorns, cinnamon, bay leaf, nutmeg, allspice, vanilla bean, cloves, and cardamom, grind it all up and make hard-packed balls a little bigger than ping pong balls. They would give the Prakashs gifts of these raw cacao balls and Minty would, in turn, parcel these out to friends, some of them going to the Krishnus. These balls were crude, meant to be grated, and the powder used in baking or in making drinks.

The spiced chocolates that the Thieberts had amassed were quite different, related Nayan. They were little delicacies, conched to truffle-like smoothness. They gave Nayan the idea to re-evaluate the villagers' cacao balls, add an emulsifier to them, conch them longer. Viveka must look out for a new line of Rimpty's chocolates, he said.

That evening of wine and chocolates in Perpignan had left Nayan otherwise unsettled. The Thieberts and their friends talked at length about estates in Indonesia and about workers' conditions on the Ivory Coast estates, in Ecuador. They questioned him about workers' conditions in Trinidad, and he could only say that there was no need for unionization or any such thing as his father was very good to their workers, giving them, for instance, a percentage of the crop, and sometimes paying for a worker's medical care or buying school books for a worker's child. They shied away from talking too much about Trinidad estates after that, but carried on talking about production in other regions, and Nayan wondered if the Thieberts and their friends had known these things for a while, of if they had gone and searched out the information especially for the occasion so that they could have their interminable discussions on the topic. He could have gone and done research too, if they had let him know what they were up to. He felt foolish. But one positive thing he learned was that there was more money to be made in the cacao business than he had realized before. There might be the exporting of beans — of course, they would have to be the fine premium kind — to France, and chocolate candy might be infused with local spices and flavours for export as well as for local consumption.

Viveka was about to say, for the sake of engagement, that she hadn't known there were different kinds of beans, but Nayan was just then called by Anick. He answered from the table, to which she said, noticeably sharply, "Please come. I need you. Now."

As he pushed his chair back, Nayan raised his eyebrows at Viveka and wrung his hands in mock fear. He was gone so long that Viveka became uncomfortable. She got up and began clearing the table. She found herself tiptoeing and resting the dishes on the kitchen counter carefully, quietly. Eventually she stepped out onto the open patio, which was lit by a yellow bulb from a single wall sconce. Fireflies and moths flew erratically around the bulb, the glass clinking whenever one of them hit it. Frogs croaked in the bushes close to the fence, and there was a steady pulsing drone from cicadas. Viveka walked around to the outside of the patio so that she could step into the relative dark. The lights on the Pointe-à-Pierre refinery twinkled, and from the tips of the stacks orange flames throbbed upward against the night's utter blackness. Directly above, a billion stars flickered.

The brilliant points of the only constellation she knew — the southern cross — shone bold and steady. She strolled on the lawn up toward the back of the house. A light shone through a small high window, the kind one found in bathrooms. As she approached it she heard Anick's and Nayan's voices. Her instinct was to rush back down to the patio so as not to suffer the shame of eavesdropping, but then she heard her name mentioned. She stopped, held her breath, and listened. Unable to hear clearly, she tiptoed on the grass until she was just under the window. She could make it back to the area of the patio in seconds if she needed to.

"But the Krishnus are old friends, Anick," she heard. "Our families have known each other for years now. I told you how close Viveka and I were before I went away."

"Don't you understand, Nayan? Is my business you telling. Not just yours. I don't know her for years. Is shameful what you saying. Is shameful for me, but for you too. Don't you see that? Is because you drinking too much."

Nayan's voice was stern. "Shameful? I am shaming you? And I have had no more to drink than you. I have had two glasses and a half of wine. Don't start with that nonsense. You want to start controlling everything I do?"

Viveka thought Anick was indeed brave to provoke such ideas when a guest was in their house. That sort of provocation could erupt in a huge quarrel, and even if the quarrel were put off for a few hours until the guest had left it would still cause a sourness in the air that would be only too noticeable. It wasn't what a woman should do, Viveka reflected, and one shouldn't need to be told so — this was knowledge one just absorbed and grew up knowing.

"Why you tell her these things?" Anick insisted. "Tell me this. Why you tell her, and you don't tell Bally and his wife? Is because you too shamed to tell them. You want them to think you so big. But you tell her, like you confessing. You really drink too much — I don't care what you say. We eat a whole meal and you talk the whole time. You never even say if you like the food, but you say how my parents make you feel stupid. You don't even ask her about herself. You take advantage of that girl. Is because she is not like other people. She can be my friend and you making me shamed in front of her. Besides, I hate it you talking bad all the time about my country and my family. How she can be my friend now?"

Viveka thought, So, after all, it *does* matter that it is me who is here at dinner! I am your friend now, Anick, more than his. You and I, we can be friends. We will be. She tried to be as quiet as a blade of grass so that she could hear more.

"Oh Christ, honey," Nayan's voice said. "Come on. For God's sake, be reasonable. She is downstairs waiting, she will think there is a problem, and there is *no* problem. We're having fun. At least I am. Don't spoil it. And does she look like she is having a bad time? I'm telling stories. I am reflecting. She is the kind of person who I can do that in front of. Why do I have to *tell* you that your food was good? Is there any of the bourguignon left in the dish? The dish is empty. What better compliment is there? We don't have to discuss everything, Anick."

"Oh my God. Look who is talking! You discuss everything to this stranger. And you tell her all kind of lies, too."

"I have my pride, Anick. I know what to say and what not to say. I am not, in fact, discussing everything. You want to see me tell her everything? I can do that, you know. Let me see then if she will have a frigging thing to do with you."

"I sick of all of this. I just sick of this."

"Oh Christ, just cut it out. She is going to wonder what the heck is happening. Fix yourself and let's go on out."

Viveka quietly hurried back to the patio.

Together, all three finished clearing the table. Anick put away some things and then rather abruptly she and Nayan indicated that they would take Viveka home. When Anick excused herself for a minute and went back upstairs again, Nayan took the chance to say that what he had liked best in France was lying at night with Anick, listening to children shouting things he couldn't understand, to the click of adult heels on the sidewalks as they passed swiftly beneath the window, a car going slowly down the lane looking for parking, the ping of a bicycle bell. They were in France, and France in all its Frenchness, all its self-assuredness, went on around them, and no Frenchman was in bed with her, the most beautiful woman he had ever seen, but he, from Trinidad, was.

Viveka listened with the evening's now-habitual forced grin on her face and wondered if perhaps Nayan really was a bit drunk.

IT WAS A SHORT DRIVE THROUGH LUMINADA HEIGHTS FROM NAYAN'S house to Viveka's, but long enough for Anick's razor-like silence to divide the space in the car into three uneven parts. She occupied the largest space. Nayan, who had become noticeably silent, had a smaller share. Judging by the way he avoided looking at Anick and the way he gripped the steering wheel, hands clocking in at five to one, he seemed aware and nervous of his share. Viveka was given, it seemed to her, an incidental sliver in the back seat. She felt a little sympathy for Nayan, but only a little.

The developers of Luminada Heights hadn't been generous with street lamps. Light flickered weakly here and there from the houses they passed. Down in the distance the outline of the oil refinery at Pointe-à-Pierre was shimmering with dots of brilliant silvery light. Now it looked like a rambling fairground of castles, rollercoasters and ocean liners butted together.

By the grace of darkness, Viveka, from the back seat, watched Anick. Anick seemed to be looking out the rolled-up window. Her reflection could just barely be seen in the glass. Viveka imagined Anick seeing herself and her life as she imagined Viveka might have seen her that night, especially in the light of the stories her husband had so indiscriminately revealed. She wanted to assure Anick that she had heard it all with a grain of salt, and longed to hear Anick's version. Or a different story all together. Anything from Anick, anything that was not about her and Nayan. Her profile was so perfectly set that it was as if Anick had turned just so, so that Viveka might watch her. Her face was thin, but not unhealthy or pinched in its thinness; on the contrary, it was lean and something else indescribable. A woman who, when she spoke to her husband spoke so harshly, who had been so determinedly quiet at dinner, should not, to Viveka's mind, have looked as soft and vulnerable as Anick did staring out the window. Viveka wanted to slip her hand onto Anick's shoulder, press her shoulder to let her know everything was all right. But she didn't, in fact, know anything, and couldn't know whether anything, let alone everything, was or would be all right. And although she imagined Anick discreetly raising her own hand onto Viveka's, squeezing it in acknowledgement of camaraderie, she dared not take such a liberty. Then, much too quickly, the car pulled up at the gate to Viveka's house.

As Viveka unlatched the gate and walked slowly to the back door of her house, her mind travelled to the places that Nayan had talked about: Toronto, Whistler, Perpignan, Paris, the Louvre. The Mona Lisa! Imagine: he had seen it! And had not been impressed. She tried to imagine skiing, but this was difficult. She was more able to conjure up going to the symphony. And she was curious now about chocolate that was as bitter as Nayan described, the chocolate that French people liked.

The Prakashs

ANICK SNATCHED UP A BRASS ROSEBUD VASE. NAYAN MIGHT GUFFAW at that, but she knew he wasn't amused. She raised the vase, and he ducked and shielded his face with his hands. But Anick wasn't crazy; she knew better than to aim directly at him. The vase hit the wall to the side of him.

It was Nayan's turn to scream. "Are you mad, or what! You think I told her everything? I told her nothing. I should have told her about the kind of person you were before I came into your life." He was not finished but Anick shouted back, interrupting him, wanting to know what, just what kind of a person would that be?

The kind of woman who one day slept with a man, and the next with a woman, the kind no sane man would have risked taking. Lucky for her, Nayan snapped, that he had come along. And if he had not been insane then, she was making him so now. After he had showed her what love was really like.

Anick couldn't believe what she was hearing. "Nayan, you know about Yves. You know I loved him. You know I lived with him for a year. What are you saying? Why you tell her I live with my parents? You tell her so many lies. Lies about me."

"Lies? I was protecting you. And myself. Did you expect me to tell her that you lived with other people before me? That you had no discrimination about who and what you loved? I know what I am doing. I know people in my country and how they think. I don't want people thinking — knowing! — that my wife was a host to others before me. Why did Yves leave you? Tell me again. Why? No. Don't bother. Because no matter how many times you tell me I can't understand it or believe you."

The words seethed between Anick's clenched jaws. "You foolish, Nayan. You too stupid. Yves leave me because he want to own me, and I do not want to be own by anybody. He was too jealous, possessive, oppressive. Words you should learn."

"He left you because you were — you were a..." But he couldn't say the word.

Anick tried to be calm, but her voice trembled. "Nayan, You know very well that Yves and I finish because I did not want to cook his meal and clean up after him and wash his clothes only. I want to do other things. He want a wife who stay at home and look after him and have no friend. Yes, is true, I still loved him. I loved Phillipe too, and Stephane, and after Stephane I love Anh Tuen, and you know I loved Anna Marie. And now I love you. I cannot help it who I love. I do not love a man or a woman. I love this person or that one. And when I love that person nobody else exist."

"I can't believe you just stood there and gave me a list of people you slept with. I don't know if it is because you are stupid that you talk so much rubbish or if it is because you can't speak English properly. Look I don't want my friends, or anyone in this country for that matter, knowing all of this disgusting nonsense, you hear?"

Nayan had indeed, and naturally, only told Viveka so much and no more. He hadn't told her that when he met Anick, she and her lover, Anna Marie, had only recently ended a relationship Anick had imagined would last forever. Anick was a mess then.

He hadn't revealed that this was why she left Perpignan and went to Whistler to be with her cousin. He deliberately hid the fact that he knew very well Anick was using him to quell that hurt. And he also did not reveal to Viveka that he had wholeheartedly believed, known deep inside of his very soul, that he — *he* — could change Anick, show her what love and happiness could look like.

AT THE RESTAURANT IN WHISTLER, ANICK WAS BEING HARASSED BY one man after another, even as she could think of no one else but Anna Marie. Nayan was unusual. She saw him watching her, but he didn't say to her the things other men, including his group of friends, did. He was nice enough, foreign enough. And how could she not have been lonely? When he asked her out, she had felt she could say yes and be safe with him. He was indeed sufficiently different from the other men, and he was such a distraction from her heartache. It was not difficult to be intimate with him, but she had no intention of falling in too closely with him. That is why she was so reckless as to tell him about Anna Marie on the first date. It was as if she was cheating on Anna Marie, and all she could do to quell that odd sense was to talk about her. To tell him all about her. It hadn't occurred to her that night, as she told him of this woman she so loved, and of how broken her heart was, that he and she would go on another date. She could see that he was perturbed, even a bit put off by her revelations, but she didn't care. In fact, that was just as well, she had thought.

Then, on subsequent dates, he seemed to become more and more intrigued, as men tended to be, by her interest in women. He wanted details. She wouldn't tell him too much, holding those intimacies close to her heart. He would persist, ask her what it was that women did to each other, what it was that made her like being with a woman. The only way she had been able to respond and still be respectful of those intimacies, and at the same time not anger Nayan with a refusal to engage with him in such a manner, was to employ the strategy of appearing to educate him. But it took hardly a sentence or two before he would become aroused, wanting nothing more then than to show her, as he would say while in the act, what real sex was and what a real man was like.

Then, once they were married, Nayan's fascination with the subject waned. Furthermore, shortly after they arrived in Trinidad, he was suddenly disgusted. He told Anick he hated that part of her life, that he was appalled, even tormented, by the idea that she had once loved women. Since then, she had dreaded the day he would throw all that she had so recklessly told him back at her. And now, that day had come. She had to fight the breaking of her heart at what she had sacrificed in herself by marrying him. In a strange place, in a family whose ways were so foreign to her, with this man whose body did not comfort her well enough, whose presence bent her spirit and heart, she felt more acutely than ever before all that she had given up.

ALTHOUGH RAM PRAKASH SUFFERED HIS SON'S MARRIAGE AS IF HE rather had lost his son, he was not unaware of the prestige Anick's Frenchness, her beauty and charm, brought to his family. She brought them the attention of the business world in a manner his cacao, chocolates, and citrus by themselves were unable to accomplish. The Prakashs had not before received so many invitations to dinners. It was not lost on them that these invitations were so that their friends could entertain Anick and Nayan.

People built parties around Anick. They threw these parties after making sure that she was available. They had food catered, and their homes rearranged, and pieces of furniture and accessories bought with her eyes and approval in mind. Behind her back, and in spite of his love of this new attention to his family, Ram accused Anick of attracting people by lasciviousness and ugly flirtation. His son might have been worth three hundred dollars an hour in cash; but even Nayan knew that this worth had been increased by Anick's presence in his life in ways that numbers and dollars could not measure. On his return to Trinidad, despite his lack of previous business experience, he was asked to sit on the boards of a number of charitable organizations. He joked to those who invited him that they were really after his wife, and they joked back that he was not at all a foolish man. He went to one or two meetings when he was asked, but the unpaid work of being on a board did not interest him.

Anick, for her part, hated the attention most of the time, but there were times when she enjoyed it just as much. She had joined a family with what seemed like a bottomless pool of cash at their disposal. She began to have her clothing designed especially for her by a well-known designer in the north of the island whose clients were often photographed by the local paparazzi for the society pages of the daily newspapers and for the Caribbean's glossy lifestyle magazines. She took Nayan to this designer, too, and they dressed him, and he and she soon became one of the most photographed couples in the Caribbean, although Nayan always looked a little lost and posed in those photos.

Anick pushed and pulled Nayan into a world of high living and society that he and his family, in spite of their business connections and wealth, had not previously easily participated in. He felt as if Anick were trying to reeducate him in her ways, to her liking. Rumours and gossip ran rampant in those circles about this one's wife sleeping with that one, and it was all taken lightly, as if for granted. There was, to his mind, just too much freedom among these people, and Anick swam, goddamn her, like a fish in this company. There was talk of parties where only women congregated, and even ones where men — men who were married — met one another, and that was going too far for him. Much too far. Particularly because he knew his wife had particular tendencies to start with.

Nayan felt acutely that Anick was embarrassed by him and his family. And he, in turn, was embarrassed by his whole situation. He was no longer Ram Prakash's son. He was Anick's husband. If in public he appeared to relish this, it was because he could not do otherwise.

Before he had returned to Trinidad, Rimpty's cacao and chocolates were sold in grocery stores, mixed on the sweet shelf with Cadbury, Bentley's, Lilly's, and Nestle. But on his return, Nayan had managed to secure a stand for Rimpty's alone, with a banner that showed a man much like himself looking out at the buyer he was courting, grinning and holding a plump heart-shaped chocolate between his thumb and fingers, that hand hovering at the parted lips of a woman who was watching him with eyes that suggested that chocolate was a precursor to other pleasures. Nayan, the son of Ram, was becoming the face of, and synonymous with, Rimpty's Cacao and Rimpty's Chocolates.

Still, even though people were beginning to talk about his business acumen and in spite of his occasional unfortunate boasts of how much he was worth in dollars, Nayan felt as if he was worth not a damn cent. He drank more now than he had ever done. And he easily became quite inebriated on very few drinks.

His routine was to come home sober from work, but rigid with tension, the veins in his neck like large green worms pushing up under his skin. He would look for Anick and curtly tell her he was going to see his mother, and then leave her to do whatever it was she had so clearly busied herself doing even though she knew it was the time he would be home. He would leave his shoes just off the rug in the living room in the meagre section of the house he and she had to themselves, and march directly to the kitchen in the main part of the house. From the fridge he would pull a beer, and he would hoist himself up on one of the counters, grunting his displeasure, words barely able to escape his gritted teeth. His mother would make him fresh roti and baigan choka or pumpkin, and while he waited for the food he would drink another, perhaps two more beers. Eventually he would get the words out, but now they would be slurred: His father had no respect for him or his ideas. His father was old-fashioned. He had been sent to university to do business, and now his father wouldn't listen to his ideas, wouldn't agree to cultivating quality beans for export or making a new chocolate. If only he could be given the chance to prove himself.

He would later retreat to the living room in his part of the house, fall asleep in front of the TV he had turned up loud, the unread newspaper folded on his belly. Eventually he would make his way to bed well before Anick. She would likely have hidden herself away on the outside patio, talking on the phone with her family and friends in France. He had the sense that she was bad-talking him or his country. Or she would be in the little room they called an office, writing letters — no doubt letters of complaint.

ALTHOUGH SHE ATTRACTED MUCH ATTENTION AND NO ONE THOUGHT her shy, Anick guarded her privacy fiercely. She might have been in demand initially at the homes of neighbours and friends, but after a time it was noticeable to her parents-in-law and to Nayan that she kept a distance from these people. She seemed to give more of herself to people she was unlikely to come in contact with too often. She more easily accepted the invitations that came to her and Nayan from acquaintances in the north, the capital. She would ask for the chauffeur for a day, and reluctantly Nayan would jeopardize that day's relationship with his father to secure the man, and Anick would take off for lunch with people they hardly knew. He couldn't understand why she wouldn't take to family friends closer to home. He sweated with worry about what, exactly, of herself she might have been giving, and to whom.

The only people in the south Anick did not shy away from were the members of the Krishnu family. She and Viveka were making small steps, Nayan noticed with a little happiness, toward becoming friends. Viveka was one of the people Anick would speak with on the phone, and apparently Viveka had begun to brush up on her high school French. Informal French conversations on the telephone with Viveka, in fact, had become a pleasurable project for Anick, and this made her just a little more pleasant for Nayan to be around. It occupied her, and separated them from each other with some calm for at least a hour in an evening — although Nayan did sit in front of the TV more than once and wonder what on earth the two of them might have in common. He hoped his wife wasn't making a fool of herself with an old family friend. In the meantime, in the peace and quiet of his living room, he would dull himself with one ice cold beer after another.

By the time Anick got into bed, Nayan was an immovable snoring weight, unaware of her presence. He awoke before she did and left the house for work, already entirely consumed by strategies for making his autocratic old-fashioned father understand the direction in which Rimpty's, by hook or by crook, must head.

Anick's parents sent her packages of goods unavailable in Trinidad, things that they knew she missed. There were regular treks to the post office at the wharf at the foot of Luminada Heights to pick up jars of Dijon mustard, champagne mustard, coarse honey mustard, slabs of nougat, marzipan, jars of Beluga caviar, and for Nayan, chocolates they collected for him, among them always one or two that had been made with fine premium from Trinidad. From the first, Nayan was peeved that Anick's parents felt they had to furnish her with these items, as if he and Trinidad could not offer her things that would adequately satisfy her demanding tastes. He was, too, irked by their gifts of chocolate. He interpreted these as her family trying to show him what quality chocolate was — and he was now well aware that his family's estate grew a strain of cacao that produced a bean French chocolatiers wouldn't have considered worthy of an exhalation. Even as Anick helped Nayan develop a presence in Trinidad society, and even as Anick was afforded luxuries she could only, before her marriage, have dreamed of, in private the two of them were growing apart.

The quality of Rimpty's chocolates eventually became a source of contention between Nayan and his father, but it was only one of many quarrels brewing in the Prakash house. Ram Prakash could not warm to his French daughter-in-law, even though he was pleased that his son was doing the kind of socializing he had never before had the skill for. Ram saw this as purposeful. It was, to his mind, work. Whenever Nayan and Anick returned from a party he would call Nayan into his home office and sit him down. He would close the door, take out his date book, and ask Nayan who he had met that might be of use to their business, if he had made any appointments to meet with these men, if he had opened — or even better, closed — any deals.

He often held his hand out to Nayan and said: Come, shake your father's hand. Let me see how strong and firm that handshake is. You could close a deal with a handshake, you know, boy, even before you state what it is you have to sell. When you meet a person — you haven't even told them what you want, but you have shaken their hand. That is the beginning or the end. Right there. That handshake. And let me see your face when you do it. Look right in my eyes. The eyes and the hand. Let them do the first talking.

How Nayan wished he could wrench himself away, jab his father in his chest with the butt of his elbow.

As Nayan flirted, eventually only on occasion, with the cream of the country's businessmen and their wives, he came to see more than his insular father could have: He, Nayan, needed to transform more than his dress, and to rely on more than his wife. He and his father needed to diversify Rimpty and Son. He would pay attention to how he lived his life — not just in the service of making more and more money, but also by paying attention to "quality of life." He would blend sound business practice with personal interest and passion. Nayan would begin importing — but not just anything. He would furnish the country with the variety and quality of goods, luxuries, conveniences, and services he had observed in France. He would instill in Trinidadians a pride in themselves while creating something Trinidadian that was synonymous in the outside world with quality. A Frenchman, he had noticed, took it for granted that pen and mountain had the same name, but was too close to the source to know that the rest of the world held the pen in high regard but might not know of the mountain. What if the name of the Prakash business, and the name of the produce of that business — Rimpty's — was changed to the name of the area where they had their estate and where cacao was grown in abundance: Rio Claro? And what if that product and place name became known in major international centres, synonymous with the highest quality cacao and chocolate in the entire world? What might that little piece of intervention on his and his father's part do for the spirit of the Trinidadian? What would it do for Nayan's own sense of self?

During his short visit to France, Nayan had experienced again and again how small the rest of the world saw him to be. In the streets he had come face to face with what appeared to be an almost official reproach for his colour. He was not unaware of these slights but had no stomach to speak of them to Anick. His money — rather, his father's money — which he had doled out in France with the generosity of one who came by it easily, could not buy French respect. The shade of his skin stained every transaction. The more scorned Nayan felt the more money he spent, and the grander the restaurants he took Anick to, and the more extravagant the presents he bought her, her parents, himself.

In France he had watched, albeit sideways, the lives of non-white immigrants. He walked in the Maghrebi neighbourhood of Perpignan and scrutinized the Moroccans, Algerians, and Gypsies when he thought neither they nor his wife was looking. He found himself ashamed of these people — the few blacks, notably Haitians and West Africans, and the Indians and Pakistanis he saw there — and yet, he was equally in awe of them and their communities. From the distance of the outsider he detected in them an understanding of the world, its ways with them, and how to navigate, slide past, or use those ways to their advantage. It was a sense and knowledge vaster than his, a useful one, and in this — even though he was the son of Ram Prakash — he saw his own inexperience and ignorance. If being Ram Prakash's son was of no consequence to anyone in France, at least that fact gave him the temerity to transform his loathing into ambition. He would to show the world that he and his fellow countrymen knew what quality was, enjoyed good service, and indulged in the finest luxury items. He would one day show all this to Anick's parents. He would show white France, and the immigrant populations there. He would show Canadians. He would show other Trinidadians. He would show Anick.

Now, from the privacy of his home office, and certainly without his father's knowledge, he wrote to companies in Europe and had their catalogues and sales pitches sent to him, and taught himself what European standards of quality and class looked like, what items created the impression of being in the know and having expectations. The Trinidadians his wife was attracting regularly left Trinidad and went abroad to spoil themselves, and he had it in his mind to provide them — and not only them, but people who were more like himself — with some of this.

Although he had been at school in Canada for four years, Canada hadn't drilled a gaping hole in his sense of self like his short visit to France had. Canada had offered him before-unknown experiences, too, but not experiences that his wife and the kinds of Trinidadians with whom she enjoyed socializing relished and hungered after. For one thing, there was too much blending of all the races and classes on the streets of Toronto. It seemed as if almost anybody — with hard work or a good dose of luck — could make leaps in economic status. This meant that people who worked in Trinidad as store clerks or as servants or as unskilled labourers went to Canada, worked for a while, and returned to Trinidad, having come to expect a standard of commodities and services that only the wealthier Trinidadians had access to. This irked the Trinidadians who had been born into ready-made comfort. It was their workers who acquired fancier tastes, expectations, manners, and a sense of self-worth in Canada, things that made these workers feel as if, even after they returned to Trinidad, they were entitled.

Nayan knew he was one of those Trinidadians born into money and a particular comfort but not into the understanding of an international sense of style. He had felt in France that while a notable few were born into fortune, the French, by dint of being just that — French — regardless of their class came into the world with a sense of style as part of their heritage. He didn't know if this was true, but they certainly made you feel that they were the owners of all things cultural. And, of course, they were only encouraged in this when they were copied by others everywhere. High-society Trinidadians often left the island to purchase this international style. They went abroad to buy their home furnishings and clothing. And they didn't go to Canada to shop but to Europe. To London, England, Italy, and France.

It had been easy in Canada. He had been able to get away with his small-country brand of princeliness; he knew that he was to the white Canadians he called friends an entertainment. They had accepted him, he knew, in good part because of how flush — and generous — he was even while he appeared to be what the mother of one of them had flirtatiously called "charmingly unpretentious." Adrenalin flowed through him to show those Canadians, and all of France, to show the Trinidadians who were so enamoured of his French wife, to show every corner of the world, that he was not a small backward man, and that Trinidad was not a small backward island. Yes, he would start by revamping the family business. He thought about opening a department store that carried only designer and museum-quality items, and making Anick the "face" of it.

He excitedly spoke with her about this idea and she laughed out loud before becoming angry that he would use her in such a way when neither he nor she had expertise in this kind of buying and selling and she would only make a fool of herself. She was disdainful that he would think to procure these kinds of goods and then put them up for sale. It was her sense that anyone who owned such goods had never been without them. Things of monetary value were not bought but were inherited, and then passed on in an unbroken chain. She wanted Nayan to help her, rather, to pull together classical musicians from the various schools she had heard about across the country and to fund the making of a symphony.

It was his turn to laugh, and to point out how little she understood of business.

Anick tried to tell Nayan about businesses and family foundations that gave back to society through their patronage of the arts, and that this in itself was good business, but as usual when she felt belittled, angered, or frustrated by Nayan and by her present situation, she was unable to find a language they shared to express herself. She ended up sounding like a simpleton, and Nayan took perverse pleasure in pointing this out to her, imitating her particular pronunciation of English words, and the phrasing and construction of her sentences. She dared not complain about any of this to her parents for fear of worrying them and because she did not want to admit, or appear to have made, a very big mistake.

Meanwhile, Nayan knew better than to talk with his father about the luxury-car detailing business or the haberdashery shop he imagined, all under the umbrella of a new "Ramayan Enterprises" or perhaps "Ramnayan Enterprises" or "Ramnayana Enterprises." He played with his and his father's names, and even added his mother's into the mix and he came up with Ramanayaminty Enterprises, which, despite its length, was his favourite. He obsessed over, under, around, and behind the pros and cons of buying up the entire strip of land that was Maracas Beach, and then about the design and details of the three hotels he imagined, each one rivalling the next with its extravagance and understanding of what five-star and pampering meant. He dreamt of wiping out whole neighbourhoods and replacing them with tropical residential architecture, homes whose interiors consisted of only the most exclusive sourced goods. He wanted to be known as the man who knew *the finest*, as a style-maker. He and Anick would travel far and wide to do all sourcing.

In the end, Nayan knew it was wisest to stick with and make the most of what was already in his hand. He would begin in his own backyard. They wouldn't have to embark on an entirely new direction but rather could make significant changes replanting the entire estate — not all at once, but five acres or so at a time until the whole was updated with one of the more modern varieties of cacao developed in the Agricultural Department of the University. The Trinidad Selected Hybrid, he knew from his research, produced a heftier, denser yield of pods that were the source of that fine premium cacao so cherished abroad. His cacao would be of such a superior quality that it would surpass that of the Ivory Coast, Madagascar, Venezuela, Ecuador, and all other chocolate-producing countries to become the main ingredient in the world's, and France's, top-ranked chocolates. He would encourage his father, too, to use this same cacao in the production of a better, more refined chocolate that would be sold right here on the island to the ordinary Trinidadian on the street. There would be a true chocolate alternative to the generic milky-sweet thing that passed for chocolate now, the only thing available to the people of a country that gave to foreigners the best of what it had and kept the least for itself. He would educate the palates of Trinidadians so that no foreigner, no Frenchwoman and her family, could look askance at them.

NAYAN'S HUMBLER AMBITIONS, NOT TO MENTION THE LOFTY ONES, were ill-received by his father:

"You live abroad four years, and it was four years too long, boy. You go abroad and come back feeling as if you know more than an old man like me. You think because you are the first in this family to get a university degree that you know more than me? Your wife likes one kind of chocolate so I must make that kind of chocolate. I never hear more! Well, my wife likes jewellery, but not just any kind of jewellery. She likes diamonds. You think I picking up and moving to South Africa, or opening a diamond necklace and earring store?"

Quarrels between the outdated autocrat (as Nayan thought of his father) and pie-in-the-sky entrepreneur (as Ram thought of his son) erupted every day. But business strategies, cacao, chocolate, citrus, modern methods and style were not the only, or even the real, issue between the two.

Curse words punctuated the mumbled rambles Nayan aimed at his father, who would invariably be out of earshot. Ram, for his part, alternately slighted Nayan and Anick, and hurled abuse at Nayan, and Minty was in tears over it all. Anick, her skin cold and clammy in the heat, her hair forever wet about her forehead and neck, sought refuge from the strife in letters written and read and in phone calls made from the little office, now unused by Nayan, that she was able to make her own.

Nayan dared not do outright battle with his father. He fought Anick instead. With her, he began to sound like Ram, who, having caught her lying on the lawn on a beach towel in her bathing suit, had called Nayan into his bedroom, shut the door, and shouted, "What is she doing parading half-naked like that in my yard for all the neighbours to see? This is a Hindu house and we have Hindu values in this house. This is not a country club. What kind of slackness is this? She and you making my blood pressure sky rocket. I don't care if it is the back of the house. How many times I have to say this? Sunning, my arse. An Indian girl would know better."

Nayan attempted to respond, but his words were an unfortunate mix of apology and incredulity at his father's old-fashioned intolerance. Ram cut him short and lashed back, "What? You correcting my English, my comprehension, now? You crazy? Don't back chat with me, child. I don't care that she is lying on a beach towel. My backyard is no beach. Standing up, lying down, sitting in a chair, as long as she is wearing that damn skimpy thing you call a bathing suit, she is parading herself as far as I am concerned. You don't understand my English, or what? You want me to start speaking that damn nonsense the two of you can't even manage between you? What is wrong with you that you can't keep you wife in check, boy? Even inside my house that dress she is always wearing — a dress with no sleeves, only string to hold it up, all her back exposed like she is at the beach. I call that nakedness and parading."

It wasn't long before Nayan himself began to criticize Anick for these very things.

On another occasion, Ram watched Anick eat roti and curried goat with a knife and fork. That night, Nayan approached the television room on his parents' side of the house to overhear his father snapping, "I am not eating at the same table with a woman who is eating roti with a knife and fork, making me feel like a country-bookie in my own house because I eat my food with my hands like I and all my ancestors and every Indian worth a grain of salt have done since time immemorial. He is teaching her all kinds of things — he can't teach her to use her hands, or is she just too highfalutin for our ways?"

Nayan soon became embarrassed by the ethnic French foods Anick cooked at home for his parents, who had no interest in adventure with food. He tired, too, of her French accent, which not only showed itself for company who would be moved by its novelty or in moments when it might have aroused him, but existed every single time she opened her mouth. The constant fumbling for the right word, the inversion of sentences, the accents placed on the wrong syllables, the substitution of whole French words for English ones or a French pronunciation for an English one. These idiosyncrasies that had once charmed him now angered him, and never went away.

Still, once out in public Nayan paraded Anick like she was a trophy. He no longer, however, took lightly the harmless flirtations with other men he had once encouraged, and neither did he find the men's attentions to Anick provocative.

EVENTUALLY, NAYAN BEGAN TO STAY AWAY FROM HOME FOR AS LONG as possible, coming in late, too inebriated to converse with anyone. Anick continued to complain about being left alone with his mother with nothing to do all day, no one to speak with, unable to invite friends to visit her at home. She complained about not being taken to movies or concerts or art galleries, and about not being able to move about the city or island with any freedom. In response, Nayan began to pick her up after work and deposit her at the house of one of his friends, Baldwin Kissoon, a man whose family owned a grocery store, a tire shop, and a garage that outfitted cars with stereo systems. Bally, as he was called, was married to a quiet woman named Shanti. They had three small children and lived on narrow but busy Rushworth Street above the garage.

Nayan would leave Anick upstairs with Shanti and the children, and he and Bally would go down to the road-level garage where cars to be serviced were haphazardly parked, tightly packed, on the asphalt driveway, the pedestrian sidewalk, and the road in front of the house. In Bally's office at the back of the garage there was a glass window that looked out onto the shop. The door and walls of that office were thick enough to dull the sounds of the audio tests, the *voomp voomp voomp* of the base in particular. Here, Bally would show Nayan small items he had snuck into the country from Miami, Florida, under the radar of Customs — radar detectors, CD players, global navigation systems. After a little while, Nayan and Bally would go to the Red Stallion, a bar that was little more than a rum and roti shop, a short way down the road. The owners, two brothers, were generous with the size and flow of the drinks they served, and the four men together would occupy a special, reserved table. They would fantasize about importing and exporting together and Nayan would talk about wanting to enter into business ventures on his own, without his father. Still, he would never reveal the details of his real ambitions. He didn't want to give his ideas away, and he also knew that these three friends would not understand creating and selling the particular lifestyle that haunted Nayan.

When Nayan, made brazen and shameless as the evening wore on, complained to Bally, Bally would remind him that children tamed a woman. A child, a boy in particular, would please Nayan's father and mother, and might even tame them too, while the gift would also warm them to Anick. Nayan felt, though, as if he were holding on to his marriage by a tether too frayed to take the huge and binding leap into fatherhood. When he said this to Bally, Bally advised that children were also the glue that kept marriages together, something that he considered important in a small place like Trinidad. He gave his opinions freely. One should marry only for the right reasons, and love was the least of them.

"You married for love, not so, boy?"

Nayan nodded.

Bally laughed and sucked his teeth at the same time. "Thought so. You have more money than brains, boy. You know why I marry Shanti?"

Nayan, as crude as he allowed himself to be when he socialized with Bally, was not keen to know.

"You don't see them hips, boy? Don't get me wrong. She is a good girl. I know she isn't a beauty queen, but she born to be a mother. When I tell you — she is a real good girl in the house. A man can't ask for more. And what you do outside of the house have nothing to do with what you doing inside. That is the beauty of the thing. Inside. Outside. Two different things. You get what I saying?" He advised Nayan, "Have two or three children, and do it quick. Don't waste time in that department. It will occupy your wife. Then provide for her and the children, so not one complaint along those lines could be made about you, and then you live your life as you please. As you please, boy!"

Nayan did wonder if he had more money than brains. Whatever had existed between him and Anick when they had first got together in Whistler and later in London, Ontario, and then in France, had ended within weeks of their arrival in Trinidad. And now Anick recoiled when he came to her. She shrugged off his romantic overtures, and faced with his urgent desires she found a thousand things that needed her own urgent attentions or she started a serious and effectively dulling discussion. She no longer touched him, no longer let her fingers linger and trace his body as he remembered her doing in a manner that had once driven him dizzy with every form of desire, from a primordial pining for the touch and love between two human beings, any two humans, through a range of feeling with her as its specific object, from unabashed lasciviousness to the readiness to hand over his present and his future to no one else but this person within whose body, when he entered it, that desire was diffused and his intention to keep her for himself made clear. He had wanted her to become pregnant in those days, had wanted her to publicly carry his child, a child who would be half her and half him. But now a child could come, with such coolness between them, only by force, and into a relationship that he was quite unsure of wanting.

The thought that others wondered just what it was that he had — besides money — that could have attracted to him a woman like Anick played on his mind and emotions. Nayan wondered what these others would think of him for marrying a woman who, before marriage, had lived in a way that was so contrary to everything he had been taught was proper in a woman and a wife. What if they knew of her past affairs with other women? What would they think of him then? Even though it was well in the past, this was a major aspect of what drove him apart from Anick now.

For a time, Bally thought that Nayan was an idiot for complaining about his wife when he, Bally, would give anything to have a woman like Anick bring up his children, cook his food, lie with him in his bed. In time, he realized that Anick was not the type of woman who would consent to live above a store on a busy road, nor to stay at home to look after him, the house, and children. Bally wanted to help his friend, and offered his wife's company. Shanti could show Anick, by example, how to keep an Indian man's home, while Anick might inspire Shanti to be less shy, to lose some weight, dress a little less conservatively — in short, inspire in him the kind of chivalry and desire he felt, without speaking of it to Nayan of course, for Anick.

But what happened was that one of the children came to look forward to Anick's visits and waited up for her arrival. Anick was obliged to read stories to him, change him into his pyjamas, and tuck him into bed. At first it was sweet, cute, funny, but although Shanti tried to show her best face, resentment coloured her cheeks. Bally treated Anick as if she were the child's surrogate mother, and this irritated both women. It was not Anick's favourite way to spend an evening. Still, Shanti sewed well, and there was much looking at magazines and talk of what would look good on Shanti, what would look good on Anick, and what of these Shanti might make. The women even went out on their own in the daytime, with a chauffeur provided by Nayan, to the fabric store down the road. But Anick could only do so much of this kind of socializing, and no more.

Meanwhile, Anick was not unaware of Bally's attentions and fielded his underhanded advances, not daring to tell Nayan. Neither Nayan nor Shanti knew that Bally phoned Anick at home, and that she as often entertained his calls as she chided him for them. In the end, though, she couldn't understand why Nayan chose to have such a close friendship with a man who was not as educated as he, and whose background was so different from his. In France it would not have mattered to Anick that a man like Bally did not know his father. Nor would it have mattered in France that Bally, having not inherited anything, had to rely on himself for a future. His fortitude and acumen, viewed through one of that culture's lenses, might well have been lauded. But within the Trinidadian culture Anick was slipping into unconsciously (even as, at other times, she rebuffed it consciously), Bally was sorely lacking. His heritage could not be determined, and his longevity in business had no precedence.

And so the once-carefree Frenchwoman, in trying to grab onto a slippery foothold in Trinidad, finally chose sides. She begged Nayan to make an effort to befriend businesspeople with longer and more presence in business — the ones, for instance, who took pride in their work and country, paid attention to the architecture of the buildings that housed their businesses and to the design of their homes, and certainly those who patronized charities and the arts. These were often the same people who holidayed abroad, not just in Miami for the sole purpose of business or profit, profit, profit, but in London, Paris, Venice, Delhi, Mexico City, places that packaged and sold their histories. They went for the sheer enjoyment of getting away and of learning, experiencing the new. These people were, too, the same ones who tended to have holiday homes on the small islands in the Gulf of Paria, an archipelago known as "down the islands," and had yachts, racing boats, and racing horses, and who had expressed the desire umpteen times to get together with Nayan and Anick.

But Nayan now accused Anick of wanting to spend time with these people because they were so worldly that they would accept or even laud her strange sexual deviance. He had watched them carefully and he saw suggestions in some of the men and the women of homosexual tendencies. He spotted signs that he was unable to adequately articulate. Trying to warn Anick, he could only say, "Well, don't you see how short her hair is? And how big her hands are?" And, "Why does he have to wear a bag like that? He is not in Paris or Rome. There isn't anything a man carries around that can't fit in his pants pocket. He wears it because he wants to hold a handbag."

What frightened and angered him was that he couldn't be sure what these apparent signs actually meant. He watched every interaction Anick had with these particular other women, to see how they looked at each other or touched each other, and feeling vulnerable by association himself, he monitored the other men's interactions with him. They so easily touched each other, but not with the slaps on the back or big animated handshakes he shared with Bally and other men who were more like himself. The gestures of these men were small, too delicate to be coming from real men. They seemed so reserved and polite and good-humoured, clean-humoured, on the outside, but who hadn't heard of their transgressions? These people Anick liked so much better than his simpler family friends such as Bally and the Krishnus, these rich types who did all this travelling, the ones from the other islands and from Port of Spain, too — despite the longing for acceptance they incited in Nayan, they made him a little sick.

Nayan demanded to know what Anick felt was lacking in him and his family. Pressed to answer, she accused him of using Bally's insufficiencies to boost his own ego. Such transparency in Nayan only angered him. He could not openly fight Anick in his father's house as he might have fought had they been in a house of their own. So he found quiet but deeply cutting ways to respond. He stayed away from home even more often, and drank everyday, even with his lunch. He declined, as if out of spite, invitations from the people in the north, and those from anyone of interest to Anick, in favour of spending time with Bally or having a drink with his workers. Anick had no choice but to forgo those invitations and instead visit with Bally's wife — if, that is, she didn't want to stay at home with Nayan's parents. And she certainly did not.

WHEN, A COUPLE OF WEEKS AFTER HER DINNER AT THE PRAKASHS, Viveka invited Nayan and Anick to her parents' house for a meal that she herself would cook, Nayan implored Anick to go without him. He would call Viveka and tell her that Anick was free but that he had a previous engagement, and he would take the opportunity to see Bally about some business. He didn't tell Anick that he wouldn't be able to bear watching her be the centre of attention, a position that made him feel ridiculed. He imagined, with disdain, Anick and Viveka tossing between them the names of artists, musicians, writers, cultural movements. And he imagined himself and the rest of his family made out to be dolts.

Viveka

FOR TEN DAYS, VIVEKA HAD RESEARCHED VARIOUS COOKING TRADItions and recipes. The information she devoured on food and chefs of the highest regard internationally cited either French or Chinese or both traditions as having the major influence and as the two greatest culinary traditions in the world. If she had come across a statement like that in one of her courses at the university she would have flown into an intellectual tizzy about who had the power, investments, and narrow-mindedness to make such ridiculous declarations, but now she merely seized on the notion and decided to match Anick's meal of boeuf bourguignon with something Chinese of equal grandeur. After hours spent at the university's library and on the Internet, she put together a meal of several courses that consisted of regional recipes cited as "authentic" by their Chinese author-chefs. As there had long been a good-sized Chinese population, and therefore a tradition of Chinese food, in Trinidad, ingredients such as dried mushrooms, dried tangerine peels, five-spice powder, Shaoxing wine and more were easily available.

Devika and Vashti set the table, and even though there were the four Krishnus and only one guest, the table was rather formal. They did not have the style of dishes in which authentic

Chinese courses would have been served, so they made do with the best there was: white bone china dishes with a heavy twenty-four-karat gold border, and the heavy cut-lead crystal wine and water glasses from Brazil, and the silver-plate cutlery that was otherwise kept in a locked buffet cabinet drawer and used only for special guests. Viveka's mother had made for the top of the buffet cabinet a lovely arrangement of flowers from the garden, yellow and deep pink gerberas, white chrysanthemums, with long unruly strands of purple baby bougainvilleas dramatically waving out of it all. There were candles, too. Nothing had been spared for this sole guest. For anyone else she might have thought it too much, but Viveka was pleased.

The meal turned out well, but sadly for Viveka, there wasn't much comment on the food except to say, My God, this is a lot, a veritable feast! And conversation at the dinner table was strained. Usually, a dinner with friends at that same table would have been a lively affair and laughter would fill the room, a good mix of lewd jokes scattered like chips on a gambling table by Valmiki and even by Devika — once she had sipped a glass or two of wine. And there would be some pertinent gossip, some local politics, some local news, and catching-up types of conversation. But this evening was subdued. Anick's hesitant English, and the Krishnu family's inability to see that, in order for her to comprehend, a certain amount of background information was necessary on just about every person, place, or thing that they spoke of, resulted in conversation that was restrained. No one was at ease.

After groping about in the dark forest of cultural difference for topics of mutual interest with this unusually private guest, Valmiki raised the subject of hunting as a pastime. This intrigued Anick. She was interested in the flora and fauna of the Trinidad forest and had finally been taken on a short walk into the forested cacao lands in Rio Claro, but said flatly that she was appalled by hunting as sport. Viveka intuited that Anick was hoping for a discussion on the ethics of hunting, but Valmiki wouldn't have thought to argue with any guest in his house, particularly a woman. He wasn't really interested in the flora or fauna and couldn't tell Anick much about the birds he had taken from the forests. That topic appeared and disappeared like a shooting star.

As everyone fumbled through the dinner, they occasionally heard the birds whistle to one another from their cages. Now Valmiki felt self-conscious and childish for having trapped them. What Devika wanted to talk about — Anick's parents-in-law and the cost of vegetables at the market — irritated Anick. She was unable to hide her irritation, and Viveka was embarrassed that her mother could talk of nothing else, not even to show an interest in Anick's past or to hear her opinions of Trinidad and life here. After dessert of cold red-bean-and-tapioca soup, Devika and Valmiki made their apologies and retired earlier than usual.

Vashti was curious about Nayan's foreign wife at first, but out on the patio as Viveka and Anick bonded over their mutual interest in the fine arts, literature, philosophy, and other subjects, she became bored. She drifted into daydreaming, and eventually roused herself and turned in.

Once she and Viveka were alone, Anick initiated the French conversation practice they had begun by phone over the past couple of weeks.

"D'accord, mais je suis... timid," ventured Viveka.

"Pas timid. Timide. Tee-meede."

"Tee-meede? Oh, okay. Je suis timide. Is that better?"

“Oui, tres bien. Mais, c’est mieux si tu developpes un bon accent des le debut.”

“Oh my God. I didn’t... Je ne comprend pas... a single mot... tu as dis. You’ll have to... Lentement... Okay, okay. Let me try this.... Pouvez vous parler plus lentement, si’l vous plait?”

This kind of exchange seemed, oddly, more intimate to Viveka than when she and Elliot had kissed. It was a little frightening, and yet she felt brazen. She had pushed Elliot away, but now she so easily laid the vulnerability of fumbling for language like a cloak on the ground for Anick to tread on.

It was Anick who eventually called the impromptu session to a close and the two women reverted to English. It was as if they had been in a movie theatre, watching something beautiful yet a little illicit, and suddenly the movie had ended and the lights had come on. But now that they were alone, Anick spoke English with much less hesitation than she had done at the table, and this too seemed intimate. There grew between them a boldness and a closeness that both frightened and weakened Viveka. There had been wine at the dinner table, they had drunk modestly and eaten heartily. That had been a couple of hours ago, and now Viveka felt as pleasantly drunk as if she and Anick had just shared a magnum between them.

EVENTUALLY, NAYAN ROLLED HIS CAR UP. VIVEKA COULD SEE HIM making his way in drunken bliss to the door. Anick appeared suddenly sober in the glare of his presence. He wanted to sit with them on the patio, stay for a while, but Anick insisted on leaving right away.

After they left, Viveka locked up the house and readied herself as quietly as she could for bed. She lay wide awake for hours thinking about what had transpired between her and Anick when they had been left alone. Anick had been sitting on the loveseat of the patio set, and Viveka, at first, on an armchair. She had gone to the kitchen to get them both drinks of sorrel, and when she returned she tucked herself into the loveseat, managing in that small sofa to create enough space between them for still another person to slide in. Both women now looked straight out into the darkness of the garden, the lights of Pointe-à-Pierre shimmering beyond.

Anick had rested her hand in the space between them, close to Viveka's knee, and Viveka could feel Anick's hand as if it were a flame as big and bright as one on the oil rigs in the gulf. She glanced down at it, so much wanting to pick it up as if it were a delicate leaf, turn it over, and examine it. She was distracted from conversation by this proximity, and felt a suffocating weight in her chest, heat coursing up and down her body. In the quiet that fell between her and Anick, Viveka's legs tensed. She wanted to cry and laugh at the same time. Anick turned to look at her. Viveka hoped more than anything that her face gave nothing away of these delightful and terrifying sensations. She glanced toward Anick, who was still watching her intently. Anick smiled and Viveka looked ahead again, now staring at the Pointe-à-Pierre jetty, watching every single building and light out there. She tried to count the lights.

There was an awkward moment, and then Anick said, "I feel something. Do you feel what I feel?"

Viveka felt as if she had been hit. Her body was drained of all previous sensations, as if a cold gust had come in from across the gulf and stunned her. She felt the need to blunt Anick's words, make a joke of them quickly, kill the strange and frightening thing that Anick was perhaps about to say.

"An earthquake?" Viveka had snapped over a chuckle of indignation, and just then Nayan's car had pulled up outside.

Anick looked as if her heart had stopped beating. She made a sound, somewhere between a wince and truncated gasp. Viveka didn't know if this was in response to her words or to Nayan's arrival. Their parting was awkward. Anick didn't seem to know if she should give the accustomed goodbye hug and kiss on the cheek. Viveka came toward her and pressed her cheek to Anick's. She took Anick's hand. It was no leaf. Anick squeezed hers back, lightly, but in that lightness was the weight of the evening.

Now Viveka relived the touch of cheek and hand, and each time without fail felt a rush of dizzying desire. It was weakness, daunting and wonderful, that began in her toes and washed quickly upwards, to land between her legs, gripping her there in ecstasy, and then it made its way back down again. Over and over. She put the back of the hand that had held Anick's to her mouth, and with her lips closed, brushed it. As if it had a mind of its own, her mouth opened and again brushed the skin of that hand. She came down hard now, her parted lips to that hand, teeth pressing into skin, and this made her cry out. The sound was thankfully muffled. She flicked the tip of her tongue, moistening the area, finally eating that part of her hand as if it were the fleshiest part of a ripe mango. She heard again her lame words, "An earthquake?" Surely Nayan would have responded differently if Anick had said those words to him. She tried to imagine how he might have replied, or what some chivalrous man would have said, and she was caught in a riptide of confusion and excitement. What if she had said something as simple as: *Yes. I, too, feel something*?

THE NEXT DAY, ANICK CALLED VIVEKA TO EXPRESS HER GRATITUDE for one of the lovelier evenings spent so far in Trinidad. Still, it seemed that no immediate time or space could be found for them to visit again. This was a small but painful relief to Viveka. Thoughts of Merle Bedi's fate played in her mind. Later that week, she took a trip down to the Harris Promenade to see if she might spot Merle, and was both grateful and sad that Merle was nowhere to be seen. She had no plan for what she might do or say had they come face to face.

As the next few days passed, Viveka oscillated between two poles. She decided one minute to still whatever thoughts and feelings Anick Prakash had stirred in her. Such thoughts and feelings were dangerous tricksters out to trip her up and land her, like Merle, out on her own, family-less. And Anick Prakash, being the root of such thought, was even more dangerous. A troublemaker. Brave. Stupid. Disrespectful of Trinidad, its people, its ways.

But there was always the other pole: the desire to see, speak with, touch Anick Prakash was like the pull of a tidal wave against which Viveka decidedly did *not* want any cautioning or power.

But Anick had withdrawn. There was that one phone call of thanks, and a few days later, one other phone conversation — so brief, it left Viveka feeling shunned. She had mustered the courage and called Anick just to say hello, perhaps for a little French conversation, but Anick was oddly formal and distant. For several days afterwards, Viveka spent most of her time in the study with her feet up on the desk, locked at the ankles, and a book on her lap. She would stare in the direction of her feet and wonder if Anick had ever really said, "I feel something. Do you feel what I feel?"

During this time, Viveka withdrew from Helen and lost interest in volleyball. She spent more time than usual sleeping. In bed, she would not kiss her hand nor touch herself while imagining kissing and touching Anick Prakash. She would rather clutch her pillow as she curled into the smallest ball she could make of herself, and as fast as she could, she would fall into a heavy, sad sleep.

After a week or so of this, the reality of the larger situation dawned on Viveka and she was appalled at herself—appalled that she had not before been affronted by Anick's disloyalty to her husband, to Viveka's friendship with Nayan, to the Prakashs' closeness to the Krishnus. She didn't know who she felt more loathing for, herself or Anick.

Soon, it was nearing the year's end and the beginning of a school holiday. Viveka thought of Anick occasionally but with bitterness. Had Anick meant to provoke her, or simply to mock and expose something she thought she detected in her? Viveka felt twinges of what could only be termed hatred toward Anick for making her feel things that confused her and that could easily have got her into unimaginable trouble. Not so unimaginable, actually, for hadn't she seen how much her mother had suffered from her father's philandering? And Merle Bedi's fate was indeed very real.

Around this time, Viveka noticed that her face seemed to be getting more angular. She stood in front of the mirror and pulled her hair back so that its length disappeared. She was even more certain now that she looked like Anand would have, had he been alive. If he resembled their father in photographs taken at the same age, he would have been rather handsome. Viveka, too, looked like her father, but that only made her ugly, she thought, not handsome. She let her hair fall again and held a pair of earrings from a dish on the dresser up to her ears. Her heart sank. She actually looked more frightful with them. Should she, she wondered, dress more like a woman and look rather ungainly, ugly even, or dress the way she liked to dress, in her T-shirts, jeans, slippers, her long hair parted to one side and left hanging down, no jewellery save perhaps for a single plain ring? Like this, she was almost invisible. She preferred it that way. It was as if she had slipped into a crack where there was no gender-name for what she was. It was feeble consolation to think that she was still developing. How long would that process take, she wondered, and what on earth would she evolve into? At least she had brains — something to fall back on. The ugliest people had a place — even in her mother's mind and, she had noticed, in many other people's minds, too — if they were smart enough.

She would use the holiday to take care of her friendships. She would resume contact with Helen who, like Viveka, on account of their family's financial stability, did not need to take on holiday employment. She would consider playing volleyball again.

She would study, too. She was refining her goal of becoming a literary critic, and was currently enjoying the notion of becoming a Naipaul scholar. She would embark on a study of early East Indian communal life in Trinidad, in the countryside, in the town and in the city, and she would theorize on the gulf between the cacao Indian and the sugar Indian. It would be one small step toward understanding Naipaul's work and Naipaul himself.

What she couldn't know was that the Prakash household was unravelling.

III Chayu

24 Weeks

Your Journey, Part Three

FROM SAN FERNANDO, THE JOURNEY DUE EAST BY CAR TO RIO CLARO begins at the San Fernando Roundabout. Within seconds you're in Cocoyea Village. The road is high, and on either side the land slopes into deep valleys of gently billowing sugar cane. The air becomes increasingly thick and sweet at the back of your throat, announcing your proximity to the sugar-cane factory at Sainte Madeleine. The ancestors of the Indians who worked these fields carry with them the stigma of impossibly hard manual work, for little pay, done under blazing sun amidst the threat of snakes and scorpions. You pass them, one of them immediately, an Indian man, risking life and grey limbs by walking on the edge of the shoulderless, two-lane road he must share with vehicles — from bicyclists to buffalo-led water carts. The man you have just passed is serious, appears to be humourless; sweat trickles down the side of his face. He is gaunt, and you attribute all of this to the common idea that the Indian leads a harsh life mired in notions of the irrevocability of one's fated lot in life.

Continue to travel due east, on an instant incline that undulates toward and well past your destination, riding high above sea level, and if you haven't become nauseous from the winding roads and near misses of cars flying around blind bend after blind bend, heading straight for your vehicle — or so it seems — you will be wide awake, fearfully watchful, expecting that if only you can spot the moment of impending impact your seeing it might aid in stopping it or allow you, at the very least, the opportunity to witness exactly how you were killed.

You pass wooden houses on either side of the road. They perch on stilts that reach far down the slopes, while a plank or two of wood connects the front of the house directly to the roadway. From the houses' eaves hang lush baskets of ornamental ferns. Some less-precariously situated houses have banister staircases from the house down to the yard, and then from the yard back up to the road. These staircases are lined with red milk and paint tins containing anthuriums, ferns, philodendrons, and other plants that are lush and bursting with caring. Curtains billow in open windows and rocking chairs trembling in the wind on the modest verandas look as if they have only just been abandoned in favour of some quotidian chore.

You pass little hubs of activity — cars pulled up in the paved driveway of a small grocery store attached to a bar, a roti shop, and opposite, a tire repair shop and air-conditioned hair salon advertising that it rents and sells videos of the latest Indian movies. The traffic has eased, but the pace continues easily, if only to keep up now with the quiet and calm of the land so far from the big town, lifestyles away to the west.

Then, quite suddenly, you're in the centre of the island, high above sea level, in the low mountains of the Central Range. Citrus, banana, peewah grown in small plots are now offered for sale roadside, but to stop on such narrow roads and make a purchase is to endanger yourself, the seller, the cars behind and ahead. Still, the stalls dot the road here and there, and in between, tied to lamp posts and water-stands, are wreaths and Christian crosses made of palm fronds, spent flowers tucked into them, topped with handwritten signs that say "R.I.P."

A little farther on, brilliant flame-coloured pods begin to dot the forests, and in time, fields of cacao planted in neat straight rows begin at the road's edge and stretch deep into the forest. The road meanders now with the most dangerous U-turns.

An hour has passed since leaving San Fernando, and finally you arrive in the village of Rio Claro. The last three miles of road into Rio Claro boast no less than thirteen well-patronized rum shops, a Catholic Church, a Pentecostal Church, the Open Bible Church, and a mosque. Hindu temples and shrines are not visible, but Hindu homes stand out with their collections of jhandi flags filling one corner prominently. The edges of the red-, saffron-, and white-cotton triangular pennants are frayed from billowing brightly in the breezes from the Atlantic Ocean on the eastern shore of the island, another forty-five minutes or so around the bend from here.

Just off the main road, still going east, you turn left at the first main road, and ask anyone—and they will jab their forefinger decidedly in the direction of Chayu.

The Prakashs

ENOUGH WAS FINALLY ENOUGH WHEN RAM AND NAYAN HAD STOPPED speaking with each other. Minty found unusual courage to speak her mind to Ram about his lack of respect for his son and his son's wife. Her stand produced no change in Rams's attitude toward his son and daughter-in-law but resulted, rather, in hours of silence smouldering between her and him. And Nayan couldn't make mention of his father to his mother without frothing curse words she didn't know he knew. She demanded in vain that Nayan have respect, if only when talking to her. She lost weight and slept little. Nayan, meanwhile, did not even come to eat supper, his mother's cooking, anymore. Morning and night there was the scent of beer on his body.

Minty knew it would be better for Nayan and Anick to be living on their own. They could move to Chayu. It was a little over an hour away, although admittedly deep in the central forest. Currently, there was a caretaker living there with his family, but he could easily be removed if Nayan and Anick wanted to go there. Minty ached to suggest it, if only because she remembered what it had been like when she had married Ram and lived with his parents in Chayu. How she had loved his parents, and they her. She had come from a devout Hindu family with Trinidad origins in the canefields, and who later owned a dry goods and hardware store on the north coast of Trinidad. The Prakashs were Hindu, too, but they were more relaxed about it, and unlike her parents, they knew more about the whole of Trinidad, not just the place in which they lived. They took part in the lives of the workers on their estate, and in the life of the village, and had opinions about politics on the island. They knew of the French origins of Chayu and even spoke the patois of the area.

Ram had been an interesting young man, unlike the Indians she knew who were more insular, but his parents spoiled him, gave him anything and everything he wanted, and he seemed to dislike this about them. He was at odds with them, if only because he needed to find his own way in the world. There were quarrels between him and his father, and Minty had thought then that things could not be worse between a parent and a child. Ram's father had bought the land in Luminada, in San Fernando, as a gift. She and Ram had a house built and they moved out of Rio Claro. In San Fernando, Ram became a born-again Hindu, and Minty found herself trapped in the role of a Hindu wife that she thought she had fled in marrying into a cacao family. Nayan came late in their lives, and Ram changed yet again with Nayan's birth. The autocrat she had run from by leaving her own family behind bloomed before her, right there, in her very own house in Luminada.

And now, how much worse were things between parents and child? She could not have imagined such bitterness or the kinds of words spoken between her husband and her son. The time had come for Nayan to leave their house and to find his own way, too. But, as his mother, and under the current unpleasant circumstances, she dared not suggest this without it seeming as if she didn't want him and his wife living with her and Ram. And Ram would have thought her mad, had she made such a suggestion. Thoughts of what her life might have been like had she married a professional man, or even a simpler man, a school principal perhaps, someone from her own background in the north, ran through her head frequently. That was where they stayed, too — in her head.

Meanwhile, communication between Nayan and Anick had been reduced to hissing, and Ram and Anick made sure not to be in the same room together. At meal times, all four scattered, eating separately. Nayan slept in the guest room while Anick, in her bed alone, cried a great deal.

Finally, Anick gave Nayan an ultimatum: either they begin to look for a house of their own or she would return to France. But Nayan was not ready to leave his parents' home. He feared that if he did, he would not be able to keep as strong a hold on Anick. He suggested alternative strategies for dealing with all that was going on in his parents' house — for instance, that Anick should go do something constructive with herself: join a fitness centre, or take a cooking class, or take up sewing, maybe start a fashion business with Shanti.

Minty tried to console Anick in broken English, which she thought might be better understood by her daughter-in-law, a French word remembered here and there from high school days tossed in. Her sense of self-preservation stopped her from trying to build any sort of bridge between her husband and daughter-in-law.

It was in the midst of all of this that Ram suffered a heart attack. It did not debilitate him, but after he recovered it was unanimously agreed that Nayan and his wife should move to Rio Claro, to Chayu, thirty miles away as the crow flies, an hour-plus by car.

The decision had the effect of washing a slight calm over Anick and Nayan, and even brought between them some tenderness. Anick could finally imagine an end to her claustrophobia. She would soon live in the very landscape Nayan had wooed her with. Furthermore, she welcomed the idea of living in a house that had French origins. The caretaker and his family would be removed. Anick was promised that they would be offered a decent place not lacking in basic amenities. She would restore Chayu — not to the way the Prakashs had kept it, but to its origins. There, not only out from under the thumb of Nayan's father but away from all the wanting and missing that had distracted Anick and caused rifts between her and her husband, she and Nayan would create a life for themselves, begin a family, get involved in the betterment of the community of Rio Claro. And she could make a home with some of herself in it, perhaps, and invite friends there. Not just for dinner or for Sunday lunch — which was most likely, given that Rio Claro was on no one's regular route, and several hours out of the way — but for overnight weekend stays. She would be able to resume her connection with Viveka Krishnu, perhaps invite her to visit. For her friends, there could be walks in the forest, tours that included watching pods being collected and transported out of the forest on baskets that hung on either side of the donkeys, viewings of the fermenting process, of the drying sheds and the roasters. Perhaps she could invite artists to come out and paint the cacao when it was in pod — the scarlet and the cadmium yellow pods, pendulous amidst forest greens and burnt umbers. Perhaps there was a chance for her, after all.

Anick still felt that old loss whenever Nayan touched her body and she his. But it was tolerable. It was only now, after all the time she'd been on the island, that she felt any closeness to him. How he had finally brightened, and how much!

The change in Nayan, on the verge of becoming the man of his own house, came about almost instantly. As soon as the caretaker and his wife had been given notice and plans were underway for the move, Nayan began coming home early, his drinking lessened, and he was respectful to his father and to Anick, too. At last he could see his dream materializing of an estate that produced fine premium cacao. His father wouldn't be coming to the estate too often now except as his visitor, so he would be able to uproot the old plants — even as few as a row at a time — and replace them. He would one day export high-quality beans and chocolates, and import luxury items to the island. This he would have to do without Anick's knowledge, but it could be done, as she would have no dealings in the business side of things. And he would be the head of a family that was solid, unthreatened, and entirely his. It could all happen out of Chayu, in Rio Claro. He would become a big man in the village and eventually help turn it from a village into a town, and one day into a small city. Sooner than that, however, there would be a Rio Claro chocolate line, called "Chayu," and that line would be available for purchase in specialty stores internationally.

Everything would, after all, turn out just fine.

Anick

THE ROMANCE OF LIVING DEEP IN THE CENTRAL HILLS WITH TROPICAL forest all around, in an original French plantation house, initially caused Anick to tingle with a feverish excitement and even the condition in which she found the house, one of almost total disrepair, did nothing to quell this enthusiasm.

The house was off the main Naparima-Mayaro Road. One had to negotiate roads that were not wide enough for two cars to pass each other. They were pocked with holes, some large enough to cut the already meagre width by half. It amazed Anick to know that there was in Trinidad an unfathomable asphalt lake with pitch enough to pave a good portion of all the roads of the world, yet most roads in Trinidad were deplorable. Hours after the long drive to Rio Claro and then the bumpy one into Chayu, her bones felt jarred and trembling, and her stomach continued to churn. But the sight of the once-great house, soon to be her and Nayan's home, set upon a mound of lawn with the dark forest behind and the brilliant deep-green cacao fields running down into little valleys at the sides, made her want to weep with a childlike joy. It didn't matter that even from the road, before one began the rough drive up an uneven gravel pathway, one could see that the house had not been cared for recently. Only a metre here and a metre there of the cast-iron cresting on the ridge of the roof remained intact, and the cast-iron and timber finials were either bent or the tips broken off. The dormer windows had lost their louvres, leaving the interior open to the elements, and the once elaborate timber fretwork that had decorated the eaves, gables, and the wraparound gallery wall was reduced to a chip here and a chip there. Most of the paint on the wood structure had been shaved right off by rain, or flaked up by the sun's heat, leaving barely a trace of its former turquoise.

Chayu had been a working estate house from the days of its French origins, its attic a drying platform for the cacao beans. The attic was still being used today for that purpose, and the sweet, earthy odour of beans infected the air inside the entire house.

Inside, the house was spacious but plain. The kitchen and eating area were large enough to accommodate the feeding of workers. In the kitchen was a window with an awning and a deep sill into which was set a single enamel sink. There were shelves, but no pantry or cupboards. The floor, covered in a chipped, once lemon-coloured linoleum, sagged and rose and sagged again.

The old bathroom and the toilet from the earliest days of the estate were outdoors, some paces from the house, but a bathroom had since been added inside by Nayan's grandparents. It was unused, though, as the plumbing had rusted out and never been repaired. The bathroom's wall tiles were broken, and black mold sprouted on the sloped floor of the long-unused bathing square.

Anick hired an architect, who put together a team that included an historian and restoration contractors, and together they came up with a plan to restore Chayu to its colonial origins while modernizing it for daily residential living. Such a project cost Nayan about as much as having an entirely new house built in the city, and Ram and Minty were appalled. They could not understand why the old house could not have been simply made functional, the amenities brought up to date slowly, and blamed the fancy wife for making her husband, their son, spend his father's money so frivolously.

The renovation took almost three months to complete, with the work stopped intermittently by inclement weather, by material shortages, by the seizure and contestation of imported materials at customs, and by sick or slack workers. During this time, Anick and Nayan lived in a rented house in Chaguanas, a bustling town in the centre of the island, about a forty-minute drive from Rio Claro. Anick paid for English-language lessons from a neighbour, a young woman who had finished Advanced Level examinations in French and was awaiting results. The young woman was studious, religious, and serious. She did not find Anick's accent amusing, and had little patience with literal translations from French into English. Anick was inspired, and somewhat shamed, into improving her English at a rate that won her quiet respect from Nayan.

It was a ten-minute drive, twenty in rush hour, from their temporary house to the chocolate-making factory. Nayan's days were spent at the factory doing the work his father had done when he'd been in better health. Late afternoons, Nayan raced from there to Rio Claro, trying to arrive before dark. Once there, he haggled with the various contractors, who seemed to find daily that they had under-priced materials and miscalculated to such an extent that they simply could not carry on the work without an advance or assurances that he would meet the regrettable increase in their quoted price. At home, Nayan was exhausted and quiet much of the time.

Anick had wanted to be involved in overseeing every nail that was hammered, every new set of louvres or fretwork crafted and installed. She had gone to Chayu with Nayan a few times, but her presence disrupted the workers. With more English words in her head and on the tip of her tongue, she was inclined to ask questions incessantly, give opinions, make comments, all in an accent, however much slighter now, that took contractors and workers valuable time to decipher and raised Nayan's ire. He started going to Rio Claro on his own, the excuse being that he was leaving to go there from some other work-related location that made it inconvenient for him to come all the way back to Chaguanas to fetch her. In response, Anick asked for a driver to take her there in the daytime when Nayan was unable to be present. The idea appalled him. If she went to Chayu without him, she would be walking among construction workers who had no loyalty to him. She would be tying up a driver that the company would likely need. She would be in the way of the architects and the contractors. She would make him feel small, as if his wife were in control, and among men like these, this would not be understood. He took her, instead, on weekends when there were no workers around except for a watchman. He took note of her suggestions, likes and dislikes, and on his weekday visits he passed on the ones he felt had merit.

On the days when Nayan did spare a driver, Anick did not go to Luminada where she would have been obliged to stop in on her in-laws, but to Port of Spain to housewares shops and boutiques, looking for items with which to furnish her new home. And she took the opportunity to lunch with a friend or two, the ones she saw little of nowadays.

Three months in a rented house in the hot, humid and busy centre of the island might as well have been a year, but eventually Anick and Nayan were able to move to "Chaillou." One of the restorers had found that time and weather had rubbed almost smooth an incised text on the gable of the pavilion-like entrance to the house. A wax rubbing revealed the words *Le Ciel de Chaillou*. When Anick told her father of the discovery of the plaque, and of the French words on it, he immediately replied, "But of course, Chaillou must refer to David Chaillou, France's first official chocolatier, appointed to the court of the chocoholic Queen Marie Therese." The original French owners of the estate obviously knew the history of chocolate in France and had named it in honour of David Chaillou—"Chaillou's Heaven." It was a pleasant irony to Anick that she had ended up living in this particular estate, this particular house. The discovery of the name of the house was, to her mind, like unearthing an umbilical cord to France. It gave her a humorous sense of "right of presence."

But the connection, and her talk of it in this manner, irritated Nayan. He had an ornate brass plaque made, on which was inscribed the single word *Chayu*. This is how the house had come to be known, with a name that sounded Indian enough, and so, according to Nayan, it would remain.

ONCE ANICK WAS ABLE TO MOVE IN, THE HOUSE BECAME HOME FAST. It was airy and light. In the early morning when mist clung to the ground, it was cool—so cool, so damp, one had to wear a sweater and socks. The forest had its own earthy smell, but the air around Chayu was cacao-scented some days, and on others, when the fermenting was happening, it reeked of an earthy sweat-like odour and sweetness—sweetness that was almost turning to rot. Early morning, the estate workers could be heard entering the fields, chatting quietly as they headed out to clean or pick or gather fruit. And when the sun burned off the mist, the forest gave off the rank odours of decaying matter, leaves, too-ripe fruit that had been left unpicked and fallen to the ground. From the earth itself rose the odour, oddly, of fresh fish or ocean sand. The workers said that this was the scent of snakes. Anick disliked mosquitoes more than she feared snakes, and fortunately the house was shrouded in nearly invisible netting that kept out not only snakes and mosquitoes but scorpions, birds, frogs, bees, lizards, and flies.

Throughout the day it was not entirely quiet, but the sounds were a kind of music to Anick. Workers came and went around the house. Women on their way to or back from the town a taxi ride away slapped their rubber slippers on the asphalt, chatting with one another in English that Anick was just beginning to catch. And there was the burbling of schoolchildren, or children who were not at school but swung cutlasses as they went down the road to cut hands of bananas from some one else's property or to pick peas or dasheen. A car passed Chayu occasionally, but off the main road there was hardly any traffic save for the donkeys that were used on the land, and the one-ton truck that belonged to the estate and transported sacks of roasted beans to the factory outside of Chaguanas. There were, always, the kinds of sounds that one welcomed: the shriek of a parrot; parakeets squabbling incessantly; once in an anticipated while a bellbird's mournful tocking; the wind fighting its way through the coffee, cacao, and citrus trees and getting snared in the banana clumps; the apamat and the silk cotton trees creaking high above all the others; and if it rained, the heft of each drop, known by the shape and quality of the sound it made on the variety of leaves all around, sounds that Anick eventually—eventually—came to take for granted.

She became more at ease in the country, recognizing neighbours and entering into lengthy conversations with them about their lives and about life in Rio Claro, in which they seemed much more interested than life elsewhere in Trinidad. This always amused Anick, since the island was so small she thought of it as a whole, all the parts entwined and entirely dependant on each other. On one side, her neighbours were Hindus, and on the other Muslim. Anick had attended the Pentecostal Church down the road, only once, on the invitation of the pastor and his wife. It took no skill to see how divided such a small village could be, divisions by colour and by religion, and by the size of a house or the materials from which it was built, and by one's children going to school or not. At the Pentecostal Church she enjoyed the singing and clapping and found catching the spirit intriguing, but the church service was no more to her than that.

Anick discovered that she was a presence in the neighbourhood, not only because she was the only white woman, but because she and her husband owned the largest property, the biggest house, had the fanciest car, and were the employers of a good percentage of the village population. If resentments ran underground, they did not show. Anick now made an even greater effort to speak and understand English, as she knew that her lack of communication skills in such a place would not be "cute," as they had been in San Fernando or in Port of Spain. The result of her making extra efforts and learning the names of neighbours, visiting people, and allowing herself to be visited in turn, was that she was looked out for *by* the villagers as much as she came to look out *for* them.

As she became more at ease in Rio Claro, however, she began to miss her friendships in Port of Spain and the acquaintances she had made with people on the other islands. She was in touch with some of these people by telephone, but the drive to Rio Claro interested few of them. She would stand at her bedroom window sometimes and look out at the land with its neat rows of cacao trees, and then interrupting that neatness the chaos of tall trees and the broad-leaved vines that hugged them, and gripping their branches the bromeliads with their central spear-like stalks that seemed to be aflame, and she would wonder if she should broach being in touch again with Viveka Krishnu.

Meanwhile, Ram and Minty drove down to Rio Claro regularly so they could enjoy quiet evenings on the now-widened gallery, sitting in the antique rocking chairs Anick had sourced and purchased, the scent of the various states of their cacao marking the village air. Each trip, they hoped that they would be invited to stay the night in one of the two spare bedrooms, but Anick had firmly made it clear that she needed Chayu to be fully her own before she would let them spend more than a few hours in a house they had once lived in, and might naturally take to bossing in again. When no invitation came from either Anick or their son, Ram and Minty would reluctantly rise, say their peevish goodbyes, and head west again, only to return in a day or two.

Viveka

WHEN, ABOUT A MONTH AFTER MOVING INTO CHAYU, NAYAN CAME into San Fernando especially to visit Valmiki as a patient, Valmiki returned home and went immediately to the study to find Viveka. The younger Prakashs were finally experiencing a second honeymoon, he told her, as if he felt some duty to do so. Anick, he reported, had fallen in love with the forest, and was taking an active interest in the cacao estate and in the social life of the village. Nayan, he beamed, had invited Valmiki to bring his hunting friends some Sunday to hunt on the estate land. He ended his report with the news, strangely disheartening to Viveka, that Nayan was finally ready to consider fatherhood.

Viveka listened to all of this with a well-performed glimmer of passing interest. Anick quite disgusted her now. She was unequivocally relieved that Nayan and his troublesome wife no longer lived just around the corner.

And then, some days later, Nayan phoned Valmiki, asking him to pass on an invitation to Viveka to visit him and Anick in Rio Claro. He had arranged the details of the visit on Anick's suggestion: Viveka would travel there and back with Nayan's parents during one of their frequent evening visits.

The invitation unsettled Viveka. She fussed to her parents and Vashti that Anick had not been in touch since just after the dinner she had so painstakingly made, and now wanted her as audience for her new house. They reminded her that it was Nayan who had phoned with the invitation, to which she whined back, "To Dad, not to me. What does he think I am, a child? He is so old-fashioned. And I am surprised at Anick. She is just like him."

Vashti simply told Viveka she was being overly dramatic when she knew very well that she really wanted to go. Devika, at first, thoughtfully encouraged Viveka to go with Ram and Minty, but when Viveka continued to protest, and indeed, did so theatrically, Devika grew terse. Finally she was brusque: "Why is she bothering you so much? What is it that you have with her? Either decide to go or stop talking about it."

Valmiki watched Viveka closely, and then he said, "Just do what you want to do, Vik, don't worry about what anyone else thinks."

This angered Viveka further. She looked at her father as if he were daft and responded, "What makes you say that? It has nothing to do with what anyone thinks. I'm just not sure she and I have enough in common, and Nayan sure doesn't interest me."

This stopped the conversation. She could tell, though, if only to save themselves and the day, her family had all decided to let her have the last say.

DURING THE DRIVE TO RIO CLARO, VIVEKA FIDGETED IN THE BACK seat of Ram Prakash's car. At four-thirty in the afternoon, progress along the narrow road was slow. Having just left work for the day, many people congregated at the taxi and bus stands. There were some private cars on the road, but mostly regular taxis, maxi-taxis, and buses. It had been a hot day, the journey was to be a long one, and outside the car it was noisy and smoggy with vehicle exhaust. Even though the use of air-conditioning put great stress on the car's cooling system, Ram kept it on. After some pleasant chitchat, Minty nodded off and Ram turned on the radio. Viveka leaned back and tried to relax. Pedestrians outside her window were noticeably wilted in the heat and glare. Viveka, on the other hand, was chilled in the air-conditioned car.

Before leaving the house, Viveka had tried on everything she owned, trying to find something that was both appropriate for a visit and that she would be comfortable in. She ended up wearing her "uniform." She could see that her mother was on the verge of commenting but then changed her mind. Viveka knew that any comment would have been disparaging and so interpreted her mother's quiet as an expression of exasperation. Rather than feeling triumph at this, she felt defeat. Now she felt shy to ask Ram to turn the cold air down, so she simply made do by rubbing her bare arms. She looked out the window and wondered what Naipaul would make of this particular present-day Trinidad. What had really changed for these people since Naipaul's depictions of them? He hadn't ever really paid attention in his work to the presence of blacks in the country, but now his cane-and-cacao Indians seemed outnumbered by people of African descent.

Viveka tried to imagine seeing Anick again. She decided that she would be still, cool in Anick's presence, not too talkative, not too quiet — she would project a fine balance of interest, disinterest, and aloofness. But as they finally neared Rio Claro, she wanted, in one breath, to get out of the car and find a way back to San Fernando, and in another to have Anick to herself, to ask her why and what and how come.

With each turn of a corner that brought her closer, Viveka's body tightened. In less than half an hour, too long and too short, she would arrive at Chayu. When she stood next to Anick, they would all see that she was uglier than ever.

Viveka looked at her hands, clasped on her lap. They were small but thick, her fingers short, indelicate. She gripped one with the other. On a volleyball court one might have called them strong hands, but now she felt as if they only confirmed the fact that, as a female, she was inelegant. The idea that Anand's spirit lived inside of her, was pushing himself upwards, through her, taking over her body, her mind, her manners, had seemed lately more plausible than ever. It was as if he insisted on living again through her — a thought she cherished at times, particularly when alone in her bedroom or the bathroom, flexing her biceps, sucking in her cheeks to make her face more angular, slipping her thumbs into the loops of her jeans and commanding a cowboy-leans-back-on-the-fence pose. She certainly often felt as if she knew what it would be like to be him, and as if she knew, too, the kinds of women he would be drawn to. He would be drawn to Anick. But then, who wouldn't be? And Anick might well have thought Anand interesting. Desirable. The thought sent a current through her.

And then, just as the sun was setting, the car arrived, all too suddenly, at the turn-off from the main road. Viveka's head swam. She would do her best, pay compliments all around regarding the house, and she would be a good enough, innocuous guest.

The area they were driving through was a poor one, and golden light from the sunset in the west highlighted every detail. The two-room houses, all with little verandas, and all exactly alike, like barrack houses, were of unpainted wood. They perched on high stilts. The Hindu houses could be identified by the religious prayer flags collected in the yards. Viveka decided that she would make conversation with Nayan and Anick about the plight and flight of present-day Indians. The plight of those left behind; the flight of others to the city. Nayan was, after all, a descendant of these Indians. She could talk of a revival, of him as a pioneer of such a revival with his return to the country. She had no elegant presence with which to grace Anick's home, but she could, at least, be bright and try to bring interesting conversation their way.

WHEN RAM PRAKASH'S CAR ARRIVED AT CHAYU, THE SUN HAD SET and the sky was spread out in hues of red. No lights had been turned on. Even so, Anick's nervousness was palpable to Viveka. Her self-consciousness — Viveka wondered if it was on account of her presence, or Ram and Minty's — unsettled everyone. She asked Viveka if the drive had been long, but then she herself answered that it was stupid of her to ask, that of course it was long, and then countered that with, "Well, you know, is polite to ask if your guest's journey was good."

There were five of them, and only four chairs on the veranda. Minty sat, but everyone else stood awkwardly, and Anick did all the talking. Of interest to Viveka was the information that from the kitchen Anick had seen two howler monkeys that morning, and that every morning the monkeys could be heard, howling indeed. And a man passing in front of the house had called to Anick that he had seen a pair of toucans in the African violet tree down the road.

Ram leaned over and whispered to Minty, who got up and pulled Anick aside. Anick went into the house and returned with another chair, but Nayan immediately sent her back in to turn on lights and get drinks for them. Did Viveka like his little kingdom? he asked. She responded that what she had seen was indeed a paradise. Nayan, satisfied, turned to his father and launched into business talk: a batch of chocolate had been spoiled because of too many air pockets; some of the machinery needed servicing, some replacing. He had read that there was, available from a German manufacturer, a new grinder and conching machine that worked in combination to make a finer product. Finer than what, his father asked, and what kind of money was he talking about? Minty listened intently, but said nothing.

Viveka got up, said that she was going to explore, and ambled along the gallery. At the side of the house, still on the gallery, she peered through the mosquito netting into the darkness, hoping to catch the movement of a howler monkey in the branches of the trees. They were so elusive that if she were to see one, or even hear one, it would have been and gone in a flash, like a falling star. There was no furniture on the gallery and Viveka wondered what, in time, would be bought for it. There were some elaborate brass hooks in the ceiling for hanging baskets, she imagined, or perhaps a hammock. A dog on the grass down below shook itself hard. She spotted it and whistled. The dog turned to her and growled, and then began a frenzied barking, and she pulled back, embarrassed. Nayan ran around, and seeing that she was still on the gallery and all right, he shouted to the dog, "Shut up! Shut up!" It growled once and whimpered before becoming quiet.

Soon Viveka came to a wall that marked the end of the gallery, but she did not want to return just yet. She waited, then turned and walked back slowly, almost tiptoeing. She couldn't bear to return to the three Prakashs and their solemn, uninteresting talk of business. But she knew, too, that if they allowed her to engage them in conversation about Naipaul or cacao Indians or books, she would still have no time for them. It was not them she had come for.

The lights in the house came on, and then those on the veranda. With light in the house, the garden just on the other side of the veranda and everything beyond it was obliterated. The chirping of cicadas suddenly rose loud all around. From inside the house, there was a clatter. Through a set of louvres along the side of the house Viveka caught sight of Anick and the maid in the kitchen. Anick wore a dress in shades of deep reds, garish yellows, and verdant greens. It was made of of sheer fabric, layers sewn upon layers, and was held up by two string-like straps. About her breasts the dress fitted close. Below, it hugged her narrow waist and her bony hips, and from her hips the layers fell in uneven angles about her knees. They flounced about her thighs as she walked. With each step that took her one way, the skirt of her dress swooshed the other. Viveka watched for a moment then made her way back to the front of the house, wishing she had not come.

Anick brought out a tray of lime juice. She told her guests that it was made with limes from one of their trees, sweetened with honey collected from a nest in a tree in the forest by one of the village boys. Ram asked if the tree that the honey came from was on the estate, who was the boy, and if he had asked permission. Anick looked at Nayan and said, uncertainly, "I think so." It was Gopaul's son, replied Nayan, the retarded one, and this seemed to satisfy Ram.

Conversation continued between father and son about bank accounts and workers, so Anick offered to show Viveka the house. They entered the living room through the louvred doorway. The open interior and the polished mahogany wood floor, the wide planks a deep reddish brown, seemed like an ocean to be crossed. Lime green walls — green the light shade of the lime's pips — rose high to a ceiling of the same material as the floor.

Anick pointed to several closed doorways on either side of the living room. On one side were the TV room, her own private room, and an office space for Nayan, and on the other side were bedrooms, her and Nayan's included. She recited the logic of this architecture — the central area that was left open for air and cooling breezes to pass from the front doors and windows right through to the kitchen and out the back door. The house was indeed cool, but there was a strong complex scent, like fresh earth and decaying wood, not unpleasant, inside of it. Cacao beans drying in the attic, Anick explained. Her vocabulary, Viveka noted, had improved, although she still preferred to speak in the present tense.

"The whole area smell of cacao. In the daytime, when is hot, the air is sweet. Everything, everything is cacao. Is like you want to bath in it."

"Don't you get tired of it?"

"No, of course not. Is not like chocolate. Chocolate you only have a small piece of and is enough. But, of course, that has to be very good chocolate. I am not talking of candy, too milky, too sweet. A small piece of good quality chocolate goes a long way."

To Viveka it sounded strange, the way Anick said this, flawlessly, like a phrase she had heard more than once and was practicing now.

"But cacao is different. You don't get tired of it. Never. Is not sweet at all-at all. On the contrary, is very dark, mysterious. You must come in the daytime. I will show you the whole process, how they collect the pod, how they cut them to get the bean, how they dry the bean and then the fermentation. Is a long process.

It have all kind of smell and taste, very very interesting, before they make it into chocolate."

They went through the well-lit kitchen, in the centre of which was a mahogany table covered with an ordinary white-and-red cotton tablecloth, and cutting boards, piles of trays, canisters and a mess of cutlery, as if everything was in the middle of being sorted for storing elsewhere.

A toilet off to the side flushed and the maid appeared. "Good evening," she said to Viveka in a barely audible voice, and then to Anick, "Madam, I finish everything. I going home now. Is okay? We will finish putting everything away in the morning."

Did she want to wait for a drive home? asked Anick. Nayan would drive her once his parents had left.

The maid answered, "He don't like to go down my street, Madam. It have too much hole in the road. He does get vex and buff me, like I make the hole." She smiled apologetically.

Anick turned to Viveka as the maid went down the back step. "Lystra is so good, but Nayan treats her badly. He can be so harsh."

There were appliances of all kinds on the kitchen counters: a blender, a coffee machine, an electric grinder, a juicer, and several mortars and pestles made from different materials and in different sizes. Cupboards lined two walls and open shelves displayed colourful dishes — more, Viveka thought, than a couple really needed. Everything was in disarray and Anick explained that she was indeed sorting through things that had been sent to her by her parents, given to them by Nayan's, and that she herself had bought.

A heavy wood door on the outer wall opened to the backyard. There was a screen in it, and a metal burglar-proofing grate. Anick led Viveka back toward the interior of the house and down a hallway — Viveka could see that there was one on either side of the kitchen, running parallel to the dining room. They went past the TV room, in which there was only one couch facing a small television. Viveka imagined Anick and Nayan on the couch, Anick curled into Nayan's body, a bowl of chocolate-covered peanuts on her lap, the two of them eating from it. They passed an office, Nayan's, and came to a room Anick called her own. Anick switched on the light. The walls were painted yellow, with white trim on the base and ceiling boards. There were piles of boxes in this room, most sealed, a few opened, and Anick explained that she was temporarily using the room for the storage of household things, and Nayan was also storing some business-related things there too.

Viveka entered this room, and walked to the window. She looked out onto a sloping darkness. Stars were just beginning to twinkle in the darkening sky, which seemed to stretch into the distance forever. Anick came up behind her, and said, "Is too dark, but in the daytime when you can see the rows of cacao, is *the most beautiful* sight." She had separated out the three words and stressed each one as she looked directly at Viveka. "You hear birds, and the monkeys, and other animals, and see colours like in a carnival. The leaves of the cacao plant are like jade. You know jade? And then in between you see little flecks of bright, bright, bright yellow, and this red—" She held a hand out to Viveka and rubbed her forefinger and thumb together as if the red was a substance, "like fire or glass. Come in the daytime, I show you."

She touched Viveka's shoulder lightly to usher her out of the room.

They retraced their steps to the kitchen and Anick pointed to the hallway on the opposite side. "Those are the bedrooms. There are three. If you come to stay overnight, you will stay there. In the one next to mine. Well, is not mine alone. Ours."

Was this an invitation? Viveka wondered.

"You want I show you my little garden? Is pitch-black but I think you can still see something. In any case, is nice outside. Sometimes I like it out there better than to be inside all the time. Nayan, he don't like to go in the forest. Is his, yet he only go to see how the cacao growing and he come right back. It have places to walk in there but he don't go. He think I am crazy. Your father, he like the forest, no?"

They went down the back stairs into the yard. Viveka remembered her walks as a child, just on the edges of the forests, with her father. She remembered him seeming most at peace then. She had always been terrified of snakes, and so close to the wild she felt that it was inevitable her fear would bring her in contact with one. She could not bear to show this timidity now, though, for fear that she would seem like Nayan. She followed close behind Anick.

"What about the dog?" Viveka asked.

"He is chained. I don't know why people here chain their dogs like this, but is how it is, I have to accept it. He is on the other side of the house. He bark a lot, but he don't bite. The villagers don't know that, though. Well, that is what Nayan think. But they not stupid."

Viveka gasped and held back when Anick suddenly snapped, "Look!" But in the twilight she saw that Anick was only pointing to a barely visible fist-size frog breathing rapidly in the dirt of a lettuce bed.

Anick saw Viveka's nervousness and took one of her hands.

Anick's hand felt quite strong, and it was warm as she pulled Viveka farther down the path. Then, suddenly, Anick stopped and pulled Viveka closer, gripping her hand tighter yet. Blood pounded in Viveka's head, and her ears and cheeks turned hot. She could hardly breathe. Anick said something, but the pounding in

Viveka's head and ears had become so loud she could not hear. She tried to ask Anick to repeat what she had said, but it was as if her throat had become clogged. She wrapped her fingers around Anick's hand, made a half-stroking, half-gripping movement with her thumb, and was sure she felt a quick squeeze from Anick, and then Anick let go. She rested that same hand on Viveka's shoulder now, and pressed gently down. Together, the two women stooped. Anick put her head close to Viveka's, pointed to something, and whispered, "Look." But Viveka could see nothing. Anick manoeuvred herself slightly behind Viveka. She brought her arms around Viveka and covered Viveka's eyes with her hands. She held her hands there, lightly, but they trembled a little, and from them came a heat that burned Viveka's face. She held her own hands up and placed them over Anick's to still the trembling. Anick pulled Viveka's head toward her, and before Viveka had time to be really sure that Anick had actually kissed the back of her head, Anick released her hands from over Viveka's eyes. A pair of pinpoint lights flashed on and off in a patch of anthurium lilies. Viveka soon made out the eyes of a rabbit.

"Nayan would kill me if he know I feed the rabbits," said Anick. "But they so adorable. The land is big enough for everybody, not so?"

They turned back along the path toward the house again. Anick hooked one of her fingers around one of Viveka's. Then Anick said, "Mr. Lal, is that you? Did you have dinner yet?"

Viveka pulled away from Anick. She heard a voice off to the side answer, "Yes, Madam. Lystra give it to me before she gone home. Thank you, Madam." Anick whispered to Viveka that this man was the watchman. Viveka looked for him but could not see him. She wondered if he had been watching them the whole time.

Inside, the light of the kitchen seemed harsh and Viveka was sure that her face was etched with evidence of fear, excitement, and restraint. She could not look directly at Anick, but neither did she want to return to the gallery and sit among the others.

Anick reached into the oven and took out a stainless-steel platter holding small mushroom caps that had been stuffed with a mixture of creamed crab and shrimp. She placed the tray on the counter and asked Viveka if she would mind helping her by taking the food out to the gallery. She said, "You do not have to serve them; I will bring out a table and these plates. We put everything on the table. Why we have to serve them? They know how to help themselves. They grown-ups, after all."

Viveka liked Anick's little tirades. She picked up the platter and was about to walk away with it, but Anick caught her by the elbow. Anick glanced over her shoulder toward the veranda as she picked one of the caps off the platter. She brought the cap up to Viveka's mouth and looked directly at Viveka's lips, parting her own. Viveka felt the mushroom cap brush her lips and she opened her mouth. She offered the tip of her tongue to take the morsel. Anick rested her forefinger and thumb on Viveka's lower lip. The two women looked directly at each other now. Anick bit her bottom lip. Viveka's mouth was full. She chewed slowly as Anick stood in front of her, watching, waiting. Anick said, in a voice that quavered, "Is good?" Viveka could only nod. Her body felt unanchored.

Anick was smiling mischievously now. "You know us French girls," she said, seemingly out of nowhere, her voice soft and trembling, "we like both." She lightly flicked Viveka under the chin with the back of her forefinger, and was ready to spring away, but Viveka surprised even herself when she caught Anick's hand and brought it to her lips. If she had stopped for one second to think about what she was doing, she would never have done it. She slightly parted her lips, and lightly held Anick's finger there between her teeth, nicking the tip of that finger with the tip of her tongue.

Anick gasped. She was no longer smiling. She came closer, again biting her lower lip. Her breathing was quick and shallow. Viveka released Anick's hand, yet Anick kept her finger at Viveka's lips. She ran her finger there before stepping back.

Viveka had been holding the platter with one hand. She wanted to drop it and fall to the ground, taking Anick with her. She felt a force inside of her that was entirely unfamiliar, frightening, and exhilarating. This was what she had not felt before, she marvelled, what had been missing between her and Elliot. It wasn't simply that it was missing from her.

The tray tilted and the mushrooms slid to one side.

"Anick!" Nayan's voice broke into the silence in the kitchen. The two women started and stepped away from each other. He was calling from the veranda.

Anick's response was swift and sharp. "Yes!" To Viveka she whispered, "I hate it when he call me like that."

"Bring another beer for me. What are you all doing?"

Anick answered only, "Okay." And then to Viveka, she spoke hurriedly. "You in my mind all the time. Do you understand, Viveka, what I am saying? Is like you steal my brain. I cannot stop thinking about you. Please, come again. Come for a longer time. Please."

IT WASN'T UNTIL THE SUN HAD COME UP, THE BIRDS BRIGHTLY RAUCOUS outside her window, and she could hear her parents just rising, that Viveka finally drifted off to sleep. She had spent the night reliving and reimagining the past evening. She repeated

Anick's words to herself, interpreted them again and again to mean everything from *I love you* to *I am bored and think you would be an interesting friend to have.* Anick's finger was imprinted on the tip of her tongue, the feel of it brushing her lip. She imagined being at Chayu when Nayan was there, and when he was not. She wondered what would happen if this thing she was feeling in every atom of her being were to stay and never go away, if it were to grow and take over her good sense. If her parents were to find out that she had such feeling for a woman. If Nayan were to know that his wife made her dizzy like this.

But most of all, she imagined Anick and herself in the house in Rio Claro, with the doors and windows closed and no prying eyes around. They would lower themselves onto the floor of the kitchen, and she would lie there with Anick, holding her face, stroking her hair, and kissing her mouth. No words would be spoken between them. They would be hungry only for each other, the aromas of cacao and Anick's perfume dizzying her. Their legs would entwine, and she would lie on Anick, lightly, and when Viveka imagined this she gasped aloud into the silent night. She imagined so well the feel and slide of fabric on Anick's hips and thighs that she wondered if she had accidentally brushed Anick in those places, and in the vertiginous events of the past evening hadn't remembered doing so. She touched herself and felt her body and mind explode as she imagined the heat of their breath, close, the wetness of their tongues touching. And she wondered if perhaps she had misread Anick's intentions. If she had, what on earth would she do with her own feelings?

She would have to wait and see if Anick suggested anything more. Or perhaps she would telephone Anick to say thank you for a lovely evening, and she would linger on that phone call and hope. Hope for more words from Anick that would tell her unequivocally of Anick's intentions. But clarity was also what she did not want. When the day began to break, not wanting to be torn away from these crazy longings and imaginings, Viveka let sleep in to comfort and protect her.

PINKY, THE MAID, WAS TOUCHING HER SHOULDER. "MISS VIKKI, IS HALF past twelve. You Mom say to wake you up. Lunch on the table."

Viveka turned reluctantly. "Half past twelve? Mom told you to wake me?" She was, in an instant, drowning in guilt. "Why didn't she just come and wake me herself."

"I don't know. Your mom look like she vex. She quiet this morning."

"She and Dad quarrelled?"

"No, it don't look so. They eat nice this morning. I don't know what happen. You know how your mom is sometimes."

Viveka tried to smile, the muscles of her face still in the grip of sleep.

In the kitchen, Devika hustled and bustled, making a display of her business.

"Did you eat already, Mom?"

But Devika did not answer Viveka directly, speaking instead to Pinky. "There is food for her in the oven. Let her help herself, Pinky. I have a hair appointment that I am late for."

Viveka realized she had not heard the phone ring that morning. She was not a heavy sleeper. Not usually. The phone would have awakened her. "Did anyone phone for me?" she asked. When her mother didn't answer, Pinky replied that the phone hadn't even rung once for the morning. In the quiet that followed, Pinky said, "So, you like the countryside, Miss Vikki?"

Viveka answered, but for her mother's ears. "I don't know how anyone can live so far from the town. Anick will get tired of it I am sure. She asked me to come and visit again. I'd like to."

At this, her mother looked directly at her and said, "I don't know if your father will let you go there again so soon. What do you have in common with her, anyway? She is married, and has a house and a husband to look after."

The room bristled. Pinky discreetly made her way to the laundry room, where she busied herself.

"What do you mean *if* Dad will *let* me? Is it you or is it Dad who has a problem with me going there? I am not a child anymore. Anick is interested in a lot of things I am interested in, Mom. And she could tell me things about the village. It would be good for my paper on cacao Indians and..."

But her mother cut in. "How many times do I have to say it? As long as you live in my house, you are my child and will live by my rules. I am not a fool, you know. I don't know why you and your father get so bamboozled by whiteness."

"But, Mom, I was just talking about the cacao Indians!"

"Cacao Indians, my foot! You want a white foreigner to teach you about cacao Indians. I might not have gone to university, but I am *not* ignorant. Look, I don't want you bothering Ram and Minty to go out there with them again, you hear."

Viveka wondered if her mother could really see right through her, if with motherhood came a seventh sense, the ability to know the mind and heart of one's children. She took the plate of food from the oven and turned her back on her mother as she headed down to the den to have her lunch in front of the television.

"I don't have a plan to go again. I want to. But not right away," she muttered over her shoulder.

The phone rang just as Viveka passed it. She flew around, almost slipping on the terrazzo floor in her rush to grab it, her food sliding to the edge of the plate.

Her mother watched.

Viveka belted out an urgent and serious *hello!* In an instant her body both rose like a helium-filled balloon and tensed, and her voice lowered to an inaudible whisper.

"Who is it?" Devika asked in a tone that suggested she already knew.

"It's for me. It's Anick. Mom, can you hang up for me? I will take it in the den. I want to watch the news."

Her mother bristled again.

In the den, Viveka waited until she heard the click of the phone before she spoke. Her breath seemed to have been snatched away and she could hardly talk. Neither could Anick, save to deliver, in a voice full of trepidation, an invitation to spend that very evening and night in Rio Claro. She had already planned everything out. Nayan would come for Viveka after his work. He had, she said, initiated the idea himself. He had plans of his own — to spend the evening with friends. He and some of his workers spent an evening a week "liming" and drinking. She was normally left alone, and it was a sore spot between them. He would come for Viveka and they would all eat together, and after that he would leave and be gone for most of the evening.

Viveka knew in a burning instant that, regardless of what her parents might say to such an invitation, she was going to keep Anick's company that night.

When she hung up, she thought for a minute. It was better, she decided, to speak with her father first. She dialled his number at work.

"But you were just there last night," Valmiki protested. "You don't want to make a nuisance of yourself, do you?"

"But *she* called and asked me. I can do some research there and…"

Her father interrupted. "Sorry, Vik, I can't talk now, I have a patient waiting. Are you asking if you can go? I can't come up with any reason why not."

"Well, I'm sure Mom will."

"God, why do you do this to me?" He paused long before saying, "I'll speak with her. I want to tell you to behave yourself. But you're a bit old for that, aren't you?"

Viveka's heart thumped. She was indeed, that very night, going to keep Anick's company.

"Just remember whose daughter you are. Whose daughter are you?"

"Well, I know I am Mom's." Viveka's voice quavered, and she felt sure it had given away her immense gratitude.

"So, I won't see you when I get home, then," Valmiki said at last. "Don't do anything foolish, you hear, darling?"

Viveka and Nayan

"THE WAY SHE DRESSES, IN BED OR OUT OF BED, IT DOESN'T MAKE A difference. You see the kind of clothes she wears? Nothing ordinary. I pay through my nose, but I see people — they don't know if to watch her face, her shoulders, her ass, or her clothes. Men and women. And it's worth every penny of my hard-earned money to see the admiration, the desire, the envy."

It was already past rush hour. Traffic on the Naparima-Mayaro Road was light. A yellow evening light cast itself over the cane fields. It had not been a hot day and there was no need for the air-conditioning to be on in the car, but Nayan had it on high. A scent of flowery perfume seemed caught in the cooling unit.

"Even inside the house or in the garden my wife doesn't wear 'old clothes,' you know. And Vik, ey man, that woman doesn't wear a stich of clothing, not one stitch, whether you could see it or not, that isn't just plain beautiful. She really has taste and she knows how to keep even her husband — who sees her every single day — salivating."

Nayan irritated Viveka on the one hand, but on the other his words brought to mind the few times long ago when she had stolen into the drawer in her father's cupboard. The centrefold photos. They were all more or less alike: a single pale woman sprawled across the two pages, her matching underwear in colours that accentuated the flawless paleness of her skin. The impossible length of her torso and limbs, the heft of breasts so translucent that Viveka could see greenish-blue veins in them — and knowing even then that images in magazines were airbrushed, she determined that the veins were intended to be left there. The women filled the two pages, edge to edge, and Viveka had had to hold the magazines at arm's length to get the full effect of each woman's pose.

She thought of her mother readying herself for parties: she would rush back and forth, dressed only in bra and panties, between the bedroom and the dressing room she shared with Valmiki as she one minute chose accessories from the jewellery box, the next made her face, plucked a hair or two from her eyebrows or chin, pulled on pantyhose. Save for her shoes, her dress was the very last item she would put on. Viveka's father, who never presented himself in front of his daughters without wearing at least full trousers, would be calmer as he dressed there, too, seemingly oblivious to his wife's half nudity. Both daughters were often in the room during this routine, Vashti helping her mother choose and fasten this or that, Viveka looking on uncomfortably, making suggestions that were most often unhelpful and so ignored. Vashti would help their mother dress, but Viveka would sit in the plush armchair and busy herself with one of her father's hunting magazines, somewhat embarrassed, feelings of guilt gnawing at her for having seen the photos she thought her mother tried poorly to emulate. She stayed in the bedroom during these times to watch her mother — in her peripheral vision, of course — taking mental notes of how she was herself supposed one day to be. She would leave the room conflicted, drawn to the strange womanliness she had seen in the magazines and nauseated by the fact that it was supposed to be desirable and attractive, while on her mother, she thought, it clearly was not.

Coming back to the present, Viveka leaned her head back on her seat's headrest. They were farther into the countryside now. The light had faded and twilight gathered at the foot of the forested land. But twilight lingered long here. She closed her eyes.

"The road is too winding for you, eh? Only another fifteen minutes. You want to stop for a few minutes?"

"No, let's just drive on. I'll be okay." She was sharper than she had meant to be, but Nayan didn't seem to notice. He continued talking, now saying something about the differences between Canadian girls, and Trinidadian girls, and French girls, who were not girls but women-in-the-making from the time they were born.

She couldn't get her father's old magazine centrefolds out of her mind, and now more images came to her, as if her memory had suddenly come alive. An unsolicited image of Merle Bedi interrupted the glossy images and her heart seemed, just as suddenly, to stop beating.

Viveka sat up. In an effort to rid herself of these unpleasant thoughts, she strained to keep her attention on Nayan.

"You can't play around with a Trinidadian girl, you know," he was saying. "Her family would expect you to marry her just because you looked at her. Man, let me tell you! They are not as innocent as their parents think, you know. I could tell you the names of three different girls right here that I had before I was even finished high school."

Viveka felt herself redden, even as she knew that this was how men talked of women. Did a tongue-kiss mean she had been "had"? He wasn't so rude or stupid, she wondered, as to include her among those three, was he? She could hear her mother or Vashti, her aunts, or even women at the university who called themselves feminists. They would say: *He thinks he is God's gift to woman or what? Why men so full of themselves? Anyway, in the end they don't mean anything by it, you know, they only full of mouth. Poor things.* And these women would begin a defense of the men. Perhaps she should fall in line, lest she ended up on the Promenade, too, Viveka thought. But she had had enough, and before she could stop herself she was saying, as gently as she could, the gentleness delivered through her uncharacteristic use of colloquialisms, "Nayan, like you eat a parrot and a lion for lunch today, boy. How you talking about your wife and other women so? You making me shy with all these details."

The smile on Nayan's face twisted and his jaw hardened. He fell quiet for an uncomfortable and long moment. The air between them stiffened. On the way to his house, and in his own car, Viveka had offended him. She found herself thinking of conciliatory things to say aloud, like, *Well, you did well, you got yourself quite a woman,* and, *Well, you really broke a lot of hearts when we heard that you were married, you know.*

But he spoke before she could muster up a voice. He was now serious and thoughtful. "Listen, Vik, I find myself ready to tell you all kinds of things. I mean, as if you are a confidante or a sister who I could trust. That's not because I disrespect you, you understand. On the contrary. You're not like other people. This is why Anick likes you. Me? I know you wouldn't judge me. I just know that deep in my heart. Well, I hope you wouldn't. But you are smart. You understand all kinds of complicated things. The funny thing is, it is why, too, I would never have been able to marry a girl like you. I could never hide in front of you. You would see right through me, through and through. You would see how small I really am. What a weak man I am."

Viveka felt uncomfortably grateful, flattered even.

"And even though I know you wouldn't judge me, I don't want to be small in front of the woman I have to take care of. You know, Vik, I will tell you something: living abroad, being in Canada and travelling to France, really woke me up, you know. It's like I woke up, but to a kind of nightmare. When I was at the University of Western Ontario I could have settled into a little nest of other Trinidadians and other West Indians, or even Indians from the various parts of the globe. I could have found a kind of safety and comfort among these people, a haven from the cold — not the weather, but the cold of seeing ourselves suddenly naked, without our families, without our cultures, without the spirit and sense of self that back-home could have given us. But I chose to go to the hard places, those very cold places, and mix with people who would make me have to prove myself."

Viveka remembered that Nayan had said on a previous occasion that he had mixed with white Canadians of the same class background as he. It wasn't the first time she had noticed how a personal story — a story that justified one's actions — became nuanced to suit the context of its telling, even if the audience remained constant.

"And what I saw of myself was that by dint of being Indian — a race whose skin colour shouts that a man is amenable to bending this way or that to please anyone he perceives to have an ounce of power more than he has — in those eyes, I was their servant. Among Trinis and other black- and brown-skinned fellows up there it was easy to be a big fish in a small pond. But it was as if I would get a fever, a delirium, that would only quiet down if I could be big and respected in the biggest pond of all. How to do that?

Well, for one, I found I had to pull out my credit cards to get noticed and respect. To get a foot in. You buy a round of drinks in a pub, and you get asked back. You might have to do this a few times, but once you're in you start to show that despite your colour you are just like they are, perhaps you even have better manners and nicer ways. They take you home, their parents like you because there is something vaguely old-fashioned about you, something reminiscent of themselves, and before you know it, you're in.

"When I returned here I watched my friends and saw — I still see it — how they all think that because they are men — just because of that single fact — that they are special. Little do they know that among other men of the world, we are practically not visible. Not just in the white world, you know. Look, I have met men from African countries, from Kuwait, from India, and if only you could see how they treat us — or don't treat us, because in their eyes, too, we — the sugar-cane and cacao Indians, those of us from Trinidad, Guyana, Fiji — we don't exist. With the Indians from India we can bond over cricket, but other than that they — even they, who share our ancestors — dismiss us. As if we are poor, poor, poor copies of an original that no longer exists. They see how we run to them for accessories like cushion covers, tablecloths, like pictures to hang up, bangles to wear on your hand. We have nothing of our own making — no style, no art or culture — to show for ourselves. So many years after leaving India, after losing the language, after watering down the culture, the religion, we're groping, still shy of becoming Trinidadian. Abroad, we exude no confidence in the way we move about. How can we? We are not properly Indian, and don't know how to be Trinidadian. We are nothing."

This was not the same Nayan, it seemed, who Viveka knew. She turned and faced him, interested for the first time.

"I am not foolish, you know, Vik. Being in France troubled me. I could see how little experience and knowledge of the world I had. It is a hard thing to realize that you know so little, have experienced so little. Before I went away I bought the best clothing from the fanciest stores here, the most expensive clothing we could find in Trinidad, and when I was among my white friends in Canada, and when I was with Anick's family and their friends in France, that same clothing looked cheap, the cloth itself inferior. It is not as if we have traditional clothes so that, no matter what quality cloth it is made from, it is intrinsically ours. Like the kinds of things the Africans, the Arabs, the Indians, wear. We gave up what was ours a long time ago and are trying too late to replace it with the same things. Too much has happened to us, we can't go back, but we don't know how to go ahead. Between being ashamed of our Indianness and the new born-again Indianness you see people practicing here, men like me fell off the radar. And the only place we can be big and confident is in the ponds we create for ourselves."

Viveka was excited by this unexpected turn in the conversation. "Wait a minute, Nayan, who do you mean by 'we'?"

Nayan looked at her as if she hadn't been listening. "Indian men."

"Yes, yes, I know, but which Indian men?"

"Are you testing me, Vik? I know what I am talking about. Indian men here in Trinidad. The ones from our class."

"Oh, I thought you meant all Trinidadian Indian men."

"No," Nayan said impatiently. "Of course not the ones like Mr. Lal and the men who live all around here. I mean men from our class. What gets us acknowledgement — or what we think gets us acknowledgement — is *not* what black people have that makes them Trinidadian (they have culture, we have money — which is better?) but a profession, wealth, children to carry on our names, and friendships with the whites. I know that people envy me because of Anick, you know."

Viveka surprised herself when she blurted out, "Well, she isn't *just* white."

Nayan grinned as if a compliment had been paid to him.

Viveka added quickly, "She is really quite a nice person."

"She is white. She is nice. And, you can say it, you know — she is beautiful. You don't think so?"

Viveka wanted to pretend that she hadn't noticed. But she took courage and said as congenially as she could, "Of course she is."

What Nayan had said made Viveka think of her father. She thought of her own attraction to the white French woman only minutes away, and the words "Yes, but I am different: I am not a man," consoled her, but only a little.

"I am not a handsome man," continued Nayan. "I mean, not a truly handsome man — looks are one thing, but style and manners, those are what make a good-looking man handsome. And I know that marrying Anick, or rather, *Anick* marrying *me* is an indication of my worth. Indian fellows from here go abroad to study because they have brains and their families can afford to send them away. They are lonely, and what happens when the first white woman comes along and flashes a big open smile at them? They fall in love. Not with her, but with they way she, a white person, is taken with them. I mean, look at how many of our men go abroad and come back with white women. And usually they are not good-looking women at all, but that doesn't matter. What matters is that they are white. Neither of them could have done better. She nets herself a professional, or at least a man with a degree, and he returns to his family, his village, to the country, with a white woman on his arm. He returns the conqueror!"

With this, Nayan fell quiet.

Viveka thought how she had, as yet, no experience of the world outside of Trinidad. Perhaps, she mused, despite the fact that she was studying at university, the quality and magnitude of her thoughts would be compromised by her lack of world travel, her limited knowledge of others and other places. She wasn't in the category Nayan was referring to, that of the Indian man, but perhaps Anick would see, in any case, how green, unaware, parochial she was. She so wanted to be grand — not "in between" like Nayan or her father.

"But you have to wonder who really conquered who," Nayan suddenly piped up. "Those white women got themselves men for sure, but men who are lesser beings in those women's eyes, lesser than men from their own societies, and much less than the women themselves. This is the only way a white woman can gain a hand over a man."

Viveka marvelled at Nayan's thinking, as bitter as it was, and wondered why, if he was capable of such analysis, he made himself generally so boorish. Although, she conceded, these weren't the kinds of thoughts that would win him friends.

"You see, it was a little different with me," Nayan continued. "I got bamboozled. Because Anick wasn't just any white woman. She wasn't *only* a white woman. She had class, she was sexy, she was beautiful, she was like a movie star. It's like — a woman like her, who could have just about anybody, chose me. There was something in me that she wanted. I don't mean to brag..." Nayan seemed suddenly to change his mind about what he was about to say. "You know," he said, taking his eyes off the road to look squarely and long at Viveka, "to tell the truth, I don't feel very secure in this marriage I made. There are things about Anick — I can't tell you everything, but there are things I know, things really private, that make me feel that as much as I might have used her," he looked back at the road again, "and I am saying *might* have, in the sense that one does these things subconsciously — well, in the same way I might have used her, she has used me too." He paused as if to reflect on his own words, and Viveka wondered what secrets Anick had, besides the one she knew — that "French girls like both." She wondered if this was the very thing that Nayan knew and now hinted at.

"But isn't that always the way it is, Nayan?" Viveka's voice quavered. "Everything comes with a price. People often only give something if they stand to gain."

"It just makes me want to do all kinds of things, Vik, from being a big man in my own house, my own pond, to showing Anick who wears the pants, showing everybody. It makes me want to create the biggest cacao estate in the world, producing the best and most desired beans, and make chocolate that would put French and Belgian chocolate to shame. You see us drinking, dancing, joking, laughing, jumping up like there is no tomorrow, bathing in the sea? People abroad think of us as the jump-up jump-up people, you know, the good time people. But an angry man must, and will, lash out sooner or later. We have to lash out somewhere, after all, but the sad thing is that we lash out at the ones we love — in private, of course. The only place we have any balls is in our little kingdoms, our homes, right here in this country. This small, small place. Lord, Vik, I am tired of being a small man. I thought in my own home I would be my own boss, but I am living with a Frenchwoman who thinks she knows the right way, the best way to do everything. And the odd thing is that as much as that makes me feel small, it is also what drives me forward, and keeps me wanting to surpass her every expectation."

Nayan slowed the car now as they approached the turn-off Viveka recognized from the night before. He gripped the steering wheel for control on the rough road. After some moments of weighty silence he tapped his forehead with one of his forefingers and said, "Heaven and hell. Right here, Vik."

A man appeared on the road waving at the car. Nayan rolled down his window and the heat from outside rushed in. He spoke before the man did. "Hanuman, good evening. You drunk or what?"

"Oh God, sir, what you saying? I coming to look for you. The wife cook a goat and some of the fellows, them coming to eat. I have a bottle…"

"One bottle? One bottle is all you have? How many men?"

"Well, is about six of us. I coming to ask you to make it seven, Boss."

"I have a function tonight. Meghu having prayers for his child."

"Yes, all of we going. But we have to eat first. He aint go have food there, you know, Boss. Is only liquids by him."

"So, is me you want or a bottle?"

"Oh God, Boss, don't shame me so, na. Is you I coming to ask. Even before the goat done the wife say how it will eat good and I should go and bring you and the Madam, but…"

"No. Forget the Madam. She have company. I coming. I coming. I can't disappoint all you fellows. I coming." He looked at Viveka and then back at the man. "I just have to drop home one minute, and I'll swing back."

Nayan rolled back up his window and as he drove off explained, "That man is the foreman. He is a good worker. He doesn't drink on the job, but after work you could pickle pommecythere in him. I could leave this place in his hands and not worry about a single thing."

Viveka's face flushed. She tried to keep her voice even. "Did I just understand that you are not going to be eating dinner with..."

"Yeah, yeah." Nayan was now dismissive. He sat up high and leaned into the steering wheel with a brightened face. He seemed to push the car forward with his upper body. He appeared suddenly to Viveka like a boy who had been cooped inside all weekend and was now called out to come and play cricket with his friends. "You will be there to keep Anick company. You'll see. She only wants me for one thing, girl. But I need a break! She won't miss me if she has company."

Viveka and Anick

THE ZIGZAG OF A SINGLE LINE OF MUSIC, A MELANCHOLIC, RESONATING drone, soared from the house, greeting Viveka as she and Nayan walked to the back stairs of the house.

"Good God!" said Nayan. "She plays that damned squeaking thing over and over. A recording her father gave her. It drives me crazy. She doesn't dare play it when my parents or friends are here. They'd think I had gone crazy!"

A second melody danced around the steady pulse of the first. "What is it?" Viveka called behind Nayan as he bolted up the stairs ahead of her.

The smell of anchar masala was in the air. Viveka's mouth watered. There would likely be roti, and some curried vegetable, and a meat dish. The music had ended, but as far as her untrained ear could tell, the very same piece had begun again. The maid greeted them shyly.

Nayan left Viveka in the kitchen while he went inside to look for Anick. He called back to the maid, "I'm in a hurry. I want a glass of ice water."

The music came to an abrupt end. In a concerted attempt not to hear whatever was to transpire between Nayan and Anick, Viveka positioned herself on the top stair, and busied herself looking out the kitchen door toward the depth of acre upon acre of cacao.

In no time, her two hosts appeared in the kitchen, Nayan ahead of Anick. Nayan drank the water that was waiting for him on the table and wiped his face with the back of his hand. Anick greeted Viveka, her hands clutching her dinner guest's shoulders as she kissed her on both cheeks. She wore a simple dress and she was barefoot.

Nayan was already heading down to his car. "I'll see if I can score some goat for you all. Don't wait up for me."

He got no response from either of the women. Viveka was still clinging to the sensation of the touch of Anick's cheek against hers.

"Behave yourselves," Nayan added, to which Anick playfully threw back, "I am not telling you what to do with yourself. If you want to misbehave, nobody stopping you. So we too, we do what we want." She looked to Viveka and said, "I am right, no?"

Viveka shrugged her shoulders. Glancing at Nayan, who looked sternly at Anick now, she posed what was clearly a rhetorical question, "I guess we can do what we want and still behave ourselves?"

"Oh, come on, Viveka."

Her name rolled like a smooth cool marble in Anick's mouth. A ticklish sensation ran through Viveka on hearing it pronounced a little queerly.

"We adults: we can do what we like, no? And how we like, too. Because he is a man he can do anything, and we, we women so we cannot? Who make these rules? After all, we are not backward people. Is true is the bush we live in, but we are not backward people. At least, that is what I think."

Nayan shook his head. "She can carry on a whole conversation by herself, and sometimes it is ill-advised," he warned

Viveka. "I'm gone. Mr. Lal is already here. Send him for me only if one of you is dying."

The two women stood side by side, close, Viveka leaning into the railing. Anick pressed her arm against Viveka's. Admiring such brazenness, but not quite so brazen herself, Viveka stood firm.

Nayan made a sign to Mr. Lal, calling him over. Viveka took the opportunity to actively resist the warm leaning weight, pressing back just enough so that Anick could feel her do it, but not enough that Nayan, should he turn to wave, would notice.

"In twenty minutes the light will go," said Anick. "Well, maybe not twenty minutes. But about that. Soon, I mean. Let us make a small walk, quickly, in the forest. We will eat after, no?"

It seemed to Viveka already too dark to walk in the forest, but she decided to trust Anick. Mr. Lal, lit cigarette in his mouth, nodded to the women as they headed onto the dirt path between a scattering of grapefruit trees.

Anick walked fast, as if to an appointment. The light along the path was low now, but Anick clearly knew the dangers— where there were dips in the ground and where the heavy roots of the shade trees protruded. Viveka almost had to run to keep up with her. All the while, her host chattered nervously, saying that now they were alone she didn't know what to talk about, that she didn't want to bore Viveka, asking (but not waiting for an answer) if Viveka knew and liked the forest, if she liked going for walks, and telling her that there was a place that was all hers, "une cabine," Anick called it, that she wanted Viveka to see.

A section of the music Viveka had heard when she arrived had remained with her, the haunting sound wrapping itself around her brain. "What was the music you were playing?" huffed Viveka.

"You like it? Is my father favourite music. You like the cello?"

Viveka didn't answer directly. She knew the cello was one of the string instruments, one of the bigger ones, but she wasn't sure which and didn't wish to show her ignorance of something clearly close to Anick's heart. "I like that piece," she said instead. "It's new to me, but it has already stuck with me."

"Is like a shovel that dig deep inside my soul. Is like it remind me not to forget..." Anick stopped mid-sentence.

"Forget what?"

"Just not to forget. Not to forget who I am, where I come from, what I dream about. You know, what move me. What I want."

The path led downwards, an almost imperceptible decline over dried fallen foliage. Soon, on either side of the path was straight row after straight row of carefully spaced cacao trees. The trees were of equal height, at least two-and-a-half times the height of a person, their branches uncluttered, open, well-pruned. Plump yellow pods defied the pending darkness and stood out brightly against the trunks from which they clung. The rows of straight lines offered an attractive perspective from the path, a dizzying feeling of motion, as the two women swept past. Viveka was nervous, fearful of snakes (she was sure she had heard more than one slither in the grass right at the edge of the rough path), the uneven ground, the falling darkness, but she remained determined not to show her fear. While Anick moved lithely a few paces ahead of her, Viveka was breathless, huffing uncomfortably, unable to respond to her companion's non-stop ramble. With each deep breath she drew in the cloying odour of ripened forest fruit, not the sort of fruit found in the grocery or in the market, but fruit that gave off scent as if it were a pheromone, sickeningly sweet, insistent.

The sky, dappled behind the shade trees' blackened foliage, had become blood-red. Full darkness would descend any minute. A few fireflies circled lazily.

"Fireflies," Viveka huffed. "I had no idea they were so bright in the forest."

"Oh, this is nothing. Their light can be so bright you can see the trees on either side."

Then, there it was off to the side, ferns all around it—*une cabine*. Anick ran ahead. "Is getting too dark now. But you can look inside quickly. Is just one room. I don't put anything in it as yet. You can see. Come."

The structure appeared to have been recently built. It was a hut, but not shabby as one might expect so far from the main house.

"Is it new?"

Sweat ran down Anick's face. She appeared suddenly youthful in a way that Viveka had not noticed before. "They had a little shack here for the workers to shelter from the rain, or sit down and rest," she replied. "Nayan break it down and he make this one for me, with a door that can lock. Is mine, he say."

"So what do the workers do now?"

"I show you tomorrow. Tomorrow we can make a picnic here. You like it?"

"Yes, sure. I mean, it's getting dark. We should probably go back. But can I step inside quickly?"

Anick took Viveka's hand, pulling her in behind her. Inside, she continued to hold onto Viveka's hand. A couple of fireflies danced in the still space. Barely discernable in a room no larger than eight feet by seven was an armchair, and next to it was a small table. Nothing else.

Viveka wrapped her fingers around Anick's hand. She tugged shyly. "Your own space." The feeble phrase was meant to take notice away from the pounding of her heart, which she was sure was loud enough to be heard.

Anick turned to look directly at her. "I bring my little portable tape recorder here, and I listen to that same music and other one my father give me. He like the cello, so is all cello music, very haunting, melancholy. Like a deep-deep human voice, singing. Is nice in the forest. Or maybe you think I should listen to the forest and not play any music?"

"No, no. I am not making any judgments. I am interested in hearing what you like."

Anick suddenly let her hand go and moved to face Viveka. Viveka's heart stilled. She could barely breathe. The sounds of the forest seemed to thunder — a cacophony of monkeys howling, of the trees trembling in the light breeze, the creaking of the branches of the silk cottons, the pulsing drone of a thousand cicadas, and frogs, frogs right outside the door croaking.

Anick stepped forward. She took both of Viveka's hands in hers, lightly, and the sounds in Viveka's head subsided. Anick brought her face, her lips to Viveka's. Viveka stepped back and leaned against the wood wall of the cabin, a strange and complete relief descending on her, weakening her legs yet filling her chest, her brain, her mouth, and her fingers with an equally strange assuredness. She listened. There was hers and Anick's breathing. Quick, shallow, wanting. She took her hands from Anick's and rested them on Anick's waist. She pulled Anick to her as their mouths came together, and they breathed in each other's warm moist breath. They wrapped their arms about each other, each hungry to discover the contours and substance of the other's body. Anick brought her hand to Viveka's face, touched her cheek lightly, and their tongues, the tips only, touched. The soft sure slide of wetness, a sensation new to Viveka, imbued her with a ferocious hunger. She withdrew from Anick, who, in reaction, held on tighter.

"I can't breathe. Just a minute. Just give me a minute," pleaded Viveka.

Anick stood away, fearful that this was a repetition of an earlier rejection. She mumbled, trembling, "I am sorry."

But Viveka had already sensed Anick's misreading. "No, no. There isn't anything to be sorry about. It's just that this is overwhelming. It's so..." She couldn't find the words. Finally she said, "I don't want to ever stop kissing you, Anick." In a voice so soft she almost mouthed the words, she said, "Kiss me again, Anick. Please."

Anick leaned against Viveka, who wanted nothing more than to be crushed by the weight, but Anick was light, and her touch was light, and Viveka feared she would want more now than she would ever be able to get. They explored each other's mouths with their tongues, their bodies with their hands. Anick's neck was wet with perspiration. The tips of her fingers were like ten eager tongues.

Through the thin fabric of Anick's dress Viveka caressed Anick's breasts, moving her thumb across the hardened, thick nipple. Anick's breathing quickened, and she made sounds of pleasure that fanned Viveka's fire. No touching had ever felt this good and true and right to her. She so wanted to place her cheek on a breast, to slip off the straps of Anick's dress and put her lips to the firm mound, but she stopped herself, for as true as all of this so surely felt, she feared, too, crossing a boundary, crossing into an aloneness from which there might well be no return. So she felt the goodness and trueness of the moment and held on to Anick, pressed her mouth against Anick's, wanting to take everything that was offered. Then she as quickly stopped herself again. How she wanted to collapse on the wood floor and wrap her body around Anick's. But fear held her back.

Drenched in this new desire, the two women went slowly back to the house by the staccato light of hundreds of fireflies. They stayed close, their fingers entwined. Viveka peered ahead, her eyes open as wide as possible, turning back often to make sure that Mr. Lal or some unknown forest dweller was not approaching or following them.

THE MAID HAD ALREADY GONE HOME. A GROUPING OF SERVING bowls sat on the counter, a large tea cloth thrown over them to keep flies away. The table in the dining room was set. Anick turned on the stereo and the cello suite began. She had burned herself a CD with that very suite copied three consecutive times. When the third round of it ended, a concerto began, the cello leading, pleading, playing ahead of the other strings and wind instruments.

Viveka watched Anick listen to the music. Her body jerked and swayed, the movements small, almost involuntary, but still perceptible as Anick moved about the room, getting them drinks, doing quick mundane chores before serving out food.

They could, between the two of them, have eaten all there was on the table — roti, mango anchar, curried shrimp, pumpkin, curried same — and the remaining food in the pot on the stove, and still they would have been hungry. They picked at the food on their plates, grinning shyly, staring at each other, the dimmed light of the dining room laying bare their desire.

Finally, as if of one mind, they pushed back their chairs, stood up, and walked side by side down the corridor toward the room in which Viveka was to spend the night.

Anick left Viveka for as long as it took to return to the kitchen to lock the back door, and close and lock the windows and doors to the rest of the house. She turned on the lights in the TV room and in her study. From outside, the lights of these rooms could still be seen. She lit a mosquito coil and returned with it to the guest room.

Viveka and Anick kissed lightly at first, but their passion grew and they pushed and pulled each other, their mouths locking, tongues probing, tasting, hands searching frantically, bodies taking turns turning, lying one on top of the other. It eventually fell that Viveka lay atop Anick, Anick's dress pulled up to her waist, and Viveka's fingers, having parted the narrow band of panty fabric between her legs, discovered a viscous wetness that took control of her mind and her fingers, and as if she had done it a thousand times before, she knew what to do to make Anick's entire body pulse beneath hers. Anick's arms were wrapped around Viveka, pulling her tighter and holding her more urgently than Viveka had ever been held before. With each thrust of her body, Anick kissed Viveka's face and sighed and moaned in pleasure. Viveka's body was an electric current of pleasure, but she was spurred on more by her desire to give Anick all that she so clearly wanted than by any need of her own. Then it was as if Anick's pleasure opened as wide as it could, and she burst, and burst and burst. She continued to pulsate, and to cry out softly, until she collapsed and sobbed.

Viveka pressed the length of her body against Anick's to still all the pleasure and anguish that had surfaced. Anick's hair around her face was wet, her skin damp. Tears suddenly ran down Viveka's cheeks and she wiped them fast so that Anick wouldn't know. She had felt, during the initial moments of their lovemaking, a sense of having taken on the form of a young man's body. Her body had become, albeit briefly, Vince's body, and in other moments Anand's. These two were suddenly young men, sturdy, muscled, handsome. As handsome as Anick was beautiful. It was strange how Vince and Anand had grown into such young men; this was the strongest sensation of that sort Viveka had ever had — of not being what she looked like, female. And yet, she knew now more than ever that her feelings and her way with Anick were hers and hers alone. Not a boy's. Not a man's. Whatever she was, these feelings were hers. She wanted to reveal all her secrets to Anick, to tell her of the time when she was a little child, the time when she and Vashti and Anand had gone for a drive with their parents to the wharf, the time when the painter from up the road had come waving a scythe at them, the time when her parents were bickering and she was trying to warn them about the man who was angry and waving the scythe. She had tried to save them all, but the others had never seen the man, and then Anand had disappeared. This story had always made sense to her, but suddenly, lying there with Anick, the story seemed, for the first time, unlikely, as disjointed and senseless as a dream. Perhaps she could be finished with Anand now. And with Vince.

Viveka and Anick lay like this for some minutes, and then the touching began again. The second time was longer and there was no crying, but instead an urgency to know and have more. Eventually, they rolled out of the bed and went to the kitchen, drank water, ate squares of chocolate from the stack that Anick had hidden away, pieces of bars sent to her by her parents.

The third time was interrupted by a whimper from the dog. Anick heard it first and she bolted up out of the bed and ran into her bedroom. Then Viveka heard the sound of Nayan's car. The car hummed on the street. Viveka shut the door to her room. She pulled a T-shirt and sleeping shorts from her overnight bag, changed, and got under the cover of the bed. She heard the shower in the next room turned on. The car horn sounded, two quick pops. The dog barked excitedly now. The shower turned off. The gate down in the yard opened. Viveka imagined Mr. Lal awakened from his slumber, moving slowly. The car rolled in, and the gate scraped shut. The barking stopped, a whimper and the tinkling of the dog's chain-link leash the only sound now.

Anick opened Viveka's door, pulling her nightgown around her body. The ends of her hair were wet. She whispered, "Good night, sweet Viveka, I won't stop thinking of you." She pressed two fingers hard to her lips, then offered them to Viveka. Viveka whispered back, "'Night," just as Anick drew in the door and silently shut it.

At the same time, the kitchen door was being less quietly unlocked.

AFTER NAYAN HAD LEFT FOR WORK THE NEXT MORNING, MUSIC similar to the Bach Viveka had heard last night, but pieces far longer, played quietly in the house. The music filled her with delicious longing. When, shortly after rising, the two women left the house to go down to the cabin and Anick gave to Viveka the tape she had played the previous night, Viveka felt as if an entirely new world was opening up for her. She had not heard such music before last night, yet it was as if it was part of her being now.

"I can make myself another one," said Anick. "Take it and listen to it when you alone. Each note enter your body when is quiet and you can concentrate. Is like love, and it make you long to give love and long to get love. Not the kind of love like between two people. Is something bigger. So big I don't know what it is, but is very real. Only some people can know this. I know you will know."

Nayan's driver was to come before noon to fetch Viveka and return her to her parents' house. They had to hurry. They took cups of iced chocolate milk with them. They met workers along the path, caught sight of them between the baliser and pineapple plants, in the groves of cacao, clearing the gullies, hacking off ripe pods, and transporting baskets, one between two people. They heard the braying of a transport donkey. Several paths ran off to the sides, the main one splitting off several times. Viveka marvelled that Anick had been so sure of her directions the night before.

They spent little time in the cabin. Viveka was certain that anyone seeing them in there would know instinctively of their passion. She kept just enough of a distance from Anick to dispel questions others might have about their closeness. Soon they had walked well past the place where the cabin was, toward the workers' hut. Viveka could hear the workers chattering, laughing, sometimes raucously, from a small distance. The hut was a low thatched-roof shelter with no walls. On its clay floor was a long table and two benches, one on either side. There was a hammock and a stand-pipe from which water dripped into a pool. The moment Anick and Viveka were in sight, the chattering and laughter quieted. The men straightened themselves and were formal but warm with Anick.

"Good morning, everybody," said Anick. "Is my friend. She come to visit."

The men nodded, and salutations were muttered back. One of them approached, a bottle in his hand. He removed his hat.

"Madam, I just get honey from the tree." He pointed to the crown of a far-off and very tall tree. "Take a bottle. I have plenty."

Anick told the man to keep it, that she still had the three bottles he had given her not long ago. But she asked if he might let Viveka have a taste.

The man was pleased. He opened the bottle, and Viveka held open her palm. The honey was black, like molasses. It was unlike the more common honey from bees that lived and fed in fields of flowers in the central plains or in the dry dunes at the seaside. Its taste was almost rancid, like an old and dirty dish cloth, yet it was as cloying and compelling as any other, more conventional honey. Viveka very forwardly asked if there was enough that she might take some home with her. The man was only too delighted to oblige.

When they walked away, Anick confessed, "Nayan, he hate that honey. Is too dark for him. He say it taste like sweat. Is true, no? But I like that it come from the forest, and that man risk so much to get it. He have to climb so high, and he don't wear nothing to protect his body. He take the comb with his bare hand. Is a talent, no? It make him proud to do this. Is why I take the honey. But I don't know what to do with it. I have six bottles in the house. If you really like it, I give you all."

AS THE CAR APPROACHED SAN FERNANDO, THE LIGHT OF THE DAY became whiter, harsher. Viveka urged herself to — in Anick's word — *remember.* She had had a glimpse of who she was, of what her desire looked like for her: she wanted to feel again and again all that she had with Anick. Several times, an image of Anick's face as they had made love — made love! That is what she had done, she had finally made love — came to her, or the sound of Anick's voice after a touch from Viveka, and there in the back seat of the car Viveka shivered.

But with this ephemeral knowledge came another thought: the dreadful possibility of losing her family. Which was greater, she wondered — to be all that you were, to be true to yourself, or to honour one's family, one's society, one's country? Her family, despite everything, was her life. She could never be without them. She could never do to them what Merle Bedi had done to her family. She wondered if her family could do to her what Merle Bedi's family had done to Merle. Again she felt an urge to go and find Merle, to talk to her. Take her away. But away to where?

Viveka

OVER THE NEXT SEVERAL WEEKS, VIVEKA FOUND LOCKED INSIDE OF her — not unlike her previously unknown ability to be stirred by classical music — a power and strength, physical and mental, that spilled over into how she communicated at large. She had become bold.

To her family's surprise, she got over her fear of driving rather abruptly. She announced — rather than asked — that she would be playing volleyball with Helen's team. Her father was pleased that he was finally being spared the burden of granting or denying permission. The announcement was received by her mother with only pursed lips and a general curtness, but Viveka was used to this and chose to ignore it. In general, the family was so stunned by this new tactic of Viveka's that they let her take her mother's car to go to volleyball, and even as far as Rio Claro to visit Anick.

What Viveka's parents and Nayan did not know is that Anick, driven by a chauffeur, would come to see Viveka play volleyball. And Viveka showed up for games as much for Anick as for the pleasure of the sport.

Helen was surprised, found it curious, that Anick would come such a distance so regularly to see Viveka play. And she expected Viveka to join the team and their friends for after-game drinks. Wayne was often there, these days accompanied by his cousin Trevor, who was visiting from Toronto and who, according to Helen, was ready to settle down and was looking for an Indo-Trinidadian wife. Spending time with a team of very independent, and mostly non-Indian, young women, Viveka could only disinterestedly wish him the best. Helen did not hide her irritation when, after the games, Viveka visited in the stands with Anick and joined the team at their regular pizza house too late to participate in the camaraderie. Helen and Wayne numerous times extended to Viveka invitations on Trevor's behalf to accompany them to dinner, to a movie, to the beach. But unlike the other women on the team, who tried in vain to capture Trevor's notice, Viveka had time for, and interest, in only one person: Anick.

On the court Viveka was as if on a stage, ever ready to show off her abilities. And she was particularly spry if she knew Anick was watching.

One notable day, she had one eye on the ball and one on the stands, awaiting her love's arrival. She was semi-crouched, trigger-ready. She saw the player on the opposite team leap for the ball and knew what was coming. She was ready to impress. The coach's dictum rang in her head like a bell, "*You* hit the ground first. The ball? Never." Towering at the top of the net, the woman lifted her cupped hand and the ball made loud contact as she spiked it into Viveka's team's attack area, a section of which was vulnerable. But Viveka had already slid into place, and the hard, outstretched cradle made by her bare forearms blocked the descent of the leather, firing it back high. One of the teammates behind her shouted, "Yes!" The *slaap* of the ball against her skin reverberated in the air. She felt so good these days. *This* is how she wanted to be always, her mind primed for high-speed analysis, her body its instant respondent. She felt like wind, a hurricane over open sea.

Scarlet welts on her arms were already blooming. They would intensify to a rusty rose by the end of the evening. The stinging felt good, told her that she was indeed out on a court doing what she wanted to do. But in becoming conscious of that good feeling in her body, of the thrill of having just made the kind of play she dreamed about, she lost focus. She pushed long bangs damp with sweat out of her face and glanced away, into the stands.

A handful of spectators were scattered there to watch the practice games. On one side, a group of bongo-drummers were immersed in their own incessant groove. But for Viveka, the bleachers might as well have been empty. She was suddenly disheartened. The ball remained in play and the opposing team, as if they saw her lapse, returned it directly at her. Crouched behind her in readiness, Helen screamed, "Vik!"

Viveka lashed at the ball with the palm side of a sloppy fist. It shot right out of the court.

Viveka followed the ball out, her body moving sluggishly in spite of the monologue in her head about how good she could be. Even as she muttered the words, "Focus, focus, focus," she couldn't help scanning the stands again.

The women on both teams wore fashionable and very short shorts in light fabrics that swished sportily as they moved. *Of course they would dress like that*, her mother would have scolded had she been there, *because not one of them was of Indian origin and other people don't have the same values.* Viveka, however, wore shorts that reached her knees and looked like something more likely to be worn by one of the basketball players on the neighbouring court. She looked different. Ever since that transformative night at Anick's house, knowing the wet heat of Anick's body against hers, she had relished the difference.

The women on the other side of the net, having been given the point, embraced, thumped one another on the back, and grunted, "A ya yai, a ya yai."

Vik's captain shouted to her, "Focus, girl. Take it easy, and focus."

A group of five young black men on the basketball court on the other side of the fence had stopped their own play and to watch. They began imitating the women's cheer to the rhythm of the drumming coming from the stands. "A ya yai, a ya yai," they repeated at length, gyrating their hips while jabbing the air with pointed forefingers. Viveka's coach smiled with only one side of his mouth. One of the men came up to the wire fencing. "Pssst. Ey, you. Sweetie Pie, I make you miss the point or what? Is me you watching so? Ey. *Vik* is your name? Is short for something? Watch me, na, girl."

Viveka turned, surprised to hear her name, and then turned away again, blushing that she was singled out. Oddly, it felt good, yet a rush of hot panic rose up her neck and over her face. The referee blew his whistle to signal his impatience. The half-smile disappeared off the coach's face. He folded his arms high across his chest. The young man, undeterred, called again, "Girl, you are the prettiest one on the court. All the other girls on the court ugly, for so." The women on both sides broke into a chuckle. Viveka didn't know how to take the man's comment or the women's laughter, for she was not like them, it was true. She knew most people would argue that these others were the pretty ones, and she — well, they might have said she was unusual, or asked why she didn't grow her nice, thick, black hair, or why she didn't wear earrings, or, off court, a dress.

The man, encouraged now, leaned into the wire fence and called directly to her, "Vik, Aloo Pie! Smile, na. Why you so serious?"

The two coaches and the volleyball referee convened and spoke briefly. The opposing team's coach stepped away and ambled close to his side's end line. The referee returned his attention to the game. Viveka's coach, arms still folded high, walked toward the man by the fence. His pace was hesitant, his eyes soft yet fixed on the man.

The man was undeterred and continued, "What a Indian girl like you doing playing in the park? Your dad and your mom know you here?"

Viveka was close to shouting at him to mind his own business. She weighed which was more prudent: standing up to him or ignoring him. Fortunately, the women on both teams, hearing the name-calling as a slur, had their limits too — they sucked their teeth loudly, over and over, in a show of heightened, united irritation, and in an instant they switched their minds right back to their game, shutting the fellow out. Viveka rejoined the competition, but less fervently. Her back tingled. It felt naked.

The man bounced off the fence laughing and broke into play with his group again.

It was they, those same basketball skylarkers, who eventually alerted Viveka that there was a new presence in the stands. Suddenly and noticeably quiet, they had stopped shooting hoops and were staring into the stands. There Anick was, seated and looking straight out at the volleyball court. The men were talking quietly among themselves. Viveka heard one of them say to another, "Boy, leave the woman alone, na. You don't have wife and child enough to mind? You shooting with us or what? If you leave, don't came back, and by that I mean don't even come back tomorrow."

A hot and thudding flush of mingled relief and happiness coursed through Viveka. She felt invincible and grinned wide like a grouper to realize that, even so, she felt like herself, not like Vince her imagined boy, and that she hadn't felt like him in a good while now — and she suddenly charged, heading harder and faster than was necessary for a play that was not hers to take. She collided with her partner, to whom that ball ought to have belonged. Neither of them made contact with the ball and both fell to the ground hard. Viveka jumped up and hugged her mate in excited apology. They resumed play and Viveka thought how odd, how great, to feel on the court like that boy she used to be, and who had slipped out of life so quietly. What a wonderful thing the mind was. She was elated. Feigning deep concentration now, it was several minutes before Viveka looked across to the stands, casually, and when she did, she behaved as if she had only that very moment realized her friend was there. She waved. Anick reservedly wagged in front of her a tightly rolled-up magazine. One of the basketball players had spotted this exchange and waved back to Anick, and then he, too, burst into a flurry of hard competitive play.

Viveka took on a slight limp, rubbing her right knee, and asked to be substituted. To her embarrassment the coach made a greater fuss of her knee than was necessary. Since it was near the end of the game, she asked to sit it out in the stands. Carrying her water bottle and unnoticed by the basketball players she limped onward, her gait that of a wounded but proud and decorated warrior. When she reached the bleachers she did not turn to see if her coach was watching; she bounded up the four tiers like a white-tail doe to Anick's row. Anick stood to greet her with their usual hug, but Viveka, breathless and grinning, put her hand quickly on one of Anick's shoulders, pressing her back into her seat. Viveka leaned in and over the drumming whispered, "Not here."

She set the water bottle between her and Anick and sat down, aware that Anick's presence had, as usual, caused a small excitement in the stands. She hoped the novelty would wear off fast.

It was unusual for a white person, let alone a woman — foreign or local — to come to the park, whether it was to play on a court or to sit in the stands. And this particular white woman, wearing large European-style sun glasses — there was not another person in the stands wearing sunglasses — drew attention, as she always did. Just the way she walked, the authority with which she held the ground beneath her feet, as if she had the idea that she could have almost any thing she wanted simply by wanting it — just the way she casually ignored every eye on her — from all this, onlookers knew she wasn't from this place. Viveka was easily captivated by this look of Anick's, but was shy of it too. She didn't want to be like all the other people Anick had told her about, liking her for her looks. And while it was quite a thrill to be the one Anick had come to watch, Viveka was uncomfortable sitting next to her. She felt exposed. Taking advantage of the loudness of the drumming on the far side of the stands, she and Anick spoke frankly to one another, Anick in her native French, Viveka in a version of it that would make sense only to someone set on understanding.

Anick pouted. "What do you think I will do? Can't I give you a hug? People hug in this country. I know this."

"Yes, yes. I know. I'm really glad to see you — you can't imagine." Viveka's tone was pleading. "It's just odd here." Then she brightened, "Besides, I am disgusting. I am completely drenched in sweat."

"That doesn't matter to me, you know that."

"But it has to matter, Anick. Just trust me. My God, it's way too hot for humans, don't you think? Hey, I thought you'd never arrive. Ca va?"

"The driver came for me late. Sorry. Is better than nothing, no?"

Viveka leaned forward to glimpse Anick's feet. Anick wore open-toe sandals with little heels on them, and her nails were painted a bright red shade. Viveka looked back up and fixed her eyes on her team directly ahead, but out of the corner of her eye she was concentrating on her own left foot and Anick's right. Centimetre by centimetre she swung the tip of her sneaker toward Anick's sandal-clad right foot. When the edge of her shoe met the hard leather of Anick's sandal she exerted enough force to move Anick's foot a fraction. Anick stiffened her leg and slid her foot closer, so that the area from her ankle down the edge of her foot pressed against Viveka's. Viveka's eyes were riveted now on the court. The light in the sky seemed to dim, the drumming was silenced by a louder reverberation throughout her body. She stared ahead, grinning.

There came quickly, however, the familiar moment when each other's company was not enough. What kind of conversation does one have, Viveka mused, what kind of communication, when time is limited and the exact moment of its ending is unknown, yet forever imminent? Viveka decided to bring that moment into focus. "Nayan, sait-il ou tu est?"

"No. He thinks I went to the grocery, so I can't stay very long."

With that, Viveka switched to English. "Christ. We're both going to get into so much trouble." She laughed nervously.

"Let's go away, Vik. Let's leave this place."

Over the past couple of weeks, every conversation between them had deteriorated faster than the last into recognition of the difficulty of this love between them and the need, growing ever more urgent daily, to do something about it. Anick had spoken again and again of wanting to return, with Viveka, to Canada — either to Toronto or Montreal or Vancouver — where there were thriving communities of people like the two of them. There, she said, they could disappear if they wanted to, and reinvent themselves. But it never seemed to Viveka as easy to deal with as it did to Anick.

"How far is away, Anick? We'll never get far enough away. You know Nayan will find you wherever you go, easily, and even if I leave this place my own parents will still suffer publicly and privately because of what I am. Going away won't solve a thing for us."

"But you're not yourself in this place. You're so jumpy."

"You've never seen me anywhere else! Why do you think I'm not myself here?"

"I know what you're like when you're alone with me."

The conversation was interrupted by someone higher up in the stands, calling out Viveka's name. Anick and Viveka both turned, Viveka's heart suddenly racing. Then relief flooded her. It was only Wayne's cousin, Trevor. She wondered how long he had been up there.

"It's that guy. Trevor. Remember I told you about him? Helen's boyfriend's cousin?"

Anick huffed. "The one you said is interested in you."

Helen had told Viveka that Trevor was asking after her, and Viveka had twisted this information into a white lie for Anick's benefit, a lie meant only to provoke the delight of a little jealousy. She had said it to Anick in a moment when she had felt a little ungainly, a moment when the boy who would usually rear up so handsomely out of her felt weak and not forthcoming.

"Oh, come on. I don't think he is *really* interested. In any case, if that were so, he would be *so* barking up the wrong tree! I am already taken, aren't I?" Viveka was grinning.

Anick was not. "He flatter you and you like it."

"Shh, Anick. Don't make a scene. This is uncomfortable."

"Don't make a scene? So that's it, I guess. Our visit is over, then?"

Viveka was as disappointed as Anick by this turn of events, but her disappointment was eclipsed by the more dire realization that, unknown to them, Trevor had likely been watching them for as long as they had been together. She quickly scanned her memory of the past five minutes, which seemed now interminably long, wondering if there had been any incriminating interaction between her and Anick. Anick arched her back and pulled her bony shoulders in, as if folding herself in two lengthwise. She clutched in both hands the tube she had made out of the magazine. Her knuckles protruded hard and had lost colour.

Viveka stood up to distance herself from Anick, and waved Trevor down toward them. Anick stood, too. She faced Viveka squarely, jabbed the magazine into Viveka's chest and blurted, "Did you know he was going to be here?"

Viveka took a small step backwards. It was in moments like these that she wished she could speak French flawlessly. And it was in these moments, too, that she wouldn't dare try. Her body ignited with the feeling that she had been sorely misunderstood. Anick's accusation caused her to feel a physical, piercing sensation of injustice. She managed to say calmly, honestly, that she had had no idea Trevor would be here.

Anick lost her composure. "You are going to go out with him. You will go for drinks with him soon. I just know it. Mais, pourquoi pas? C'est facile, ca, eh?"

"Stop, Anick, stop. Don't do this. I spent the whole time on the court waiting, looking for you."

"*You* are worried about how much trouble we are going to get into. I don't care, Vik. Don't you understand? I don't give a shit—I don't give a lonely little piece of shit. I just want..." She stared into Viveka's eyes as if she were boring the end of that sentence into Viveka's brain. Then her shoulders slumped and she looked utterly dejected.

Viveka felt as if her insides were collapsing. *A lonely little piece of shit.* How like Anick to mix up her words when she was distraught. Yet in mixing them up, she expressed so much. Viveka pulled her lower lip into her mouth and locked it tight between her teeth. Her entire body, every place that Anick had ever touched, was aching to hold Anick down, or tight, or just hold on to her. But Viveka's mind steeled itself. There mustn't be a scene. Not ever, and especially not now.

Just before Trevor reached them, Anick uttered in exasperation, "My God, Viveka, you can be so fucking cold."

Viveka had never heard Anick use this expletive before, and again she felt a searing sensation deep inside. Anick sidestepped Viveka and quickly edged her way out of the row of seats. She vaulted down the last few tiers of bleachers. Perhaps she heard Trevor's voice rise over the competing noise of the drummers: "Well, yes. Hello, there. I was looking forward to... oh, who am I kidding—I was praying, I'll admit it, that I'd see you this evening. So, did I chase away your friend?"

As she and Trevor chatted for some long minutes, Viveka tried not to show her heartache. She noted, with only a little pleasure, that Trevor remained focused on her and showed no interest in her beautiful friend.

THE FOLLOWING SATURDAY MORNING, VIVEKA WOKE LATE. SHE WAS alone at home. There was an oddly amicable note on the table from her mother.

"We went to the Mall. There is roti and pumpkin in the oven. Heat it up. We'll be back before lunch—about two-ish. Enjoy. Mum."

Viveka frowned. Whatever had overcome her mother? Why would she tell Viveka to heat up her food as if she were an imbecile?

She sat in front of the television with her plate of lukewarm roti and pumpkin, wondering what Nayan was doing at that moment, and if Anick would be able to telephone her. The phone rang, and having just had that thought, she knew in her heart that the universe was on her side. She plopped her plate down and raced to answer it.

But it was Trevor. He wasted no time. "I have a proposal. I was hoping that you might give me a tour of the town this evening. How about dinner first, and a drive later?"

When Viveka hesitated, Trevor added, "I called earlier for you. Your father answered, and since you weren't able to come to the phone, I decided to ask him if I might take you out."

"You what! That was pretty bold of you!" The oddness of the note from her mother now made sense.

"It was, wasn't it! Your mother said she was going out, but that if you wanted to see me, it was alright with her."

"I thought you said you spoke with my father. You spoke with them both? I'm sorry that you did so before asking me!"

"Yes, but I know what it's like here. My own father was an old-fashioned Indian man through and through when it came to his daughters. I imagined yours to be no different. Your father put me on hold — he said he had to check with the boss. I could hear your parents talking. I had to wait for about three minutes. No kidding. I thought he had forgotten about me. Then your mother came on the phone and asked if I knew where we were going for dinner, and she made some suggestions. So if you can't come up with a place I have a list from her. Are you free tonight?"

Viveka was livid. In her best tone of civility she said, "Ah, so finally I have a say in this. But I am not free tonight."

Trevor made a show of having correctly anticipated her response, one of disappointment, and ended with a promise to call again.

When they returned home, Viveka's parents had an air of controlled excitement about them. They hovered about her, trying to make conversation with her, but didn't bring up Trevor and neither did Viveka.

And later, as Valmiki, Devika and Vashti napped, heat sapping everyone's energy, Viveka and Anick clung to each other's voices and stories via the telephone, their painful words to each other at the volleyball game earlier that week forgotten.

Devika and Valmiki

IN DEVIKA'S EYES, VIVEKA HAD BEGUN TO DRESS EXACTLY LIKE THE person she kept hoping her daughter would not turn into. With no discussion, let alone permission, Viveka cut her hair short. Her parents were irked, yet curious in spite of themselves. Now Devika, too, saw the ghost of Anand in their daughter.

Anick Prakash visited Viveka at the Krishnu house often these days, but usually when Valmiki was at work and Devika out at a luncheon or appointment. Devika bristled the few times she saw them together on the patio, or down by the garden railing, leaning against it, oddly close to one another, a quiet between them that made them seem closer than was to her mind and good taste natural. She watched, horrified and at the same time mesmerized. They were an odd pair indeed, these two young women, listening to classical music, engaged by talk of novels, ideas, and theories Devika had no interest in, speaking unabashedly like ten year olds in their ridiculous gibberish of French and English.

Viveka also went twice, sometimes three times, a week to Rio Claro. One morning, Devika could contain her disapproval no longer. She called Valmiki at his office to complain that Viveka had yet again asked her at breakfast if it was alright to take the car and go out with Anick, this time to a lecture on the calypso as a socio-political medium. At this last, Devika shouted, "What the hell do you all think I am? A fool?"

Valmiki ignored the question and simply asked what she had said to Viveka. Devika replied: I told Viveka that she was going out too often. That Anick was a married woman. That their friendship was strange. It was unnatural. That if she wasn't careful, didn't put a stop to this nonsense right away, there would be a scandal. Single women should not have married women as friends. Marriages broke up because of that sort of thing. And the single woman was always blamed. Devika began to cry on the phone. "It is you who is to blame. You know damn well that you are the one who has brought this on us."

The words "What the hell do you mean by that?" sprang instinctively to Valmiki's mind, but he knew better than to ask: he did not want an answer. Neither of them would have had the vocabulary for the ensuing conversation.

"You and your daughter are going to ruin us," Devika carried on. "How dare you do this to me? You should not have returned here after you finished medical school. You knew even then, didn't you, you knew that you were..." But she couldn't finish.

Valmiki wanted to retort, "You knew about me too, and you stayed with me." But that one ill-advised comeback would have led to verbalized confessions and regretted accusations and a conversation he imagined only too well: So, what are you saying? Devika would ask. That I shouldn't have? And he: You knew who and what I was, but it served you well to stay, you have not wanted for anything materially. And then she: I didn't know when I let you touch me before we were married. And I didn't know when I married you, but you did. You knew very well what you were doing. And you lied when you didn't tell me... I wanted a man to love me, a real man.

That sort of conversation he needed to avoid. How would he and Devika carry on after that? He could never leave his two daughters. The scandal would ruin all four.

To avoid all of this he remained silent, a profound silence which, to Devika's mind, was an admission of all she herself had no language for.

But admission, silent or explicit, was not what Devika wanted. The impossible — a reversal of time, a whole other life — is what she so deeply, deeply wanted. How clichéd to wish to close one's eyes, and on opening them again find that the life before had only been a bad dream. But it was all she had, such clichéd wishing. She closed her eyes. When she opened them, she snapped, "Why the hell don't you take responsibility and talk to your goddamned daughter?"

He didn't know how to talk to her anymore, Valmiki muttered, and Devika was about to begin again — Valmiki detected the beginnings of another controlled explosion. He wanted to tell Devika that he couldn't have this conversation right now; he had patients waiting to see him. But she just carried on and he was overcome by the familiar weariness that welled up in him at the onset of quarrels with Devika. She had a tone that made him want to slam the receiver down, the door shut, his fist on the table, but he never did any of those.

It had always, always, always been left to her — now she was... what was that tone... *screeching* — to discipline the children because *he* didn't want to alienate them and *he* always had to be the good one, and she was left to be the nasty parent. Or so she would accuse him.

Valmiki had stopped listening.

Really, he asked himself, what the hell *was* Viveka doing? He hated the question, for he knew the answer. She was beginning to live the life he had made choices to avoid. It was his doing. His fault. But how dare she? How dare she think only of herself. Had she no good sense after all? No sense of loyalty—if not loyalty, then responsibility—to her family, to society? To him? And why wouldn't she have loyalty? They, he and she, had their differences, but those differences were their thing, their special thing they shared with each other to bond. There was no small love between them. Had she no discretion?

Defeated, Valmiki whispered into the phone, I have patients waiting, I can't do this anymore. Devika was answering back, *Can't do what anymore? Are you threatening me?* as he quietly rested the phone back on the cradle.

Viveka and Valmiki

IN MID-JUNE, MINTY CALLED TO SPEAK WITH DEVIKA. IN A WEEK'S time, she and Ram were hosting an anniversary celebration luncheon for Anick and Nayan. It was late notice, she apologized, but those two couldn't make up their minds, as usual, about anything. The party would be held at Chayu and the entire Krishnu family was invited.

It was almost midnight when Viveka was finally alone and could telephone Anick. She knew that if Nayan were at home he would be asleep by now, and he slept so soundly that the ring of the telephone would not awaken him. She quickly let Anick know that she was perplexed to hear there would be a celebration of the marriage, and that Anick dared to allow her in-laws to invite her, Viveka, to witness such an event.

Anick insisted that it had been Ram's and Minty's idea. She had begged Nayan not to allow it, but he wanted the party. He and she had fought over it, but winning an argument with her had become more important to him than the party itself, and he won. He won because she couldn't fight him in a language that was not her own, in a country where she herself had no one but him — and Viveka, she quickly added.

Numerous times in the past Viveka had asked Anick why, if she really didn't like being with Nayan, she continued to stay in that marriage. And each time, Viveka had received a slightly different answer from the time before, as if Anick herself were trying to figure out the answer. She had offered once that she had always been an accessory for anyone who loved her. Everyone — men or women — fell in love not with her, but with what they called her "beauty." They wanted to be seen with her. They were in love with themselves, Anick theorized. With Nayan it was different. His foreignness and the differences between them were a gulf she felt would never be bridged, and because of this, she might be able to maintain her independence. She did not have a profession and barely spoke English, and so she felt insecure. And because she was on her own and naive, and Nayan wanted so much to give her everything, she just, she had to admit, betrayed herself.

Anick never answered that she had married Nayan because she loved him.

Viveka muttered the same questions again tonight, but, exasperated, she meant them rhetorically, asked of the heavens rather than of Anick. "Why on earth would a person leave the town and go to live so very far away? If you were closer, at least... Well, maybe we could have talked about all of this face to face rather than whispering on the telephone at midnight." Her questions met with quiet, and so Viveka continued repeating herself. "I don't understand why, in such a hopeless marriage, you would leave the town and go to live in such a remote village? And above all, I don't understand why you remain in this marriage. To tell the truth, I don't understand why you married a man in the first place."

At last Anick had new, albeit partial, answers. She said, "Everybody think the French, they so enlightened. They think

French and enlightenment go together. But that is so simple, no? The French, especially outside of the city, they like everybody else. My parents, they are the same. French does not equal enlightenment, Vik. It does not mean freedom. Get that into your head. It would be easier for my parents if I marry a man from Morocco, Algeria, or from Senegal or Trinidad, than if I choose to live with a woman."

The people in town she had met, she continued, Nayan's friends, most of the people in Luminada Heights, were too conservative. You had to conform to old-fashioned ways and attitudes so as not to make them uncomfortable. She felt as if she were an exotic animal in a cage, her every action watched and commented on all the time. And there was that constant, petty competitiveness among Nayan's and Ram's and Minty's friends. People were always struggling to match up, trying to impress. The place had strangled her and therefore was more dangerous for her than the forest. Even so, she had come to love the land of the island, the food, aspects of the culture, the climate of Trinidad. She didn't know how to begin the process of leaving the Prakash family. And if she were to leave, how would she manage? Where would she go?

There were answers to these last, Viveka knew, but she also knew that she herself could not help Anick to leave Nayan or San Fernando or Trinidad. If she did, neither of them would be able to find anyone in their regular circles who would help them. It would cause a public scandal, and there would be the very real threat of physical harm being done to both of them. It would be the scandal of the century. She had to stop asking these questions of Anick.

"Your English isn't that bad, Anick. You can win an argument if you want."

"When I talk with you is not bad. But I can't even think when Nayan start to argue with me. Vik, you know if he find out..."

Viveka didn't need to hear the end of that unfinished sentence.

In any case, the anniversary luncheon would happen.

RAM AND MINTY HAD THE FOOD CATERED. THERE WERE MINI DOUBLES for appetizers, pholourie balls and sahinas with mango anchar dips and tamarind. They hired a barman who was kept busy mixing rum drinks, and gin and vodka martinis. Champagne and red and white wine were served.

It was as if everyone of note in the upper echelons of San Fernando society had moved themselves, intact, to Rio Claro for the day. It was an older crowd, full of Ram's and Minty's friends. Even Nayan's close friend Bally and his wife Shanti had not been invited. Nasser and Cynthia Khan, who owned Khan's Clothing and Household, were there. And Tessa and Sam Bisessar, who owned Imperial Furniture and Rug Emporium. Several other business acquaintances from San Fernando were there, and some of the Prakashs' Luminada neighbours. They all brought to the country, to the forest's edge, their town finery. Gold dangled from the ears and necks of the meagre women, and their wrists held bangles, the jewellery studded not so discreetly with diamonds and sapphires and rubies. Talk of karats and sizes, hands held up and fingers splayed to display all, was had and got out of the way early. There were dresses in fine linen, and pant-suits in silk. And all the women wore open-toed, high-heeled, patent leather sandals. The men were more casually dressed. Several wore light slacks and all wore white shirts, as if in uniform, and very shiny dress shoes. Their large gold Rolexes and Pateks glistened against their dark, hairy wrists, and strong scents of the latest, most expensive colognes did good battle with the catered food and with the cacao roasting in neighbouring properties.

Nayan kept the music going, a mix of steel-pan orchestral works and a solo electronic keyboardist much loved by this older crowd. The music was played just loud enough for its melodies to be heard and a little sway encouraged in the hips of the guests. Amidst laughter and excited chatter, the clink of ice could be heard as glasses were shaken to mix the melting ice with the ingredients of the beverage. Anick asked around if anyone wanted to see the land, but Nayan laughed, and the guests chuckled. They looked at themselves and at each other and remarked that no one had brought a change of clothing.

Viveka, keeping herself in the background, marvelled at this — and at how her own fear had disappeared. Had no one thought they might take a walk into this tame forest?

Valmiki and Devika stood chatting on the veranda with other guests. Valmiki kept his back to the forest, nervous that if he were to look at it, his manner of looking might expose him. He prayed that the man who in a different forest some time ago had witnessed him raise his gun to a wet and shivering dog had not identified him, had not spoken of him to anyone. In a place so small it was likely that someone other than his immediate hunting group knew of his leanings. It had been a cowardly and bullying thing to do — to think he could shoot that dog — but it had happened in an isolated moment borne of the craziness of feeling out of control in his own life. But who here at this party, he wondered, would stay long enough to hear this explanation, to try and understand what he had gone through all of his life just so that he did not rattle the security, comfort, and knowledge of all who were at this very gathering, and the rest of Trinidad's "big society"? He put his hand on Devika's waist. She shifted, looked down at his hand and then, questioningly, up at him. He ignored her surprise, kept his hand lightly on her waist and continued to engage the conversation of the man before them.

Viveka had been to Anick and Nayan's house several times now, and there was always amicability between her and Nayan. Anick usually assured her, and Viveka hoped it was true, that Nayan didn't suspect anything about what was going on between the two of them. But he didn't pay Viveka much attention at the party. He hardly seemed to notice her. She imagined that this was a function of familiarity, as she had recently been so present in their house.

Nayan and Anick, meanwhile, were easy enough with one another, but Viveka noticed that they never touched, not even in passing. When together speaking with guests, they stood apart. Viveka was curious about this but it pleased her too, especially since whenever Anick passed her on the veranda she brushed Viveka with her arm, whispering delightful teasings.

"You look delicious. I want to devour you."

"Hmm, maybe you find other women here attractive?"

"You remember what you do to me last time? I am thinking of this now."

As the main meal of curried goat, roti, curried pumpkin, dhal, channa, curried mango and rice was being spread out by servers on the table, Anick brought a morsel of the pumpkin and roti on a side plate especially for Viveka to taste. This did not go entirely unnoticed. More than one guest called out, "So how come she is getting special treatment? Are you going to bring me a little plate too?" As much as Viveka was flattered, she cringed just a little.

Viveka stood aloof and apart from the other guests, a rum and Coke turning watery in her hand. She looked out in the direction of the cabin, imagining the forest flora there, its jade and umbers like a lifeline she tried to hook with her eyes. When she was spoken to she was amicable enough, but she encouraged no lengthy conversation and maneuvered herself away. It frustrated her that the second question every guest asked her, after how she was, was where was Vashti. It made her feel as if the others saw her as a child. That used to be alright, feeling like a child, even at twenty years of age, all because she still lived at home. But having fallen in love, having made love with Anick, she no longer felt like a child.

When Anick finally came up to chat, they strolled out of earshot, turned their backs to everyone and faced the forest greenery. Viveka held her body awkwardly, stiffly, as if one foot was ready to bolt and the other to accompany Anick wherever she went.

None of this went unnoticed by Devika nor by Valmiki. When Anick returned to her guests, Valmiki watched Devika walk over to Viveka, who was now leaning against the veranda wall and looking in at the party like a critical voyeur.

"Why are you just standing around like a coonoomoonoo? Can't you go and talk to people?"

"I'm not a coonoomoonoo, Mom. You know I am not comfortable at these kinds of things."

"Well, why did you come then?"

"What! This is different. Anick is my friend."

"And Nayan. Remember that. And you're damn right, this *is* different."

"What do you mean? Of course Nayan is my friend. I know that."

"Then you better watch yourself."

Viveka straightened herself. "What do you mean by that?"

"You know exactly what I mean by that. You *better* watch yourself."

Devika's mother's face was severe and she was shaking with restrained anger. She turned and walked back to where she had been sitting.

After the main meal, the buffet table in the dining room was cleared and a cake brought out and placed onto it. It was much like a wedding cake, but a chocolate one covered in white icing, and there were two little plastic people on top — a male and female couple holding hands. A waiter was about to cut it when one of the guests caused a ruckus, saying, No, no no, it should be cut like a wedding cake. A cheer went up and although Nayan and Anick protested, they in the end obliged. Everyone gathered around the table as the barman and server stepped up to the occasion with quickly passed glasses of champagne.

Viveka entered the living room area but she hung well back, a glass of champagne in her hand, if not for toasting at least for a show of civility.

As the guests grinned and some of them heckled, Nayan cut the cake and offered a forkful of it to Anick. She, in turn, was immensely shy and awkward, but encouraged by several of the women to reciprocate, she too cut a piece and made to offer it to Nayan. It fell off the fork, and the two of them scrambled in vain to catch it. Anick tried again, Nayan cupping her hand throughout to steady it. There was laughter and teasing, but it was done. The guests were not satisfied; they tapped their glasses with cutlery and called out, "Kiss, kiss, kiss!" Nayan giggled like a teenager. He embraced Anick and planted an awkward kiss on her lips.

There were calls for a speech from Nayan, and so he thanked his parents for the party, the guests for coming such a distance "into the bush," and Anick for putting up with him for the past two years. Then he turned to Anick and said, "Shall we tell them?"

Anick's face fell noticeably. She swiftly pulled Nayan close and turned away from the guests. The two of them now faced Viveka, and she could just make out Anick's sharp voice: "Nayan! We agree not today. Why you ask me this?"

He put his hand up to the waiting guests, turned and winked at them, grinning with confidence, and then turned back to Anick. He whispered, "Come on, honey. This is the best time."

She hissed, "But we agree last night, and you promise again this morning."

"Look, we're having a big celebration and I want to tell everyone now. I don't understand why you want to keep this a secret."

In a controlled whisper, she held firm. "Fuck you, Nayan. You always get what you want. I won't fight with you in public. Do what you want. You don't care about me. I am not going to forget this."

He laughed. "Yes, I do get what I want," he said, and he turned around. Anick turned too, her face red.

Nayan looped his arm around Anick's shoulder, pulled her reluctant body close and announced, "We have good news."

Before he could finish there were cheers, shouts of "Yes!" and low impressed moans of "No!" Glasses were raised in the air. Minty and Ram hugged the two of them. Finally the happy noise subsided and Nayan resumed. "The baby will be born in April."

As Devika made her way with the other guests to congratulate the couple, Valmiki headed forward too, glancing over at his daughter.

Viveka was pale. She looked as if she would faint.

Valmiki retreated quickly toward her. He took her glass and draped an arm around her shoulders. He turned her away from the revelling, congratulatory crowd and ushered her to the veranda. "It's hot in there, eh? Stay out here with me."

Viveka was trembling.

Valmiki whispered, "Catch your breath, Vik, stay calm and catch your breath."

Viveka couldn't help herself. She covered her face with both hands. Tears welled fast.

They faced the forest. Valmiki could imagine its interior. The scent of the earth, dying flora, rejuvenating soil, and Saul. Beautiful, handsome Saul. The sweat on his back, salty, yet so sweet on the tongue. He hadn't seen Saul in several weeks. The more time Viveka spent with Anick, the more he had avoided Saul.

"This is a happy moment, Vik. Don't spoil it for Anick. She is your best friend, isn't she? She'd want you to be happy for them. Come on, get yourself together. Let's go back inside."

"No, I can't, Dad. I'm sorry, I don't know what's wrong with me."

"It's the heat. I'm sure it is. Shall I get you some water?"

Viveka thought her father an idiot. He imagined he knew her so well, but he knew nothing about her. If only he knew how she felt, as if she couldn't breathe, as if she had lost control of her bones, as if she were about to fall down right there and die.

Valmiki, for his part, was suddenly determined. He would put an end to his relationship with Saul. He would make do with Devika, whom he had robbed of a fuller life. He would try to give her some morsel of happiness by being more present for her. Perhaps, he reasoned, the universe would then be kinder and in some miraculous turnabout allow his daughter the freedom to love in any way she wanted, and in so doing spare her the double life he was forced to live. Otherwise there were so many casualties in these pretenses. Devika certainly, but Nayan and Mrs. Joseph too, as well as Anick, Saul, and, of course, himself. He did not want this for his daughter. He would make a deal with the universe and call Saul tomorrow. Meet him at The Golden Dragon. This time they would not take lunch in a room at The Victory, they would remain in the restaurant. He would end it over a nice meal. He would call his lawyer — he would have to make up some plausible story, but he was up to it — and he would sign over the house on Fellowship Land to Saul, the house that Saul's wife, in any case, thought Saul had bought. It was the least he could do for Saul. And that would be that: He would never see Saul again. Even if this meant he would spend the rest of his life without air in his chest, that he would slowly shrivel and die of loneliness, there was no sacrifice too great for this daughter.

"Look here, Vik, think about yourself. This is a small place. It is not a kind place. Get yourself together right away. Don't do this to yourself, honey. Please."

He wanted to tell her to leave this place, to go far away, but he held himself back. She had always been a strong child, stronger than he had ever been. She would do what she had to do. He knew this about her. He only hoped that in this instance she would do the right thing. He could not lift and carry her. He could not set her down on the correct stepping stones, but he could nudge her like a herding dog. The actual steps would have to be hers. "This place is too small for you," he said. "Take a deep breath, and leave this behind. There is so much more waiting for you elsewhere. So much, you can't imagine."

Viveka looked at her father, and seeing a strange, urgent, almost pained understanding in his eyes, she quickly averted hers, wondering if, after all, he knew something of what was going on inside of her. She pulled away from him, and stepped forward. Could she take the car, go home on her own? Perhaps he and Devika could catch a ride home with one of the other guests? To her surprise, Valmiki pulled his bunch of keys from his pocket rather quickly and handed it to her. He grabbed her by her shoulders, squeezed them and put his lips to the top of her head. There was so much he wanted to say to her.

"I love you, darling."

The words were whispered, but she heard them.

Anick and Viveka

ANICK CAUGHT A GLIMPSE OF VIVEKA AS SHE WENT DOWN THE veranda's stairs and out of the house. She pushed her way through the guests, excusing herself. But just as she reached the veranda, Valmiki caught her. He held Anick by her shoulders and said, "She's going home. Let her go. She isn't feeling well."

Anick's face crumpled. Valmiki gripped her hard. "Stop it, Anick. Don't make a scene. You can call her later. Nayan's coming; get hold of yourself."

But Anick broke away from Valmiki and ran down the stairs. Valmiki let her go; as she glanced back, Anick could see that he had caught Nayan and was congratulating him, saying with studied lightness that Viveka had been complaining about a headache and nausea all morning. He and Devika had told her not to come but she had insisted, and now she had a temperature. Anick had gone to tell her goodbye. Valmiki's voice carried on, asking Nayan how the visits to the obstetrician were going. And fortunately, before Valmiki's attempts to hold Nayan back could become too obvious, Nayan was called back into the dining room to regale the guests with stories of his hopes and dreams for the child that was to be born.

The Krishnus' car was parked among a long line of guest cars out on the road some distance, but still visible, from the house. Viveka was already in the driver's seat trying to back the car out of a tight spot when Anick approached. She rolled the window down. Silently, tears ran down Anick's face.

Finally Viveka spoke. "I don't understand why you didn't tell me."

"I only found out yesterday, and I couldn't tell you on the phone or here today. I wanted to tell you first."

The pregnancy was an answer to all the questions welling in Viveka's head. There was no need to ask them. She was too stunned to feel anything more than confusion. She stared in the direction of the house as she spoke. "I guess I am really stupid. I hadn't realized that you two still slept together. I am an absolute idiot."

Anick was silent.

"How come you still sleep with him, Anick?" As soon as the words were out of her mouth, she regretted them.

"Oh, Viveka, he is my husband. I cannot tell him no every time."

"Do you want to — are you —" She didn't know, really, what she wanted to ask.

Anick hazarded an answer. "I don't know what to do. I cannot stay with Nayan any longer. I am not in love with him anymore. I love only you. We can wait until this child is born and then you and me and the baby, we can go away together."

Viveka glared at Anick in disbelief. "You think you can take Nayan's child, Ram Prakash's grandchild, and go your own way?"

"We can go away together," Anick repeated desperately. "You and me, we can be a family." It was as if the particulars of her situation, the reality of Nayan, the Prakashs, of Viveka's own family, of their position in Trinidad society, had vanished from

Anick's comprehension. Viveka glanced again at the house. Then se gripped the steering wheel and readied herself to drive away.

She wanted to tell Anick to get inside the car with her right away. What would she do then? she wondered. There was no hideaway on a small island. Drive to the airport, abandon her father's car there and get on the first plane going anywhere? The outside world, which had always seemed unfathomably grand, suddenly felt too, too small. At the same time she knew she had to get away. But no, not with Anick. In a way she had, minutes ago, already left Anick.

"Say something, Vik. I am so sorry. I didn't want this to happen. But, please, say something. Say you will wait and you will go away with me."

Viveka looked at Anick. She wanted to get out of the car and hold her, wrap her arms around her. "Do you love Nayan, Anick? Tell me. I need to know."

"I told you already. But is not that I love him or don't love him."

"Do you love him?"

"I don't hate him, Viveka. Is just that —"

Viveka cut her off. "I don't understand you. I don't understand this push and pull. You seem to have done that to him from the beginning. Don't do that to me."

Anick reached a hand into the car, to the back of Viveka's head. She grabbed a handful of hair and gently closed her fist on it. "Vikki, I have no life without you. Do you understand this? I love you. Only you."

Viveka thought, *I have no life here*. She started the engine of the car. Anick let go of her hair and stepped back into a clump of flowering cock's comb. She remained there until Viveka had backed out, driven off, and disappeared.

THE AIR-CONDITIONING IN THE CAR WAS SWITCHED ON, THE WINDOWS rolled up.

We have good news... the baby will be born in April... Oh Viveka, he is my husband. I can not tell him no *every time... you better watch yourself...*

The words formed an endless loop in Viveka's mind. Her limbs felt limp. Thoughts of Anick came to her, and each time she felt a gripping sensation deep inside, as if pleasure and pain entwined there. As she neared San Fernando, a thousand realizations buzzed in her brain: all that she and Anick had felt between them had been real; she had felt more open and authentic than she had ever felt before. Big. Full. Full of purpose. How could any of this be wrong? She had to find a way to be all that she was, regardless of how society would view her. She could not live clandestinely. She would not. Nor would she not let her present sadness devour her. She had to train herself to remain above it, otherwise she would become like Merle. There simply had to be a place where she would fit in, and she would find that place.

She thought of her and Anick's first kiss, of her fingers sliding inside Anick, of Anick gasping and thrusting against her, and she determined not to go mad. Of the tip of her tongue encountering Anick's heat and wetness, of how good that had been, and she promised herself that she would find a way out. She thought of lying on Anick, Anick gripping her tight, whispering into her mouth, against her cheek, and tears welled in her eyes. She thought of her parents holding her back from participating in sports, trying to break who she was and redesign her so that she didn't bring notice to herself and shame to them, and she wept uncontrollably. She recalled hovering, moving her body against Anick, and the strange, absolutely true feeling in those moments that between her legs there was an appendage, a phantom one that swelled with all her desire and something baser, too, something more bestial and demanding, something that could enter and penetrate Anick, empty itself into her. How many times had she wished that she could cause Anick to become pregnant, and how often had the futility of the wish made her feel inconsequential and invisible? Tears poured down her cheeks and she made sincere bargains with a God she hadn't really believed in before. In exchange for honesty, integrity, a lifetime of service, she prayed that she and all people like her be granted the freedom, so long as it did not hurt anyone, to love whomever they chose, to love well, and have that love returned without judgment. She implored, and her thoughts rambled on, and she made promise after promise and apology after apology for anything she had done to put big and small obstacles in the path of her way of loving. She thought of Nayan and the hurt he might have been caused, and apologized to him — then quickly decided that Anick and Nayan had been hurting each other so much, it was their love that should have been brought to an end, not her love with Anick.

She had to leave. That was clear. But leave how, and go where? What if she were to find a haven in the Trinidad Anick had told her about, in the north of the island? But in her heart she knew that there was nowhere on her small island far away and safe enough. After all, it was not only her security but that of her family, her mother and her father and Vashti, that would be affected.

By the time she arrived home in Luminada, Viveka was drenched in sweat, her face and neck tear-stained. She had no map of her future, but she knew who she was. She would not be diminished because of it.

IV Valmiki's Daughter

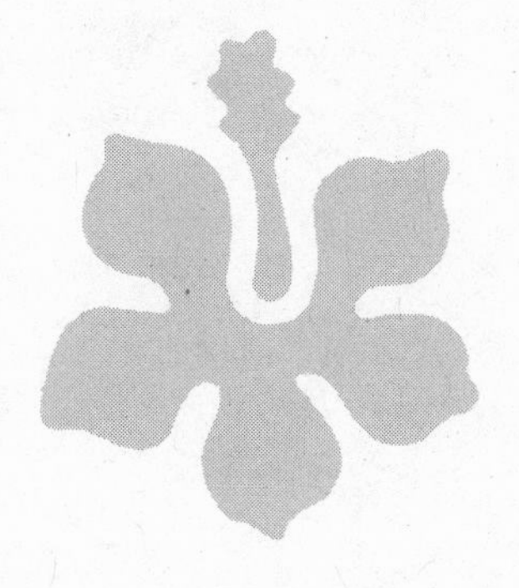

Your Journey Home

YOUR JOURNEY BEGAN IN SAN FERNANDO. YOU VISITED LUMINADA Heights with its magnificent views, and continued inland, east to Rio Claro. Now, you'll circle back to San Fernando, where your journey abruptly ends. All that has changed along the way is landscape. Implicit in an ending is a beginning — destination rendered futile. In any case, as the saying goes, wherever you go, there you are. There you are.

The Krishnus

THE LARGE PICTURE WINDOW LET IN THE EVENING'S HARSH LIGHT but not its heat. Without a wind, everything except for two blue-grey tanagers hopping erratically up and down the length of a yellowing coconut tree branch appeared still. The two birds slapped each other with their wings and pecked at each other's beaks in elaborate gestures of quarrelling, or perhaps courting. Viveka could imagine the ruckus they made, but nothing that went on outside was audible inside the cool, air-conditioned room. The garden sloped away on this side of the house. The lawn, lushly green, had been cut the day before, edged tightly where it met beds that had been plumped with fresh black manure. This, and the precise, trimmed clumps of flowering hybrid hibiscus shrubs that were her mother's pride, amounted to a picture framed on two sides by heavy damask curtains.

The bed in the guest room where Viveka sat was a mountain of colourful boxes, presents wrapped in iridescent foils with wedding bells and brides and grooms printed on them. Her mother sat on the edge of a chair, a shawl wrapped around her against the cold from the air-conditioner. Vashti hovered about excitedly and Trevor leaned against a wall, watching, as Viveka untied the ribbons and tore the wrappers off. Viveka called out what the gifts were: a wand blender, a punch bowl, ladle and glasses, a Waterford water jug, a crystal ship's decanter, and so on; and who its sender was: Molly and Angus Ramsumair, Auntie Joan and Uncle Peter, Allan and June, Auntie Sylvia and cousin Mohan, and so forth. Her mother jotted these down in a notepad. The cards ranged from the simplest tag exclaiming *Congratulations On Your Marriage* to epistles that went on and on for pages — thoughts on Two Hearts, Two Souls, Pledges, Pathways, and pronouncements that Love Stirs The Heart, wishes that included Hopes And Dreams and Growing Deeper Day by Day. Many of them were flecked with sparkle dust, points of which stayed on Viveka's fingers and made their way to her face. Some of the gifts were so beautifully and craftily packaged that her mother would rise, pull the shawl tighter and come to the bed, take the package from her, examine it, and then go back to her armchair.

Trevor nodded acknowledgement every once in a while, and Vashti took the unwrapped, recorded presents and passed judgment on each: "Oh my God, this is so heavy, how can you fill this and then lift it and pour from it?" "They got this from Bisessar's Furniture and Rug Emporium — I saw these there, and this was, by far, the nicest one." "You see, if we had gone and chosen gifts from Landry's, instead of letting people just buy whatever they wanted to, you wouldn't have gotten three of this and two of that, and none of these dreadful patterned glasses. Why did we invite them anyway?"

The cards and tags Viveka collected in a shoebox, and the bows she shoved into a clear plastic bag for recycling. To the side, an extra-large black garbage bag overflowed with scrunched-up paper, and a deep cardboard box held smaller boxes that she broke down and made flat and placed on top of a variety of protective packing material.

After a while, Devika told Vashti to take the full bag of papers out to the garage and to fetch a new one. Vashti opened the door and the sizzling crescendo of moist ingredients dropped into hot oil screeched in the air, then subsided quickly with the clatter of a metal spoon urgently stirring it all. In an instant, the guest room was flooded with the aroma of anchar masala and its signature note of roasted cumin. The family looked at one another and made noises of appreciation and anticipation. Pinky was currying mangoes.

These days, every day was festive for Pinky. It was as if her own daughter was marrying. Viveka worried that four days from now, the day of the wedding, she would have gained so much weight that the outfit being made for her would fit poorly or not at all.

Vashti shouted out to Pinky to come bring a new bag, but Devika shook her head. "She is doing her work. *You* go and do it," she said.

For two days in a row Viveka had worn a sun dress, a flimsy thing with spaghetti straps, close-fitting at the waist and falling to mid-thigh. With encouragement from her mother, Vashti, and Helen, she had had three of these little dresses made by a seamstress who used patterns found in a *Vogue* sewing book she showed to her customers. As Viveka smoothed the dress and tried to fix an image in her mind of each gift with that of its sender, Trevor was saying, for the second time since they had begun opening the gifts, that they could buy this item, or that one, for much less than it would cost to ship them.

Valmiki, home from work now, entered the room just in time to hear Trevor ask how Viveka was planning to trek all of this to Canada. His heart lurched at the umpteenth realization that this daughter was marching onward, past them all, past him. He put on his best face and answered, "Oui, papa! Trev, boy, this is a lot of loot, in truth. Let's open up a little shop, you and me, and make a little money, man. This could be the start of an empire!"

Valmiki stooped down to look at the unwrapped gifts. "Who is this from?" he wanted to know of an eighteen-inch giraffe ornament, the fire of its crystal flickering in its belly when he picked it up. He fingered an Indian-silk bedspread with a glass-beaded border and embroidered elephants that hung on the back of a chair and wanted to know who had sent that, too. Winking at Devika, he said, "I didn't know the Williamses have such good taste! You don't think this would look good on our bed?" If no one else heard the tremble in his voice, Devika did.

Vashti was rummaging through the gifts on the bed again, her brow scrunched up now. "Hey, did Anick and Nayan send us anything?"

Devika pursed her lips and Valmiki grinned too widely for comfort.

Trevor watched Viveka as she answered, "Us?"

Vashti caught herself and, embarrassed, muttered, "You know what I mean." Then she bounced back with, "In any case, are you two planning to have children? You never wanted any, Vik, so in the end I will inherit all of these gifts. So, I ask again, what did Anick and Nayan send us?"

"They sent something, but it's buried under here. We'll get to it eventually."

"You're lying. You probably opened it already."

Devika said warily, "Why do you two have to speak to each other like that? Be nice, Vashti."

Viveka unwrapped a large picture box and, with some effort, out slid a low-relief picture set in a deep frame. A grainy photographic image, silk-screened onto moulded plastic: a panoramic scene of Niagara Falls. A light set inside the frame at the top suggested that the image could be illuminated. Everyone erupted into laughter. Before Viveka could read the card, one of those that went on for pages — Sacred This and Vows That — Valmiki burst out, "Wait, wait. Let me guess. That is from your Aunt Radica."

"My aunt?" Viveka asked, with feigned indignation. "She is *your* mother's sister. And you're dead-on. Who else would send something so . . . so . . ."

Trevor filled in, "Redolent. Prosaic."

Vashti untied the length of electric cord attached to the picture and plugged it into a wall outlet. A fluorescent light flickered and then the scene was bathed in a harsh light. Seconds later, to everyone's surprise, a cascade of previously imperceptible optical fibers woven into the silk-screen image animated the falls.

"Trevor is right," Viveka blurted out, shoving the item toward Vashti. "We can't possibly take all of this with us. Here, Vashti, I bequeath this to you."

The faint ringing of the phone outside of the room could barely be heard beneath the laughter and the hum of the air-conditioning. Pinky knocked and opened the door, letting in the weighty scent of masala-fried hot green mangoes. The aromatic sourness made Viveka's mouth pucker and fill in an instant with saliva.

Pinky glanced at the colourful disarray, broke into a quick grin of approval, and announced, "It's for Miss Viveka."

"Oh," Viveka said, disappointed to be disturbed. "Can you ask them to call back?"

Looking intently at Viveka as if there were no one else in the room, Pinky said more quietly, "It's Miss Anick."

Vashti groaned. "You shouldn't have told her who it is. Now we are going to have to wait. I bet you're going to take it, aren't you?"

"Yeah. I know she has to go out this afternoon, and if I don't take it I won't be able to get in touch with her for the rest of the day." Viveka got up, folded some wrapping paper, and shoved it into a bag, studiously avoiding any show of haste.

Vashti babbled to Trevor, "Everything always gets put on hold for Anick. When they get on the phone they talk for hours."

In Viveka's peripheral vision, a vision sometimes more accurate than frontal, she saw Trevor straighten, steel himself.

Devika, her eyes hardened and jaws clenched, stood up as Viveka walked out of the room to the telephone. As if permission to start and stop opening the gifts were hers to give, Devika said, "That's enough for today anyway. You can open more tomorrow."

Viveka could hear Vashti saying to Trevor, "Do you speak French? The two of them, they speak French together all the time. Well, Vik pretends she can speak it. As if they don't want anyone else to know what they are talking about. She'll probably tell you, though, because now it's you she'll have secrets with."

Just before she picked up the receiver, Viveka saw that Valmiki had interceded and invited Trevor to have a beer on ice with him out on the patio.

Viveka and Trevor, Part One

TWO MONTHS EARLIER, VIVEKA HAD BEEN IN HER BEDROOM CURLED up in an armchair, a textbook in her lap. She had been sitting there for about forty minutes and had read only two pages. Little interested her these days.

Devika entered without knocking. "I just want to let you know," she began without pause, "we're having people over for lunch on Sunday. So don't make other plans, eh."

"Is there an occasion?"

"Well, we haven't had anyone over for a while." Devika went to the window and opened it wider. Then she walked over and sat on Viveka's bed.

"Who's coming?"

"The Rattans. The Williamses. Joan and Rodney De Cairies."

"That's it?" Viveka said, feigning disinterest. It was with a good measure of relief that she noted no mention had been made of any of the Prakashs.

"We invited the Clarkes, Helen, and Wayne and his cousin Trevor also."

At this Viveka slowly uncurled her legs and let them down onto the floor. Devika responded to the frown taking shape, and the questioning twist of Viveka's mouth.

"He asked us if he could take you out once and you never responded. We thought it was only polite to have him over. In any case he is leaving the day after, so you don't have to worry that we're pushing you on him, or him on you."

Over two months had passed since that invitation. Trevor had returned to Canada shortly after, and Viveka had not heard from him since. She had almost forgotten about him, actually.

"But, Mom, he asked *me* out, not you all."

"So what? You want to ask him out? You know you can't do that. He might be living abroad, and might have adopted foreign ways, but he must know that a good girl from a good family would never take it upon herself to reciprocate in that way. And he had the decency to call and ask us if he could take you out. He is that kind of man."

"Things are changing, Mom. If I wanted him to come over, I could have asked him myself."

"Child, don't be crazy. How could you do that? You mean you would call him up and invite him on your own to go out with you?"

"Well, not to go out, but maybe to come here. But that's only if I wanted to. I mean, I would ask you and Dad, and then yes, I would do it myself. Where he comes from, people at my age don't have their parents doing things like this. At my age people don't even live at home with their parents, come to think of it."

"But eh-eh, so what, now? You want to leave home, now? As long as you're living here, you'll do things the way your father and I are comfortable with. Look, don't make a problem out of this. Why does everything have to be so complicated with you? We just want to have him over, that's all, and to have a nice pleasant day. Your father is looking forward to it. Don't spoil it for him, Vik. Now, what are you going to wear?"

TREVOR AND VIVEKA FOUND THEMSELVES LEFT ALONE, WHILE EVERYone else went inside the house into the air-conditioned living room. She showed little interest in him, but still he told her of his life.

He seldom spent his time off in Toronto, he told her. He was a mechanical engineer and worked with one of the major airlines. Because of his seniority he was afforded unlimited free trips worldwide, as long as space on a flight was available. He worked four days in a row and then would have four off. Sometimes he worked five days in a row so that he could take five off. A couple weeks before he had spent three days in Tahiti.

That seemed strange to Viveka. Surely it was too long a distance between Toronto and Tahiti to go for only three days?

But that's the point, Trevor told her. That he was able to do it. The sheer craziness of it. Before that, he and a co-worker had been in Argentina, and before that he had gone on his own to Lisbon. He and his colleagues chose places based on seat availability on a flight. Sometimes they arrived at the airport with a change of clothing, a toothbrush, that sort of thing, all in a small carry-on bag, and took whatever was available.

Trevor paused, then suddenly asked where Viveka's beautiful friend Anick was. Viveka was caught off guard; she hesitated. He reminded her that he had seen them together at volleyball practice. Wayne and Helen had told him about Anick, and he had expected to see her here. Mention of Anick made Viveka's stomach rise and fall like a kite in an erratic wind. She wondered, and worried, what Helen and Wayne had said about Anick. She shrugged, and Trevor carried on, "I thought she must have been a very special friend to come and sit by herself in those stands to watch you play volleyball. And then when she walked off the way she did that time I came to speak with you, without even looking at me, I thought to myself—hmm, she's got a thing for Viveka. So, has she?"

Viveka thought this a bold conversation. She noted that Trevor had waited until no one else was present to make mention of Anick. Since he was leaving the island again the following day she, in equal measure, challenged him. "What makes you think it wouldn't be the other way around?"

"Nothing at all. Is that how it is?"

Viveka didn't answer.

"Fair enough. It's hard to pin you down, isn't it? I like that. You're pretty complicated."

Her mother often threw it at her that she was too complicated for her own good, but the way Trevor said it was almost a compliment. He kept his eyes on her and this made her blush. He took advantage of the moment.

"So, I was wondering what you would say this time if I were to risk having my ego bruised and ask you out, again, to dinner. After all, I think your parents like me, and I have a list of places from your mother still to go through."

"What do you mean? Aren't you leaving tomorrow?" Viveka's blush turned into a moment of panic. This flirtation was harmless enough precisely because Trevor was around only momentarily. She wanted to tell him that he was wasting his time. That she was already inextricably and deeply in love. That even if she never saw Anick again, her heart would always belong to her.

"Well," Trevor began slowly, all the while keeping his eye on Viveka for her reaction, "I am considering returning in a month's time."

"For what?" She did not mean to sound as hostile as she did. Trevor was oblivious to her truculent tone.

"To have dinner with you," he beamed, and added, "because I am able to do it, and for the sheer craziness of it. What do you say?"

THEY WENT TO THE LOUNGE AT THE VICTORY HOTEL. THE TABLES were arranged to give the illusion of privacy. Groupings of large planters that contained tall plastic trees — banana, and palm, and the baliser and haliconia shrubs, little clumps of jungle — divvied up the room, creating caves where couples could steal a little more than time.

Trevor sat back comfortably in a deep love-sofa, the palm of his hand flat on the seat cushion next to him, as if indicating a spot that was available. Viveka sat in a chair opposite. She was not at ease. She thought of Anick, of how, at a party or in some public place, she would strike a pose in the presence of a man who was paying her attention. Viveka used to enjoy watching her, knowing that Anick was teasing the man and her, but that it was she who held Anick's entire attention. She looked around the lounge and noted that there was not a woman there who did not appear to be posing.

Trevor, she had to admit, was unusual. He led a more interesting life, she supposed, than most men she knew. Since they had last talked at the party, he had been to Delhi. It was his first time. His father's ancestors were from there. He had sent her a post card with a picture of a building within the Red Fort. It said on the back, *This is my new favourite destination. I bet you'd find this place fascinating. You'd be looking for your ancestry in every corner. I am. It's here, I can feel it. I bet you would too. In other words, I wish you were here with me.* That he had thought of her so far away, in India, had, admittedly, flattered her. Since it was a postcard and it had arrived in a pile of the household's mail, it was very likely that her mother had read it.

Although he had lived abroad for many years, Trevor returned often to visit family and to indulge in his love of Trinidadian cultural life. He knew the island's nooks and crannies well and offered to take her to remote parts of it on future visits. He clearly noticed that she neither accepted nor declined his invitation, and he grinned at this.

Trevor did not eat, but he consumed three beers rather quickly—his dinner, he told Viveka. She had a shrimp cocktail and a Bentley with gin. He wanted to know, he said, every detail of her life. She reluctantly offered a few more sketchy details on subjects already familiar to him—her course work and volleyball. Even though Anick was at the front of her mind, Viveka didn't speak of her, and this time Trevor too made no mention of her.

When she returned home, just before ten-thirty, all three members of Viveka's family were sitting in front of the television watching a late-night movie by way of waiting up for her. There was an unusual, excited kind of attention paid her by her mother and Vashti. They wanted to know what she and Trevor had drank and eaten, exactly what kind of work Trevor did, and if he had siblings, and how long he had lived in Canada and why. Viveka told them she thought he was on the prowl for some meek woman to wash his clothes and cook his food. Her mother, at that point, became quite irritated and said that relationships were a give and take. Her father interjected, humour intended, that in most cases the same person who was giving was also the one taking.

Viveka was embarrassed by the sudden attention. Still, in a way it felt rather good.

HOW EASILY THEY LET HER USE THE CAR TO TAKE HIM TO THE AIRPORT.

On either side of two sections of the highway, fields were ablaze. Ribbons of glowing cane leaves spiraled upwards and sailed through the air. They floated back down as grey strands of ash. Although she had the air intake vents closed off and cold-air blower turned on high, the sweet smell of the burning cane fields, the heaviness of the smoke, managed to enter the vehicle. An unpleasant cold draft was hitting her upper left arm. She fiddled with the louvres on the vent to redirect it. Turned on low volume, the cello suite could barely be heard.

Curbside at the airport, Viveka left the car engine idling and remained inside. She gripped the steering wheel. Trevor hesitated, stared ahead.

"I had a really good time, Viveka."

She tapped the steering wheel with her fingers to the beat of the music, and said, "Yeah. Me too." There was no need to be effusive.

"But I've been thinking. You're an expensive date!" Trevor was solemn. "I can't keep coming to see you like this, you know. We have to do something."

Viveka felt a sense of doom at Trevor's words. There immediately arose inside of her that particular hunger she had only known in relation to Anick. It was a hunger but it did not come from her belly. It was Merle Bedi's hunger. It was bigger than she was, and would not easily be quelled; it would, rather, forever gnaw at her. She knew this. But she was determined not to become Merle Bedi. Nor to become Anick.

She, rather, had to do something.

"Like what?" she said, but not waiting for an answer, she quickly offered, "Get married?"

"That's what I was thinking," Trevor replied jovially, adding, "It's always a means to an end, isn't it. Would you like to?"

She wondered why he would say such a thing. *It's always a means to an end.* Did he know how true his words were? Perhaps he, too, like everyone else it seemed, had his reasons. If he had, they didn't interest her. "Where would we live?"

"Well, in Toronto, I suppose. We'd travel a lot, I think you might like that. But we'd live in Toronto. That's where my work is. So, what do you say?"

Viveka thought for a moment. Finally, as if agreeing that they should make a left turn rather than a right at a fork, she shrugged and said, "Okay. I guess so. Let's."

Trevor chuckled. "I will have to speak with your parents, then. Won't I? Don't say anything. I'll return in a few weeks and we'll surprise them. What do you say?"

He held her face in his large hands and kissed her mouth. His skin smelled like burning flesh.

Viveka and Trevor, Part Two

ON THE WAY TO THE AIRPORT A MONTH LATER, VIVEKA HUMMED TO the taped Bach cello suite she had long ago memorized well.

How happily her parents had let her take the car for this trip, too.

Waiting in the midst of a small and animated crowd, Viveka's eyes were fixed on the guarded, tinted doors ahead. She could have stepped out of the crowd and waited for Trevor closer to the doors, but she wanted to see him before he saw her. The automatic sliding doors parted and he, tall and skinny, squinting into the late afternoon glare, emerged from the air-conditioned Customs and Immigration Hall. He was met by a blast of dull, suffocating heat. He scanned the crowd for her. She held back for a brief second, shielding herself behind a woman with a mass of frizzy hair that exuded an odor of petroleum jelly. Trevor spotted her nevertheless, and so she broke into a broad smile as she shouldered her way through the crowd.

He came to her grinning and hugged her long. She returned the embrace, noting a faint cologne rising off his shirt. She felt as if she were on an escalator that was moving more swiftly than normal. Her greeting was a quick, nervous, embrace, cooler than he — and even she — expected. A long lash of cane ash floated down in front of him. He blew at it and it broke apart, some of it catching in his hair and on his shirt.

Crossing the street to arrive at the parking lot she reached for his bag, a black canvas knapsack so light he was able to sling it over one shoulder. He nudged his shoulder upward, out of her reach, and said gaily, "Thank you, thank you. I can carry it, my dear." She hadn't looked at him, but could hear the grin in his voice.

He took the key from her and opened the trunk. The white car had turned a dusty grey from the ash that had settled on it in the short time it had been parked there. He dropped his bag in and handed the key back to her.

Trevor dozed in the car, snoring so heavily that Viveka felt he could have been anywhere, and not necessarily in her presence. She took her eyes off the road to look at him. His head was tilted back on the headrest. He wore a black polyester/cotton shirt with tiny green palm trees printed on it, along with yellow martini glasses and pink flamingoes. His head was thrown back on the head rest, and his lower jaw had dropped. His breathing rattled in both directions against his epiglottis.

In the hope that Trevor would be awakened by it, Viveka turned on the CD player. The Bach cello suites. Viveka's lungs felt suddenly bereft of air; insatiable desire mixed with regret rose in her chest. She hit the button to turn off the CD player with more force than was necessary.

A COUPLE OF DAYS LATER, VIVEKA AND TREVOR SET OUT FOR THE beach. In the village of Maracas, on the only road that serviced the north's most popular beach and the fishing villages that dotted this coast, traffic alternated between crawling no more than a car length or two ahead, and standing still. Cars coming from both directions met at the entrance to the beach's parking lot, and formed a loosely linked chain of thrumming metal. The air inches above them shimmered in the heat.

Drivers wilted inside their infernos, each awaiting a hard-to-come-by vacancy in the sole, over-full lot. Their passengers had abandoned them along the crawl-route to the lot. Loaded with beach paraphernalia retrieved from the trunks, these escapees joined ragged groups that ambled on the road. The road had turned into a hot, noisy playground. The air just above the softened asphalt danced in waves. A slow parade of people in bathing suites, some wrapped in sarongs, some with towels around their waists, strained under the weight of Styrofoam coolers or boxes and baskets that contained food. Their rubber slippers slapped at the asphalt as they toted canvas bags, rolled-up grass mats, bright towels slung over their shoulders, and hoisted impatient, excited toddlers in their arms. Those without footwear bounced swiftly across the road, lifting their legs high after each protracted step, and blowing as if they felt the heat of the asphalt on their tongues. There were shrieks at children to watch left, watch right before crossing. And there was a constant shuffle of young women — high school girls, really — with movie-star-thin bodies and swimwear intended to fulfill only legal requirements, and strutting in their wake young hairless boys, surfboards like trophies clutched under their arms. All of this, and more — children armed with spades and buckets, heedless of the fact that they were on a roadway, a couple of sombrero-wearing men with guitars, a cacophony of car horns, and the boom-boom-booms from "sooped-up" car stereo systems — contributed to the impression that the state of the roadway was part of the general beach outing, and no one was in any hurry.

Those who remained inside their cars did so knowing well that they could be trapped there for what would seem like hours.

The air floating into the cars was thick, and as the cars limped on, it reeked in turn of carbon monoxide, of pee in the bushes, of coconut-flavoured sunscreen lotions, and nearer the vendor stalls, of oil used in the frying of bakes, shark and king fish. By the river, the stench of stagnant water repulsed, and then suddenly, on each cooling and heaven-sent breeze, was washed away by the salty scent of sea water.

In the driver's seat Trevor had angled himself, partially resting his back against the door, his eyes closed. His exaggerated breathing conveyed ire. As the car had idled in the same spot for too long, the fan had gone into high gear with a sudden and frightening soprano-like whir, and so he had switched off the engine. Viveka's door was ajar, and all the windows were rolled down, but still it felt as if an electric heater was on at full power. Breezes from the sea were infrequent and when they did ripple in they were disappointingly warm. Trevor dangled one arm out of the window, down the length of the door, and leaned his head against the door frame. With his fingers he tapped the hot outside metal of the door in time to the beat of a calypso wailing out of the car behind. His other arm extended across the interior, and he rested his hand loosely on Viveka's leg. He jerked his head slightly in time to the music. Even so, there was an air of impatience about him.

His eyes remained closed as he said in a voice low with weariness, "I will never stop loving this country. Too bad it's run by a bunch of disingenuous incompetents."

"They say people like you should return," Viveka offered. "Not for a holiday, but permanently. To try to make things better."

Trevor opened his right eye and looked at her. "This heat, and..." He sat up and pulled his hand from her lap, balled it tight and with his thumb rigid he pointed to the back, pumping his fist at the row of cars behind. The sharp parson's nose of his fist alternated accusing jabs at the endless row snaking ahead, and he continued, "This kind of inanity would kill me. You would think they'd have cleared that land over there and created another lot, or better yet, they'd ferry people in by public transport and alleviate the area of this kind of congestion, and..." he waved his hand in a circle in the air, his index finger now stiff, pointing toward the roof of the car, "...all this fucking pollution." He closed his eye and leaned his head back again. Viveka suppressed a smile at his use of the word *inanity.* The way, too, he stressed it, i*nan*ity. The same rigid hand came back down, rigid but now studiously weightless as a feather, to rest on her thigh again.

Inanity and fucking in the same sentence. How easily "fucking" slipped out of his mouth lately.

With his eyes still closed, Trevor spoke in such a low voice that all she heard was *short hair,* and several seconds passed before all the words of his question materialized in her consciousness.

"Have you always had such short hair?" is what he had said, she realized.

When she finally answered, she sounded terse without intending it. "Only most of my life."

Viveka had never said *fuck*, had not even whispered it when no one was around to hear, which is not to say that she hadn't tried it out in her head. It was a word scrawled on public walls, heard shouted angrily in the streets by people she would not have known. It was not a word used by people she knew, except, she imagined, in the privacy of their own heads, too. It is true that Trevor said it only when they were alone, but more often now than when they first met.

He opened the left eye now, leaned his head forward again and squinted at her. "You like that boyish look, don't you?"

"I don't think it is boyish."

"No, no, you're right. It isn't boyish."

As if out of nowhere, Trevor then asked how she and Helen had met. "What about the two of you?" he added.

"What do you mean? What kind of a question is that?"

"Well, even though you still won't tell me just how close you are, I know you're close to Anick. And you're not like girls from here. It's why I am attracted to you. You're not the kind of woman Trinidadian men like. Women like women like you. You've never actually told me, you know. What about you and Anick?"

"Oh, come on, Trevor. How would you like it if I began questioning you?"

"I don't mind at all. Ask me anything you like, as long as you don't mind getting an answer."

Viveka blushed so much that Trevor began laughing and said, "So, how does she feel about us getting married?"

Viveka turned her face away. Trevor persisted.

"Does Nayan know about you two?"

"Know what? I never said anything about us."

"You don't have to..."

Trevor waited for Viveka to respond, and when she didn't, he said, "How long have you been lovers?"

"We *were*. We're not anymore."

He shut his eye, rested his head back, and drew lines with the tip of his baby finger, back and forth, on the soft skin of her thigh. She looked down. She had had her legs waxed the day he arrived, before meeting him at the airport. They glistened because she had rubbed them first with baby oil, and then with sunscreen lotion.

Last evening they had been sipping rum and Cokes, reading the newspapers quietly on the patio at her parents' house. Trevor had looked up from his paper abruptly and asked Viveka if she was going to keep her last name once they were married. She noticed that he didn't ask if she was going to take *his* name, but if she was going to keep her own. She had said, simply, "Yes." He picked up his paper again, leaving her staring into the sliver of sea visible on the horizon.

Now the large splay of his pale pink hand with prominent green veins, like vines under his skin, rested on her leg, his fingers curled loosely. The tips of them fell against her inner thigh. The first time he had taken her hand in his, several long weeks ago now, she had felt as if she were cheating. A nervous quiver had spread through her stomach then, and she had withdrawn her hand altogether.

Sitting here with Trevor in the car now, the hem of her wispy dress pushed up a little, noting the dark, almost black hairs on his knuckles, seeing the lower part of her body with his hand wrapping her thigh — it all looked like it belonged rather to someone else. His index finger drew a lighter, longer line to the mound of the softest flesh just before her panties. The air went out of her. Blood surged suddenly through her and began a rhythmic pounding between her ears, and she gasped. This time, she found herself tightening the muscles of both legs, of her bum, and then, involuntarily, she tilted her pelvis toward his hand. She tried to remain still, not parting her legs as her body, to her surprise, ached to. But Trevor just as lightly lifted his hand away, brought it to his nose. He felt the bridge with the tip of his middle finger and then raised his hand to his head. He combed his fingers through his hair and then dropped the same hand on the brake handle, leaving it there. His eyes remained shut all the while.

The coursing of blood in Viveka's body had accelerated, overtaken itself. Her temples and forehead throbbed and ached.

She thought she should say something, but, besides being shy about what her voice might betray, she could think of nothing appropriate. She wasn't even sure if it was right to interrupt, to try to reel him in from wherever he had gone and left her. She rearranged herself in the seat, smoothed her dress back down, and straightened the hem, as if doing these things would erase what she had felt. Now she felt a twinge of sadness, confusion, and an odd emptiness, and she thought of her parents in their car, on long drives together, her sister, Vashti, and she in the back seat, the long periods of wordlessness between them. Often, from the back seat she would hear one of her parents puncture the quiet with something muttered, inaudible to her and Vashti, and the other would grunt back a monosyllable and they would both seem satisfied, stilled again. Save for the murmur of the air-conditioning unit and the cold air shooting from it in puffs of whiteness that smelled like table salt, quiet would overcome her parents again and the sound in the car would be the sound of contentment.

But this, here, was not contentment or a simple quiet, it was silence, and it was not *between* her and Trevor, it was not one shared. It was the sound of something unfinished and awkward. How much is enough time to let such silence be? Didn't he feel what she had felt? Hadn't he intended to make her feel this way? How could someone send you to such a giddying place and not have gone there with you himself?

TREVOR AND VIVEKA IDLING THERE IN THE CAR, IN SUCH HEAT, IN SUCH a long queue on the roadway, waiting for space in the parking lot had begun to seem ludicrous. The beach, once they got to it, would be crowded. They would do what? Throw out a towel on the sand and lie there? Head into the water? Trevor would probably take her hand as they leapt the waves, and when the waves were too high he would grip it tight as he led her beyond the breakers and into the calmer water where the swells grew, but did not break. And out there, if he became distracted and distant, Viveka would panic, as she was not a competent swimmer.

He came and went so easily. Lost in his thoughts one minute, talking about anything and everything the next.

He loved the North Coast, insisted on coming to this coast. She would have preferred Mayaro Beach on the east coast. There would have been no scrutinizing what everyone else was doing and eating, no listening to what others were saying. But here they were in the car, and he had shut her out by closing his eyes, and now by taking his hand from her thigh and placing it on the hand brake.

Suddenly, as if even with his eyes closed he knew her thoughts and could be both irritated by them and in agreement with them, Trevor shifted his body upright and gripped the steering wheel with both hands. "Oh, fuck this, man," he breathed out and swung the wheel outward. He pressed his hand flat on the horn and heaved the car forward in such a surprising and erratic motion that pedestrians scattered, halted cars sprang into action and swerved inward to make room for him, and the ones at the bottleneck scattered like repelled balls of mercury. Through the cacophony of blaring car horns and cuss words, Trevor cut his way up the road, past the second beach, screeching ahead as if driving a rented car. Viveka pressed her body into the back of the seat, and so as not to look as horrified as she was, she bore a tense smile. Leaving the disordered queue of cars behind she felt entirely submerged in deep water. She was compelled to say something, but all she could do was whisper, "That was some move there."

For a long while he said nothing. Finally, tilting his head toward the edge of the road he said, "There are numerous coves and bays down there. Let's pull off the road and climb down."

They were now far from the two popular beaches. She had never before been to the beach with a man — just her and a man — and now that they had left the crowds behind she experienced relief that she would not be seen there, at a public beach, alone with him. She hadn't even realized, until now, how stressful that had been for her. Unlike her mother, and her father too, who worried about what others might say about this or that, it was not the possibility of rumours that troubled her, or the possibility of developing a "reputation." Rather, she did not want to be seen as someone who could be owned by someone else.

SO, IT WAS ON THE NORTH COAST OF THE ISLAND, ON A STRIP OF SAND too slim to label a beach, that he lay on top of her.

He had eased the car off the roadway, thumping over thick rabbit grass and nettles until the car's nose shoved at a fat stand of rozay. Glistening shards of emerald sea flickered between the foliage, but there was no hint of a beach or a bathing place below, no clearing that would have suggested a path down to the water's edge. Viveka had remained in the car for some seconds after Trevor had switched off the ignition, and stared ahead. A ghostly residue of sound hung in the air — the engine's hum, its groan on the ascents, the tires crunching gravel, the car lurching over humps and into the bellies of the heat-deformed asphalt that surfaced the road. She had felt suddenly sad, and realized that is was because she didn't know the French word for emerald.

In the mountains cicadas sing in the daytime. She knew this, but still, in the brilliant sunshine, it surprised her. That, and the rustle of leaves. The ocean, even though it vibrated in the distance, was too far away to be heard.

To arrive at the dash of sand well below, Trevor had shoved and trampled his way through the foliage. Viveka followed. The rozay fronds, like barbed feathers, finely sliced the surface of her exposed skin, and the sun and sea salt on the wind made the tiny crisscrossing beads of blood, like little hardening rubies, sting. But it was only the surface of her skin that stung, and it was as if she stood some distance from herself, watching — not feeling — the pricks. From that distance she marvelled at the vulnerability of human skin making contact with grass that appeared to be stately and benign, but that was edged with barbs so minuscule they were not visible from even half a meter away.

They arrived at a place where the land fell abruptly to the sea. The surf's pounding on the shore below was relentless. One loose pebble on such a descent was all it would take and one, or both of them, Viveka imagined, could be catapulted into that water. She asked Trevor if he was sure this climb down was a good idea. He said it always looked this way, as if it were a straight drop, but from experience he knew that it was not so, and that if they made their way down one step at a time, she would manage, and they would find a little nook in which they could just sit, or lie quietly. He was sure of it. She should stay close if she was worried, he said, and hold his hand.

But Viveka was worried about her mother's car left on the lonely road where it could be robbed, peeled of its tires, seats, dashboard, stolen, or hit by another passing car that would not expect to come upon a parked vehicle there. She said nothing.

The sound of waves hitting the cliff just below troubled her. She stumbled more than once, her heart lurching in fear, but she did not reach out for Trevor. She tried to say in her mind, word by word, in French, "I am climbing a steep cliff down to the emerald sea."

He said something, but the wind snatched his words away and the crashing and the suddenness and the cold and the wet beads of salty surf that jumped up from below and snapped at her made Viveka reluctant to ask him to repeat what he had said. He didn't seem to need a response from her, so she remained quiet and set her foot, her hands, and her bum where he did. It was awkward in a dress, even in a short one with an airy skirt, but more so because he was a good foot taller than she, and so his steps wider than hers.

The words came to her: *Aujourd'hui, je suis descendue la falaise et j'ai aperçu*...and then in English she thought: *I am descending a cliff to the emerald sea, but the sea is not below, it is high above. I am descending in order to rise.*

Once below, there was, as Trevor had promised, a place, although it was only a sliver of sand. It was a breeding ground for sand flies. They swirled in masses so dense that together they looked like a black shimmery veil, and their numerous beating wings sounded like the whir of motorized toy planes.

It was not what she would have called a beach. A beach to her mind needed to be long and wide enough for more than two people to picnic there—for a large Trinidadian family, with extended relatives and their friends and friends of those friends—a crowd large enough to form two full teams for volleyball, enough friends to play the bat-and-ball version of cricket.

IN SPITE OF ITS ISOLATION, VIVEKA WAS UNEASY AS SHE AND TREVOR lay naked there. The pelagic odour of seaweed when it begins to decay curdled the air in the cranny of this tiny bay.

"First time? With a man, I mean?"

She nodded, embarrassed.

Against such malodorous air it was impossible to moderate her breathing — one panacea, she thought, to the relentless push-push-pushing. When Trevor accidentally slipped out of the small progress he had made — he assured her it wasn't her fault — he had to start all over again. She did as she was told — raised her buttocks off the sand — and he slid one arm under her and brought her up yet higher.

"Breathe, just breathe," he sputtered. Viveka closed her eyes tightly and breathed slowly, deeply.

Her body was host to the flies. Welts had formed fast, each one already a fiery point of sweet itching. Her body marked easily. It would be difficult to keep private from Vashti what she had been up to.

He offered her his shirt full of sand, and she took it to wipe herself.

"I guess that was a little different, eh?"

"I guess," she said.

Trevor took the shirt when she was done, waded naked into the water to his waist. He dropped down to his neck to protect his body from the unrelenting attack of swarm after swarm of the nasty black flies. Viveka watched him. His back was to her, and he was busy wringing the water from the shirt. He shook the shirt loose, slapped and whipped the air and the flies hard with it. His buttocks were small, drooped, and she had just had sex with him.

Viveka's Father

VALMIKI LED TREVOR OUT OF THE HOUSE, LEFT HIM AND RETURNED with two beers. The two men walked off the patio onto the lawn. They strolled over to the heavy wrought-iron fencing, and looked out toward the yellow-grey waters of the Gulf. Below were the roofs of the houses of neighbours they knew well, people who would come to the wedding and who had already sent gifts.

There was little conversation between Valmiki and Trevor. Both of them were uneasy, both waiting, Valmiki knew, for Viveka to show herself again.

The town was small. And here Valmiki was, looking out toward the sea yet feeling imprisoned.

He had already told Trevor that he had organized the driver to take them all to the airport the day after the wedding, but he told him again now. Trevor thanked him, as he had done before. Each of them was bearing up under the burden of too much knowing.

Valmiki pointed to a flock of three brilliant scarlet ibis limping through the sky just south of the jetty. With his eyes planted again on the roofs of the homes of neighbours, invited guests to the wedding, he knew it was too late to speak with Viveka. Too late to stop her. Too late to ask her if she was sure that she was doing the right thing. To ask her what on earth she thought she was indeed doing. Times were different. In his day he had had no choice, but she had choices, and even as he thought this he felt the relief, instantly, that she had made the one she had. If he were to question her, he should have done so weeks ago when this talk of marriage first arose. But then, as now, it was as if one of his feet was trapped in a cement block, the other dangling to the side uselessly.

When exactly had his Vik so suddenly reared up and gone away from him?

If he were forced to put a thumb to time, he would say that everything had begun to unravel the evening Nayan had brought Anick to the house for the first time. That was the same day he had almost shot a helpless dog in the forest. The very day Viveka had taken a taxi to school in defiance of all that he and Devika were, just because they wouldn't let her play volleyball.

But it wasn't that easy, was it, to pin it all on a day? Perhaps it had begun, rather, when he, Valmiki, had decided to leave the only person he had ever really loved, Tony, and to court Devika Sankarsingh.

Perhaps questions were not what he had to give, but advice. But what would such advice be? Viveka would, in the end, like everyone else, have to cut out her own path.

He had no advice and his glass was empty.

Epilogue

24 Months

TREVOR LEANED AGAINST THE PATIO'S RAILING. HE WOULD NOT FACE her.

After a long silence, and although they were alone, she whispered earnestly, "Do you still want to go through with this?"

"Have I indicated otherwise?"

They both stared out at the lights just beginning to twinkle alive on the Pointe-à-Pierre jetty.

"How long do you think we'll last, Trevor?"

"Is that a serious question?"

"Well, you know who I am."

"What do you mean by that?"

"It's a serious question. How long?"

Trevor took a drink of his beer before he looked at her. "Five years, give or take, I suppose. How long do you think?"

"I would say two."

"Two! Oh, come on, Vik. Show a little courage! I am exhibiting a mountain of it, wouldn't you say?" He was terse.

It was a while before she could respond. She looked up at him, tears welling. "You'd be surprised, Trevor," she said. "You'd be surprised at my courage right now."

Acknowledgements

A DEBT OF GRATITUDE, IN NO SMALL MEASURE, IS OWED TO MARGOT Francis, Aline Brault, Brenda Middagh, my brother-in-law, Shekhar Mahabir, and my brother Ramesh. My sister, Indrani Mootoo, braved the Naparima-Marayo Road and drove me into the trenches of Rio Claro. My memories of that complicated area — bucolic on one hand, treacherous on the other — include discovering with her, much awe between us, the forest, the cacao industry, the farmers, and, outside the scope of this book, the frightful surprise of foreign intelligence officers combing the area for drug and gun smuggling and underground militia camps. Thank you, Indrani, for our adventure. If it weren't for Dr. Brinsley Samaroo and his enviable ease with, and knowledge of, the island, I wouldn't have come so close to the cacao lands or met Bjashanand Hanooman. Thanks so much, Brinsley. At the time of the writing of this book, Hanooman was the agricultural officer for the Rio Claro area. I couldn't have had a more perfect or generous guide. He and his wife, Lutchmin, spared no trouble, imagined what I didn't know to ask, and gave me a fascinating introduction to the French-Indian world of cacao from which I drew. For this I am immensely grateful.

Thank you to Sarah MacLachlan, to everyone at House of Anansi Press, to book designer Ingrid Paulson, and to my agent, Maria Massie. Words are paltry to try to express the depth of my gratitude for my publisher and editor Lynn Henry, who, to understate it, always "gets it."

With every good reason and no need for explanation, I would like to express very special thanks to Sarah Declerck.

Any resemblance of characters in this novel to persons living or dead is purely coincidental.

© JULIE WILSON

About the Author

SHANI MOOTOO was born in Ireland and grew up in Trinidad. She has lived in Canada since the early 1980s. Her acclaimed first novel, *Cereus Blooms at Night,* was published worldwide and was a finalist for the Giller Prize, among other awards. Her second novel, *He Drown She in the Sea,* was on the longlist for the International IMPAC Dublin Literary Award. Mootoo is also an accomplished visual artist. She has lived in Vancouver and Edmonton, and now lives in Toronto.

Anansi offers complimentary reading guides that can be used with this work of fiction and others.

Ideal for people who love talking about books as much as they love reading them, each reading guide contains in-depth questions about the book that you can use to stimulate interesting discussion at your reading group gathering.

Visit www.anansi.ca to download guides for the following titles:

The Outlander
Gil Adamson
978-0-88784-828-5

The Law of Dreams
Peter Behrens
978-0-88784-774-5

Die With Me
Elena Forbes
978-0-88784-804-9

Long Story Short
Elyse Friedman
978-0-88784-803-2

The Spare Room
Helen Garner
978-0-88784-838-4

Gargoyles
Bill Gaston
978-0-88784-776-9

The Order of Good Cheer
Bill Gaston
978-0-88784-816-2

Cockroach
Rawi Hage
978-0-88784-834-6

De Niro's Game
Rawi Hage
978-0-88784-813-1

The English Major
Jim Harrison
978-0-88784-835-3

Returning to Earth
Jim Harrison
978-0-88784-786-8

True North
Jim Harrison
978-0-88784-729-5

Day
A. L. Kennedy
978-0-88784-808-7

Paradise
A. L. Kennedy
978-0-88784-738-7

The Withdrawal Method
Pasha Malla
978-0-88784-817-9

The Tracey Fragments
Maureen Medved
978-0-88784-768-4

Alligator
Lisa Moore
978-0-88784-755-4

Valmiki's Daughter
Shani Mootoo
978-0-88784-837-7

Atonement
Gaétan Soucy
978-0-88784-780-6

The Immaculate Conception
Gaétan Soucy
978-0-88784-783-7

The Little Girl Who Was Too Fond of Matches
Gaétan Soucy
978-0-88784-781-3

Vaudeville!
Gaétan Soucy
978-0-88784-782-0

The Big Why
Michael Winter
978-0-88784-734-9